THORNS of CHAOS

Jeremiah Cain

VYLETRA LLC

vyletra.com

Published by Vyletra LLC, Mobile, AL
vyletra.com

This is a work of fiction. Names, characters, places, and incidents are a product of the author's imagination. Any resemblance to actual people, living or dead, or to businesses, companies, events, institutions, or locales is completely coincidental.

Thorns of Chaos / Jeremiah Cain. – 1st ed.
Hardback ISBN: 978-1-7348024-2-9
Paperback ISBN: 978-1-7348024-3-6
Ebook ISBN: 978-1-7348024-4-3
LCCN: 2022918334

First printing March 2023

Cover and interior illustrations © 2023 by Jeremiah Cain
Book Layout © 2017 by BookDesignTemplates.com (modified by J. Cain)

CHAPTER ONE

Efflorel 30, 831

A frenzy of drumming erupted from the flickering firelight of a cave's tall entrance as a dozen hands slapped taut leather in an escalating tempo. Black smoke billowed from the portal's craggy zenith.

Laisren stepped forward. Behind him, a small village of simple roundhouses stood vacant beneath a setting sun. His bare feet touched the cool, rough stone of the cave's inviting mouth.

His kilt was a patchwork of irregular panels of black leather clutched together by thick hemp thread. His belt was thick, its buckle, a spiral of rusted iron.

The upper body of the twenty-four-year-old man—thin and fit and pale—was naked but covered in crimson tattoos of infernal sigils and arcane runes. They protected him. They empowered him. They connected him to the primordial force that formed the foundation of all reality.

Laisren touched his fingers to his heart, to the tattoo of a downward-pointing, acute-angled, seven-pointed star. He could feel the drumbeat in his chest, vibrating down his core with chaotic energy. He breathed deeply, drawing the power inward.

His lips curled in a slight grin as his cold hazel eyes stared, without blinking, into the flickering darkness. Laisren—a handsome man with a pale, smooth face and disheveled black hair curving just past his eyebrows—stood at the threshold of ecstasy, peering in.

Again, he breathed. This time, he extended his arms from his sides, raising them slowly as he extended his black feathered wings from his back.

"Hail Ig-ní-sek-het," Laisren intoned. "She who creates herself."

Crossing his arms over his chest and folding his wings at his back, he entered, his gait methodical, as he rounded a slight decline.

A bonfire blazed at the center of the large cave. Black smoke surged upward, scorching the stone above it before rotating out in thick ripples along the ceiling.

Eight old, dusty skulls on six-foot pikes circled the fire, with men and women writhing among them.

All three dozen people were winged, like Laisren, and bore similar tattoos. Those who wore clothes dressed like him, yet a slight majority wore nothing but ash.

The drums grew louder and faster, and the crazed dancing of those around the fire followed pace. They leaped about and shrieked, as if madness had overtaken them.

Others pursued other games.

To his left, Laisren passed pairs of men and women, creating their own heat as they pressed their bare, slick bodies together, licking, thrusting, calling out in fervent, ferocious debauchery.

Laisren inhaled a portion of their energies as he passed them.

To his right, a naked man shouted as he whipped a leather strap against his own stomach and chest.

Laisren inhaled a portion of his energy as he began to pass.

The man grabbed Laisren's wrist, stopping him. He kissed Laisren's lips, and Laisren reciprocated with lust as he slid his hand under the man's soft brown wings and down his lower back, past his waist, to the bare, silky skin below.

They would continue this later, Laisren resolved. But not yet. He had a task.

Pulling away, Laisren continued to a small stone platform about three feet in diameter and a step up from the surrounding floor.

There, he stood still and well postured with his head slightly bowed, eyes glaring out, arms at his sides and palms forward. His feet spread slightly apart. He breathed in all the surrounding chaos—the beating of the drums, the cracking of whips, the shrieks of pleasure and pain, the mad cackling, the crazed dancing, the heat of the fire, the reek of smoke and sweat and beer. Within his mind, Laisren amplified them all into a sort of internally raging madness, a madness amplifying and swirling, overtaking his mind until he could think of nothing.

Clarity within the eye of the storm.

The sounds fused, becoming one, until they were but a distant, high-pitched tone.

Laisren closed his eyes, his mind blank, and envisioned a single point of crimson light within the dark. It expanded, forming a beautiful, unclothed woman. Her skin was fire. Her wings were fire. Her hair was long and black. Her eyes were crimson light.

She stood within a void with her legs together, her arms by her sides and palms forward. Her fiery wings stretched wide. She looked at Laisren, and he accepted her forceful gaze with horror and delight.

She raised her hands upward, and when they were above her head, a symbol—formed of crimson light—ignited. It was an inverted, seven-pointed star—the same symbol engraved as a mark on Laisren's chest.

The star dissolved into innumerable streaks of crimson light that darted erratically throughout the void.

An ancient energy flowed through him, vibrating through the lowest depths of his being and filling him with pleasures unknown within the mortal realm.

"Hail Ignísekhet," Laisren intoned. "She who creates herself. Goddess of Chaos. Archdemoness of Wrath. We honor you."

—

A wave pushed up on the beach, twisting around his toes, his legs, his brown leather kilt, and butt. As it withdrew, the water pulled some of the sand from beneath him, causing him to sink slightly into the shore.

He ignored his reed fishing pole. It'd already gotten him the large salmon lying beside him on the sand. Instead, Finn gazed across the darkening waters of the Hyvile River.

Twenty-five miles wide, the sparkling water of the immense river—lit orange fading to greenish blue—appeared to stretch forever. To Finn's left, in the east, the sun had nearly sunk beneath the tide.

Finn laid his arms across his drawn-up knees and watched the gentle waves. A pleasant wind flowed over him.

He was a toned, shirtless man of twenty-five with pale, freckled skin. His feathered wings were shades of orange, with dark gray at the furthest tips. Finn regularly washed his hair in limewater, thus stiffening it to short, messy spikes and bleaching it white—though his ginger roots showed. Skinny with a somewhat boyish face, he thought himself unattractive, but many had differed with compliments, which he liked.

The last of the sun sank below the river, starting the last night of the dark season. Or the first night of the light season. He wasn't sure.

Someone slapped the back of his head.

Finn jerked around to see his best mate—usually.

Lann was two years older than Finn, and they'd known each other as long as they remembered knowing anyone at all. As a boy, Lann had been a younger friend of Finn's brother, but over the last ten years or so—with the brother having moved to the capital and Lann and Finn remaining in the fishing village—they'd grown close.

Lann was a brawler and looked the part. He'd competed in minor playful skirmishes with other local lads from surrounding villages. It didn't interest Finn, but it was nice, sometimes, to have a fighter looking out for him.

Lann's wings were like a falcon's, in shades of brown with touches of white. His hair, matching in brown, was dreaded and bound in a messy ponytail, with the ends hanging to his mid-back. He was more muscular than Finn, particularly in his arms, but of a similar height. Too, they dressed about the same—brown leather kilt and bare feet—but Lann wore leather bracers on his forearms.

Like Finn, Lann bore a purple tattoo on his left chest: an obtuse-angled seven-pointed star, a *Septogram*. Within it, a triangle of three spirals merged into its center.

"Good evening to you, Lonnie," said Finn.

"What are you doing here still?" Lann asked. "The others sent me to find you. We're to leave for the temple village soon, you know."

"I'm relaxing some here before the festival. 'Twill be all on in a bit."

"Aye, and I bet you didn't get a gift for the chief druidess."

"Feck's sake," Finn said. "What d'you get her then?"

"Me wife made a basket of flowers, same as most."

Finn huffed. "I'll have to buy something off the Dayigans now."

"With what, you pauper?"

"I've got a ..." Finn looked around. "A fish."

"A fish says he."

"'Tis a lovely fish, this."

"Go on. Give it a fool's try," Lann said. "But hurry up, or the procession will leave without us. I'll come along, so you don't get lost. Or gutted."

Finn jumped up from the shore and spread his wings before pushing them down to gain lift.

He kept a low flight of about thirty feet and could see their village as he passed.

A dozen rowboats—wicker frames covered in skins—lay inverted in a line on the shore. Just past where sand turned to grass, but before turning to forest, a small cluster of homes stood within a fence of long, thin branches woven horizontally between rough posts. Each of the houses had low mud walls and tall conical roofs of thatch.

Finn saw that all the villagers had gathered outside around the houses. Many held torches. A few children chased each other just above the roofs in aerial frolics.

Down the shoreline, Finn continued flying toward the Dayigan fort.

Ominous walls of thick logs, standing two stories high and sharpened, surrounded the roughly square fortress at a hundred and fifty feet across.

When the Dayigans had first arrived four years ago and built their walls, Finn's people were aghast that they would rip down so much of their forest for such a pointless thing. The structures inside the walls were wooden too, with roofs shingled with green-painted wood. Wooden docks extended from the fort out into the river. Three large sailing ships—not built from these forests but from some forest somewhere—rocked within the tide.

At each corner of the fort, a tower extended higher, and from the center of each, a mast held a smaller horizontal pole at its peak. From each, an emerald green banner hung like a warning in the wind. In gold thread, it bore the sun and both moons in an upward-pointing triangle. A downward-pointing triangle, below the first, represented the distant island city of Dayigo. It screamed, "This is ours now, not yours," a sentiment echoed by the fort's inhabitants.

Finn knew better than to enter the fort. Instead, he landed on the shore just outside the wall.

There, the ground was planked over in a level boardwalk. Stalls ran along the edges. The area should have been bursting with goods from all across the continent, but it was empty.

Holding his salmon like a smelly newborn, Finn stared, disappointed and unsure what to do.

Lann landed beside him. "Won't get much trading done here."

"'Tis market day, is it not?"

"Aye, it were market day when it were day," Lann said. "But 'tis not day no more. Come on then, let's go back. Chief Kaie will have enough gifts without yours, so."

"I've come this far, though, haven't I," Finn said. "Might as well see if someone's about."

Finn walked forward and stepped up on the boardwalk. He stopped and gasped, clutching his fish to his chest.

A Dayigan soldier stood guard. He was Human—a race like the Terovae, but without wings. They had hairy faces, and though some were thin, like Terovaes, others could grow wider with either muscle or fat. This soldier was larger in the muscular variety, and a suit of chainmail, covered by a green tabard, armored him.

The soldier eyed Finn but didn't turn his way.

Finn had also found Humans to be a little angry all the time.

"Go on then," Lann prompted behind Finn. "'Twill be midnight 'fore you're done."

Finn breathed deeply and approached.

"Good evening to you, Dayigan friend," Finn said. "Hate to be a bother, sir, but I've come for a quick trade, and I'll pop off."

Maintaining his rigid posture and staring forward, the Human replied gruffly. "The market's shut for the month."

"Aye, that be true," Finn said. "And I hate I missed it, but 'tis a special night, this. Tonight, my people—the Feah, well, all the Five Tribes really—celebrate Midyear's Eve. That's the end of the dark season and the start of the light season. I'm sure your God Déagar would have a special place in his heart for that, right? *Light* season, like. And you see, there's this tradition where we all get a gift for the chief druidess, and I, fool I am, forgot. And to make things worse, me brother's a temple guardian and his wife—my sister by marriage—she's not only a druidess, herself, but no less the second-in-command of our whole fecking tribe." He breathed. "So, 'twill go well noticed if I show up with naught but empty hands and shrugged shoulders, won't it now?"

The soldier said nothing.

"Right," Finn said. "What can I get for this then?" He held up the salmon. "A basket of eggs would be lovely. The druidesses use them for the beernog."

"There's plenty of fish in the river. We can get our own."

"That be true, yes. But this fish isn't in the river, is it? No, this fish is ready and waiting for yourself. And that saves you all the bother of fishing it out."

The Human turned his head toward Finn and glared a moment. He snatched the fish by its tail. He held it, looked at it, and threw it.

The salmon flew a limp and uneventful flight to hit the boardwalk's edge, head slapping wood with a spray of blood. It fell to splat on the beach at the water's edge.

The Human chuckled. "Looks like 'tis in the river to me."

"Fucking Human!" Lann charged forward to fight.

The soldier drew his sword. "You want to fight me, savage? I'll gut the both of you before you can—"

"No call for that," Finn said. "We're all friends having a chat like."

Lann stopped but glared.

Finn walked to Lann and patted his chest, now flexed along with the rest of his tense body.

"I don't think he wants to trade at all," Finn said. Turning back to the soldier, he added, "We'll be on our way then. Good night to you."

The soldier didn't lower his sword, and Lann didn't relax.

"The village'll be waiting for us now," Finn insisted.

Lann spit on the plank-covered ground.

Finn pushed Lann's shoulder to turn him.

The Terovaes flew away.

CHAPTER TWO

Both moons shone large in the sky, and the forest buzzed as people danced and laughed. Drummers played a merry beat, accompanied by rapid wood-winds. As Treasa navigated the crowd, she inhaled the sweet fragrance of the many flowers that adorned everything they could adorn.

Buttercups, daisies, cowslips, and gorses—all yellow, the color of Goddess Larissa, the protector of their lands, whose domain included the hearth and the life-giving soil.

This village, the temple village, Treasa's home, kept its structures scarce, small, and simple, with the least possible alteration to the forest. They built homes where the surroundings dictated and formed them of natural materials, often with living roofs and walls. Other homes perched high in the massive trees, trees as wide as ten feet, and towering into the night.

"Happy Midyear, druidess," a man said with a polite nod.

"And a happy Midyear's Eve to you, as well. May the Three Mothers bless you and yours."

Treasa almost wished she didn't have to wear the thin white linen gown of the druidesses. People did make a fuss when they saw her. Of course, she didn't truly mind and had put in extra effort to look particularly nice tonight. Her toe-nails and fingernails were filed, buffed, and painted yellow.

Her pale face showed a slight, artificial blush. Her auburn hair had shine and bounce, and her reddish-brown wings were neatly preened. Since the many visitors were unaccustomed to seeing druidesses, Treasa felt the need to impress.

Each of the Five Tribes that comprised their people had its own region, which could, on some overly formal occasion, be called a chiefdom, but was almost exclusively called "lands"—this was the Feah lands. Each chiefdom was further divided into nine parishes. These visitors here now lived throughout the capital's parish, but all came twice a year to celebrate in the capital, the temple village.

"*Moyra*," Treasa called with a wave to a woman at a distance.

The other woman had a fighter's build and was dressed in a leather bodice, showing her athletic stomach. She also wore a short leather skirt with a thick belt. Her hair, in chunky braids along her head and tipped with brass balls, was light brown and matched her wings.

They hurried to one another and embraced.

"I figured you'd be in the temple," Moyra said. "We're headed there now." She lifted her hand to show a basket of primroses.

"*Oh*, they're beautiful, them." Treasa touched the basket. "The chief will be delighted. I actually left the temple to come looking for yourself. And"—she smiled at the ten-year-old girl with white hair and wings, just behind Moyra—"I see you there as well. How's my favorite niece now?"

"Excited," she said with a giggle. "Happy Midyear's Eve, druidess."

"Happy Midyear's Eve to you, Alannah. May the Three Mothers bless you. But ..." She looked at Moyra. "Where's my brother gone?"

Moyra shook her head exhaustedly. "That husband of mine," she sighed. "Your *husband's* brother went off to who knows where, so I sent your brother off to find him. And the two of them silly eejits both went missing altogether. The village had to leave without them. Ah." Moyra looked past Treasa. "There's your Cal though."

Treasa looked back to see her husband and her twelve-year-old son approaching from the crowd. Upon seeing Treasa, the boy ran up to her, wrapped his arms around her waist, and set his head on her side.

Treasa placed her hand on his back, just above his orange wings.

"I was just telling Treasa," Moyra said to Cal as he stopped by Treasa. "Lann and Finn have run off."

"Have they now?" Cal chuckled. "Well, with my little brother, 'tis no doubt for some mischief. They'll make their way here, you be sure."

Treasa looked at Cal for a moment. He was a handsome man of thirty, a year her senior. His hair, eyes, and wings were all dark brown. His hair would have come down just past his ears, but he kept it pushed back sloppily.

Cal asked the boy to take Lannah to the temple. "We have adult matters to discuss here."

"Boring matters," Ubaz said. "Come on then. We'll have us a race."

The children jumped up from the ground and flew over the crowd.

"Be sure to run 'round the fire when 'tis lit," Moyra called. "Or wicked Faeries will snatch you up." It was unclear if the children had heard.

Treasa leaned to Moyra. "The Dayigans are here. In the temple village itself."

"Fuck's sake. What do those bastards want here?"

"They're here for the festival, of course. The chief invites them every year, but they've never come before now."

Moyra rolled her eyes. "Can't she *uninvite* them, all the same?"

"*Moyra*," Treasa chided. "The Midyear Festival is open to anyone who wishes to attend it. However, you and Lann are two of our best warriors. The chief requests that you simply *keep an eye out for any trouble with them*."

"I didn't bring no weapons, and Lann'll be pissed on beernog within three hours. But aye, I'll keep them Humans in line, yes."

"The chief druidess thanks you. As do I. Please, let's not mention this to anyone else but Lann. Hopefully, 'tis nothing."

Moyra nodded. "Course."

—

Though the merry music played on and the many revelers danced, Treasa paced and chewed her thumb. An X of brown leather straps now crossed her upper body, over her white dress. It held a scabbard between her wings, where she kept a knobby wooden staff in case of trouble.

"Will you calm yourself?" Cal said with a smile. "You'll rut the grass down to dirt."

"I will not, no. I don't have a pleasant word to say to them. They hate us. They don't pretend not to hate us."

"You'll do fine, love. Maybe Chief Kaie will even make you the official Dayigan ambassador after this."

"You shut your mouth, Calvagh ó Ríona," she said and smiled.

He returned the smile but looked past her. "Here's your man now, *Ambassador Treasa*." Cal pointed two fingers.

Treasa looked back, seeing three bearded Human men approaching. Each wore an emerald green tabard bearing the Dayigan symbol in yellow thread, this over chainmail and circled by a brown belt weighed by a sword. Leather gloves and boots matched the belt. Rigid and guarded, they walked as if they traversed some filthy place they wished not to brush against.

Treasa rolled her eyes at Cal before she stood taller and hurried to the man leading the triad.

"Commander Beadurinc?" Treasa asked.

"Yes." He eyed the surrounding festivities with clear revulsion.

"Good Midyear's Eve, Commander. I am Vischief Treasa, and this is my husband, Calvagh."

"Well met," he said firmly to Cal. "This is Captain Osgar." He motioned to his right, to a soldier with wavy blond hair to his shoulders and a matching neat beard. "We were told you'd be showing us some sort of savage ceremony tonight."

Cal glanced sideways at Treasa, who was evidently invisible to the Dayigans. "My wife here," he said, "will be showing you the, em, *savage ceremony* there, friend. She's an archdruidess and second-in-command of the Feah Tribe. I'm only the temple guardian, myself."

"A *soldier?*" the Dayigan said, impressed. "I suppose someone has to protect a temple full of women."

Cal looked at Treasa again and gained a large, dopey smile as he no doubt saw how annoyed she grew with each word from the Human's mouth.

"*Right*," Cal said at length. "Well, I'll leave you to it then. I need to be off. I'm in the ceremony, you see."

"Fear not, temple guardian," the commander said. "We will assure that no harm comes to your pretty wife."

Cal released the laugh he'd been holding. "Right. You do that, sir. You keep her well safe for me."

Treasa glared at Cal playfully.

He approached her, leaned in, and whispered in her ear, "Do try not to kill our guests, please, love."

"I can't be making promises now." She kissed him. "Ancestors give me strength."

He smiled at her again, jumped up into the air, and flew away.

"You kiss your husband in public?" Beadurinc said. "You savages are quite uninhibited with your affections."

Her smile dropped. "You might want to stop saying 'savage' now, Dayigan." She talked slowly and overly kindly, as if to an idiot. "We are *the Fe-ah tribe*. Or, if you like, outsiders often call the people of the Five Tribes, as a whole, *Drevites*."

Taken aback, the commander looked at Treasa. Her tone had clearly vexed him, but he soon produced a faint grin. He examined her with his eyes.

"Right." Treasa forced a smile. "If ye three would come this way, the chief has partitioned us off an area to stand and watch the ceremony."

—

Centered in the village, the Feah Temple of the Three Mothers resembled a grassy hill but with a stone-framed entrance at its front. Before the entrance set a seven-foot-tall standing stone with gray steps—of thin, irregular slate—circling down around it.

A dirt path led from the steps, and a crowd gathered excitedly along it. They chatted while keeping an eye on the temple.

From the temple's entrance, a sinister man emerged.

The crowd grew silent.

The sinister man, the Winter King, crouched ferally as he walked. He kept his fingers flexed in a form reminiscent of claws as he made swiping gestures at the onlookers lining the path. Growling and hissing, he darted at the children. The onlookers feigned playful fright, and the youngest jumped away.

His hair was wet with oil. His skin was ashed in thin, chalky layers of white. Black ribbons layered his wings. Otherwise, he wore a black cotton loincloth that hung past his knees to tattered fringes.

Four drummers, dressed and painted like the first, followed out of the temple and kept a somber beat.

The Winter King meandered the short, curved path to a slight hill. On it stood a mound of sticks, logs, and shriveled leaves. Alone, he ascended the hill and stood before the mound.

"*Hear me, world of Perdinok!*" he screamed in theatrical villainy. "*I am your king and God!* My kingdom stretches to all four corners of the world. I have corrupted all women, all men, and all children with the Dark Light. No one acts as guardians of nature. No one honors their ancestors. The world is wicked throughout. Thus the sun," he stretched his clenched fist to the night sky, "O mighty Jerah, has turned away from us, leaving the world in everlasting winter. *Hear me, Perdinok! I have won, and no one stands against me now.*"

"Is that your husband?" the commander asked Treasa. They watched from beside the path in an area circled by small stones.

Treasa whispered, "He is, but right now, he's the ancient Winter King."

"He's not wearing much."

From above, a woman's voice shouted, "You are wrong, foul Winter King."

The king crouched and looked upward, searching with wide bestial eyes.

The onlookers began clapping and cheering as a woman descended from the sky. She, a woman of thirty, wore a ring of yellow flowers atop her head with others braided into her long silver hair. Her wings were silver, too. Her flowing gown was bright yellow and belted with a golden cord.

When her feet touched the ground, all went silent.

"I stand against you, foul Winter King," she said. "Mother Lágeya, who is Nature, has sent me here. I am Goddess Larissa, her daughter. Though your kingdom stretches the world, Mother Lágeya's spirit is a living river flowing through every plant and animal, imbuing the hearts of mankind. She is in all. She is the One Soul."

"Lies!" cried the Winter King. "I rule all of mankind. And nature is dead."

The Dayigan commander leaned to Treasa. "That's your chief calling herself a Goddess?" His tone held an accusation.

"She's playing the part, yes," Treasa said, growing vexed.

Goddess Larissa stood resolute and silent. She knelt and touched the soil. Three living stems burst from the ground in a triangle around her.

Treasa leaned to Beadurinc. "The three plants represent the three elements—sea, soil, and sky. By the power of Mother Lágeya, the chief has brought the elements together, in this case using the 'sea'—the water vapor—in the air. As you see, she's used it to make the plants."

Large leaves grew from the sides of the stems as they grew ten feet tall.

Treasa continued. "Of course, druidic creations are not nearly as grand as those made by Mother Lágeya herself, so they only last an hour or so before they divide back into their parts."

They blossomed into sunflowers.

"Here," Treasa said, "these particular flowers also represent Jerah, the sun."

"Witchcraft," the commander growled.

Treasa huffed and leaned away.

"Nature lives," Larissa proclaimed, "and all people who bear the Septogram over their hearts are safe from your corruption. *They* are the guardians of nature, and *they* honor their ancestors."

The onlookers set their hands on their hearts, where all Feahs, age thirteen and up, bore the tattoo of the obtuse seven-pointed star, the Septogram, in purple ink.

The Winter King fell to his knees as if he'd succumbed to some great weakness. He called out dramatically, and afterward, he remained kneeling on the hill.

Seven druidesses, all in flowing white gowns, ran from the temple and frolicked down the path. They wore shoulder bags, from which they grabbed handfuls of petals and threw them out into the crowd. Some threw rings of flowers.

Treasa caught a flower ring and offered it to the commander. He folded his arms in annoyance. Unbothered, she shrugged and set it atop her head.

When the druidesses reached the woman in yellow, they knelt around her.

Larissa stood postured and held her hands high above her head. "I call to my father, Jerah, who is the sun. See us! With his might, I vanquish you, Winter King."

She reached toward a far-off torch, hung in iron on a tree, and motioned as if pulling it toward herself.

The torch's fire flared and flew in her direction. The flames turned bright yellow, reshaping into a bird with strikingly long tail feathers. The bird of yellow fire flew steady circles around Larissa, creating a ring four feet from the ground.

Standing in unison, the druidesses drew unlit torches from their bags and lit them from the ring. Around the Goddess, they danced, skipping and yelping with glee as they held their torches high.

"Go!" Larissa pointed. "And end this everlasting winter."

The druidesses ran up the hill.

Where the Winter King had knelt, now knelt a wicker reproduction of him. A woman grabbed it up, sounded a shrill trill, and threw it onto the mound of sticks and logs.

All the druidesses threw their torches into the mound until a great fire burned.

Larissa thrust her hands into the air, and the firebird flew high and burst into brilliant light.

"I call Mother Lágeya. Bear witness! I call Mother Larissa. Bear witness! I call Mother Ashatra. Bear witness! True Light powers bring us the season of light. Blessings from the Three Mothers. Blessings from the True Light!"

And the crowd—save for the Dayigans—cheered. "Blessings from the Three Mothers. Blessings from the True Light!"

Larissa announced, *"Summer is here!"*

The crowd applauded, and music erupted throughout the temple village. As they danced and frolicked, the people swallowed up the path. The fire became the center, with people circling it and flying over.

Treasa, filled with delight, looked back at Commander Beadurinc.

The commander kept his arms crossed across his stomach as his narrowed eyes watched the scene. He seemed to boil with anger.

Treasa nearly asked him his opinion of the ceremony, but his silent displeasure was so apparent that her questions lingered unsaid on her lips.

Finally, the commander said, "You *honestly* believe this display of debauchery and sorcery somehow honors the True Light?"

She forced a smile. "Mother Larissa is a True Light God, same as your God Déagar. She is his sister, you know."

He still watched the festivities with the same anger. "The Supreme Patriarch of the Church of Déagar is currently leading a team of scholars to reevaluate the ancient texts. They are exploring which texts are true, which texts are partially true—and thus need to be reedited—and which texts need to be burnt completely. One finding by the team is that the so-called 'pantheon' was a mistake. God Déagar is the *only* God; his brothers and sisters are demigods at best."

Treasa huffed with annoyance, done with this man. "If that's what you choose to believe, then believe what you like. You came to *our* festival to experience *our* culture, and I've shown it to you. I have no intention of converting you to our ways."

"*Your ways* are a disgrace to the True Light. And your people are filth."

Treasa clenched her jaw as she glared daggers at him. She breathed slow breaths through her nose as her heart pounded in her breast.

Cal landed just beside her. "Did ye enjoy the show?" he asked with a smile. "I tried to push my performance even better, with it being your first time here. Impressive, was it not?"

Treasa and Beadurinc remained locked in tense, staring silence.

Cal lifted a basket. "Would you have yourselves some nice oatmeal biscuits?" He paused, looking at them. "What?"

"You still wear that demonic guise on your nearly naked body," the commander said.

Cal looked down at himself. "I do, yes. I have to play the monster a few more hours still, 'til the children go off to the temple for bed. That's when the real fun begins."

Another tense pause.

"The commander," Treasa began calmly, "was just explaining to me that our culture is a disgrace to the True Light, and our people are filth."

Cal paused for a moment, soaking in the words. "Right, what's the idea saying shite like that to us?"

"Cal," said Treasa, "leave it."

"No. Just 'cause ye think yourself civilized, don't give you the right to be shitey arseholes."

The commander smirked and glanced at the blond captain, as if Cal's outburst had confirmed something.

The captain nodded.

"I think the guided part of the tour has ended now," Treasa said. "Come on, Cal. The Dayigans will be good on their own."

"Good to leave our lands." Cal threw the basket of biscuits at the soldiers' feet.

CHAPTER THREE

A few paces from the hill holding the bonfire, Finn combed his fingers through his spiked white hair—a slight tidying up to keep looking nice—before he approached a large iron cauldron. He held up a tin cup.

"Can I have a bit more, love?" he asked of the woman in her late fifties, who stood behind the cauldron.

"Course, dear." She dipped a ladle in the milky depths of the beernog. "You *are* staying out of trouble, aren't you, lad?"

"I am that, aye. For now. But the night's young yet?"

She laughed as she emptied the ladle into his cup. "You need to find yourself a nice boy to start a home with. And stop running around like you do."

He smiled. "Right now, though, I'm just looking for a *wicked* boy to start the night off with."

"Oh, Finn," she laughed. "You're wild as a wee imp, you."

"That I am, love." He took a drink from the cup.

Lann slapped Finn's shoulder as he came from nowhere.

A splash from the cup spilled on Finn's center chest and rolled as a white line down his stomach to his navel.

"Come on, Finn," Lann said excitedly. "I've found your brother and me wife and sister. We all have a spot up this way."

Finn took another sip. "My thanks." He nodded to the woman while lifting his cup. "Even better than last year's."

"Wears well, too," Lann added.

"Happy Midyear's Eve," Finn called, as Lann pulled him away by his shoulders.

—

The festive crowd within the wooded area thinned somewhat as Finn followed Lann outward, though the fire remained not too far behind them. The music, though a tad softer, still filled this new area.

They neared a wonky circle of five worn wooden benches.

"There the two of ye are." Moyra stood from a bench and approached. "By the Mothers, I swear if I hadn't married you meself, the two of ye would've run off together."

Lann grabbed her around the waist. "Nah, Finn's too sweet for my liking, love. I like 'em well mean." He tickled her sides.

She laughed wildly. "Oh, I'll show you mean." She punched him in the arm.

He stopped and looked at her with a bit of fake sad.

She kissed his arm. He kissed her neck. She kissed him deeply on the mouth. She shrieked as Lann grabbed her and pulled her close. Their passions flared.

Finn passed them and turned his attention to his brother and brother's wife. They sat next to each other on a bench.

Cal had washed up from playing the Winter King, and the black ribbons were gone from his brown wings. But he still wore the black, tattered loincloth, and a few remnants of the white body paint showed in random streaks on his skin.

In stark contrast to the festivities all around, Cal and Treasa were slouches and long stares at the grass.

"The two of you look like your falcon's just died," Finn said.

"'Tis those fecking Dayigans," Cal grumbled.

Moyra came up for air. "I been watching them like you asked, Treasa." She sat on a bench facing them and leaned in. "The three you was with, joined up with five more. For a couple of hours now, they've just been sitting on the edge of things, watching everyone. 'Tis well disturbing, them."

"I don't understand why they're here at all," Treasa said.

Finn took a seat. "I don't understand why we're giving them a thought. 'Tis Midyear's Eve, this. I'm not letting them Humans take a piss on our festival."

Treasa sighed. "Finn's right."

"That's not something often said." Lann laughed as he took a seat next to Moyra.

Moyra slapped Lann's shoulder. "Cheeky bastard."

Treasa stood up and pulled Cal to his feet.

"Though druidesses and temple guardians may not drink," Treasa began, "I raise an imaginary cup to my friends. *Happy Midyear.*"

"*Happy Midyear,*" the rest said together.

"Now ..." Treasa smiled as she grabbed Cal's hand. "Let's go dance 'til our feet fall right off."

Someone slid his hands over Finn's shoulder, down his chest, and rubbed the top of his slim stomach. He kissed the side of Finn's neck.

Finn turned to see Kyran, a man two years older than himself, who lived in a village just north of here. Only a thin layer of chalky blue ash coated his lean body. Nothing else.

Finn extended his orange wings to brush up Kyran's sides.

"I was hoping I'd find you 'round here." Finn beamed a blissful smile.

"And 'twould seem you have now." Kyran set a ring of yellow flowers atop Finn's spiked hair.

Kyran kissed Finn's lips as Finn spun around on the bench. Once facing, Kyran positioned his arms on either side of Finn's neck, and Finn set his hand on Kyran's waist. Finn began kissing down his stomach.

"Looks like we lost Finn," Lann said. "Come on, then. Let's go."

"I'll catch up with ye," Finn called back.

—

Near the blazing fire, a writhing mass of men and women danced and drank and played. With all the children now in the temple listening to old stories before bedtime, the crowd had turned more sensual in their frolics, the music, faster.

Treasa held her husband's hand as they entered the area. Close beside them walked Lann and Moyra, his arm around her waist.

Cal placed his hand on Lann's shoulder and shouted over the noise, "Looks like you're low on nog there, friend. You might want to fetch some more for yourself."

Lann looked in his cup. "Nah, I'm good for nog, see."

Treasa neared Lann and gave him a stop-being-an-idiot stare. "Lann, *go*. I need some time with my husband without my little brother lurking 'round."

He looked at her and looked at Cal. "Right. Come on, Moyra. I think there's a nice spot way over yonder on the other side of the fire hill."

Cal grabbed Treasa, and she giggled as he pulled her into his arms. He gazed at her for a moment, smiling.

"You *are* beautiful, you," Cal said. "Know that?"

"I've been told so. And you're not too bad to look at yourself."

He kissed her on the lips tenderly but with a passion that tingled down her body.

He whispered, "I quite love you, Treasa."

"And I love you, Cal."

He kissed her again, this time on her neck. His lips trailed downwards, down her cleavage, left bare by the low cut of her white gown. His lips moved onto the thin white linen itself, kissing her breasts.

Treasa stepped back and gazed lustfully into his deep-brown eyes. She danced slowly, in complete contrast to the quick music surrounding them. Her entire body moved like a flame as she raised her arms high.

She watched Cal watching her. He was like someone enchanted, his eyelids partly closed and his lips holding a slight grin. *Such a cute man,* she thought.

Treasa neared him. She ran a finger, leisurely and seductively, down the center of his bare chest and along the ridges of his hard stomach.

His grin grew larger.

She slid her fingertips onto the tie at the hip of his black loincloth. She yanked the tie and pulled away the cloth. Holding it behind her back, she kissed him. She ran laughing from the crowd.

With a playful smile, he ran after her.

—

Two men and one woman—naked save for colored ash—danced wildly by the fire. Each twirled a thick baton lit on either end with flames.

Their dance was quick and animalistic. They spun themselves and spun the flames, throwing batons to one another.

The flickering light glistened on their heated skin.

The woman cried out in thrilled shrills as the men, with increasing speed, juggled the fire around her.

—

Kyran shoved Finn against a thick, rough tree as their lips and tongues caressed. The kiss was deep, unrestrained, and long lasting, and hunger consumed the fervent men.

Kyran's chest, painted ashy blue, pressed its growing heat against Finn's own as Kyran eagerly unfastened the outer buckle of Finn's leather kilt. The inner buckle, on the other side, came next.

The kilt fell to ankles, leaving Finn as bare as his sexy cohort. They ground their bodies together with their manhoods swelling, skin to sensitive skin.

Together, they spun around, Kyran's back to rugged bark.

Finn dropped to his knees, to the blue-painted rod standing hard from dark curls. Finn smiled wantonly. He licked it, base to hooded head.

Kyran, squirming against the tree, sighed in pleasure.

With a mischievous grin, Finn tongued a drop of clear nectar into his mouth, savoring the taste before wrapping his lips around the source.

—

Lann clapped his cup against Moyra's and against the cups of the other revelers gathered at an outdoor table.

Nearby, the bonfire reached its brilliant arms toward the night, as those with Lann laughed and joked.

A merry song broke out as the group lifted their cups and swayed them to the beat.

Lann curled his arm around Moyra. He squeezed her against him as they sang.

—

Down her naked body, Treasa's white gown flowed, crumpling at her feet.

Cal, his loincloth tossed aside, took her hand, and she stepped out from the ring of linen.

She put her hand on his shoulder, pushing him down as he knelt before her. He kissed down her thin stomach before kissing deeper between her thighs.

Treasa grabbed his brown hair and pushed herself harder against his face.

The surroundings blurred, and the music became a distant sound. Her entire body tingled as she writhed against his mouth. Her breathing hastened through an open grin.

At length, she slapped her hands down on Cal's shoulders, yellow-painted nails clutching his skin. She leaned her weight against him as her balance faltered. She called out, surging with delight.

Treasa, panting, clamped her hand under Cal's jaw and pulled him upward.

She kissed him on the lips as she glided her hand down Cal's side to his waist. Her fingers traced the V-line muscle at the base of his stomach, sliding down between his legs. She touched his swollen length before she circled it with her fingers. She guided him inside her.

—

Kyran grasped the tree in front of him as he spread his wings to full span.

Kissing the back of Kyran's shoulders and neck, Finn pressed his body against him.

Kyran arched his back, offering up his tight blue ass.

Finn grabbed himself and aimed. He entered slowly but with force, gripping Kyran's waist as he pushed deeper.

Lost in ecstasy, Kyran moaned as Finn's thrusts became faster and with greater force.

—

Among the massive trees, Finn walked side by side with Kyran, their arms over each other's shoulders. They were both stark, bollock-naked, and they sang a nonsense song they made up as they walked. When neither of them could concoct a next verse, they broke out into silly laughter.

Kyran looked up and down Finn's body. He chuckled. "You've taken half the blue off me for yourself."

Finn looked down at himself, smeared with ash-based body paint. "Aye. I need it. 'Tis ash from the sacred fire. 'Twill keep wicked Faeries at bay."

"You *are* a wicked Faery yourself," Kyran laughed.

"Am I now?" Finn grabbed Kyran up and swung him in a circle before kissing him.

Kyran stopped, turning serious. "I ..." He stepped back. "I'm leaving the Feah soon. Permanent."

"What, the whole tribe?"

"Aye. I met someone, a fella up in the Frelon tribe. He's got a little place on the Teréyi Sea. Wants me to move in with him, proper like."

"I," Finn began but stopped. The words were such an abrupt turn. His eyes drifted to the ground, and his whole body felt as if it had sunk. "But we got a fun thing here, you and me."

"Aye, and you got the same fun thing with half a dozen other lads in the Feah too."

"A whole dozen, surely." Finn gave a mild laugh.

Kyran chuckled. "You're a right satyr, Finn."

"*And you.*"

Kyran nodded but didn't laugh. "Not no more, though. The Frelon bloke is talking marriage. And a proper home. Don't you want more than just fucking about?"

"Fucking about suits me though, don't it? I rather like fucking about. Happy for you, though." Finn sighed. "I'll miss you."

Kyran moved closer and set his hand on Finn's cheek. He looked into Finn's blue-gray eyes. "You're more than what you think you are, Finn. I wish you could see it."

"I'm just"—Finn shrugged—"just plain me, s'all."

They lingered in that moment. Finn was certain Kyran could see the sadness in his eyes. He tried to force a smile, but it was short-lived.

Kyran's eyes were sad, too. "I ..." he began. "I just came here to tell you. To see if ..." He looked away.

He could stop Kyran, Finn knew, knew too that Kyran wanted him to. For years, they'd shared a wonderful friendship.

"I love you, Finn. You know that, right?"

Finn paused. "I'm not really much to love, am I?" Finn forced a smile, as if he'd meant it as a joke. "You'll do better with the Frelons. I hear the sea's grand."

"Right." Kyran sniffed. "It is that. Had a visit there myself. Well nice."

"I will miss you. It wouldn't be right, though, to keep you here when you could have better there."

Kyran stared as if hurt, as if Finn were supposed to help him.

"That *is* what you want," Finn asked. "Right?"

"It is, yes. But let's not get all weepy teary on Midyear. I told you, now you know. Now, give us a kiss 'fore we head back to the others."

Finn gave him a slow kiss as he held the other man against him. It was nothing like before. A finality marked their embrace. Finn held him, not wanting to let go but knowing he must. It was for the best.

"Fucking za," said a nearby man. "What in God Déagar's name is this *filth?*"

Finn looked up, clearing his eyes with his finger.

The Dayigan commander approached with another soldier.

"Leave us be, you old smelly troll," Kyran said.

"Leave *you* be? You are the ones brazenly performing your disgusting debauchery in my very path."

"Debauchery, says he," Kyran laughed. "Should have seen us a few minutes back." Kyran turned around, pushing his ass against Finn's groin, and began exaggerated moans.

Finn stepped away, not sharing in Kyran's jest. The Human's word had him feeling ill. *Filth*, that's what he felt like. Ashamed, he covered his stomach with one hand and hid his groin with the other.

The Dayigan's next words, dripping with hate, were a jagged sword. "You are evil perversions," he said. "The True Light has no room for things like *you* in our holy kingdom."

Finn stared in the commander's general direction, dazed and hurt. He wanted to shout back, but he was numb with sorrow. He wasn't sure why the stranger's words affected him so thoroughly, but they throbbed through him and spun in his head. Finn found a part of him believing the commander that he was disgusting.

Finn looked at the blue ash smeared down his body. "Sorry," he said, downcast. "We'll be on our way then."

"Don't you apologize to them," Kyran said. He lunged toward the commander.

Finn grabbed him, holding him back.

"You'll get us killed," Finn whispered harshly as his arms grappled around the flexed chest and stomach.

Kyran struggled forward, his wings slapping Finn.

"Your Faery friend is right," the commander said. "Best flit off like good little savages." He drew a sword.

Kyran stopped his struggle but remained tense in Finn's arm. He stared at the commander.

"Go," Finn said to Kyran. "I'll have a talk with them and meet up with you in a bit."

"I can't leave you here on your own."

"'Tis no bother," Finn said. "To be fair, 'twas probably a startle, walking up on two naked blokes shifting. We'll just have a friendly chat; that's all. Should resolve easy enough."

Kyran relaxed, and Finn let him go.

After glaring at the commander, Kyran flew away.

"I think there's been a wee bit of a misunderstanding," Finn said to the soldiers. "Everybody here—you, me, and all— just wants to have a fun night celebrating Midyear, right? Let's stop all this bickering, friend, for at least tonight. Sound good to you then?"

The commander stared at the shining steel of his blade. His words were slow, with controlled hate. "If we were in the Holy Dayigan Empire, I could run the pair of you through, and they'd celebrate me. But these savage lands are so soft on wickedness and witchcraft that you're overrun with it. And blind to it."

"Why have you even come here?" Finn grew annoyed. "If you hate us, why not go back home?"

The commander paused a moment before a slight smirk curled within his beard. "To save you from your wickedness."

He swung around his sword and stabbed the other soldier in the gut.

Horrified, Finn's eyes widened as he watched the commander yank his sword upward inside the agonized man. He twisted the blade.

Deep red flowed, splashing onto the forest floor.

The commander released the sword, letting it fall within the dying man.

"Praise God Déagar," the commander said, "the one and only God, protector from the Dark. You are the Greatest of All. I praise your name, majestic and holy, without ending. By your fire, guide us safely to Laqyigo. Astha'will-miabé."

Panicked, Finn backed away.

The commander aimed his finger at Finn. "Murderer!"

"No," said Finn, head spinning.

The commander pulled a horn from his belt. He blew.

More soldiers came. Five.

"Murderer!" the commander shouted again.

The festive music faded. Other Feahs rushed into the area, looking at Finn and the dead soldier.

"He's lying." Finn backed away.

"Arrest him," the commander told his men.

Four Dayigans moved forward.

"Stop where ye are," a woman commanded.

Finn looked to see Treasa standing among the trees and pointing a knobby staff toward the Dayigans. Cal, returned to his normal kilt, stood beside her, his bow armed and aimed. Behind them, a crowd gathered.

"This is none of your concern, woman," the commander said. "This pervert assaulted me and murdered my man. We will take him to our post. Men, continue."

The Dayigans continued toward Finn.

Treasa thrust her staff forward, sending a twirl of wind at the soldiers. It hit the ground.

Vines erupted from the ground around the four soldiers' feet, wrapping their ankles and wrists and binding them in place.

"This is Feah lands here," Treasa maintained. "If he's a murderer, as you claim him to be, then he's under the Druidic Circle's jurisdiction."

"The Dayigan Army is the strongest in the world," said the commander. "You play a dangerous game, little girl."

Treasa kept her staff aimed. "One you'll lose, little boy."

He chuckled. "Detachment, stand down." He didn't seem defeated, but more like one who couldn't be bothered with this trite conflict.

Treasa withdrew her staff.

The vines wrapping the soldiers withered and browned, dissolving as dust to the ground.

"Temple guardian," Treasa commanded. "Arrest the accused."

Cal complied, rushing to his brother.

"You all right then?" he asked.

Finn nodded, confused.

Cal patted his little brother's shoulder as if checking for soundness. "We must go to the chief. Come on."

As they walked away, Finn heard the commander, pompous as ever. "Be assured, I will follow up on this. That *killer* will die."

CHAPTER FOUR

Silently, Finn followed his brother down a dirt rut formed from centuries of travel. His shoulders and wings drooped, weighed by the preceding encounter. The thick trees on either side kept their garlands of yellow flowers, but the music had stopped, and the passing people were rustling with worries, whispers, and sullen stares.

Cal, too, remained silent as they neared the temple. Finn recalled their father when he was angry after Finn had done something wrong, which was often. Five years older than Finn, Cal had often played the part of assistant father. Now, Finn was like a boy, in trouble and unsure of what he'd done wrong.

Even as they neared the temple, it looked barely different from a hill, two hundred feet across and thirty feet high. Tall grass covered it, and a cluster of small trees grew near its apex.

The path led to a rough standing stone about seven feet tall. The stone bore the same mark as on Finn's chest—an obtuse seven-pointed star, a Septogram, around a triangle of three spirals. Here, the symbol was two feet across, with its carved lines charred black into stone.

Finn looked at the symbol, said to be the oldest symbol of the True Light, given by Mother Lágeya to protect mankind.

You are evil perversions, the commander had said. *The True Light has no room for things like you in our holy kingdom.*

Finn looked away.

He followed Cal around the steps that circled the stone. These steps, rising about three feet, were formed of thin slate stacked so naturally they appeared as if they just happened to be there. The two sides converged into a slight alcove in the hill behind the standing stone.

There, a rectangle of three massive stones framed an entrance. Above it, similar stones framed an open window.

Without a word, they entered a narrow, low tunnel. It was not carved through stone, like a mine, but was edged in stones—large, thin slabs that covered most of the masonry wall.

The moonlight faded as they followed the slight decline for forty feet.

A thick wooden door marked the tunnel's end. Finn knew it to be locked. This shortcut was not the way.

Instead, he followed Cal, turning right and entering the dim, turquoise light of a wider, taller corridor. From the ceiling's wooden planks, supported by thick logs, dangled countless threads of turquoise light.

Finn gazed up at them as he followed the decline around the gradual semicircular corridor. When he was a child, the druidess who'd led the children down this path would teach them something of bioluminescence—the natural light from certain plants, insects, and sea life. The amazing lights above them were specially cultivated fungi.

But the druidess always kept her lesson short, for this walk around the inner sanctum was meant to be done in silent contemplation, as those who walked it prepared to enter the holy place.

After two hundred feet, the ramp ended, and the wall to Finn's right stopped at a thick vertical log still covered in bark. The wall to his left continued its same curve but was covered in thick vines with sparse, velvety magenta flowers glowing like a wall of stars.

Cal and Finn now stood in a large hall. The high plank ceiling angled upward to the vine-covered wall. From its rafters hung large yet simple brushed brass chandeliers with thick white candles.

To Finn's right, several long ten-foot-high wooden shelves were butted together at obtuse angles, one after the other, following the curve of the outer wall. On the shelves, skulls were set neatly and evenly spaced. Clean of dust and carved with delicate spiral designs, these skulls were from the greatest of the ancestors.

Finn had never liked to stand before the many watchful eye sockets. To him, nothing in his life made him worthy of standing before them. He lowered his head and drew his arms across his naked body.

Cal seemed unmoved—this had been his home for a decade, since he and Treasa had left the fishing village to pursue druidic life.

"You know where the temple garments are, right?" asked Cal, motioning to a low doorway through the wall of shelves.

Finn nodded.

"We'll need to wear them in the Temple Grove. There's a small pool in there and a sponge so you can clean the paint off you."

"I've been here before." And after a wait, "Are you mad at me now?"

Facing Finn, Cal's eyes turned sad. "Of course I'm not, you silly fecker. I ..." He sighed. "I'm worried. About my baby brother. Those bastard Dayigans ..." He looked down.

Finn stepped forward and extended his arms for a hug.

Cal held his hand at the center of Finn's chest, stopping him. "No." Cal cracked a slight smile. "I will not be having a naked brother hug."

Finn stepped back. "Oh, right."

"Get dressed. The chief will get this sorted out."

—

Finn could feel the calm energy of the inner sanctum, called the Temple Grove, as he passed through the large stone-framed entrance and stepped his bare feet onto the trimmed grass. He could hear a harp, its music delicate.

The room was a hundred-foot-wide heptagon, its roof sloping toward a thirty-foot apex.

A ring of thin five-foot stones—resembling headstones—circled close to the outer edge of the room. Toward its center, seven thick oaks grew in a circle from the grassy ground up to support the thick black wooden rafters, limbs twisting around them. Many large orbs of lavender light hung from the high-up branches of the trees.

When Finn was a child, Chief Morgana—the chief at the time—had always called upon the fireflies to fill the room on New Year's and Midyear's Eve. Finn could see that Chief Kaie still followed the tradition. Points of yellow-green light danced throughout the room.

Finn followed Cal over knobby roots into the circle of trees.

Centered on the dome ceiling was a circular opening to the night. The circular portal, thirteen feet across through ten feet of roof, held an acute version of a Septogram, called a Faery Star. Here, thick bars of brushed brass formed the star, and it was set into a brass spiral.

Below the opening, a thick monolith of rough gray stone stood thirteen feet. Each of its four sides bore the same symbol as the standing stone outside, but here the symbols glowed purple. Before it sat a stone altar, the size of a table, filled with a display of yellow flowers, fruits, and crystals.

Beds of straw and fur clustered throughout most of the lawn. This was not the normal configuration. Tonight, the temple hosted all the children of the parish. Some children snuggled in their beds, but most, circling the druidesses, eagerly listened to old stories Finn had heard many times before.

The druidesses differed from when Finn was a boy, but otherwise, it was how he remembered it from the fire festivals of his childhood. Somehow, this comforted him, despite all.

As the two men entered, some children turned their way. Cal and Finn each wore, like all the boys there, a white linen skirt. The girls wore white linen gowns, and the druidesses wore their normal white dresses.

A twelve-year-old boy with orange hair and wings leaped up and ran to Cal.

"Is it time to go home already?" Ubaz asked.

"'Tis not, no," Cal said. "Our Finn's got into a bit of trouble, and we need to see the chief."

"Trouble?" Ubaz gave a concerned look Finn's way.

"'Tis nothing we can't sort out." Cal tousled Ubaz's hair. "Right, go on back to the other children now."

Ubaz raked his hair out of his eyes. "The chief's in there." He pointed with a bit of annoyance and hurried back to the group.

—

Treasa, Lann by her side, stood surrounded by a gathering mob. The people wore their festive costumes, flowers and ribbons and merry designs of body paint. But they were not merry. They demanded answers Treasa could not give. They questioned why the Dayigans remained in Feah lands. They called for justice and vengeance.

"Enough!" Treasa shouted. "The Druidic Circle shares your outrage—we do—but we must remain calm."

"Calm?" a man shouted back. "You know Finn didn't do what them Humans said he did. They should pay for making lying claims against a Feah."

"He's not wrong," Lann said to Treasa.

She glanced at her brother and gave a vexed shake of her head. She again addressed the group. "To be fair, we don't know what happened. True, I find it hard to believe our Finn up and murdered someone. We will find the truth, present it to the Dayigans, and I'm sure they'll be reasonable about it."

"Reasonable?" a woman scoffed. "There's a fecking laugh."

"You might want to remember," Treasa said to her, "nothing's happened to *any* Feahs but words. *Words*," she repeated to all. "A Human died tonight, not a Terovae. Our people were insulted and threatened, but in the end, they were just words. We will not fight over words. We will remain peaceful until we can't be peaceful anymore."

The crowd stared at Treasa but was silent. Anger was the loudest emotion, but it wasn't the most prevalent. Treasa could see the fear in them, the worry. The same mix of feelings throbbed through her, and she prayed, by the Three Mothers, that it was not so apparent.

"Now"—Treasa controlled her wish to scream—"'tis Midyear. I invite ye all to return to your merrymaking or return to your villages. We'll tell ye more when we have more to tell."

The crowd wilted, and muttering, they moved away, some in defeated amble, some spreading their wings and heading up into the night.

Treasa stood still beside Lann.

"We can't fight against the Dayigan Empire," Treasa said, perhaps to Lann, but more to herself.

"I know."

"If a bunch of angry Feahs flew up to that fort of theirs looking for a fight, we'd just end up with loads of dead Feahs."

Lann nodded.

"We need a plan first," she said. "Find Moyra and the both of ye watch for any trouble—from Dayigans *or* Feahs. I must return to the temple now."

—

"I can't believe it," Chief Kaie said. She was about Cal's age, and although she wasn't from the fishing village, she'd become friends with Treasa as a child. Thus, Finn had known her, somewhat, before she'd started her druidic studies. Even then, she'd been a smart, determined girl with long silver hair and wings. Now she was a thin woman of thirty in a long purple velvet cloak over her white druidic dress and an elegant bone necklace.

"'Tis the utter truth," Finn said, "every word of it. The Human commander killed his own man. I give you me word on that, Chief. And 'tis said, '*Keep true to oaths, for he whose word is meaningless is meaningless, himself, and cannot be trusted.*'"

Cal elbowed Finn in the arm. "The chief druidess knows the Tréréaldéag. You don't need to quote it at her."

They were in Kaie's study just off the Temple Grove, and the large stone-framed doorway behind Finn showed the massive grassy room centered with trees. *This* room was plastered white, though the texture of the stones beneath showed. It was a ten-foot by ten-foot room with a large rectangular section of the ceiling open to allow one to fly up to Kaie's second-story living quarters. The entire upper border of the room was sunken a few inches, holding a purple fire to light the room. The sparse furnishings—a table, two simple chairs, a few bookcases, and the chests of drawers—were all stained white.

After a thought, Kaie rested her hand on Finn's upper arm. "Of course, I believe you, Finn. I'm just surprised, that's all, that they'd go to such lengths. And to what end?" She sighed. "I was thinking, true and well, if they came to our festival and got to know us ..." She shook her head.

"That's the trouble though," Cal said. "They didn't get to know us. They were hateful arseholes the whole time. Seems to me now they only came here to start up trouble."

"Could be true," Kaie said, "them coming here to start trouble. If they just wanted to murder Finn, they would have, then and there, without the show." She turned to Finn. "And thank the Mothers they did not."

Finn glanced downward as the uneasy thought washed over him.

Cal leaned toward the chief and lowered his voice. "Do you think it part of the *other matters*, Chief?"

Why Cal lowered his voice puzzled Finn. He was the only one there, besides the two, and could hear. Obviously, Finn wasn't supposed to know what the "other matters" were.

"Most likely." Kaie looked up past Finn and Cal. "Ah, Treasa, 'tis yourself. How are our people faring?"

Finn looked back to see Treasa standing just inside the thick stone-cased entry.

"They're scared, angry, and confused, Chief. As am I. Is there hope we can convince the Dayigans that this is all a big misunderstanding?"

"'Twould seem they know, already," Kaie said. "Finn, we might as well let you know—there's been reports throughout the Feah lands. People are disappearing without a trace. Some blamed the Dayigans, but we had no way to be sure about it. Some of the victims' own families blamed it on wicked Faeries, and that hasn't happened in ages. Either way, we hadn't any proof."

"Well, here's your proof here." Cal grew angry. "And my little brother about vanished altogether for it. We need the Humans gone. Now."

"You sound like the hooligans outside." Treasa approached her husband, her anger increasing with each step. "Would you have us storm the outpost of the largest army in the whole world? Of the largest empire in the world? If we did anything like an act of war against the Dayigan Empire, we'd need to militarize the entire Feah tribe to defend ourselves. And, *and*, we'd still end up dead as old stones."

"Stop fighting," Finn yelled. "Please."

Cal and Treasa stood, panting, as they looked at one another.

Finn looked past them. The boy, Ubaz, was peeking in the entrance.

Treasa turned to see the boy's head dart behind the casing. She went to him.

"You be a good boy and go play with the other children. We're having grown-up talks in here."

Another druidess hurried to the boy and ushered him away.

After Treasa returned, Chief Kaie said, "The both of ye are right. We need the Dayigans gone, aye, but we can't fight them. Not on our own. I sent word to the other True Light nations, asking them for help."

"And they'll help us then?" Finn asked.

Kaie shook her head. "They won't."

Finn looked down, staring at his toes.

"Disappointing as it is," Kaie said. "I, at least somewhat, understand the reply from the kingdom to our south—across the Hyvile River. They, Dinikimera, said they wouldn't help because they're a *trade nation*. They apologized, actually, but they need to stay neutral, says them. But they said they would set up a trade route with us, so we wouldn't need to use the Dayigans. And without them needing to set up a post here. They even said they'd waive all tariffs for three years."

"Sounds promising, that," said Cal.

"'Twas nice of them, aye," Treasa joined. "But the Dayigans aren't here to trade with us, not really."

"Treasa's right," Kaie said. "Like Dinikimera, our lands mark the dividing line of the continent. We think the Dayigans are wanting to set up trade with West Bikia, not with us. Or something; who knows? We've nearly stopped trading with them as it is, and they couldn't care less about it."

"Real neighborly of Dinikimera though," Finn added.

Kaie nodded. "Aye, it was, true. I contacted the Reyigans to our east as well. Not quite so neighborly, them." She sighed. "Well, just read it for yourself."

From a table, Kaie grabbed a folded page of parchment with a broken blue-wax seal. She extended it to Finn.

Finn looked at it without taking it. He looked at Kaie. "Can't do a thing with that, Chief."

She moved the page toward Cal.

Cal looked away, as if he'd seen something interesting in the corner.

Treasa huffed and stepped forward, taking the page. "We're teaching Ubaz to read."

Cal shrugged. "'Tis your time to waste, love."

Treasa unfolded the page and read:

"Dear Chieftainess Kaie, whilst we sympathize with the plight of the Drevite people, your extremely unorthodox version of the True Light is at odds with long-held virtues and morality that are upheld by the Kingdom of Reyigo and the Karulent Alliance at large. Someone could misconstrue our sending you aid in this matter as an endorsement of your way of life, which could potentially confuse our people, especially our children, during this time when we already blah, blah, blah. We hope you understand. Blah, blah, blah. Impressive signature."

Treasa lowered the page to her waist and stared.

"That's what that Human commander said to me," Finn said. "That we weren't good enough to be calling ourselves True Light."

"We have to do something," Cal said.

Kaie took the page from Treasa and folded it. "First, we must inform the other tribal chiefs of the situation here in the Feah. It might move to their lands as well. Treasa, do me a kindness, please, and help me write four copies of a letter."

—

Treasa held, as a pen, a reddish-brown feather as long as her upper body. It was one of her own primary flight feathers, molted years ago. With it, Treasa meticulously scratched black carbon ink onto rough paper as she leaned over a white table. Kaie, beside her, did the same with a similar silver feather. Centered on the table, a small brass cauldron held a fire.

Treasa concentrated on each word, not only writing them with ink but also willing every letter to exist on both a physical and nonphysical level. She charged them into existence and empowered them. Writing here, with a quill from her body, was a ritual.

Thus, Treasa tried to ignore Cal, who paced the room. And Finn, who sat on the floor and fiddled with a pebble.

Finished, she set the quill down and lifted the page to review for any mistakes.

The gist of it was simple: the Dayigans intentionally killed one of their own and blamed it on a Feah man; the reasons were unknown, but it could be part of a greater scheme that could affect all the Five Tribes. She saw no errors.

Treasa rolled the page and touched it to her forehead while she concentrated. Afterward, she placed it in the cauldron's fire, letting it slide in.

Finally, Treasa looked to the room's edge. There, a horizontal bar supported by white wedges lined a part of the wall. On the bar perched two ghostly ravens.

"Heed, O Ravenshade," Treasa said. "Take these words to the chief of the Allar tribe."

The Ravenshade spread its wings of black mist and flew toward the cauldron. It dove toward the fire and, with its talons, snatched up the twisting trail of black smoke.

It flew away with it, out of the room, up toward the circular opening centered above the Temple Grove.

A druidess stood in the doorway. "Forgive me for interrupting, archdruidesses."

"No bother at all," Kaie said. "Come in."

"One of them Humans, the leader, is at the front of the temple, Chief. He's demanding to see you. And he's demanding ..." She looked at Finn. "Says he, 'the murdering pervert,' Chief."

"Feck's sake," Cal grumbled. "The nerve of him."

"I'll go," Finn spoke up. "If 'twill help out the Feah—"

"You will not," Kaie said firmly. "You're *our* murdering pervert, and I aim to keep you alive. Treasa, I must finish this last letter. Do send that ogre of a commander on his wretched way."

"Aye, Chief." Treasa pulled the staff from the scabbard between her wings.

CHAPTER FIVE

Treasa stood within the temple's dim outer chamber—
the Hall of the Ancestors—and looked at the many
skulls arranged on their shelves.

"Ancestors give me strength," Treasa said. She breathed.
She released her left hand from her staff, holding it with only
her right as she turned it vertically. It looked like a walking
stick rather than a weapon, though without her leaning on it.
It made her appear less threatening. She would not be a
fighter, she decided, not yet.

Treasa walked up the sloping corridor to the exit on
ground level. Behind the standing stone, she could smell the
faint metallic burn of magic and feel the prickles in the air:
the commander had tried to force entrance.

She twisted around the stone and descended the steps. All
signs of festivity were gone, save for a few sad remnants of
garlands. There were no Feahs.

The only people Treasa saw were Commander Beadurinc
and ten other Dayigans. All eleven Humans wore identical
emerald green tabards emblazoned with the symbol of their
homeland in yellow thread. This covered a thick suit of
chainmail. Treasa saw it as a bunch of hot and heavy nonsense and knew it would do nothing against a spell.

Beadurinc's hand crossed his stomach and remained on
the sword sheathed on his belt. "I asked to see your chief."

"Demanded, more like," Treasa said. "And I'd wager only after you realized you couldn't enter our temple. The ancestors protect us."

The commander scoffed. "That big magic rock protects you. Magic is the realm of the Gods alone, witch. Only the wicked dare trespass. Hand over the savage who murdered my footman."

"We have no savage like that here, sorry. You might want to have a look at your reflection, Commander."

Beadurinc moved his hand down from the pommel of his sword, and his fingers circled the grip.

Treasa lifted her staff and angled it to drop diagonally across her into her other hand. "What do you *truly* want? We figure you want to establish trade between Bikia and West Bikia. Is that it?"

"What we want"—he began to slide his sword from its scabbard—"is to save the Drevites from the wickedness that plagues you."

His words took Treasa off guard. "I don't understand. What does that mean, save us?"

"Forgive me," Chief Kaie said as she exited the temple. "I should have come sooner, but a chief druidess has much to do on Midyear's Eve, you know." She passed her second-in-command and neared the Dayigans.

Another druidess, staff in hand, took a position next to Treasa.

Kaie circled the commander as she looked him up and down. "*Commander*, I knew Humans get more muscular than Terovaes, but you, sir, are like a mighty bear."

He clicked his sword back into its scabbard and stood taller. "Indeed, my lady. The army of the Holy Dayigan Empire is the strongest in the world and only promotes its best to commanders."

"'Twould seem they chose wisely with you, yes. What do you want with some wee fisherman from an outlying village?"

"If you mean the pervert who killed my soldier, we seek justice."

"Bollocks." Kaie smiled. "Why are you here, Commander?"

"He says he wants to save us," Treasa said.

"Save us, is it?" Kaie asked. "Do we be needing saving, Commander?"

"Witchcraft and perversion overrun your lands. We can help you return to the Light, but you must first hand over the murderer."

Kaie looked at him for a moment. "Well, how can I argue with that? Witchcraft *and* perversion, says he. We can't have that, can we, Vischief Treasa?"

Treasa said nothing. Only watched.

"Very well." Kaie said. She turned to the druidess beside her second. "I suppose you'd better be getting him, then."

"What? No!" Treasa objected. "We can't do that, Chief."

"I can do what I like, Vischief. And you might want to stand back, or I'll be restraining you." Kaie told the other druidess, "Go on, do as the brave commander asks."

The druidess glanced at Treasa. "Yes, Chief." She hurried into the temple.

—

Kyran flew a helter-skelter path, twisting through the maze of thick towering trees. His head spun. He felt as if his aching gut would soon vomit up through his mouth, already tasting of regurgitated milky beer.

Kyran tried to push himself to fly higher, above the trees, and above the maze. No. He descended, nearly to the ground.

As his stomach tightened, he hacked a deep, visceral cough. He fell, bare feet slapping the ground with force. He ran four steps before his knees buckled. Hitting the ground, he rolled.

Kyran pushed himself up with his arms, and the sick came, splashing on the grass with that horrible, caustic taste and scent.

I shouldn't have left Finn, Kyran thought through heaving gags.

He panted, staring at the mess and hoping no more would come.

An older man, gray hair and wings, ran up to him. Kyran didn't quite recognize him, but the man called him by his name before trying to help him up.

"You know better than to fly when you're pissed, lad," the man said.

With most of his weight on the man, Kyran walked, barely. He mumbled, "I had to get away."

"Here, have yourself a seat."

"No." Kyran slid off the man to melt into a crumpled seat against a tree. He'd skinned his arms and legs. Nothing major, but he'd feel it tomorrow.

"They're chasing me," Kyran said—attempting urgency but aware it sounded garbled and sleepy.

"Are they now? And who be chasing you, lad?"

"The Humans."

The man scoffed or laughed; Kyran wasn't sure. Either way, the amusement stopped as something hit the man's head. He fell.

With blurred sight, Kyran stared, trying to figure out the man's sudden need to lie stomach down on the grass, head to the side, eyes closed. Kyran looked up.

Two Dayigan soldiers stood over him.

—

Angry but silent, Treasa waited outside the temple as she watched Chief Kaie chatting pleasantly with the Dayigan commander. Her heart pounded adrenalized blood through her veins. She'd need to act. Soon, the other druidess would return with Finn. She couldn't let the Dayigans take him. The three soldiers would pose little issue, but Kaie ... *Would I need to fight my chief druidess?*

Kaie laughed boisterously, as if the commander had said something hilarious. She placed her hand on his arm.

After an eternity of anticipation, the other druidess exited the temple, circled the standing stone, and descended the steps. Finn was not with her.

Instead, in her hands, flat in front of her, she carried a decorative wooden box.

Treasa's anger melted into curiosity as she watched the druidess approach the commander and present the box.

"What is this supposed to be?" the commander asked.

"'Tis the murderer, that," Kaie said. "You didn't expect us to keep him alive, did you? A man like him could be well dangerous."

Kaie opened the box's hinged lid, showing its contents: black ash.

The commander grew angry. "What do you take me for, woman?" He slapped the box out of the druidess's hands.

It hit the ground, spewing ash across the grass while expelling a dusty cloud.

Kaie remained calm. "And here I thought you wanted him."

"Bring him to me *now*."

Kaie stared into his eyes as she smiled innocently. "The only murderer I know of is *here*, Commander."

His eyes on hers, he crossed his hand to his sword.

Another voice, a man's, shouted from above. "What have you done with him, you shite-eating ogre?"

Treasa looked up to see Lann, his brown wings wide as he descended.

When his feet touched the ground, he ran at the commander.

Beadurinc drew his sword.

Treasa readied her staff, pointing it at the commander.

"Lann," Kaie commanded, "you *will* stay back."

He stopped. "These goat-fuckers kidnapped the wee Kyran fella."

"Is this true, what he's saying?" Kaie asked the commander.

"Yes, I gave the order. I have no way of knowing if they have completed it. He is an accomplice to the murder, and I will try him as such."

"You think me a fool, Human?" Kaie asked. "You killed your own man yourself."

The commander chuckled. "Absurd. Who told you that? The murderer?"

Kaie said nothing.

"As I thought." The commander scoffed. "The drunk fool grabbed my sword, and when my footman scolded him for it, your pervert stabbed him dead." He nodded curtly. His stance conveyed some victory in his words.

Treasa looked to Kaie but couldn't tell if the chief doubted Finn's account.

The Dayigan showed no sign of deceit. And, ever so slightly, Treasa found herself wondering if Finn's story was missing something.

Lann spoke up. "You're not believing this troll of a Human?"

"Lann, get in the temple."

"Aye, Chief," he grumbled. He gave another hateful glance to the commander before retreating inside.

The commander maintained that same pompous grin, as if he had achieved something. "The trial will be in *two days*. 'Tis in your best interest—and the best interest of the accomplice—that the accused attends."

He turned from her and commanded his men. "You ten, remain here and guard the pagan temple. *You will not let that pervert escape.*"

—

Cal still paced. It seemed to Finn he would've tired himself out by now, but no. Finn tried to ignore him. He tried to hold confidence in the Druidic Circle. They'd handle this. Surely.

Finn remained seated on the floor but had moved so his back leaned against the wall. He tried to think of sunset on the river shore, when the arriving night was anticipation and excitement, when the last thing he could have foreseen was this night twisting into nightmares. Sunrise would come soon. Finn wished the sun would wash away this night with all its horrors. But he knew it wouldn't.

Lann entered.

"What's going on out there?" Cal asked as he stopped pacing.

"That commander brought ten of his soldiers to fetch our Finn. And they say they're not leaving 'til they do."

"Fuck's sake," Cal said. "Why are Humans such bastards?" He turned to Finn and approached. "I won't let them have you, you know that, right?"

Finn sighed and nodded before looking down.

"There's more." Lann lowered his head, his manner grave. "They ..." He knelt to Finn. "They got your Kyran. Snatched him up, like."

"No," Finn said. "They can't have."

The chief entered, followed by Treasa.

Finn jumped up and rushed to them. "Chief, we have to get Kyran back."

"We will. We will. And I needn't tell you there'll be repercussions for attacking a Dayigan fort."

"Damn the repercussions, Chief," Lann said. "They've taken one of our own."

"Could we," Treasa began, thinking, "perhaps contact the other True Light nations again? Things have changed now."

"They've made their positions clear," Kaie said. "Finn, is there no chance there's more to your story about the attack?"

"I didn't have a sword on me. I didn't have nothing on me, in truth."

"He said you grabbed his sword." Kaie put her hand on his arm. "If it was an accident, we can work with that. But you must tell me."

"It were just like I said, Chief. The Dayigan commander came out of nowhere, calling me and Kyran all kinds of things. Kyran flew off. And then the Human swung 'round his sword and killed his own warrior. Deliberate like."

Kaie nodded. "Right, thank you, Finn. Were you listening, Treasa, when I was talking to the commander, or were you just standing there pouting like I'd truly hand over our Finn?"

"Plotting a defense, to be honest."

"Right. 'Twould seem the commander has loads of ideas on how to 'improve' the Feah lands. And wouldn't you know it, those, says he, who don't agree with those changes mightn't need to be living here at all. He didn't say execution directly, but he got real quiet when I asked him where they'd go. Save us, indeed. So, we can assume whatever mockery of a trial the Dayigan commander is planning won't be fair in the slightest." She folded her arms and paused in contemplative silence.

The silence lingered as all eyes remained on the chief.

Treasa spoke up gravely. "Whatever we do, we must do it quick. The trial is in two days, and they *will* kill Kyran."

"Aye, I suppose they will," Kaie began. "Our magic is for healing people, caring for nature, and communing with the ancestors. But I know you've been exploring other uses."

Treasa nodded, downcast. "I have, yes. I feared this moment would come. I've modified a few druidic spells, and Moyra has taught me how to use my staff as a weapon."

"Mothers help us," Kaie said, as she raised her fingers to her forehead. "We have to do it. Treasa, tomorrow, you will assemble a team, go to the Dayigan fort, and retrieve Kyran by force."

CHAPTER SIX

O n the grassy floor of the Temple Grove, Treasa sat cross-legged, her back straight, her wings extended, and her hands set palm-upwards on her knees. She gazed at the rough, impressive stone before her, centered on the room. The massive oaks formed a circle around her. She tried not to think of the impending mission. Instead, she felt the warmth of the sun as it embraced her skin. She felt the energy of Mother Lágeya, she who was Nature and in all things: the One Soul.

Peace and calm filled Treasa as the room became but a pleasant bath of energy, filling her and revitalizing her.

"You look well calm, considering." Her brother's voice shattered her meditation.

She turned to see Lann taking a seat on an oak root beside her.

"'Tis a forced calm," Treasa said. "I need to recharge my inner seid by drawing the One Soul into me."

"You mean, charge up your magic."

"I do, in part. Coronal seid powers magic, but also creativity and intuition and other *mental* feats. Vital seid strengthens the body, enhances endurance, and helps a person excel in other *physical* feats. You would also do well to take up meditation."

"It must do wonders for endurance," he joked. "You've been telling me the same damn thing since we was teenagers and haven't give up yet."

Treasa shot him a vexed look. "Because it is true. Taking a wee bit of time every day to make yourself better wouldn't do you any harm, Lann."

She stood up and dusted the seat of her dress. "But I've done enough for now. I started just before noon and that's been an hour now."

"More like two. Cal awake?"

"He, Finn, and Ubaz were still sleeping when I left our apartment. But that's been a while."

"Lannah's still sleeping as well," Lann said. "We had the hardest time getting the wee lass to nod off. She didn't understand why we had a room in the temple here, but she's old enough to know something's wrong." He paused. "You and Cal. Me and Moyra. With the four of us all going to the Human fort tonight, she and your Ubaz could both be ..."

He didn't say the word *orphans*, but he didn't need to. The word had remained lodged in the back of Treasa's brain since the moment she'd selected her team. But it was the best team, she knew, both in ability and unity. Nevertheless, she feared what her decision might bring.

Lann looked away, as if he'd seen something past the trees. "Moyra's in with the chief now. Kaie's checking and reinforcing her armor. She wants to do the same to ours as well. And Cal's."

Treasa looked down at the purple knot tattooed on her forearm. "My armor's good. But it could do with some reinforcing."

She began walking toward Kaie's study.

"Treasa," Lann said.

She stopped and turned back to him.

"I ..." he began. "That is, I just wanted to say ..." He cleared his throat.

"I love you, Brother."

He glanced down and nodded. "I you, Sister."

—

Under the pale blue larger moon and the lavender-tinted smaller moon, Treasa crouched on a high limb of a shore-side tree, her hand resting on its rough bark. Her eyes remained on the Dayigan fort.

The vertical log walls stood two stories before their sharpened peaks ascended higher as parapets edging a rooftop walkway. She could see soldiers patrolling the walkways, one on each side. Each corner guard tower held another soldier. Centered atop the towers, wooden masts displayed emerald green flags.

The ten-foot width of the walkways covered half the thickness of the walls, with the other half, under green wooden shingles, angling downward to end over a courtyard. Treasa wanted to see into the courtyard itself, but even at her height, her distance and angle offered only a glimpse inside. There, she could see only the green-shingled roofs of four large houses, one in each corner, but she couldn't determine how many soldiers the courtyard held.

"I can't see in properly," Treasa said back to Moyra and Lann on another limb.

"I'll fly over to better see in," Lann said. "And I'll take a piss on the lot of 'em whilst I'm up there."

"He means it, truly," Moyra said wearily. "He's done it before."

"It were Finn that said it first," he said. "Joking like. But we talked ourselves into doing it for real."

Cal flew in, pausing a moment in the air before landing next to Treasa. "Did I miss anything?"

Treasa shook her head. "A story about our brothers being idiots."

"Not bothered then. Had enough of those for a lifetime. He's livid, our Finn, 'cause we left him."

Lann chuckled. "We'd do better with wee Ubaz than him. Finn's me mate, but he's shite in a fight. Least Ubaz can use himself a bow."

"He has heart," Cal said. "Finn, I mean. The chief had to tie the bugger up just to keep him in the temple."

"If we could focus on the fort now, please," Treasa said. "I've been in there before. Cal knows. Four years back when it was new and Morgana was still our chief, the Dayigan commander invited her, Kaie, and myself into the 'trade post'—that's what he called it, a 'trade post,' and that's what Chief Morgana had given them permission to build. She was already annoyed with them for using so many trees and building it so large. When we got there and saw the inside, she was utterly furious. She kept her calm, our chief, but I could tell.

"The whole time," Treasa continued, "that fecking commander kept calling it a trade post but kept blatantly showing us how strong of a fort it was. 'Twas full of soldiers—three hundred at the time. The entire tour was a show of power, and the bastard was rubbing our noses in what they'd built right here in Feah lands."

"But why?" Moyra asked. "Build it, I mean. That's what I never understood."

"It doesn't matter right now," Treasa said. "What matters is, I know where they keep their prisoners. They clearly copied the whole place from their homeland, so 'tis more meant to keep out other Humans than Terovaes. The outer doors—one in the front and one in the back toward the river—are large, thick, and well-enforced. But we can just fly straight into the courtyard, where the doors are meager or nonexistent."

"Was it the doors that's the problem then?" Lann joked. "Here I thought it were all them armed Dayigan soldiers aiming to kill us."

She glanced at her brother for a moment and gave a vexed shake of her head.

Treasa spread her wings and reached back, pulling her staff from the holster between them. She stepped from the branch. Hovering in place, she stared at the fort. Focusing her mind, she held her staff with both hands and thrust it high above her head.

"Hear me, Mother Lágeya, she who is Nature and the One Soul that flows through all. Empower me. In your name, I summon the flying insects that sting and bite."

A wasp buzzed past her. A few mosquitoes followed.

"Come stinging insects!" Treasa shouted. "Come biting insects! And be my army."

The buzzing grew louder from all sides as swarms amassed as black clouds above the trees.

"Know your target," Treasa commanded. "*Know your target.*" She lowered her staff and thrust it toward the fort. "Go!"

As one, the swarms moved, buzzing like a blob of blackness and funneling in a downward spiral into the fort.

Treasa's body grew weak. Lightheaded, she fell. She felt her body being caught, and she was in Cal's arms.

He flew her back to the branch.

"The insects won't attack us." Treasa shook off the dizziness. "But I can only control them for *one* hour. Then I must send them away or they'll be stinging us as well."

"You heard the woman." Moyra drew her weapon, a wooden mace topped with a bronze head circled by three rows of thick knobs. "Stop gawking and let's go in. That boy needs us."

They jumped toward the fort and flew. Treasa moved to the front.

The soldiers in the towers and the soldiers on the walls already shouted and cursed in pain as they swatted frantically at the tiny invaders.

Treasa pointed to the front wall and led the group toward it.

The soldier there—grimacing as he fought a dozen insects biting his skin—drew his sword and shouted, charging the Feahs.

Moyra acted first. Her mace crossed the soldier's sword. The fight began.

An arrow shot from the tower behind them, striking Moyra's bare shoulder just above her wings. But her unseen armor held, causing the arrow to hit her skin as if against something hard—cutting her but not piercing as it deflected. Blood oozed from the shallow slice and dripped onto her feathers. Moyra fought on.

"To the tower," Treasa commanded her husband. "Lann, to the other."

The men drew maces and leaped up, flying to the separate points.

Rushing to the wall's edge, Treasa looked into the court-yard. A large house was set in each corner—the closer two, long and two-storied, and the further, single-storied and square. These houses hadn't been here on her last visit, when the fort already held three hundred men. In the large sandy field between them, fifty soldiers ran in circles to escape the surrounding swarms. Others futilely hid behind crates, barrels, or the like.

Thin green doors on either side of the yard, on both levels, led into the fort's walls. There, more soldiers scrambled within large bunkrooms filled with insects. Some men desperately tried to wrap themselves in wet sheets. At the back of the courtyard, the ten-foot green doors—leading to the river—stood wide open, with soldiers retreating to the water's safety.

Treasa felt bad for them. She was not the sort who enjoyed torturing strangers, and as she watched their terrified faces, a part of her wanted to send the insects away.

A scream sounded from the tower where she'd sent Cal. Treasa turned to see a Human falling. He slammed into the ground, blood pooling around him. Treasa watched his broken body in horror.

He was not dead—not yet. His bloody, shaking hand lifted as if reaching. She could heal him, she knew, but she doubted the Dayigans could. The mosquitoes came to him, buzzing around him, covering his bloody body as they feasted.

She turned away.

Cal landed beside her. His eyes, wide, his face, blank.

Treasa stood and looked at him. She nodded. "You had to."

Moyra knocked her opponent unconscious, while Lann descended from the tower.

Had Lann killed, too?

"The prison is right below us," Treasa said. "A lot of the soldiers are fleeing to the Hyvile, and I doubt they'd go swimming if they knew we were here. We still have the surprise. Cal and Moyra, get that back gate shut. We want the men outside to stay outside. Moyra, melee. Cal, archery. Lann, you're with me. We're going for Kyran."

—

Lann and Treasa landed in the courtyard in front of the large doors leading through the fort's front wall. This was not the main door leading outside but a smaller, thinner set of doors, and Treasa remembered a large hall opened beyond it. She was certain she could break it down.

Treasa glanced at the man who'd fallen from the tower. Covered with crawling, biting insects, he struggled to drag himself ... somewhere. But the skid marks of his blood showed that he'd only moved a foot.

"Treasa!" Lann shouted.

Two soldiers, swords drawn, ran at the Feahs.

Treasa held her staff firmly, blocking a forceful blow from a sword. She pushed forward, throwing the soldier back long enough to swing her staff around and club him in the side.

He staggered sideways, nearly falling. He regained himself and swung again.

Lann and Treasa fought fiercely, meeting strikes with blocks and striking hard in return.

Three soldiers on the second-story walkway shouted as they drew swords. They ran down the stairs to charge the Feah.

"We got more coming," Lann strained to say as he fought.

"I see."

A hornet stung her opponent in the face. He tried to ignore it, to fight on, but Treasa gained the advantage. Using the moment, she swung her staff.

One firm blow struck against his skull. The soldier fell.

Treasa thrust her staff at the three approaching soldiers and screamed, voice echoing ethereally. *"Focus!"*

All the insects in the court rose up at once and focused their attention on the three.

Treasa stared in horror at the nightmare she'd conjured as all the men's exposed skin swelled from countless stings. Their screams twisted within the deafening buzz.

The soldiers ran toward the house in the back corner of the fort, fleeing behind it. Two other soldiers, uninvolved, fled simply at the sight.

Treasa waved her hand and released the insects' focus. They swarmed in various directions.

She returned to Lann. Her goofy little brother stood panting with blood splattered down his chest and arms. He clutched his bloody mace in a dangle. A bludgeoned corpse lay at his feet.

"Lann." She stared, dismayed, sick. She regained herself. "We must hurry. This way."

Treasa turned to the double doors at the front, and Lann ran at them, kicking where the two met.

"Stand back," she said, aiming her staff at the ground.

Wind spiraled from staff to ground. There, a diagonal tree erupted and crashed through the doors.

Treasa grabbed her head as a wave of dizziness caused her to stumble.

Lann rushed to her, but she stood on her own.

"I'm good. Calling all the swarms here was a massive spell that used up most of my magic before we began. I can still command the swarms, but if I use any more magic, I'll—"

"You'll be seid depleted." Lann cut her off. "And 'twill tap into your vital energy needed to keep you alive. I know. Me sister's a druidess, if you haven't heard." He cracked a smile across his bloodied face.

Treasa sighed. "Yes."

"You'll be fine with your staff as just a staff. Let's go."

"Drevites!" a man called behind them.

Treasa turned to see Commander Beadurinc. Blisters covered his visible skin, but he retained his pompous posture as he held his readied sword.

"We've come to rescue the man you've abducted from us." Treasa gripped her staff. "We *will* take him home."

"Fine," the commander growled.

"Fine?" Treasa asked and glanced at Lann.

"Yes," said the commander. "Send away your infernal insects, and my men will fetch your filthy savage."

Treasa again looked at Lann. The need to fight twisted with mistrust of the Dayigan. "Why should we believe you?"

"I swear by God Déagar, the Greatest of All," said the commander, sheathing his sword, "no more harm will come to you or your fellow invaders if you comply. And you may leave safely."

Treasa nodded exhaustedly. She flung her hand upward.

The insects, all of them from every part of the fort, flew upward and dispersed.

The commander glared at her for an angry moment as he folded his hands across his stomach. "I'll have the prisoner brought here, Vischief."

CHAPTER SEVEN

Treasa, Cal, Lann, and Moyra stood wearily, centered on the courtyard of sand.

Hundreds of Dayigan soldiers glared. They stood on the edges of the yard and the second-story walkway railed in green logs. They stood atop the walls.

Treasa tried to ignore the many hateful eyes. Instead, she focused on her haggard group. Countless cuts from arrowheads covered Cal's body, and his armor was nearly depleted. Moyra's armor had nearly popped as well, and she showed multiple large bruises and a long but shallow cut across her upper arm. Blood covered Lann, though most was not his own. Treasa's injuries were minor, but she hadn't enough remaining magic to heal a needle prick, if need be.

By some grace of fate, the Feahs were getting what they came for, but Treasa felt defeated.

"You've made additions," Treasa said to the commander. "These four houses in the courtyard; they weren't here before."

"Yes," Beadurinc said. "The two-story buildings to our left and right are additional barracks, allowing this ... *trade post* to house five hundred men."

"Five hundred?"

A motion stirred behind the commander—at the doors Treasa had smashed with a tree. The tree she'd conjured had half decayed and looked more like melted foam than wood. Two soldiers, stepping through, dragged a prisoner.

"Kyran," Treasa gasped.

He could barely walk. The soldiers lifted his limp body by his arms. Dark blood coated every inch of his naked body. His face was beaten beyond recognition—his features were swollen, jaw broken, eyes black. Fierce lashing had torn the skin of his body as if from whips holding bits of sharpened steel. The lashings covered him—front, back, and legs. One of his arms was broken with bone pressing out against his skin.

In shock, Treasa stared, her eyes watering, her mouth trembling to say something. But no words came.

Kyran strained to lift his heavy head and look at her.

She couldn't tell if there was recognition in his swollen, bloodshot eyes. She wanted him to know he'd be safe now. He'd be home soon.

The soldiers threw Kyran to the ground beside Beadurinc.

Kyran lay limp and motionless in the dirt.

"I had planned to save this sinner," the commander said. "I'd planned to purify him of his wickedness and make him someone worthy of returning to the Light."

Treasa closed her eyes and tears rolled down her cheeks.

"But your *interference* has taken that from him," the commander said. "These *savages*"—he raised his sword to the courtyard—"have attacked us with wicked magic and stolen this reprobate's only chance of redemption."

He looked Treasa in the eyes. "This is *your* fault."

The commander thrust his sword downward, stabbing it between Kyran's wings.

"No!" Cal shouted.

Treasa ran to Kyran as the commander stabbed deeper.

She thrust her hand toward the commander, shoving him back in a twisting wind.

A final grunt of pain, and Kyran was dead.

"You ogre!" Treasa screamed. "You broke your vow to your own God. You swore we'd all be safe."

"I swore *you'd* be safe—the invaders, not the prisoner. And I intend to uphold that vow. Return home. Tell every one of your godless savages what happens when you come into *my fort!*"

With clenched fists, Treasa glared at the Human. "By the Three Mothers, I vow, *we are not done, sir.*"

"Far from it. We wished to save that *thing.*" The commander smirked. "Now, because of your actions, he is dead. And I assure you, Vischief, when we catch the murderer—and we will—his fate shall be ten times more severe."

Treasa looked back at Cal.

He seemed near panic.

"Go," she commanded. "We'll get Kyran."

Cal jumped up and flew away.

—

Finn, sitting on the floor at the end of a dark hallway, his back against the stone wall, hiked his knees to his chest. He rested his hands atop them and stared, his face frowning with worry.

Tall structures, each one or two stories, lined either side of the hallway. They didn't seem quite like part of the massive stone room around them. The wooden buildings were more like oversized bits of furniture; their roofs were flat and didn't quite reach the slanted ceiling above. Their lower doors met the floor on which Finn sat. The upper doors stepped out to simple, unrailed balconies—small things just enough for someone to land on and enter.

One of the second-story doors—painted in a thin coat of happy yellow—led to Cal and Treasa's apartment. They weren't at home. Finn tried not to think of that, of their current conflicts, or if they remained alive.

The hallway was not directly lit. Instead, a ten-foot, square passage framed in thick stone sat at the end opposite Finn. It borrowed light from the great room beyond. Though dim, the light allowed Finn to see the simple—almost childish—paintings on the wooden walls. Thick, green, twisting, swirling lines were meant to be vines with oversized leaves and flowers. To Finn, the paintings were consoling, not only in their presence but in the happy moments he imagined for their creation. Finn imagined merry druidesses laughing while they painted. Perhaps Treasa had been among them. Perhaps Cal. In his daydream, Treasa tapped a dot of pink paint on Cal's nose. Cal was suddenly perturbed while trying to hide a smile. Treasa started laughing. Ubaz started laughing.

The imagined scene was in contrast to the present, in which Finn's whole body was tense and his guts twisted with anxiety. His hand atop his knee fidgeted, with his thumb darting around his fingers, popping his knuckle, and clicking his fingernails.

A memory flashed in Finn's mind. He thought of walking side by side with Kyran, their arms over each other's shoulders as they sang made-up songs. Finn thought of laughing with him.

Finn wanted to scream, but he kept his attention on the paintings as if he could absorb joy from them.

He wanted to help them—Cal, Lann, and all. He wanted to be the sort who could help them, not the one left behind. But mostly, he just wanted everything to return to normal.

Finn heard his name shouted from the larger room. It was Cal.

Finn jumped up and ran down the hallway, through the stone-edged portal, and into the grand Temple Grove. He saw Cal.

"Finn!" Cal called again, with desperation in his voice.

"I'm here."

Cal—not dressed for the temple and bloodied—rushed to him and grabbed him tight, like a parent finding a lost child. "We have to get you out of here. Out of the temple, out of the whole fecking parish."

Finn stepped back. "Where's Kyran?"

Cal froze, his sad eyes searching for anywhere to look but at his brother. "Never mind him."

"Cal." Finn's voice cracked. "What happened to him?"

Chief Kaie approached them. She stood near but quiet, her head bowed slightly.

A few distant druidesses watched and whispered.

"What happened?" Finn shouted.

Cal shook his head, his eyes watering. He answered toward Kaie. "That bastard ... That dirty rotten bastard of a commander threw Kyran to the ground like he was nothing. And killed him right in front of us. He was beat beforehand, as well. Awfully beat. Like ..." He shook his head.

Finn lifted his hand to his forehead as he sat on the grass. Dizziness throbbed through him. He could barely speak but managed, "Are you ... are you sure?"

"Yes, I'm fucking well sure, Finn," Cal shouted. "I'm sorry. I'm sorry."

Kaie asked about the other members of his team, and Cal said they'd stayed behind to collect Kyran's body.

"They're safe," Cal added. "The commander vowed we could leave unharmed. But just so we could tell everybody about our bleak failure. But Finn's not safe here. We have to get him as far away as we can."

Eyes on the grass, Finn muttered, "He was about to get married, him. To a fella up in the Frelon tribe. Kyran said he lived on the Teréyi Sea. I don't know his name." He looked up at no one in particular. "We have to tell him."

Kaie nodded and set her hand on Finn's shoulder. "I'll send a Ravenshade to the Frelon chief. I'm sure she can figure out who the man is, and she can let him know."

"Will they help us?" Cal asked. "The Frelons? Or maybe the Rúcahs to our west."

"I'm afraid the other tribes aren't in any better position to handle the Dayigans than are we."

"But if all the Five Tribes united ..." Cal tried.

"No," Kaie said firmly. "Uniting against the Dayigans won't mean a thing more than many deaths in all the tribes."

"I'll go to the Dayigans," Finn said. "Keeping me alive isn't worth starting a war over. I'll turn meself in."

"Stop saying that," Cal said. "The chief's already told you that's not to happen."

"That's well brave of you, Finn," said Kaie. "But we know their commander knows you didn't kill his man. So we know he's not really trying to prosecute a criminal. Whatever he's planning, I'm not thinking your death will solve a thing. But I *do* think he'll kill you all the same, though."

Kaie thought for a moment. "We need an ally strong enough to deter the Dayigans from attacking altogether. And

Cal's right; we need to get you out of the area. Come here with me."

—

As Cal and Finn followed Kaie into her study, the purple fire along the tops of the walls ignited and spread along the upper border.

Kaie waited in the center of the room until Cal and Finn were inside. She motioned to the large doorway.

The threshold rose as a large slab. With the scratching of stone on stone, it rose until—thud—the door sealed.

Silence.

"I'm not sure what ye know about the departure of the former chief," Kaie began. "Treasa shouldn't have said a thing, but ..."

"Not the slightest word," Cal said. "'Twas maddening."

Kaie nodded. "Now, 'tis time ye know, but no one else. Do ye vow by the Three Mothers to keep this secret?"

"Aye," Cal said. "I vow."

"And me."

Kaie paused, as if debating whether to continue. "Three years back now, Chief Morgana went out in search of a powerful ally in the very same fight we face today." Her voice was grave. "Do you know of the *Anordúla?*"

Uncertain, Finn glanced at Cal.

Cal shook his head. "I do not. What is it?"

"Well, in ancient times, when the Five Tribes were one and calling themselves the tribe of Drevok, our ancestors teamed up with a tribe of Humans called the Gels. And together, we fought against the dark Faeries who wished to destroy the world."

"Everybody knows that bit, Chief," Finn said with a smile. "When we was wee, we heard them stories here in the temple every New Year's Eve. And Midyear's Eve. Our ancestors fought with a grand good Faery called Adalheidis."

"Aye." Kaie nodded. "And we won and cast those dark Faeries back into their dark realm. But we cracked up the walls between our realm and theirs, with the damage extending throughout the lands that the Five Tribes now call home. The five druidic circles—the Feah, the Rúcah, the Allar, the Frelon, and the Caróg—were founded to guard those cracks and make sure nothing comes through, especially on New Year's Eve and Midyear's Eve, when the walls are the thinnest."

"And ye be doing a fantastic job at it, Chief." Cal thinly hid impatience. "You and the rest. But what does any of this have to do with the ninth century and a madman coming for my brother?"

"By the Mothers, Calvagh ó Ríona, if you do not hush up and let me tell my story, I'll kick you right out and just tell it to Finn."

"Aye, Chief."

She turned to Finn and grinned. "He was like that when we were children. Do you remember?"

Finn nodded. He glanced at his brother.

Cal turned red with annoyance.

Kaie leaned to Finn and turned somber. "There's a bit we leave out of the stories." She stood upright. "When the druidic circles were founded, there was a sect that didn't agree with the rest. That sect thought, instead of guarding the planar cracks and trying to seal them, we should harness the chaos energy flowing from the dark Faery Realm itself."

The words horrified Finn, and he could see Cal was similarly affected.

Kaie gave a curt nod. "That's shut you up, hasn't it now? Imagine what the ancient Drevites must have thought, hearing *that* right after they'd just fought a war against dark Faeries. The sect argued that the risk was worth the power our people would gain from it. The sect began calling themselves *the Anordúla* and kept trying to gain support. In the end, our ancestors had no choice but to banish them. And they vanished from history altogether.

"Now," Kaie continued, "to the ninth century, as requested by our Cal here. Do you remember how delighted we all were when Chief Morgana welcomed the Dayigans to our shores?"

"We threw a fecking parade for the bastards," Cal griped.

"It seems well mad to think about now," Kaie said. "Just four years ago, but so different."

Both Cal and Finn gave downcast nods.

Kaie looked downward. "'Twas meant to be so fantastic, trading with all the other nations for miles upon miles. It wasn't until after they built that fort of theirs that Morgana knew they were a threat. Knew, too, we was stuck with 'em, lest we do something drastic."

"The Anordúla?" Finn asked.

Kaie nodded. "There's no reason to think they still exist. But Morgana aimed to find them. She wanted me and Treasa to go with her, but we weren't having it, not then. But things have changed for the worse now, and the other True Light nations won't help us."

Finn digested the words as Kaie walked to a chest of drawers on the back wall. The dark Faeries and their magic were things Finn had learned to fear as a young boy. Tales of Faeries luring away children to drown or eat were well known among his people, as were tales of adults seduced into equally grim fates. Too, Faeries trapped the souls of the dead, enslaving them long after death, if not forever. The time of the dark Fae was a time of waking nightmares. The idea that Finn's own chief had left to seek this forbidden and dangerous magic made him feel sick in his stomach.

Chief Kaie returned from the drawers and held a Y-shaped stick, stripped of bark, smoothed, and varnished. A few runes were carved along its length.

"Morgana enchanted this rod and gave it to me and Treasa. She hoped we'd use it to find her when we—said she—'came to our senses.'" She held out the rod. "I want you to take it, Finn. Find Morgana and, hopefully, find the Anordúla as well."

Finn stared at the stick but didn't take it. His heart pounded as if the chief had offered him an angry snake.

"I don't want to leave the Feah, though," he said. "I can't."

Kaie set her hand on his arm. "I won't make you find Morgana, but either way, you have to leave the Feah lands. Not forever, but for a while."

Cal joined. "We can't just send my brother out alone to who knows where."

"I'm sending ye both out to who knows where. If you'll go. I don't plan to truly use chaos magic, but restoring peace to the Feah lands is of the utmost importance. If we can show the Dayigans we have chaos magic and could *potentially* use it, it should be enough to make them leave our lands for good."

Finn looked to Cal for answers.

Cal paused. "I must speak to Treasa."

—

When Treasa entered the Temple Grove, she seemed broken. Finn watched from afar as Cal approached the haggard warrior. She threw down her staff, and Cal hugged her in a lingering embrace, the kind in which the contact between two people attempted to battle the sorrow within them both. Arms pulling the other as close as possible. Despondent faces. Silent tears.

Cal stepped away, his hand still holding hers, and guided Treasa toward Kaie's study. He signaled Finn to follow.

Inside, the three of them waited in stunned silence as the thick stone door rose from the floor. It thumped.

Treasa sat on the floor, centered on the room. She listened as Cal recounted Kaie's words from earlier.

"Do you think we should do this?" Cal asked.

Treasa had been watching the floor. Now, she turned her head toward Cal as he stooped to her level.

"You saw what they did to Kyran," she said, her words bitter, her face blank. "Not just when he stabbed him, but the bruises and cuts already covering his body. They tortured that boy with a brutal hate unlike anything ..." She controlled her breathing. "... anything I've ever seen before."

Finn clamped his eyes as tears rolled down his face.

Treasa clutched her shaking hand to her forehead and raked her fingers back through her auburn hair. "Is that what that hateful commander will do to our little boy if he gets ahold of him? You know our wee Ubaz is like Finn and Kyran. Will the Dayigans call him a pervert, torture him; will they murder our little boy whilst we watch?" She inhaled a deep breath. "The commander will not stop unless we stop him," she whispered. "I saw it in his eyes."

She looked up at Cal and said, "If the Anordúlas are our only choice to stop this, then they're the only choice we have."

CHAPTER EIGHT

Finn sat against a thick tree, one of the seven oaks that circled the large standing stone in the center of the temple.

Four days had passed since Kyran's death. Finn thought about him every day. Cried for him every day. Kyran had only come to the Feah's festival to say goodbye to Finn. It was Finn's fault, he reflected, that Kyran was not happy, married, and living by the sea.

Finn couldn't attend the funeral. Kyran's body had been placed high in the Tree of Silence for Nature to take. Finn wasn't allowed to leave the temple—not since that last night with Kyran.

But he'd soon leave, leave the temple, leave everything.

"Finn." Treasa approached from behind him.

Finn stood and dusted off the seat of his white temple garment.

Treasa, bleak as she faced his general direction, held out a rolled-up sheet of leather twenty-two inches long. "This is yours."

Finn took it. "'Preciate it."

"Lann got it. He's been round to your house and sorted anything that needed sorting."

Finn untied the waist of his temple garment, and the cloth fell to the ground, leaving him naked.

"I hadn't meant for you to change here." Treasa tried a half smile. It was short lived.

Finn looked to the ground. "Sorry." Still watching the ground, he wrapped the leather kilt around his waist and fastened the straps and buckles.

His own clothes. He'd thought they'd make him feel more *him*. Instead, they only reinforced that it was time to go.

"Cal's waiting for you at the spot you're supposed to meet," Treasa said. "Do you remember where to go?"

Finn nodded. "I'm sorry he had to leave you and Ubaz."

She inhaled through her nose. Paused. And exhaled just as slowly. "'Tis not your fault, Finn. None of this is."

Finn turned his attention to the sun beaming through the brass star in the ceiling. "That's my exit, is it? Up through there?"

"No. The gaps aren't big enough to fly through. And squeezing through would be too slow. You'll need to rush out the front of the temple."

He swallowed dryly. "And they'll be shooting at me?"

She placed her hand on his forearm. "Trust in the armor Kaie gave you."

Finn looked at his forearm, where his skin reddened around a fresh tattoo. It was an elaborate knot—a design portraying a continuous line twisting around, over, and under itself. This one was roughly square and circled by runes.

"'Twill still hurt when the arrows hit you." She looked into his blue-gray eyes. "But you cannot let them be a distraction to you. You must fly fast and keep going. Don't let them deplete your armor."

Treasa was afraid for him. He saw it in her eyes, and his own fear twisted in his gut.

Lann entered and approached. "There's thirty of the bastards out there now. But that's not the worst of it: two of them are Terovaes."

"Terovaes?" Finn asked. "With the Humans? How's that?"

"We knew there were Dayigan Terovaes," Treasa said. "'Twas only a matter of time before they sent some here to us. It does change things, though." She looked at Finn. "It means they'll be chasing you into the sky."

"It means we can't be sending our Finn out there at all."

"We have no choice, Lann," Treasa said firmly. "The Dayigans have to see Finn leaving the temple. Alone. Maybe after that ..." She sighed. "Maybe they'll leave us be."

Silence lingered for a moment.

"'Tis no bother, Lonnie," Finn said. "I'm a fast flier. You know that."

"You better fucking be." Lann gave a sad smile. "You better fly like the fucking wind on fire."

Finn nodded. His body felt numb. "I'll see you soon, mate. Both of ye. 'Twill be all right, soon enough."

—

Finn stood in the tight, shadowed entry tunnel of the temple and stared at the standing stone in the sunlight just outside the entrance.

He breathed.

"Ancestors, help me."

He ran.

As soon as he hit the light, Finn spread his wings and jumped. He shoved his wings downward with all his might, pushing himself upward and missing the standing stone by a foot as he soared into the air.

About twenty feet above the temple, Finn stopped. Treasa had said that the Dayigans must see him leave, and he aimed to ensure they did.

"Feck off, ye nine-headed ogres," Finn shouted. It seemed like something Lann would say, sort of, but it was awkward from his mouth. "You'll never catch me."

Five arrows flew his way at once.

Finn tried to dodge, but an arrow struck his calf. Its steel blade cut his skin but didn't pierce.

Finn called out in pain and slapped his hand to the bleeding gash.

The two Dayigan Terovaes spread their wings and jumped from the ground. They both had brown wings, short neat brown hair, and that same hateful scowl as the Humans.

Finn thought it weird to see the Dayigan uniform airborne. It differed from the Humans'—instead of mail underneath cloth, the tabard itself was green leather and was sleeveless and V'd down the back to the belt. No undershirt, as far as Finn could see.

The trousers were black cloth. Same brown leather gloves, belt, and boots as the Humans.

Finn took all this in at a glimpse because as soon as he glimpsed it, he took off at a steep, upward angle.

Holding his body in a tight diagonal line, Finn pumped his wings with strong, concentrated beats, forcing as much air downward as possible to push him higher, faster.

Finn looked down. The soldiers were about twenty feet below him. If he had a bow and could use it, it would've been a perfect shot. But he didn't, and they did—bow in hand and quiver set between their wings. At least Finn could take some solace in knowing they couldn't shoot upward at him.

Finn's chest and dorsal biceps—the muscles near the tops of his wings—soon burned. He couldn't maintain this rapid ascent for long.

He spread his legs, fanning out his kilt as a rudder. Finn twisted his body in a tight turn, sending himself in the opposite direction in a loop that sent him flying parallel with the ground, about a quarter of a mile down.

The Dayigans wouldn't be able to copy his turn, Finn hoped. Looking back confirmed that they'd fallen back a good forty feet, but higher.

But they now had a shot at him.

Finn glided, resting his aching wings while he panted in the thin air. He'd be able to glide for a while in the vast blue, but no doubt, so could the Dayigans.

A soldier snatched an arrow from his quiver. He slowed, turning himself vertical, aimed, and shot.

The bladed point cut across Finn's left wing—shallow but painful—and took some minor feathers.

Finn, shouting in pain, recoiled his wing. He lost lift and fell.

He shook it off, thrusting himself back up, and leveled out.

Another arrow sliced his other wing close to his spine.

Finn gritted through the pain, keeping himself steady. He knew he had to lose them or they'd slice him up.

Finn dove toward the trees, branches scratching him as he plunged through the canopy.

Navigating woodlands in fast flight with a nearly twenty-foot wingspan was a frightening headache of a task. It meant yanking in his wings to avoid hitting something, only to lose all lift and needing to flap them quickly to keep flying, all while expending a lot of energy twisting and dodging trees, flying diagonally. It also meant Finn needed to focus completely on what was ahead of him, with not a moment to glance behind. The Dayigans might have been a foot from his foot, and Finn wouldn't have known.

In time, Finn had no choice but to locate his pursuers.

His feet hit the ground running, and Finn spun around and stopped.

Panting, Finn searched the skies and surrounding area, as if he were a hunted animal.

No one.

"Mothers be praised," he said.

Finn dashed for the underbrush and hid.

—

Finn's trek to the spot to meet Cal was a panicked rush. Luckily, sunset helped him hide. He kept to the forest floor, crouching and dashing from tree to tree and using any concealment he could find. He'd let himself become a rabbit hunted by hawks, but he had no other option.

The sky was out of the question. Every so often, Finn glimpsed one of the Dayigans circling above.

Finn was frightened, more frightened than he'd ever been, and the cuts on his leg and wings burned.

Finally, Finn saw Cal pacing in a clearing around an apple tree in bloom circled by small stones. From the woodline, Finn threw a stick at Cal's feet.

Stopping, Cal looked around.

"Cal!" Finn whispered and motioned him over.

Cal ran to him and grabbed his shoulders. "You took ages, then. I feared ..." The worry on Cal's face was clear.

"The clearing's not safe," Finn said. "I'm being chased. By Terovaes."

"Terovaes?"

"Working with the Dayigans."

"Fecking traders."

"They're Dayigans, themselves," Finn said. "From their empire."

"Still. Fucking bastards, then. How's your barkskin holding up?" Cal asked, meaning the armor.

"They shot me up good, but it hasn't popped yet."

Cal grabbed Finn's wrist and looked at his forearm.

The tattoo of the elaborate knot design, which had been a solid purple line before, was empty for most of its length, with only its borderlines remaining. Only a small part remained filled.

"You don't have much of it left," Cal said. "The chief should have given you stronger armor, like ours. Use your magic stick quick. We need to be going."

Finn hurriedly pulled the Y-shaped rod from under his belt and held both of the smaller ends while pointing the third outward.

Finn closed his eyes and tried to relax, to let it guide him. But his head raced with thoughts, and his heart pounded with fear and adrenaline.

"It isn't working now."

"You have to relax, like Chief Kaie told you."

"Fuck's sake, Cal!" Finn snapped. "How am I supposed to do that then?"

Cal said nothing, shocked by Finn's outburst.

Someone landed right behind Finn and grabbed him. Before Finn knew what was happening, a Dayigan clamped an arm around Finn's chest and forced a dagger to his neck.

"Don't move, either of you."

The other Dayigan hovered above them.

The first said, "Give me a reason to cut his throat." He pressed his dagger closer to Finn's neck.

Finn could see the dread in Cal's eyes as he stared.

The other Dayigan Terovae, hovering above, descended closer as he armed his bow and aimed at Cal.

Surely Cal saw him, but his eyes remained on Finn.

The soldier behind Finn squeezed his arm tighter around Finn's chest. "I might not understand the witchcraft keeping my arrows from piercing this savage's skin," he said to Cal. "But I understand that look in your eyes. That look says you don't think your magic will stop my dagger from slitting his throat." He pulled the blade closer. "The commander wants the murderer dead or alive. You choose which one 'tis going to be with your actions now."

"You don't have to do this," Cal said. "You must know the Humans are corrupt. You don't have to serve them. We can help ye out."

"We don't serve the Humans, savage. We serve the Holy Dayigan Empire and God Déagar. My home is in the empire, in a city my family has lived in for generations. Don't try and act like we're anything alike, just 'cause we're Terovaes."

He was right, Finn knew as he listened to him. His words, his accent, even the way the two held themselves—there was nothing of the Five Tribes in these Dayigans.

"Put your arms straight out from your sides," the soldier behind Finn commanded Cal.

Cal glared at him for an extended moment before complying.

The other soldier landed before Cal and yanked the belt that ringed Cal's waist. The soldier unbuckled it, and it—along with Cal's quiver, mace, and satchel—hit the ground with a thump.

The soldier continued, patting down the sides of Cal's legs, but stopped, looking at the kilt. He looked back at the first soldier. "I don't have to check in *there*, do I, Sergeant?"

The soldier holding Finn, evidently a sergeant, chuckled. "I doubt she's got much worth caring about up her skirt."

"More than you have," Cal said.

"Strap him," said the sergeant.

Finn could only watch. The other soldier opened a pouch on his belt and took a rolled leather strap like a thick belt. He forced Cal's arms to his sides. He wrapped the strap around Cal's upper arms and wings, circling his chest, pulling the strap tight, and buckling it in place. A second strap soon circled Cal's lower arms, wings, and stomach. A third circled his ankles.

"I'll come for you, Brother," Cal said. "I vow by the Three Mothers I will. Chief Kaie will make that commander of theirs give you a fair trial, you be sure."

"Trial?" The sergeant chuckled. "Trial's over, savage. We're taking the murderer in for execution."

"No!" Cal struggled at the restraints.

"Deal with him," the sergeant said.

The other soldier kicked Cal in the stomach, causing him to crash into the dirt.

Cal shouted as he twisted on the ground.

The sergeant whispered harshly in Finn's ear, "I'll let you watch this part, savage. *The True Light is the only way. All others will perish.*"

The other soldier drew his sword. He kicked Cal flat on his back and straddled him. He lifted his sword with both hands.

"Let him go, you rotten bastards." Finn struggled, even as the dagger pressed into his neck.

The soldier thrust his sword into Cal's chest. It drew blood but did not enter.

Cal shouted in agony as the soldier pressed his weight onto the sword, twisting it and trying to force it into him.

Blood flowed as thick rivers from the forming injury streaming down Cal's chest, his sides, pooling at his throat, and running down his stomach.

"Please," Finn cried. "Please, you only want me. I'll go with you, fine. But leave him."

The sergeant held Finn tighter but said nothing.

Finn struggled, pushing against him with his wings.

Cal kept screaming.

Finn elbowed the sergeant in the side.

"Fucking savage," he growled in Finn's ear. He squeezed tighter and pressed the dagger into Finn's neck. "You'll die for that." He ripped the blade across Finn's throat.

Finn shouted in horror.

But the cut was shallow. The greater pain was in Finn's forearm, where his armor tattoo burned.

Using the moment, Finn twisted while bending and forcing back with his wings.

The sergeant lost his grip on Finn and stumbled some steps away.

Finn glanced at his protection tattoo. "Empty. Fuck." The sergeant had popped his armor.

Finn dashed toward Cal, but the sergeant drew his sword.

Finn stopped and faced him, bracing himself as he looked around for answers.

Cal screamed, "Go, Finn! Fly!"

It wasn't an option as far as Finn was concerned, but he didn't bother answering. All he could hear was his brother screaming in pain, unlike anything he'd ever heard, and he needed to save him. Cal's armor wouldn't take much more, Finn guessed. He needed to hurry.

The soldier atop Cal stopped his torture and looked at Finn. "Do you need assistance, Sergeant?"

"Stay on task. I've got this little pervert."

The other soldier lifted his sword over Cal and slammed it into the pool of blood centered on his chest.

The sergeant cast a murderous look Finn's way as he lifted his sword. He seemed almost pleased to be given the excuse to kill him.

Finn looked at Cal again. So much pain. Finn hesitated for a moment. Then he flew away, taking a low flight into the thick woodlands surrounding the clearing.

Feet hitting the ground, Finn ran and dashed behind an oak. He crouched low.

He was certain the sergeant had followed but hoped he hadn't seen where Finn hid.

The soldier soon arrived. He hovered, searching, sword in hand. He touched his boots to the ground and folded his wings.

The sergeant walked carefully and quietly as he looked all around, listening.

As still as possible, Finn barely breathed, despite his silent panic. He needed to hurry. Time was short, but how short, Finn didn't know. Cal's screams rang out in the distance.

Cal's armor was stronger than his, but surely, it wouldn't last much longer.

Finn laid his hand on a fallen branch, about three inches around and long, tapering into three small bare branches. Finn lifted it. A piece fell off, thumping on the ground.

The soldier turned his way. Pausing, staring. "Run, little pervert. I don't care. Wherever you go, I *will* find you." He continued his search.

Finn waited for him to turn away. Waited. Finn jumped up and flew at the soldier.

He smashed the branch against the back of the sergeant's neck. The half-rotten thing crumbled on impact, but it was enough to cause the soldier to drop his sword.

Finn snatched up the weapon and flew. Like a harpoon, Finn rushed as fast as he could, thrusting the sword in front of him.

The soldier atop Cal looked up as Finn approached him. Finn saw the realization, the horror strike in the soldier's eyes just before the blade stabbed through his leather armor, his flesh, and his bones. Before blood erupted from his chest.

With a scream of hate, Finn flew on, lifting the soldier from his brother by the sword and taking him a few feet before slamming him to the ground.

Finn hurried to Cal and undid the buckles.

An arrow flew by Finn, but he dodged.

With the last buckle opened, Cal leaped up and grabbed his mace.

"Stay here," Cal said, glowering. He flew into the woods.

—

Cal hadn't killed the Dayigan sergeant. Instead, he'd used his mace to knock him out.

Now, Cal and Finn sat in the small clearing beside the apple tree circled by rocks. They were silent, resting, and thinking. Finn stared at the man he'd killed.

Finn half wanted to vomit. He half wanted to lie down and fall asleep. Instead, he watched the dead man, lying there as still as anything could lie.

The soldier's black cloth pants had been cut into shorts—the removed cloth made into bandages for Cal. His brown boots were beside him. Dried blood stained his green leather tabard and the ground beside him. A part of Finn nearly cried for the man who'd tortured his brother.

Finn had been charged and convicted of killing a Dayigan soldier. Now, he'd done it.

"Would you stop looking at him?" Cal pushed his brown hair back along the top of his head. "You had to do it. The Mothers know that. The ancestors know it as well."

Finn nodded sadly and turned away.

The sergeant squirmed on the ground like an injured worm. They'd bound him with the same straps used before on Cal. His buddy's sock was stuffed into his mouth.

"What do we do with *him?*" Finn asked.

Cal looked at the sergeant. "If we were like you, we'd kill you now, you know. Or leave you here, tied up, to be eaten alive by wolves. My guess, they'd go for your man there first, so you'd have plenty of time to have a nice think about what's soon to happen to yourself."

The sergeant squirmed on his side and struggled against the restraints.

"Aye, so," Cal said, "you best be thanking your God Déagar we aren't Dayigans."

Cal looked Finn's way and motioned his head toward the woods. "We need to have words. Off on our own."

—

A few paces past the wood line, Cal paused, staring at Finn.

"I'm hurt, Finn. I can't fly with my chest cut up like this. I'll have to go back to the temple and get Treasa or the chief, to heal me. And more so, the dead one needs disappearing, and the live one needs taking back to the temple so he doesn't come after you."

"And you want me to—"

"I want you to go on without me, Finn. You have to. They'll be looking for you, same as before."

"But I can't do that, Cal. Not on me own."

"Fuck's sake, Finn. You're twenty-five years of age." He stopped. "Sorry." Cal sighed. "I'm sorry. You've always had the group looking out for you, I know that, but ..." He closed his eyes and sighed painfully. "But you'll do fine, Brother. You've got your fish hook, right? And your line?"

Staring at the ground through watery eyes, Finn nodded as he touched a pouch on his belt.

"That's all you need, right?" Cal encouraged with a forced smile. "A fishing hook, a line, and the chief's magic stick to tell you where to go. Oh, and this."

From his belt, Cal removed his mace along with the leather frog that held it. He raised both to Finn.

Finn despondently took the weapon and holder, staring at the unwanted gifts. He looked up to Cal. "I don't even know how long I'll be gone for."

"We'll know that when we know that." Cal patted Finn's shoulder and pulled him into a hug. It was brief before Cal called out in pain.

Finn jumped back. "Sorry."

"'Tis fine." Cal touched his bandaged chest. "You'll be fine."

Finn wasn't sure if Cal spoke to him or himself. And wasn't sure if either of them believed it.

Cal breathed. "Go. I'll handle everything here. I love you, you silly fecker."

Finn sniffed and smiled. "And I you, Brother."

Finn turned and leaped into the air.

CHAPTER NINE

Alone. Finn sat on the wooded bank of a small river—or perhaps a large stream. Having grown up on a twenty-five-mile-wide river that—from what he'd heard—stretched the entire continent, he couldn't think of this rocky, winding thing squeezing through the woodlands as a river.

A small fire, down to embers, crackled beside him. Beside it, Finn's fishing pole was jabbed into the ground; the line twirled around it. On the grass, Finn sat cross-legged and held a sheet of curved bark on his left palm. This bark, as a plate, held chunks of cooked perch that he ate with his right hand.

Preparing lunch always offered some diversion from his travels. He'd left Cal five days ago and had no idea what had happened with his brother or the Dayigan sergeant. Finn worried for Cal and for the village he'd left behind. He was pretty sure he still traveled Feah lands, but in the northern borderlands, where villages were few and far between.

Never had Finn been on his own for so long. He tried to keep in good spirits, but alone, all he could do was think. Too much had happened.

He shoveled another handful of fish into his mouth.

He'd grown tired of wandering and hadn't the slightest idea how much further his journey would take him. Or any idea if the magic stick that supposedly guided him somewhere guided him anywhere, at all. Perhaps he'd travel all the way north to the Arctic Ocean and stare across it like a fool.

"Fecking stick." Finn looked at it lying next to him. "You've got me lost out here, haven't you now? I have a good mind to stay right here, make a hut, and be done with you for good." He sighed. "And never see me brother or Lann again."

He shoveled another bite of fish into his mouth.

The bark plate cracked and broke. His food fell to the dirt and tumbled a turn toward the water.

Finn didn't react. He just stared at his lost lunch, now ruined. "I give up here."

A black goat ambled past him and started drinking from the water.

"Don't suppose you're one of the ancestors, taken animal form to help me out some. I'm wrecked, like. And ready to give up on it all. But if I just had some information about what's going on and where I'm to go."

The goat looked back at him, staring with dumb goat eyes. She turned back to the water and continued drinking.

"Right. Didn't think so." He tossed down the rest of his plate and stood.

The goat jumped and braced herself as if ready to bolt.

"'Tis all right." Slouching passively, Finn shuffled to the goat and reached out his hand. "You can't stay here. There'll be wolves here come nightfall, and you can't fly away like me."

The goat eyed him, still ready to bolt.

Finn set his hand on the black fur of her back and petted.

"See, we're all friends here, aren't we now?"

The goat returned to drinking.

Finn knelt upstream at the goat's side and scooped handfuls of water into his mouth.

Once they'd both had their fill, Finn said, "Come on, goat. Let's get you somewhere safe."

—

Fog overtook the thick woods as Finn walked, and the goat trailed behind. He kept his arms relaxed as much as possible while still holding them before him, his hands loosely grasping the two shorter spans of the Y-shaped stick as the third pointed forward. All the while, he felt the gentle tug from the stick. He let the subtle force lead him to the unknown destination, to the position of his former chief—hopefully.

However, he wanted to go home. He needed to go home. The pain of it, of the loss, lodged behind his eyes and ached within his chest. He missed his brother and his friends, and he had every reason to fear he would never see them again.

As the fog grew thicker, sadness throbbed through him. He nearly turned back, ran back, and flew home, but he couldn't. He walked onward, guided by the tug of the stick, following the direction it pointed.

Finn glanced behind him. The goat still followed. If nothing else, he needed to get the animal to safety.

The fog enveloped him. Its cold breath chilled his skin. Trees emerged from the twisting gray only a dozen feet before he passed them. Then, only half a dozen. And then a foot. In time, the swirling fog hung so densely that he could barely see the end of the stick he held.

"'Tis all right," he tried to console the goat. Or himself.

It wasn't all right.

Something told him to go back. Sadness of loss twisted in-to fear of what would come. Panicked, his body tensed to such a degree that it shivered.

He walked onward. He had to. He needed to follow the tug of the stick and find Chief Morgana. His people counted on him. The goat counted on him.

Finn glanced back. The goat was gone. The departure of this final friend made him want to scream or cry. He did nei-ther.

Finn continued forward. Alone.

—

The fog ended abruptly, unnaturally abruptly. It towered as an undulating wall, a mile high, surrounding the place Finn had entered. Clouds, low and thick, were a ceiling block-ing the afternoon sun and casting gloom.

Before him, a small village nestled in a rocky clearing. The dozen houses matched those of his own village—round with short mud walls and steep conic roofs of thatch. A slight hill marked the village center, crowned by a large circle of trees.

Finn's attention turned to three nearby Terovae women. They held each other's hands as they danced wildly in a swirl-ing circle. They looked to be in their late twenties and their tattered dresses of dark cloth were as wild as their dance. Their hair, too, followed theme, with long tresses teased up madly. Two had pale skin like the people of the Five Tribes, but one's skin was darker than Finn had ever seen—a rich, deep brown. Her hair and wings were black.

"How are things, then?" Finn attempted casually despite a fear of the strange women.

"What? You should not be here," the dark-skinned woman said, her accent foreign. "The Fog of Confusion should have made you lose your way and pushed you from our village. How are you here?"

Finn shrugged his freckled shoulders. "I've got this magic stick here." He lifted it.

"A magic stick, says he," one of the women said, and they all had a laugh.

Their laughter only made him more uncomfortable. "Have I walked through to the Otherworld?" Finn asked. "Are ye three Faeries?"

The women had a laugh about that, too.

"Maybe we are," the black woman said. "Or maybe we are just figments of your imagination gone wild."

"Right." Finn gave a firm nod. "Well, if you mean to seduce me and lead me to some water for a drowning, you should know I'm more partial to the fellas."

The women laughed again, and Finn joined, though not as boisterously. He hadn't meant it as a joke and wasn't sure why it was funny, but if they took it as such, he decided it was better to act as if he had.

The goat bleated behind Finn. He turned, seeing her emerge from the fog. Relieved, he rushed to her. "I thought I'd lost you." He petted her back.

"And what are you doing with our goat?" a woman asked as the three neared.

"I found her," Finn said. "Is she a Faery goat, then?"

"By the ancestors, what is wrong with this boy?" the black woman asked. "It is not a Faery goat, and we are not Faeries, either. My name is Nekesa, and this is our village you have wandered into, trespassing."

"A shame, that," Finn said. "I figure returning a Faery goat to its Faery owners would get me a wish or two."

A man landed and folded his black wings behind his back. He stood tall, staring at Finn from behind a wooden mask. His skin was pale, with a light coating of black hair over his fit chest and down the center of his slim stomach to a low kilt. He bore ten tattoos, but the one that caught Finn's attention marked his chest. Instead of a Septogram, like Finn's, he bore an inverted Faery Star. His kilt of black leather was long for a man's, falling nearly to his bare feet.

"How do you come to be here?" the man demanded.

"He has a magic stick, supposedly," Nekesa said. "Take care, my chief. He will think you are trying to seduce him into a lake."

"Wouldn't mind so much with him." Finn formed a half grin.

"You should not be in our village," the man maintained.

"'Twas like I was telling your friends here," Finn said. "This magic stick is leading me to our former chief."

"Speak you of ..." the man began, his anger lost, "of Morgana?"

"Aye, that be her, yes," Finn said. "We need her help back at home."

The man looked downward—a sad glance, perhaps—but the mask showed little. "Morgana is not here," he said, his voice deepening with anger.

"But the stick here—"

"See for yourself if you don't believe me." He flung his hand dismissively. "You're here now, aren't you?"

"Right." Finn nodded, confused by the man's reaction. "I'll get to it, then. The goat will be fine here, yes?"

Nekesa nodded, averting her eyes as if Finn had done something wrong and no one liked to say.

"Right." Finn lifted the stick in front of him and let it guide him deeper into the village.

The few villagers around their small homes stopped their tasks when they caught sight of Finn. They stared. Finn glanced back at the masked man and the three women. They watched.

The stick led Finn toward the center of the village, to a gradual hill topped by a seventy-foot ring of ancient hazel trees. Their knobby, bare arms twisted upward.

He walked hesitantly up the gentle incline and entered the circle. Beyond the hazels stretched an elongated berm of stone, so worn by time it was nearly erased. A ditch followed, then another mound, then another ditch. The last of the three concentric circular berms was the base of a towering wall of mist. Finn passed through to a thirty-foot area of dirt and sparse dead grass.

In its center burned a five-foot circle of black fire.

Above the fire, a neck ring hovered and revolved slowly. Most of the ring was composed of thick wires of silver metal twisted around each other to form an inch-thick, solid rope. The ends, of the same metal, portrayed the heads of ravens with ruby eyes. The ravens faced one another, and in their beaks, each held a black gem, filling the three-inch gap between them.

Mesmerized, Finn stared. A part of him screamed he should flee, that this was a wicked place. Finn could feel a dark energy in the air. It whipped chaotically around him on all sides, even on the soles of his feet, through the dirt, as if he flew within a violent storm, yet it had neither sound nor visible effect. However, even as Finn felt these unnerving sensations, he stood motionless, staring at the strange ring as it revolved.

The stick no longer guided him. He dropped it to the dirt. Now, the ring called him forward. Somehow, he knew it would kill him. Even so, he stepped closer, willingly closer. It was like a sort of lust overriding everything else. He wanted to touch it, hold it, and run his fingers along the silvery metal cord and the beautiful raven heads.

Finn stepped close enough to the black fire that he should have felt a great heat, yet it was cold. More than cold: it seemed to drain his heat away.

He lifted his hand toward the neck ring, leaning nearer to the fire.

"I would stop if I were you."

The words woke Finn as if from a nightmare. Dazed and panting, he jerked his hand away.

Finn looked back at the masked man.

"What is this?" Finn asked, out of breath.

"This place is called a *ráth*. And that"—he gestured at the neck ring—"is the *Torc of Datura*."

Finn nodded, as if any of that had given him any kind of information. "The stick was meant to lead me to Chief Morgana."

"As it has." The man's words were bitter. "At least as well as it could. This is where Morgana died. The black flames burned her alive whilst she screamed, leaving nothing, not even ash. I witnessed it, yet helpless."

Finn looked at the fire, about a foot from him. "Suppose 'tis best I move back, then." He proceeded to increase that distance tenfold.

Once Finn was closer to the masked man than to the deadly fire, he said, "Our current chief sent me out to find our previous chief, since the Dayigans are in our temple village being right arseholes. We were hoping Chief Morgana found the chaos druidesses and they could help us out."

The man folded his arms and sighed. "Morgana found no Anordúlas. The last died millennia past. Yet Morgana, not one to concede, searched the Five Lands and gathered any whispered story or faded etching on some long-forgotten stone. Finally, she communed with the long dead of the ancient Anordúlas, learning their secrets. Thus, Morgana herself became a great Anordúla druidess," he said with pride. "Alas, her quest delivered her here."

Finn looked back at the flames that had taken her life. "So there's no chaos druidesses left ... again?"

The man nodded sadly. "There are no druidesses, no. But all in our village are Anordúla magicians, taught by Morgana. And I strive to become a druid."

"*Druid*? What's that then?"

His voice lowered with annoyance. "'Tis a male druidess."

"A *male* druidess, says you." Finn laughed. "Is that a thing now?"

"'Tis always been a thing, Finn. 'Tis just not common."

"Right. And how do you know my name?"

"I know your name ..." He reached behind the mask to untie it. "Because I know you. Or I did."

Finn looked at the face now revealed. Messy wavy black hair hung just past the young man's eyebrows and curled to the right, and on the sides, it showed only the bases of his earlobes. His staring hazel eyes had a cold glint. His handsome face, thin and pale, attempted a stern look, but appeared more sad and nervous.

"Fecking nice." Finn grew an enormous smile. "Laisren— 'tis yourself."

"You remember me?"

"Do I? *Course.* How could I forget the first lad I ever kissed? What were we, eleven?"

"The first time? You were eleven. I was ten." He remained no less aloof.

"Right," Finn said with a reminiscent smile. "Right."

Laisren had been a scrawny, pale, sickly boy, but as cute as he could be. Finn had been little different, save for the sickly part.

Finn scanned his adult body and felt a vibrant yearning down his core. "You've aged well, yourself. Quite well indeed."

Laisren gave a half chuckle, as if Finn had said something humorous.

"I was ever so sad when your mam sent you away for schooling. Ach, your mam," Finn realized. He returned his eyes to the ring of fire. "Your mam, Chief Morgana?"

Laisren nodded.

"Oh, I am sorry, Laz."

"Come," Laisren said. "'Twould seem we have much to discuss, and I have lingered in this ráth longer than I'd like."

CHAPTER TEN

The walk to Laisren's home was slow despite the short distance. Finn wasn't sure what he expected a village of chaos sorcerers to look like—perhaps bloody altars and withered nature. Instead, he saw people working in little gardens. He and Laisren passed the woman he'd seen before—*Nekesa, was it?*—who was milking the goat. A few pigs rooted behind a fence of horizontal woven sticks.

To Laisren, Finn recounted recent issues with the Dayigans. He talked to Laisren as if they'd only been apart for months. At the same time, Finn felt weird talking about such serious topics, like they were boys talking about grown-up things.

"This is mine." Laisren stopped at a cottage, larger than the rest, but similar.

Inside, the circular house had flat walls to the left and right. Each extended eight feet high—stopping before the ceiling—and partitioned off a quarter of the house on either side. The middle half was a large room with a sparse, earthy décor, mostly composed of pelts on the walls. A low fire burned in the room's center, its smoke drifting up to conic rafters and seeping through the thatched roof.

"I wish we could help." Laisren motioned to a fireside bench.

Finn sat, pulling his pipe from the pouch on his belt.

Laisren remained standing, rigidly watching the fire. "The current Anordúla possess a *technical* knowledge of chaos magic, yet not the means for practical application."

"Right." Finn finished packing the pipe. "And what's that supposed to mean?"

Another voice called out, "It means they can't do a damn thing."

Past the fire, Finn saw someone emerge from the door of another room. The person was unlike anyone Finn had seen. The thin humanoid, without wings, had sage-green skin. Fox-shaped ears, thin and white as lilies, curled to points. A leather tie-bound thick, violet, shoulder-length hair. A gray belted tunic extended to the knees.

"This is Jyoti," Laisren said. "Ze currently resides here."

"*Ze*, says you?" asked Finn.

Jyoti approached Finn and extended a hand. "Pronouns are a little different with my race."

Finn shook the hand, which felt velvety and warm.

"I'm an Afedioc. We're neither males nor females, how you understand the words. Or *both*, depending on how you view it."

Finn nodded. "I'll try to get it right. Are you two ..." He looked at zem and at Laisren. "*Together?*" Finn found himself slightly jealous or slightly disappointed while realizing how ridiculous it was for him to feel either.

Jyoti curled zeir pale green lips into a knowing grin.

"Jyoti, this is Finn," Laisren said. "We were good friends as boys before I left for the Academy. Finn, Jyoti is a friend from the Academy."

"Not as good of a friend as you, I suspect," Jyoti added. "I'm only staying here a few months to study the Anordúla."

"I've never left the Feah lands, meself," Finn said. "Is everyone in Vohcktara a Af...?"

"*Afedioc*," Jyoti said. "And no, my kind are few in Vohcktara, and that's not my home. The majority of their city is actually Terovaes, with Humans as a close second. Then there are other races—Ophiruks, Zezovaes."

Finn grinned widely, intrigued. "I don't even know what those are."

"No matter." Ze smiled. "But you really should visit Vohcktara. Their kingdom touches the Feahs' eastern border. Of course, Vohcktara proper, their capital city, is much farther east. It is an absolutely beautiful city. You'd love it."

"We were speaking of chaos magic," Laisren said.

"Yes," said Jyoti. "I was telling your friend your tribe can't do a thing with it."

"Nothing?" Finn turned to Laisren.

Laisren sighed. "Nothing on the level required to help the Feah. You know the old stories: in the ancient war, the skies above the five lands cracked between the Natural Realm and the Faery Realm. For centuries, the druidesses worked to seal those cracks. They've nearly succeeded, thus halting the chaos energy used by the ancient Anordúlas."

"But that's a good thing," Finn said. "Right? It keeps the dark Faeries out of our world."

"Dark Faery is a misnomer," Laisren said. "That is a ... *an incorrect name*. 'Twould be more accurate to call them chaos Faeries, but their proper name is *Irefaeries*. And yes, it is generally good that Irefaeries—who delight in torturing, killing, and eating people—remain far away. But as conduits to the energy of the Plane of Chaos, they were useful."

Finn furrowed his brow in confusion. "Right."

"In as many words as possible," Jyoti said, "Laisren is simply trying to say Anordúlas are learning how to use chaos energy, but don't have any to use."

"Ah," Finn said. "Sounds like a massive waste of time, that."

Jyoti laughed. "I like this one."

"'Tis good to know things, Finn. Just to know them." Laisren paused. "But Mother had planned to use Anordúla magic. That's why she went after the Torc of Datura. With it, she could have accessed chaos energy, even with the Realms closed. But—that never happened."

"So, ye *can't* protect our people from the Dayigans?" Finn asked.

Laisren shook his head.

Jyoti set zeir hand on Finn's shoulder. "'Tis a shame you came all this way to return home empty-handed."

Finn looked down. "I can't return home."

"Well, that part's an easy fix." Jyoti looked at Laisren. "You should let him stay here. Your bed's big enough for two."

Finn jolted at this suggestion, and his heart raced.

Laisren began to say something, but his mouth hung open. His eyes drifted down Finn's body.

"Apologies." Laisren looked away. "Of course, you may stay here. My home is yours."

—

Laisren, Finn, and Jyoti sat by the fire for some time. The topics ranged in their conversations, with Jyoti doing most of the talking. However, Finn's mind was too full for much chatting.

In time, Finn excused himself, went outside to piss on a tree, and didn't return indoors.

Instead, he sat against Laisren's cottage and placed his pipe between his lips, occasionally drawing a smoky breath.

"There you are." Laisren stood in the doorway of his house. "The entire village gathers for meals. I was soon to head that way. If you'd like, you may come as well."

Finn blew a plume of smoke as he shook his head. "I'm not really up for the ol' meet and greet right now. Suppose that's odd for me."

"Not really." Laisren took a seat next to him. "The boy I recall liked to think himself social, but he was slow to any gathering and quick to leave."

Finn smiled. "Do you remember we used to run off into the woods together, alone? We'd just walk around, talking and exploring places we'd explored countless times before."

Laisren was silent before replying. "Apologies. I should not have brought up those days." He stood. "I'm not who I was then, and I shouldn't expect you to be, either."

Finn looked up at him. "I weren't lying before when I said I was devastated when your mam sent you away."

"I wasn't lying when I said I'd changed." Laisren paused but didn't look Finn's way. "There was a reason I wore a mask when I met you at the edge of the village. I meant to keep it on and send you away without your ever knowing I was here. But when I saw you ..." He cleared his throat. "The village isn't very large. You can find the dining area if you wish to join us."

With that, Laisren walked away.

—

Finn sat by the fire in the center of Laisren's house. The house had been empty for a while, and all he could do was think. The attack on Cal. The death of Kyran. The Dayigans.

"You keep by that fire like 'tis winter," Jyoti said.

Finn looked back to see zem standing just inside the front door. In zeir hands, ze held a tin plate.

"I failed my people when they needed me," Finn said. "And I can't even tell them about it."

"Your people asked you to find Chief Morgana and the Anordúlas, which you did."

"Aye, but—"

"But nothing." Ze cut him off. "You made it here on your own. That's a feat in itself. Lamenting never did anyone any good."

Finn nodded. Ze was right, he knew.

Jyoti lifted the plate. "Laisren made you a plate and asked me to give it to you. He won't be coming home tonight but says you're welcome to use his room whenever you're ready."

"He's mad at me, for some reason."

"No," Jyoti said with a smile. Ze neared, put the plate down on the bench, and sat between it and Finn.

"Laisren normally seems a little angry," ze said. "And a little sad. He keeps to himself and to his studies. I can't believe he's letting someone stay in his personal space. I suggested it as a joke."

"You're staying here, so."

"I'm staying *there*," ze pointed to the door on the right. "You're staying *there*." Ze pointed to the left door, presumably leading to Laisren's bedroom. "The last time an uninvited visitor made his way through the fog, Laisren whipped him bloody, dragged him out through the fog, and gave him a warning never to speak of this place. He certainly didn't give him his bedroom."

"Laisren wouldn't do that."

Jyoti snorted. "He's done worse."

Finn's face went blank. He felt ill.

"I ..." Finn started. "I think I *will* go to bed." He stood and began to move toward the door.

"Your food." Jyoti lifted the plate.

"Right." Finn took it.

—

Once Finn entered Laisren's room, he shut the door gently and set the plate on the floor.

The room, a quarter circle, had a flat wall that held the door Finn had entered.

His attention moved to an iron birdcage centered on a small table on the opposite side of the room. It held a crimson ball of light just larger than his fist.

Finn tentatively neared the strange light and touched his fingers to the cage.

The light darted away and pressed itself against the farthest side.

"Sorry, wee light." Finn withdrew his finger and looked at the bed beside the cage.

The bed was like a dream. It was raised about a foot from the floor on a wooden platform, and its headboard was a grid of horizontal and vertical slats. The bed itself was like a massive rectangular pillow, four feet across, and covered with a sheet of black silky fabric Finn didn't recognize.

He pressed down on the bed. It was softer than anything he'd ever felt—by far softer than Finn's little cot at home.

Finn continued his exploration, searching the strange room in the eerie crimson light.

He turned back to a shelving unit he'd passed by the door. Its boards were sanded smooth and painted black. A ram's skull was the most prominent of its contents. Finn touched the bone lightly. Beside it, a wooden bowl held a collection of one-inch bones, each carved with a rune. Next was a gray marble mortar and pestle. Then, an assortment of clay jars. Peeking in, Finn saw most held what looked to be dried herbs, but one held five bird feet and one was filled with teeth.

The highest shelf held three thick leather-bound books.

The lower shelf held an orb of obsidian atop a small silver stand, a pyramid of tiger's eye, and something Finn recognized.

He lifted the smooth brown stone about the size of a potato. Near its peak was a carefully carved spiral with three lines carved below. As a boy, Finn had made it and given it to Laisren before his trip to Vohcktara.

He smiled and put it back on the shelf.

Something hissed at him.

Finn jumped and looked to see a black cat lying on a red pillow next to the shelves. Its eyes reflected the light so thoroughly that they seemed to glow crimson themselves.

"'Tis all right, cat." Finn crouched and extended his hand forward.

The cat jumped up, hissing again as it arched its back. The eyes, Finn realized, were not reflecting, but glowing. It extended bat-like wings and jumped to the top of the wall. It glared at Finn before retreating to the main room.

"Not a cat, then." Finn sighed. It was time to go to sleep.

—

Laisren burst into the bedroom. "Finn, I have great news."

Finn's eyes shot open, staring into the cylindrical silk-covered pillow. A black silk sheet enveloped him atop a bed that was more comfortable than anything he could have imagined.

"What?" Finn said sleepily as he sat up.

"It may be possible to get the Torc of Datura."

Finn yawned. "That's fantastic." He stood while wiping his eyes as he stretched. He looked at Laisren.

Laisren had frozen. His lips parted as he gazed, his eyes roaming Finn's body.

Finn looked down at his naked self. He'd awoken aroused, and Laisren's gaze only strengthened the effect.

"Sorry." Finn turned.

"'Tis fine," Laisren breathed. "'Tis ... nice."

"Nice, is it?" The word locked Finn in place, heart pounding.

Laisren's eyes roamed but kept returning to Finn. "Aye," he admitted awkwardly. "Well nice, it is, yes."

He rushed to Finn and set his hand against the back of Finn's neck before hesitating. Finn kissed his lips with a passion unlike he'd ever felt before, a slow passion that seemed to flow from the core of his being. Laisren pulled him closer, drawing their bodies together. His hand ran down Finn's back, past his waist, to the pale mounds.

The kiss grew faster, tongues dancing around one another. Finn felt as if he could release everything he was and stay forever in his embrace.

And yet Laisren pulled away.

Panting, Finn whispered, "I wanted to do that since I first saw you again."

"I shouldn't have." Laisren's hazel eyes bored into Finn's. "You're a good man, Finn. And I ..." He sighed. "I am not."

Laisren turned away toward the door.

Finn looked at him a moment more. He nearly spoke but found no words. Instead, Finn picked up his kilt, which lay crumpled on the floor. "I think I frightened your cat last night."

Keeping his eyes on the door, Laisren said, "He's no cat. He's an Irefaery, specifically a tromlee. Whilst people sleep, tromlees lie on their heads and cause nightmares. Then, they drain the person's soul."

"Right," Finn said distantly, wrapping the kilt around his waist. "Suppose 'tis best he flew off then."

"He can't hurt you." Laisren turned to him. There was a hint of disappointment in seeing Finn dressed. His eyes still held the same longing they'd shown before he rushed toward him. "I wouldn't have let you in here if I thought he'd hurt you. The tromlee is a projection of himself trapped in our world when the veil closed. His true self, along with most of his power, is in the Irefaery Realm. There, he's slept for centuries."

Finn said nothing. His head spun and his heart raced. His skin ached to touch Laisren's.

"You're protected from Irefaeries," Laisren assured. "At every fire festival, when you danced around the sacred fire and flew over it, and when you coated yourself with blessed ash, you were building up protections against chaos. 'Tis why the tromlee fled from you. And why I cannot recharge your armor spell."

Finn looked at the tattoo on his forearm, the lines still empty. "I'm protected from you?"

Laisren looked away. "As I said, I have great news. I spent all night reviewing information Mother collected about the Torc of Datura, specifically the fire that guards it. There could be a safe way past it."

"That's great," Finn said unenthusiastically, his skin still pulsing, his mind a bundle of confusion.

"'Twill take time to find an exact method, but I think it obtainable. And with the torc's power and the Anordúlas' knowledge, we can save your people."

CHAPTER ELEVEN

In a slow meander, Finn approached the Anordúlas' dining area, located just east of the hilltop ráth.

The space's most prominent structure was a small rectangular building of masoned stone. This was the pantry, and most of its goods were within. However, outside its wooden door were large wicker baskets with large wicker tops. From racks along its front wall hung drying herbs and onions and such.

Logs extended out from the pantry to support a thatched roof above a pavilion. The sides of this were open, showing four tables of gray wood with matching benches on either side. They were empty of people and meals.

The roof extended across to another wall. Here was a bread oven beside two shelving units. The shelves, positioned on the pavilion's edge, held a couple of large cauldrons, a few smaller pots, various other tools for cooking, and a cluster of tin plates and cups. To the right of the shelves stretched a long rectangular fire pit.

Finn went to the shelves, grabbed a cup, and dipped it in a barrel of water, filling it.

He took a seat on a bench with his back against a table and stared at the dirt.

"You missed lunch," a woman said.

He looked up, seeing the dark-skinned woman he'd met a week ago when he'd first arrived in the village. She exited the pantry.

"I ate already. Jyoti always brings me a plate. You're called Nekesa, right?"

"Yes." She folded her arms. "I am surprised to see you out here and not hidden away with the chief."

"Really, I haven't seen much of him either in the last few days. I've been sleeping in his bed, but he doesn't sleep there."

"Lucky for you. About the bed. If a God had a bed, it would be as comfortable as Laisren's. It's from Vohcktara."

Finn looked at her—an attractive woman a few years older than himself—and wondered if she'd confessed something. He nearly questioned her, but didn't. Jealousy was new to him, and he didn't like it.

Instead, Finn said, "Laisren's been sleeping in some cave up on the edge of the village. Says he's got books there he needs to read. So he can figure out how to save our people."

"Yes, he does get lost in his studies," she said distantly. "Well, whenever you decide you are not too good to consort with the wicked Anordúlas, we make good company." She began to walk away.

"Wait. 'Tis nothing like that."

She stopped.

"I've just been thinking a lot; that's all. 'Tis nothing 'gainst the Anordúlas. Truth be told, the little I've seen of ye, ye all seem well nice."

She grinned. "We have our moments."

"Sorry, if ye thought I were being an arsehole, keeping to meself."

"No." She approached him. "Forgive us for starting silly rumors."

Nekesa sat on the table and set her feet on the bench next to Finn. "Most people in the village had a rough, lonely path before we found each other. Everyone here but me is from one of the five Drevite tribes, and I'm sure you know the Five Tribes' views on anyone taking an interest in chaos. My people are similar, but instead of chaos magic and Irefaeries, they are more against the dark magic and Demons. But it is all grouped together as wicked and forbidden. Like the Drevites, we are raised to worship the True Light Gods and honor our ancestors."

Finn nodded. "Where are you from?"

"Dinikimera. Do you know of it?"

"Heard of it, yes," he said. "'Tis right across the Hyvile River."

"That's right. I grew up on the Hyvile."

"And me," he said happily. "Were you in a fishing village?"

She laughed, her smile bright. "No. I grew up in a city. And I worked with my family in a little shop. Do you know what that is?"

He shook his head.

"It is a place where people buy things. My family owned a jewelry shop. We—my mother, father, me, and my two brothers—would tumble beautiful stones until they were as smooth as glass. We made beautiful beaded necklaces, bracelets, earrings, everything that's beaded. My mother was the real artist of the family.

"I loved it," she continued, "but as I got older, I became more interested in becoming a priestess—that's like your druidesses, but without the governmental authority."

"So, did you become one, then?" Finn pushed himself up to sit beside her on the table. "A priestess?"

"No. I began studying for it and was doing quite well, but something about it … wasn't quite right for me. Reluctantly, I returned to the shop, but my interest never died. Three years later, Morgana entered our shop." She stopped. "Oh, but I am going on, aren't I?"

"No. Please, keep going."

She nodded. "My city, Alemiberi, is a major trade hub with items coming from all across the continents of East and West Bikia. So Morgana came there on the trail of an ancient Anordúla relic. But"—she smiled—"that did not mean she couldn't get a nice necklace on her visit. I remember she wanted something in obsidian, tiger's eye, and red jasper, which I thought was an odd request. Most items in our shop were quite a bit more colorful than that. But something about her; she interested me. Perhaps fate brought us together, yes? I took the project myself, and I decided—I did not know why—I needed to make this necklace a *masterpiece*.

"It was a slow process," Nekesa recounted. "Just finding the right stones was slow by itself, and I wanted it to be perfect. Morgana would check in on the progress, and we would talk. First, we talked about the project and other minor things—the weather, the city, small talk, you know. In time, our conversations moved to the magical properties of the stones she had selected. Finally, she confessed her genuine reasons for coming to our city. She told me about the Anordúla and her quest to reestablish it. At first, these topics frightened me. But I wanted to learn more. And the more she told me, the more I realized that the 'thing' that was not quite right for me in becoming a priestess, it was right in the Anordúla.

"After three months, I finished the necklace. But when Morgana came for it, I told her I would not sell it to her. Instead, I would give it to her if she became my teacher. She agreed, but she said it would not be easy, and it would take me far from home. I said to her, I understand.

"When I told my parents, they were furious. They said Morgana was a wicked, wicked woman and her ways would lead me down an evil path. I tried to tell them I was a grown woman and tried to make them understand, but they would not listen. My father shouted, 'If you leave with that evil witch, don't you ever come back here because you are no longer a daughter of mine.' I left. I had to, because, you see, chaos was already part of me long before I met the chief. And I never saw my family again."

Nekesa went silent after that, and Finn absorbed the words. It hadn't occurred to him that all the villagers had come from places, from families, that viewed chaos magic just as he had.

"But ..." Finn stared into the tin cup grasped in his hands. "I still don't understand." He looked at her. "Why did you have to? You don't seem wicked to me. Why would you have to use wicked forces instead of good ones?"

"Magic is not good or evil. It is a tool." From her belt, Nekesa drew a knife. "This knife is a tool too. I can use it to slash a man's throat." She sliced it through the air in front of her. "Or to cut flowers for a friend." She handed him an imaginary bouquet. "Chaos magic gives us the freedom to use any knife we choose, but it's how we use it that leads to good or evil outcomes."

"Right," Finn said, thinking. "Then why not just use a knife that won't get you disowned by your whole family?"

Nekesa looked downward as she sheathed her knife.

"Sorry. I didn't mean nothing by it. I just want to understand, you and Laisren and the rest."

"No, it is fine." She smiled. "It's the magic in my blood. Part of me. The magic I *must* use."

"Right. I still know nothing about it. Laisren won't tell me a thing."

"Lucky for you"—she grinned as she leaned so her shoulder tapped his—"I know more than Laisren."

"Really?" Finn said eagerly.

"But how do I explain chaos magic to someone with no real understanding of magic at all?"

He chuckled. "Real simple like, I should hope."

"Very true." She laughed heartily. "Let me see. Basically—very basically—you have three kinds of magic. First, you have your own, personal magic inside of you." She touched her chest.

"What are you two talking about?" It was Laisren, his words cross. He stood behind them near the oven and held a handled basket filled with various items.

"Your man here," Nekesa said, "wants to know about our ways."

"'Tis not your place to tell him."

"No," she said. "It's yours, and you haven't told him a thing."

"He needn't learn of the Anordúla."

She stood up and faced him. "Are you ashamed of us now, my chief?"

"Fuck's sake, Nekesa, you know that's not the case. But he's only visiting here." He turned to Finn and sighed. "We're ostracized by the people outside this village. I want you to have a normal life. We can't send you back to the Feah with a hundred questions about the ways of druidesses."

Before Finn could speak, Nekesa responded, "You'd keep him ignorant so he can live happily with the ignorant?"

Laisren nearly said something but looked away.

"Are the druidesses bad?" Finn asked.

"No," Nekesa said. "No, they have chosen one way, and we have chosen another. But ..." She laughed. "The *Dayigans*, they are fucking assholes."

Finn laughed at this, and Laisren chuckled.

"I'll answer your questions about the Anordúla," Laisren relented. "Actually, I came to find you. I've barely seen you, and I thought we could have a picnic." He snickered. "I didn't expect you to be at a table."

Finn shrugged. "We could leave the table and go eat on the ground. That's fine by me. I already ate, though, but I could eat more."

"'Tis more of a snack picnic, in truth," Laisren said. "Nekesa, I welcome you to join."

"Thank you, my chief, but I don't think either of you wants me coming along." She smiled. "You two go have some nice time alone."

—

On the edge of the village, next to the wall of fog separating the Anordúla from the outside world, Laisren shook out a gray blanket and let it flow flat to the grassy ground. It had a thick border of black spirals, but not the sort of spirals Finn was accustomed to seeing in the art of the Five Tribes; these spirals were squared.

Next, Laisren set the basket on the blanket and pulled out a shallow, handled black bowl with orange artwork depicting naked men in festive play. From a clay jar, he poured something into the bowl that, to Finn, looked somewhat like little boiled eggs, but some were green and some were purplish black. This was in oil.

Laisren took out two clay cups and filled them from a clay jug with something that looked like thin blood.

Finally, he grabbed a small, clay, covered dish and removed the lid to reveal something that looked very much like pale mud.

"What do you think?" Laisren said with pride at what he'd put together.

"Is it ..." Finn began hesitantly as he crouched, "food?"

"Yes, 'tis food. 'Tis Vohcktaran. I liked it when I was at the Academy, and I thought you might like it as well. These are olives. This is wine—'tis like beer, but from grapes. And this is hummus. Oh, and I brought this." He pulled a loaf of bread from the basket. "This isn't Vohcktaran, but we can put the hummus on it. I ..." He glanced down. "'Tis silly, but I thought you'd like it."

Finn gave him a look that was somewhere between confusion and hesitation.

"'Tis good," Laisren assured. "Just lie down on your left side, and I'll do the same."

Finn complied, and soon they positioned themselves with Finn's head pointed one way and Laisren's, the other. Both faced the food between them.

The snack picnic began as Laisren introduced the strange food that Finn enjoyed, particularly the grape beer. Mostly, Finn enjoyed listening to Laisren talk. Soon, they were laughing—nothing boisterous, just relaxed chats. It was the most relaxed Finn had been since he'd come to the village.

"But you were interested in Anordúla magic." Laisren spread hummus on bread with a tin spoon. "I haven't forgotten."

"Did you learn about chaos magic in Vohcktara?" Finn asked.

"No. The Vohcks know little about chaos magic. That's why Jyoti came here to study it. But I learnt of other schools of magic, which is important as an Anordúla. We use and combine rituals from other traditions."

"Right." Finn maneuvered his tongue to separate an olive from its pit. "Nekesa said you needed a lot of knives to choose from."

"Exactly. But you're jumping ahead. I heard her tell you there are three kinds of magic. That's a *vast* oversimplification, but one I'll stick with."

"Simple's good by me." Finn popped another olive into his mouth.

Laisren sipped his wine. "First, you have magic performed by using your own life force. We'll call that *seid magic*. The problem with using your life force is that you need it, to live, and if you run out, you die. But a seid magician can usually avoid that. Some people are born with a heightened life force, and some aren't born with enough to do anything magical, but they can build it up. Of course, no matter how much you have, if you're using it a lot, you're going to run low. Life force recharges rather slowly on its own, and even if you don't drain yourself dead, just being low can cause melancholia. So, what to do?"

Finn spit an olive pit into his hand and shrugged. "Indeed."

"Generally," Laisren said, "magicians who use seid magic at least use an external force to recharge themselves."

"Like the One Soul that Treasa uses." Finn dipped a tear of bread in olive oil.

"I don't think I know Treasa."

"Do you not? Lann's sister? She's Cal's wife now. And a archdruidess."

"Then yes. And that's when we move into your second kind of magic—high magic, ritual magic, prayer meeting—whatever you want to call it. 'Tis when you call on powerful beings to either help you out in your workings or to just do it for you. So now you're involving your Gods, your Demons, your powerful dead, your—"

"Irefaeries?" Finn asked. "Like the Anordúlas use?"

"No," Laisren chuckled. "A magician would be a fool to evoke an Irefaery for his workings. They're too damn unpredictable, them. But there is a subset of ritual magic in which one traps a being and forces—no. No, I'll keep it simple.

"As far as magically imploring *cooperative* entities to help you, you can get a lot done, but 'tis not free. Some might require minor tasks in return; others might demand complete dedication of your entire life. There's a large range."

"That's what the druidesses do as well," Finn said. "They worship the Three Mothers in exchange for protection and magic."

"Yes. The Druidic Circle combines seid magic *and* ritual magic, and thus they must stay subservient to the Three Mothers."

"But what wrong with that? They protect us and all."

"Do they? Because my mother sought the power of the Anordúla because the Three Mothers were not protecting our tribe, and that's the same reason Kaie sent you here now."

"Right." Finn looked down. Questioning the power of the Three Mothers was like betraying an old friend. Sadness washed over him as if he had lost another piece of home.

"Apologies," Laisren said. "I might have been gone a long time, but I was raised the same as you. I still have love for the

Three Mothers. But I realized I couldn't be a slave to them or any God any longer. The Anordúla is freedom from that. We use the first two kinds of magic at times, but primarily, we use a third."

Laisren sipped his wine. "Using wisdom first developed by an ancient Irefaery sorceress, we've learnt we don't have to call upon the power of sentient beings with demands and agendas of their own. Instead, we can evoke the *non-sentient* power of the *belief* in a powerful being."

Finn grimaced, head hurting. "I don't understand."

"'Tis fine." Laisren smiled. "You don't need to know this. You're not even a magician."

"I want to know. You said 'tis good to know stuff. 'Sides, 'tis well interesting, this."

"All right." Laisren turned solemn. "But sometimes, knowing things separates you from those who don't know them."

"Aye," Finn said. "And sometimes, knowing things gets you closer to them that do."

"Fair point." Laisren threw an olive at Finn.

"Bastard," Finn said, laughing. He sat up and threw a chunk of bread, hitting Laisren's face.

Laisren grabbed it and playfully darted toward Finn.

Finn offered little resistance, but Laisren stopped. Their eyes locked.

Finn thought of the kiss as his heart pounded.

Laisren nested his hands under Finn's jaw and stared into his sweet blue-gray eyes.

But Laisren looked away. "Three."

"What?"

"Three," Laisren said again, breathlessly. "The third type of magic. 'Tis chaos." He returned to his place on the blanket.

Finn stared, eyes full of longing, at Laisren as he took a long drink of his wine.

When he put the cup down, Laisren said, "For countless years, countless people have put a lot of energy into believing in the Gods and other grand beings. They've put so much energy into it that their beliefs have, in themselves, become very powerful. So powerful that it has etched a—copy's not quite the right word, but I'll say copy. The people's combined belief over time has etched a copy of the God's power onto the chaos-aether pairs that form the building blocks of the universe."

Finn stared at him, wanting to go to him, grab him, and kiss him.

"Are you still with me?" Laisren asked.

Finn nodded. "You use the copy of the power, so you don't have to worship the Gods themselves."

"Essentially, yes. But you make it sound lazy." Laisren took another sip from his cup. "'Tis so we don't need to *depend* on higher beings. Using the copy—actually, I like *template* better than *copy*. Using the template created by the beliefs held by many people, we can use their same rituals to call upon chaos energy to mimic the powers that we call upon."

Finn continued to stare, his smile lost, his eyes sad.

"Apologies," Laisren said. "I feel like I've lost you now."

"The opposite, if I'm being honest with you," Finn said, downcast.

"I need us to just be friends," Laisren said. "That's all we can be now. Is that all right?"

Finn nodded and stared at the blanket. "Course." He sighed. "If the universe is made of chaos, why do you need the Irefaeries then?"

Laisren watched Finn for a moment before answering. He seemed to hold Finn's same desires, but suppressed them. He looked down into his cup and said, "The universe is made up of chaos-aether *pairs* called energy. All matter in the universe—whether it be rock or air, everything—is energy at different vibrations. We can manipulate the chaos in matter, but 'tis neutralized, so we can't use it to fuel magic. There is free chaos in our realm—that is, not in pairs—but not enough to perform the impressive feats of sorcery we'd need to defeat the Dayigans."

Finn felt dizzy sick and set his hand on his stomach. "Sorry, I'm feeling a bit ill."

"No, *I'm* sorry. I've made this complicated. It really isn't. We're learning to use chaos energy to fuel the templates of Gods that people have formed with their beliefs and to manipulate the chaos in matter."

"'Tis not that." Finn stood up. "'Tis because you're complicated, yourself, and I can't figure you out. I need to be going now." He began to move away.

Laisren jumped up and hurried in front of him. "When I first got to Vohcktara," he said gently, "I hated it. Because I missed ..." He paused. "Because I was missing you, Finn. And I know I'll miss you again when you leave here. But this isn't where you belong."

Finn nodded and, without another word, left.

CHAPTER TWELVE

Finn listened to Laisren and Jyoti debate various theo-
ries for passing the black fire that circled the Torc of
Datura. They'd been talking about it for weeks. They
were in Laisren's house. Laisren and Jyoti sat on the wooden
benches by the fire centered on the main room. Finn sat on
the floor beside them.

They'd meant Finn to be part of the discussion, but the
topic was beyond him. Instead, he found himself gazing at
Laisren. He didn't mean to. He tried not to. But his eyes kept
finding their way there.

The kiss had happened nearly a month ago. It confused
Finn—why it had happened and why it hadn't happened
again.

Laisren caught Finn staring now as he and Jyoti talked.
Their eyes locked for a moment. They smiled. Laisren looked
away.

"You cannot *continue* to view the black fire as *normal* matter," Laisren said to Jyoti. "The laws of natural physics do not
apply here."

"I'm considering metaphysics." Jyoti folded zeir hands and
glanced at the rafters. "But until we know the exact nature of
the substance, I must hypothesize based on substances with
which I am familiar."

"No one wrote down what 'tis made of?" Finn joined as he scooted closer to Laisren. He flipped through the enormous book in Laisren's lap. The handwritten runes filling most of the pages meant nothing to him, but the few sketches were amazing.

"The ancient Anordúlas didn't write anything at all." Laisren stroked his forehead in frustration. "Like the current Druidesses, they did not trust such important things to text and relied solely on oral teaching."

"A ridiculous practice," Jyoti added.

"Yes," Laisren agreed. "Mother—who luckily did not share their views—wrote these books. She compiled everything she had learnt in her travels and from her conversations with the dead Anordúlas. However, the Anordúla formed *after* the torc was in place. The dead don't know how to reach it either."

Finn sighed. "I wish I could be more helpful."

Laisren placed his hand on Finn's shoulder.

"Did you tell him about the pattern?" Jyoti asked.

"The pattern is irrelevant," Laisren said.

Jyoti leaned toward Finn. "His mother determined that there is a twelve-second cycle to the black fire and there are three seconds in each cycle when one can just walk through unharmed."

"*The pattern is irrelevant*," Laisren said again, more firmly. "We cannot determine when the three-second windows are, which leaves a three out of four chance of death, which is exactly what happened to ..." He stopped and gritted his teeth before looking downward.

Finn rested his cheek on Laisren's hand, still on his shoulder. Laisren brushed Finn's cheek with his thumb.

"I'm headed out." Finn stood. "I'm to meet Nekesa. For my archery training. 'Tis important we all learn to fight the

Dayigans, says she. 'Tis the very reason Chief Morgana started the Anordúla."

"You aren't an Anordúla."

"I'm not, no. I'm just a lad whose home happens to be
down the beach from a massive fort full of Dayigan soldiers."

"Right," Laisren said disappointedly.

"We'll meet up later in the pavilion when 'tis time to eat."

———

Finn found Nekesa sitting on a bench in front of her cottage, a smaller version of Laisren's. The most notable
difference was that Nekesa's door was purple.

She faced downward, looking at a cup on the ground between her feet. She dropped a leaf, and—despite a four-foot
drop—it fell directly into the cup.

"How'd you do that now?" Finn asked.

She looked up. "Finn. I hadn't seen you." She plucked the
leaf from the cup. "It is a developmental game for new sorcerers. My skills are far beyond it now, but it has become my
own version of twiddling my thumbs."

He took the leaf from her, looked at it, and aimed above
the cup. Despite his efforts, the leaf curved in its descent,
landing a good foot from the target.

"Sorcery starts by willing the *slightly* improbable into the
probable," she said. "And in time, working your way to do the
extremely improbable."

A breeze brushed against Finn's face.

Nekesa gained a sly grin. "Did I make that breeze happen,
or did it just happen to occur? You cannot tell."

Finn, with a perplexed half-smile, asked, "What else can you do?"

"Nothing I demonstrate for show. Like Chief Morgana, I specialize in spirits, both incarnate and disincarnate." She grabbed a bow beside the bench. "Yet you are here for a different kind of training, yes? You have made good progress so far."

He took the bow. "Thank you. I don't feel like I'm ready to fight the Dayigans like me brother though."

"You aren't. But it has only been a few weeks." She leaned in and whispered, "Don't look, but someone watches you."

Finn looked back, seeing a man slightly older than himself crouched in a patch of vegetables. He eyed Finn as he pulled weeds.

Caught, the man jerked away.

"Who is he then?" Finn asked.

"Have you not met Conor? I believe he is being shy with you." She leaned in again. "He, for one, is hoping you and the chief do *not* end up together."

"You mean, him and Laisren are ..."

"No," Nekesa said and laughed. "They had their fun, yes, but I mean, he is interested in *you*. He said you were"—she raised her hand to her breast—"adorable."

"Adorable, is it?" Finn stood taller as he glanced back at him.

Even covered in dirt, the man was attractive. The men locked eyes for a moment before Finn returned to Nekesa.

"I would've been shooting over there in a flash before I came here, truly," Finn said. "But now ..." He glanced down at the bow he held. "We should probably be getting on with this training."

—

As more days passed, the heated debates between Laisren and Jyoti grew cold as hopelessness smothered them. Finn found it like watching a fire's last embers slowly die.

Laisren closed a thick black book on his lap. He sat on a bench in his main room, and Finn sat on the floor beside him, with his head rested on the side of Laisren's leg. His arm was over Finn's shoulder, and he lightly rubbed Finn's chest.

"I know what I must do," Laisren said.

—

Night. Laisren and Finn stood at the mouth of a cave in the northeast corner of the village. An unseen fire flickered within.

"Jyoti isn't coming?" Finn asked.

"This isn't zeir sort of thing."

Besides his normal attire, Laisren wore a long black leather robe—sleeveless, backless to the waist, and open in the front. He also wore a leather necklace ending at a copper square displaying a sigil. "I'm unsure if this is your sort of thing either, but I ..." Laisren paused, gazing into the flickering dark. "I wanted to share this place with you. 'Tis part of me."

He took Finn's hand, folding their fingers together.

They entered.

There was a thick heat to the cave, not only from the large fire centered therein, but also from the people. All thirty-six villagers were there. Some danced in convulsive madness. Most had stripped off their clothing and were grouped into frenzied orgies. Some sang out in lunacy. The drums pounded furiously.

Finn's heart pounded as he, in curiosity and lustful anticipation, looked at Laisren. Finn's lips parted as he licked them. He wanted to pull Laisren to him. But it would need to be Laisren's move, Finn knew.

Laisren leaned in close and shouted over the noise. "This is our ritual space, much like the Feah temple."

"Not *much* like it, from what I can tell."

"The druidesses use calm and meditation to clear their minds into a single, focused thought. We Anordúla do the opposite. We do our workings within a frenzy of noise and activities that block out all our rogue thoughts until we enter a focused trance."

"When I was a wee lad, me and Cal, my brother—you remember him."

Laisren nodded.

"When we was being too rowdy," Finn said, "our mam would say, 'You're making so much noise I can even think!' 'Tis like that, yes, this ritual?"

Laisren chuckled. "It is, actually. Somewhat."

The heat of the cave, the energy, embraced Finn like countless heated fingertips stroking his skin. He heard the moans of pleasure calling out. He locked his eyes on Laisren.

Laisren's smile faded into a look of desire. Laisren lifted Finn's hand, still in his own, to his mouth. He kissed the back of his hand.

Finn looked up into Laisren's hazel eyes. The fire flickered over Laisren's skin.

But Laisren turned away. "That's not why I'm here." He pressed his forehead against Finn's. "I've come here to call upon the aid of a Demon."

"A proper Demon or a Demon template?"

"A proper Demon."

"You can't."

"I must. We must help your people. For years, I've honored Ignísekhet, Goddess of Chaos, but I've never asked anything of her. I dared not. But now ... She could help me help your people."

"'Tis ritual magic, that," Finn said. "That's not what the Anordúlas do."

"I never said we don't use ritual magic. We just aren't bound to it exclusively."

A man from behind Finn slid his arms around him, embracing him. It was Conor, the man who, according to Nekesa, had called Finn "adorable." With a belly full of beer, he was not as shy as before and wore nothing but a smile.

"Sharing your friend with us, are you, Chief?" Conor asked.

Finn looked at Laisren, who looked sadly at Finn.

"Join him, if you like," Laisren said in dismissal. "I must perform the ritual."

"No." Finn shrugged off the embrace. "I want you. Don't you understand that? I ... I love you, Laisren. I think I always have."

"This is *not* your world, and I am *not* who you wish me to be. We'll drive out the invaders to the Feah, and you will return home. You'll find some fisherman or farmer and have a happy, normal life far from this darkness." He breathed. "Now, I must evoke the Archdemoness."

Watching Laisren walk away, Finn shouted at the top of his lungs—another sound of madness twisting within the cave.

He turned back to Conor and grabbed him, kissing him deeply, ferally, angrily. Finn ran his hands down the other man's naked body as they pulled each other together. His skin was slick and hot, as was Finn's. The man fumbled with the buckles of Finn's kilt, even as their tongues caressed with rising lust.

Finn placed his hand on the buckle of his kilt, stopping him. "No," he said breathlessly. "I'm sorry."

Finn looked up, searching for Laisren.

Laisren stood upon a stone a step higher than the cave's floor. He extended his black wings to full span and stretched his arms upward. He faced downwards, his eyes closed.

Finn stepped away from the other man.

"I'm sorry," Finn said again and ran out of the cave.

Outside, he flew away.

—

Atop the hill, within the ráth, Finn sat. He observed the ring of black fire with the Torc of Datura hovering above its center.

Finn heard the flap of wings behind him. Feet touched the ground. He didn't look back.

"I've searched everywhere for you," Laisren said. "I feared you'd left."

"I don't want to see you now."

"Well, 'tis good you have your back to me then."

Finn only stared at the wall of black flames twisting upwards six feet. He'd been watching for hours, staring.

"Should we talk about what happened?" Laisren didn't seem angry. He didn't seem anything, and Finn was tired of trying to figure him out.

"Seems to me that had fuck all to do with you. Friend."

Silence.

"You shouldn't be here," Laisren said. "Come, let's—"

"I shouldn't have come at all."

"I meant in the ráth."

"I know what you meant. And I know what I meant," Finn said. "I shouldn't have come here." He looked back at Laisren.

Laisren, slouching and looking sad, stared at Finn.

Finn asked, "How'd your chat with your Demon go, then?"

Laisren shook his head. "Nowhere."

"Right." Finn nodded. "Then I failed our people."

"*I* failed your people."

"Who fucking cares," Finn said. "They're failed, aren't they, either way? And I can't even tell them. That's the thing, isn't it? I can't even tell them they're failed. They're just waiting." Finn sighed.

Laisren said nothing. And what could he say? They'd exhausted all their options. But one.

"I ..." Finn stood up. "I found the pattern. Your mam's pattern in the black fire. If you watch it long enough, you see these little sparks of crimson."

"The pattern means nothing, Finn."

"It lasts three seconds, the spark, and then another one comes nine seconds later. 'Tis just like Jyoti said."

"I know of the sparks. I stood right here a year ago and watched my mother run at those damned sparks. And I watched her scream in agony as she burned."

Finn let the words sink in. "She ran in when the spark shined?"

"She did."

"Then that's wrong." Finn looked back at the fire. "The three-second window must be during the nine seconds the spark's *not* there."

"You don't know that."

"I have to try."

"*What?*"

Finn stepped toward the ring of fire. "'Tis the one option we have left."

"Finn, get away from there."

Finn stepped closer. He could feel flames pulling the heat from his body. "It must be the three seconds right after the spark disappears."

"Finn, I'm begging you. Just step back from it, all right? We can go home and discuss this new theory of yours."

"We've talked enough." Finn trembled with fear, but he ignored it as much as he could. "It makes sense for me to go. If I fail, you still can—"

"If you fail?" Laisren said desperately. "Fucking za, Finn. If you fail, you'll be dead."

"Our people need me, Laz." Finn lifted his shaking hand toward the fiery wall. "I'll give you the torc once I get it."

Laisren stepped forward.

"Stay back," Finn said. "If you mess up my concentration, I might enter at the wrong time."

Laisren stayed but reached out his hand toward Finn. "Just come back, all right. Please."

Finn watched a crimson spark appear within the flame. One. Two. Three. It vanished.

Finn ran in.

"*No!*" Laisren dashed forward, but it was too late.

The flames exploded, twisting upward and consuming Finn.

"No," Laisren cried as his hands hit his knees. He helplessly watched the black fires flare up and twist.

Finn shot from the fire and crashed into the ground ten feet away before rolling like a limp carcass.

Laisren ran to him, crouching to him and checking for any signs of life.

Finn's body was limp and covered in burns and bleeding cuts.

Laisren scooped Finn's upper body from the ground, holding his head to his chest.

"Please wake up, Finn. Please." His eyes watered. "I love you, as well. I should have said it. *Fuck.* I should have said it. But I thought it was best for you. Please. Please wake up."

He pulled Finn's lifeless, bloody body to his, embracing him. "Please, Finn." No response. Already so cold.

"No," Laisren whispered. Tears ran down his cheeks.

He laid Finn down on the dirt. He set his hand on Finn's chest. No heartbeat, no breath.

Laisren's scream of anguish echoed in the night.

CHAPTER THIRTEEN

Absolute darkness surrounded him, and the silence within it lay undisturbed by even the slightest sounds. He felt nothing.

A word clung to the tip of his consciousness. He grasped for it and tried to decipher it. It was something important—something he needed to remember. A name. His name. *Finn.*

The darkness faded, but not by illumination. Instead, it was as if his eyes had become unblinded. His vision, blurry at first, came into focus, and Finn saw that he stood perilously close to the edge of a cliff.

This was like no cliff he'd seen before. The ground, a circular pane of black glass, stretched fifty feet to its opposite edge. The pane was suspended—by no support he could determine—within a spherical emptiness.

Beyond the emptiness, in all directions, innumerable streaks of crimson light twisted and flashed and swirled around one another as they flowed, filling an unending black.

The sight, awesome and confusing, enthralled him so entirely that he did not, at first, notice that his body was numb. Finn looked down at himself to see that his body was, in fact, there and intact. However, his kilt looked tattered and the color of dust.

A tingling formed at his forehead and rushed down his body. The sensation mimicked times when a sleeping limb awakened, but all over his body, at once, and with a hint of pain.

When the prickles subsided, the numbness had gone, yet there was little to feel. The glass, solid under his feet, gave scant sensation. There was no wind or temperature.

Finn walked, curious and afraid, toward the center of the disc, where he saw two thrones. They looked as if they had grown up from the floor, and accordingly, their bases were like foundations of old oak trees with thick, twisted roots spreading out in all directions. This was all of black glass, as were the beautifully carved thrones themselves.

These thrones faced away from him, and as Finn—like a mouse fearing capture—walked around them, he found a woman seated on the one to the left.

The woman, in her early forties with long black hair, was strikingly pale. Her thin face and fierce dark eyes stared forward, unaware or apathetic, of Finn's arrival. Her crimson lips gave no smile. Her chin set at a perfect right angle to her slender neck, leading to her low-cut dress of black velvet bordered in embroidered runes of silver thread. The long belt—wrapping her thin waist and turning to follow down her skirt—echoed the border's design.

Noble was her posture as she sat on her throne. Her wings, like those of an immense raven, extended slightly from either side. The chair had no armrests, yet in Terovae fashion, twisted shafts of black glass extended up from either side of the seat's front. The shafts held obsidian orbs, whereon the woman kept her delicate hands tipped with black sharpened nails.

"Chief Morgana," Finn whispered, frightened to disturb her, as he knelt and bowed his head. "We thought you were dead."

She didn't look at him. "You are that boy who used to chase after my Laisren," she said. "Calvagh's brother."

"I am, Chief, yes. And you sent him away. Laisren, I mean."

"Sent him away?" she said, her words slow and cross. "You speak as if I cast him out to a deserted island. My son required more education than our tribe offered."

"Forgive me, Chief. Laisren's very smart now and back then. You were right to send him off."

She looked upward with a distant gaze. "I can feel his sadness, even now, as we speak. He weeps for you."

Heart aching, Finn glanced downward at the lustrous pitch-dark floor. "He mustn't know I made it safely. I found your pattern, Chief. The crimson sparks in the black fire. I was able to—"

"The pattern was nonsense," she said. "I was desperate at the time and grasping at straws. There is no safe way through the black fire."

"But I made it, Chief. Safe and sound."

"Did you now?"

Trembling, Finn looked at his hands and arms, truly seeing them for the first time since his arrival. And he saw what must have been true the entire time. His skin was colorless in shades of gray, his body translucent.

"Right," Finn said, disappointed. "Is this the afterlife then, Chief?"

"This place is part of the Irefaery Realm, which I partitioned off for myself. I await the Firechild. Tell me, why did you come to Anordúla?"

"To find yourself, Chief. Chief Kaie requests your help in dealing with the Dayigans."

Morgana lowered her shadowed eyes to gaze intently at Finn, as if she read every part of his being and was displeased.

He felt small and anxious. His body tensed. He wished to hide from her, yet he remained in place.

She sighed. "I have no need for Kaie's errand boy."

Morgana lifted her pale hand and slapped it back down on the orb.

The glass at Finn's feet shook. It shattered. With no time to react, he fell through the forming fissure, through a rain of black glass shards, and downward into darkness.

Frantic, Finn spread his wings, but before he could take flight, his body, once again, went numb.

He dissolved into countless crimson sparks.

—

Finn reformed in what appeared to be a wooded area, but the winter bare trees were not wooden. Instead, they were sheets of heavily rusted tin with parts broken away, showing them to be thin-skinned and hollow. The sky above them showed the same swirls of crimson in blackness as those Finn had witnessed above Morgana's throne.

With no idea where he was or where to go, Finn walked cautiously, his bare feet crunching on the smooth brown pebbles that covered the entire ground.

His trek was not long, however, until he came to a clearing. Centered there, some distance from Finn, was a large fire formed of glass in shades of red, orange, and yellow. While its individual flames were motionless, the fire, as a whole, rotated slowly and glowed.

Around it, cavorting in the reverse direction, ten bestial men danced wildly. Each stood seven feet tall and appeared, above his waist, very much like a powerfully built, hairy Human, but with ears stretching to points and head crowned with horns. Their erections were humanoid in form but not in dimensions; instead, they ranged about two feet in length and bobbed rigidly as they frolicked. A long horse-like tail marked the tops of their butts. Below, fur covered them and grew denser down their legs, which grew more bestial until they ended at hooves.

Finn knew satyrs from old Faery stories but had never seen one before. Now he watched, fear pounding behind his ribs.

"They excite you, yes?" a voice said behind Finn.

Finn turned to see a young man leaning his back against a metal tree.

"No."

He too appeared Human, or at least a wingless Terovae. He was like Finn in height and build, but younger, about twenty. His pointed ears peeked slightly from his long black hair, which faded to crimson tips and brushed his bare shoulders. His face was more beautiful than any Finn had seen—his skin, like porcelain. Beneath perfect brows, his eyes were dark and mesmerizing, with irises flecked with glowing crimson. His lips curled upward in a mischievous grin.

The stranger stepped forward and approached Finn with slow, evenly spaced steps, and Finn was certain the man wished him to better view his gorgeous body. The man was shirtless and his skin glistened even in the dim light. His chest was small but muscular, as was his slim, smooth stomach.

Finn's eyes trailed down him, past the tiny navel to where his black leather pants hung low on his hips.

"I know what you are," Finn said breathlessly. He looked into those mesmerizing eyes, now but a foot from his own. "I'm in the Otherworld." Finn couldn't take his eyes off him. "The place of wicked Faeries."

The stranger's perfect lips curled upward. "Do you think me wicked, mortal?"

Finn continued to stare at him, so close he could kiss his lips with the slightest of movement. "I think you're ..." Finn breathed. "I think you're a gancanagh."

"*Very good.* Then you know I can give you pleasures unlike anything you could imagine."

A dopey smile crossed Finn's face. *Tempting.* "No," Finn breathed as he jerked and stepped back.

Looking away, Finn said, "I'm in love, properly in love."

The gancanagh huffed scoffingly. "Love? I see the many, *many* sexual encounters written on you, yet not one shows love. Just tonight, I see you lustfully kissed a man. What was he called?"

"Colm. No, em, I mean—Conor. I'm not even sure why I did that, to be honest."

"You were hurt," the gancanagh said, "and desired pleasure to mend your wounds. It makes perfect sense to me. I would have done the same."

"No. 'Twas wrong, that. I'm in love. And now I'll never ..."

"See him again?" The gancanagh's body blurred and wavered. When he reformed, he appeared in the form of Laisren—as real and perfect as if he were standing there.

Laisren whispered. "You can have me right now."

"You don't know a thing about love, Faery," Finn said.

The satyrs turned to him and began to move, but the gancanagh raised a hand.

They stopped but watched.

Finn continued, saying, "Gancanaghs make people love them and then abandon them to misery, madness, or suicide."

"A bit hypocritical, mortal." He reformed again, this time into Kyran.

As Kyran, he said, "I loved you, Finn, so much. I only returned to the Feah, so you'd talk me out of leaving. I just wanted you to love me as well."

"'Tis not the same, that," Finn said. "I only meant to ..."

"To have fun?" The gancanagh returned to his true form. "Yes, you simply wanted pleasure and gave him pleasure in return. 'Tis not your fault he made it into something more." The gancanagh chuckled. "Mayhap you are a gancanagh, as well. I could spend the night transforming into the many poor men who fell in love with fair Finn, or we could get naked and forget them all."

Finn crouched down and stared at the countless pebbles covering the ground. "It would have been different with Laisren," he whispered. "I think maybe I was waiting for him this whole time." He snatched up a pebble and threw it to clank against a tree. "But I'm fucking dead now, so it don't matter."

The gancanagh released a long sigh that turned into an annoyed groan. "You're not dead."

"Amn't I?"

"What good would the dead be to me?" He ran two fingers horizontally through the air, and a cord of braided strands of white light appeared under his fingers.

It trailed off through the air, fading to oily black before continuing to some far-off origin. The other end came to Finn's navel.

"You're still connected to your body," the gancanagh said. "And to all your little sensitive nerves I'd like to make tingle."

"But that's fantastic."

"Not quite as fantastic as you might like, I'm afraid. It appears that someone has locked you in the moment of death. The blackness coming extremely slowly up the cord is that moment ending."

"Right," Finn said, disappointed. "How long do I have then?"

"Well, judging by the rate of motion of the nex—that's the black part—up the cord, divided by the very long length of the remaining cord up to your sexy stomach, and then the square root and the hypotenuses, I would calculate ..." He grinned slyly. "... that I am a sex Irefaery, not a mathematician."

Finn grinned. "You *are* charming, in your way."

"I really am," he said. The cord vanished. "In truth, it didn't look like the nex was moving much at all. But it was indeed moving. 'Twould seem someone powerful wanted to keep you alive."

Finn nodded. "Then I must use that time to help my people. Do you know anything about the Torc of Datura?"

"*The Torc of Datura,*" he repeated as he set his hand against his perfect jaw. "I'm sure I could think better if you gave me a shoulder rub."

"Aye, and if I touch your skin, I'll be enchanted by you."

"I've already enchanted you, mortal." He licked his upper lip and raised an eyebrow.

Finn smiled. "Do you have a name, Gancanagh?"

"That is not for you to know, mortal."

"Well ..." Finn crossed his arms and leaned in toward him. "Whatever your name is, I am in love with Laisren altogether and will remain so until I drop down dead."

The gancanagh huffed. "The torc is in there." He waved halfheartedly.

Finn looked to see a thick mist peel back around a cylindrical tower of black glass, like part of a castle, standing fifty feet tall on a hill within the tin woods.

"It can't be in there. 'Tis in the ráth in the Anordúla village."

"No," the gancanagh said, "*you're* in the ráth in the Anordúla village, projecting here. And *it* is here, projecting there."

"Course. Like the wee bat-winged cat. I have to go to it—the torc, not the cat. You can come if you like."

"I suppose I will, but don't expect me to be any help. I'm coming only because I enjoy looking at you."

CHAPTER FOURTEEN

Atop a hill, within a ring of old tin trees stood a fifty-foot tower of slick black glass. Finn, followed by the unenthusiastic gancanagh, entered through a large archway.

The tower held a single room, from floor to high-up conic roof, and there, as the gancanagh had promised, was the silver Torc of Datura.

"The fire's here as well," Finn said, pushing his shoulders down in frustration. "Do you know how to get past it?"

"I know how to use my tongue in such a manner as to take any man or woman to a place of such pure ecstasy that they would abandon everything and follow me to the ends of the world. But no, somehow, I've never needed to pass through a void flame to satisfy a lover."

"Void flame, is it? And what is that?"

"Is that important?" the gancanagh asked with little interest. "Bravo me, being unintentionally helpful. You really should give me *a reward*."

"I have to get a message to Laisren," Finn said. "If he knows what kind of fire it is, he should be able to figure out some way to get past it."

"Pointless waste of time," the gancanagh said. "Yes, the fire is in both places, but the torc is only here. You'd have him risking his life for a reflection."

"Right." Finn nodded as he stared at the fire. "Suppose I'll have to figure it out meself then." He looked sideways. "I've never done much figuring out before. There's always been someone else to do the figuring out."

"Well, I hope you don't expect me to do it." The gancanagh circled his hands in the air in a slow, gentle wave.

An item formed within an undulating blur. It was a type of furniture, a lounge framed in gold and cushioned in purple velvet.

The gancanagh, atop it, lay on his side.

"Could you tell me what void flame means at least?" Finn asked with impatience.

The gancanagh sighed. "Void is what the universe was just before it was created. It is *nothing*, but not normal nothing. It absorbs everything, even light and heat. And if you break through the magic containing it here, 'twill absorb you too and break you down, bit by smallest bit, into utter nothing. A horrible, agonizing way to die."

"I'll have you remember, that's the way I'm about to die, meself. Or am dying. I think. Do you know if void destroys a soul?"

The gancanagh yawned. "Do wake me up when you're naked." He closed his eyes.

"Fecking Faeries," Finn muttered as he sat down cross-legged on the floor. He stared at the fire.

"How's it any different now, just 'cause I know 'tis void?" Finn said aloud. "Void. Void. Vo-id. I can't extinguish it, still. I can't go through it, still. I can't fly over it, still no."

He lay back and folded his arms under his head. He stared upwards, half in thought, half in dismal surrender. "Everyone's counting on me, and I'm just fucking useless, me." Finn sighed. "Hold on." He perked up. "There's a roof over it there. Gancanagh, how's there a roof over it?"

Finn looked back to see the Irefaery fast asleep.

Finn thought for a moment. "Laisren said there's a clear wall over the fire that stretches up for miles. But that was the real-world version."

He jumped up and dashed outside. He grabbed a handful of pebbles from the tin woods and returned, just as quickly, to the black fire.

Finn threw a pebble above the fire.

It hit the unseen cylinder, stopping in midair. It shot straight down into the circle of fire. The void flames absorbed it.

Finn flew higher and threw another pebble. Same effect.

Higher. Same effect. Higher, same effect. Finn flew as close to the ceiling as he could and attempted to throw a pebble over the transparent ring. Like before, it was sucked down and vaporized.

He looked at the ceiling.

—

Finn landed on the squat, conic roof shingled in dark gray wood. He approached the area that he estimated to be directly above the fire ring.

He threw a pebble.

It passed through where the wall should be, landing with a few chinks on the opposite side before rolling down.

Finn smiled. "Mothers be praised."

—

"Gancanagh!" Finn exclaimed. "Wake up, you lazy bastard. I need a long rope."

The gancanagh stirred some on the lounge. "I didn't take you for one into bondage."

"Don't know what that means," Finn said. "But I need you to make a rope—twine, really—as long as this tower is tall."

The gancanagh opened his eyes, glanced at the roof, and looked at Finn. "Sounds to me like you need to capture yourself a leprechaun. He'll give you three wishes."

"Aye, and what's a leprechaun?"

"A leprechaun is a *Faery*, the nice ones who are sometimes inclined to help People. *I*"—he placed his hand on his chest—"am an Irefaery, the wicked ones who are often inclined to kill People, eat People, enslave their souls, drive them mad, and other fun things in the realm of general malevolence."

"I appreciate you not eating me. I really do."

"'Tis not something I particularly enjoy, to be honest."

"Still, nice of you. Could you make me some twine like how you made this bed-thing?"

"That's not something I particularly enjoy either."

"Please, Gancanagh." Finn forced a sad face with a slight pout on his lips. "I'd be ever so grateful."

"Not grateful in any way I'd like."

"*Please.*" Finn bit his lip.

"Are *you* trying to seduce *me*, Terovae? That's *my* game. I'm the gancanagh."

"Please."

The gancanagh huffed. "Fine." He swatted his hand.

A spool of thick brown twine appeared a foot above the floor before falling on its side and rolling.

"But I'm leaving." The gancanagh stood. The lounge vanished in a purple swirl. "I'll go find a rusalka. *She'll* appreciate my genuine talents."

"Thank you, Gancanagh. I'd kiss you, but, you know, enslavement and madness."

"Yes," the gancanagh grumbled. He began toward the exit but stopped. "You have half a moment left of life, mortal. Use it for pleasure, even if without me."

"I can't do that."

"Very well. But know this: As deadly as the void flames are in the Natural Realm, they are merely a reflection of these flames here—and with but a fraction of their power. Here, the void *will* destroy your soul. Be careful, sexy."

Finn nodded gravely. "And you."

In a blur toward the exit, the gancanagh was gone.

—

Finn's wings flapped in struggling flight as his arms strained around a heavy stone. Groaning through gritted teeth, Finn managed to fly the stone up onto the tower's wooden pointed roof. He pushed it up the slope, almost to the center. Again, he wrapped his arms around it and lifted. He smashed it down with force.

The roof cracked around the stone.

Finn lifted it again. He dropped it again. More cracks.

The third time, the stone crashed through the roof, almost dragging him along with it. Finn fell to his hands and knees above the hole and watched the stone plummet. It hit the inside of the unseen wall.

The wall caught it and sucked it down into the fire. It was obliterated.

Finn stood carefully, fearing he'd meet the same fate if he fell.

He grabbed the spool of twine, unwrapped a short length, and threaded it through a ball of crumpled rusted tin he'd made from part of a tree. *Would the outer wall of a tin tree still be called bark?* mused Finn as he tied the weight in place three feet from the end. To the end, Finn tied a large hook he'd fashioned from a large tin stick.

Meticulously, Finn lowered the hook through the broken roof and down within the unseen cylindrical wall. The ring of black fire looked frighteningly far down, yet he kept sight of it, as it was his only means of working out the clear wall's location.

If the hook hit the wall, it would suck it down with the twine and perhaps Finn too. The invisible well above the circle of fire was far too narrow for Finn to expand his wings inside it without hitting it. He would either touch the wall with his wings and be pulled down, or not extend his wings and simply fall; either way, hitting the fire—vaporized. Even if he managed not to fall with his twine and hook, with his tools lost and the gancanagh gone, he'd have no other means of getting to the torc. He had plenty of time to think of all these disasters as, inch by careful inch, Finn lowered the hook while trying his best to avoid any sway.

The absolute preciseness of it became almost maddening after some long length of time—Finn wasn't sure how long, well over an hour. He'd never imagined holding a string could make his arms so tired. He strained to hold it steady.

The spool was looking thin. *Was it enough twine?*

At long last, the hook neared the torc fifty feet below but stopped a foot above. The twine ended.

"No," Finn whispered, unable to react more for fear of sending ripples down the line.

As carefully as he had ever done anything in his life, Finn tied the end of the twine around his wrist, cautiously tightening it with his teeth.

A tiny wave rippled through the line, growing as it vibrated downward. Finn froze, not even breathing for fear of adding to the motion. It calmed.

Finn then, ever so slowly, leaned forward, bracing one hand on the fractured, splintered wood surrounding the hole. He carefully, extremely carefully, lowered his arm into the hole. His head, inverted, neared the dizzying drop. Fear rushed through his disincarnate being. It would more than kill him, he knew; the gancanagh said it would destroy his soul.

Finn kept his strained eyes on the hook, fifty feet down, as it brushed the torc.

He clutched the broken wood of the roof. He leaned a bit farther down.

With a slight clink of metal on metal, the hook slid over the upper section of the ring. It caught hold.

Finn released something between a stifled laugh and a stifled weeping, but he held still.

He began to pull it up.

—

The victory of getting the torc waned as Finn sat on the floor of the glass tower and stared at the black fire.

He looked down at the neck ring in his hand, marveling at the twisted, inch-thick silver rope forming the bulk of the circle and the ends designed as raven heads with ruby eyes. In its beak, each held a black gem, closing the three-inch gap between them.

"So," Finn said, "what do I do with you now then? All that effort, but you're no good to me, are you?"

"You risked your life coming here," a woman said behind him.

Finn jumped and turned to see Morgana. She stood with a noble posture, her hands folded at her waist, her wings half extended, her clothing all in black. She was like someone wicked in a faery tale.

Morgana continued, "And you risked your soul getting the torc. Why?"

Finn shrugged. "I figured loads of people have risked their lives helping me out. Seemed fitting I return the favor."

"You have little time remaining."

He nodded sadly. "I know. I feel it—death. But I still have to get this torc to Laisren."

She stared her fierce eye at Finn for a moment. "He is lucky to have found you." She paused. "Come here to me."

Finn stood and approached. He knelt before her.

"Give me the Torc of Datura."

Finn complied, holding it up with both hands.

She took it gracefully and gazed at it. "I sought it so long. Died for it." She looked at him. "The walls between the Irefaery Realm and Perdinok are closed. So it is impossible for us to send the torc back."

"Then I failed, after all that."

"I saved your body from obliteration, and by the power of my son's tears, froze you in the moment of death," she said, her voice stern. "But you have multiple fatal injuries beyond my ability to repair." She touched the torc to her throat.

The torc became animate, slithering around her neck before resolidifying.

"Do you, Finnán ó Ríona, vow yourself everlastingly to my service? It is your choice to make."

"I suppose so, yes."

"Be serious, boy," she said, her voice echoing.

Finn took a deep breath and answered solemnly, "Yes, Chief Morgana. I vow meself to you. Everlasting like."

She cast her palm toward Finn.

Finn's hands shot to his neck as he felt a dull pain. The torc, identical to that Morgana wore, circled his neck.

She said, "The projection of the Torc of Datura, the one in the Natural Realm, is now on your body."

Finn tried to look at it, yanking at it around his neck. "Does that mean this here's a projection of a projection?"

Morgana sighed as she closed her eyes. "Yes," she said, "I suppose it is."

"That's a laugh, Chief, is it not?"

"No," she said. "It is healing your body, Finn."

Finn looked up at her. "Does that mean I can go back there?"

She cracked a slight smile. "It does."

"But 'tis Laisren, not me, that should have the torc."

"But you are here, and he is not. You must wear the torc's projection until the eve of the new year, when autumn paints the woods in shades of orange and the veil between the worlds is thin. On that night, I will be able to transfer the projection to my son. In the meantime, with the genuine torc, I will send you power and guidance. Now go." She cast her hand toward Finn.

His eyes shot open as he took a long, painful breath. He sat up on the ground.

"Finn?" Laisren rushed to him and cradled his back as he gripped Finn's hand.

Agony struck, and Finn called out as all the blood and wounds on his body burned away within lines of crimson embers, leaving him healed. The tattoo on his chest burned away, too. In its place, a new tattoo formed: an inverted seven-pointed star matching Laisren's.

"I don't understand," said Laisren, his eyes darting across Finn's body as he tried to process what was happening. "Are you ... Are you all right?"

Panting, he nodded weakly as he scanned his new surroundings—the ráth centered in the Anordúla village.

Finn looked at Laisren with sleepy eyes. "I am all right, actually, Laz."

Laisren smiled. "I love you as well, Finn—I should have said before." He sniffed and wiped away tears. "I thought I'd lost you."

"How long was I gone?"

"I'm not sure. I think your heart stopped beating for over a minute."

"A minute?" Finn chuckled. "A fecking minute."

"You're healed and you're wearing the torc," Laisren said. "What happened?" He paused. "Actually, tell me later." Laisren kissed Finn's lips.

As Finn nervously kissed him, he feared Laisren would stop and leave like so many times before, but the kisses grew deeper. Finn relaxed, letting himself go within his arms, feeling Laisren's warm chest and stomach against his own and his soft tongue caress his own.

Laisren kissed Finn's neck and the top of his chest. But he stopped.

The fear returned to Finn. *Would he leave again?*

Instead, Laisren gazed into Finn's eyes for an extended moment and grinned wantonly with open lips and dreamy eyes.

Touching Finn's chest, he slid his hand downward, along the tiny hairs down the center of his slim pale stomach, past his navel, under the waistband of Finn's kilt.

Finn jolted and released a heavy breath through a wide smile.

Laisren gently pulled the tip from the top of the leather waistband. He kissed down the center of Finn's stomach, approaching the sensitive target until, finally, he licked the swollen head hiding within delicate skin.

Finn squirmed under these lower kisses as Laisren's hands moved to the outer buckle of Finn's kilt, releasing it. Next, to the inner buckle. He unwrapped Finn, cock standing firm from orange curls. He took the rigid length into his mouth.

Finn writhed, thrusting forward at a growing pace. Soon, he stopped himself. He jumped up, ripping Laisren's robe from his shoulders. He stripped Laisren and flipped him to lie with his back on the dirt. Finn took him into his eager mouth, sucking and slurping hungrily.

In time, Finn licked up Laisren's fit stomach and chest, returning his mouth to his.

The men kissed wildly with carnal passions now unleashed.

"I love you," Finn breathed as their mouths parted.

"I love you, as well."

They pushed their bare bodies together as Finn ran his hands down Laisren's sides and along the black feathers of his wings.

Finn pulled away, sitting up between Laisren's hairy thighs. Finn pushed Laisren's legs upward, exposing the hinder cleft, and moved forward.

"No," Laisren said. "That's not something I do." He panted through a smile. "Get back how you were on top of me."

"Right." Finn nodded stupidly, his mind lost to desire. He complied.

Again, their lips met in a lasting fervor.

Laisren wrapped his hand around both rods together and began grinding himself against Finn's. Finn followed his lead and began thrusting faster into Laisren's hand.

Their kisses grew more animalistic as their bodies grew hotter and slicker with sweat. Finn kissed his salty neck, his shoulder, and returned to his mouth.

Within Laisren's grip, they pumped with an increasing tempo, thrusting harder and faster.

Laisren called out in breathy moans into Finn's mouth. The hand became slippery.

Finn wasn't far behind, convulsing as he rammed into the greased hand. Finn called out as he mixed his seed with Laisren's.

Their breathing slowed. They smiled in relaxed, lazy bliss. Finn kissed Laisren's chest and tenderly licked his frosted stomach.

Finally, Laisren pulled Finn back up for a slower, affectionate kiss.

"Fecking nice," Finn said with a laugh. "I should die more often."

Laisren chuckled. "Arsehole." He sighed and looked at Finn contently before pulling him to lie against him.

Holding each other tight, they lay enjoying the blissful moment.

CHAPTER FIFTEEN

Finn woke on his side within the black silk sheets on Laisren's bed. One of Laisren's arms and a leg were around him. Finn inched backward, so their bare bodies touched.

"You're awake." Laisren yawned. "I worried for you." He sat up, and Finn rolled on his back to better see him.

"You fell asleep," Laisren said. "After we ..."

"Right." Finn smiled. "Sorry about that. I suppose I do that sometimes."

"No, I mean, it was two nights ago. I checked and found you were severely seid depleted."

"You indeed depleted my seed, that be true."

Laisren grinned slyly. "Not that sort. *Seid*. 'Tis a Gellic word, originally. It means your soul energy. Coronal seid is used to perform magic and vital seid keeps your body alive. There's no definite division between the two, so if a magician uses too much magic, he can die."

"That'd be a shame there," Finn joked. "Me, having just come back to life and all."

Laisren did not share the humor. "'Tis not something that usually affects non-magicians. I barely figured it out."

"But no bother. I'm all right now, amn't I?" Finn leaned up and kissed his lips.

The kiss lasted as Finn sunk back to the bed and pulled Laisren with him.

Laisren lay his head on Finn's chest, and Finn rubbed his messy black hair.

Laisren said, "I'll have to teach you ways to strengthen your seid." He reached up to Finn's neck and touched the Torc of Datura, running his fingers around the thick solid silvery rope. "And teach you how to use magic."

"I thought it was the necklace's magic I'd be using."

"Even acting as a conduit for greater magic drains your own seid." With his thumb, Laisren stroked the black gem held in the beaks of the ravens while his other fingers stroked Finn's collarbone. "And it is extremely important that you understand how any magic you're using works. The course will need to be quite intensive and extensive."

Finn stretched his arms and folded them under his head. "I figure I'm still too seid depleted for all that right now. As I see it, 'tis best I stay in bed all day with you wrapped around me."

"We do need to start as soon as possible."

Finn flipped him over on his wings and straddled his waist. He held Laisren's arms down above his head.

"Do we *really*?" Finn kissed his mouth.

Finn heard an elongated meow from behind them and looked. The winged black cat stood just inside the door beside the black bookcase.

"Your cat says we should be staying in bed now." Finn smiled.

Laisren returned the smile. "I'm well sure he meant we should go train and study."

Finn turned back to the tromlee and started to ask a playful follow-up but stopped. His face went blank as he watched as a crimson aura surrounded the Irefaery.

Laisren sat up and moved nearer to the foot of the bed.

The tromlee, his eyes glowing crimson, grew larger as his fur dissolved away.

Soon, he was the size of a panther but bone thin. His furless skin was black and leathery and crinkled as if deflated. His long tail was a series of jointed bones. His paws, all four, stretched into hands with long, thin fingers and claws. His wings grew as large as Finn's own, but like a bat's.

Finn glanced at Laisren, both dumbstruck.

The tromlee's voice was a slow, hissing groan through sharp teeth. "I have a gift for thee, O Lord Finnán."

"*Lord Finnán*, says he," Finn said. "That's class, there."

"Be serious, Finn," Laisren said. "What gift?"

"It is from thy dark mother, O Chief Laisren."

"My mother?"

"Aye," Finn said. "I seen your mam when I were dead. Bit scary, herself, but nice altogether. She sends her love."

"What?"

"Come," the tromlee groaned.

—

Laisren and Finn followed the tromlee out of the cottage and toward the hill ringed with twisted trees.

They did not ascend the hill itself. Instead, the tromlee stopped at a stool at its base. The stool held a beautifully carved bow of ebony wood.

"That's my mother's bow," Laisren said.

"Is it a magic bow?" Finn asked.

"It never was before."

The tromlee said, "'Tis now thine, Lord Finnán. A gift from Great Morgana."

Finn glanced at Laisren and received an assuring nod before he approached. He lifted the bow warily.

The whole thing was smoothed and polished to a metallic sheen, its detailed carvings sinister.

"Use it," the tromlee hissed.

"I don't have an arrow on me," Finn said.

"*Use it*," the tromlee maintained.

"Bit pushy, your cat," Finn grumbled. He held the bow as he'd seen others do and dragged back the string.

A bolt of crimson light formed where an arrow should sit. Finn aimed and released.

The bolt shot forward and stabbed into the hill, dissipating. The foot-wide area around the impact—both the land and the blades of grass—misted.

"That was fantastic," Finn said. "I mean, I was aiming for a tree, but still."

Laisren hurried to the spot and crouched down to examine the effects. "Remember when I told you all matter is energy at different vibrations and energy is chaos-aether pairs?"

"Aye. When we had the grape beer."

"'Tis not truly called grape beer, you know," Laisren said, and sighed. "'Tis fine." His excitement returned. "It appears you've disrupted the chaos in this spot just enough to ripple the vibrations and send the matter out of phase. This mist *is* the grass."

The mist retracted, and the area returned to normal.

"It reverted," Laisren said. "Interesting." He stood and returned to Finn. "Imagine the matter composing the grass was a bow." He took the black bow and demonstrated. "You pull at the bowstring and it bends the bow, just a little, but when the force ceases, the bow returns to normal. No damage done."

"So, 'tis pointless, then. It didn't do a thing."

"It would hurt if you did that to a person, possibly knock them out. And with enough pull on the metaphorical bowstring—with muscles well beyond a normal person's—you could break a bow in half." He handed the bow back to Finn.

Finn looked at the bow. "'Twould be well good to shoot people and knock them out without injuring them. Dayigans, I mean." He looked at the Irefaery. "What are you called, Cat?"

"I am Mephistus."

"Thank you kindly, Mephistus."

"As I said," he hissed, "the gift is from Morgana."

Finn looked at Laisren. "Exciting, right?"

Laisren lost his excitement and gained a grave composure. "'Twould appear you are chest deep in the world from which I wished to protect you."

"A world with you in it."

He smiled sadly. "True."

—

The next four months were filled with training and study. Laisren or Nekesa led Finn's courses, but everyone in the village added somewhat to the education, be it in magic or archery. Finn's brain and muscles maintained dull aches, and the constant use of magic kept him queasy and tired. Nevertheless, he was careful not to fall into what Laisren had called *seid depletion*.

Finn's preferred parts of the days were when he and Laisren were not training but alone together, laughing, kissing, embracing one another. They'd slept together every night since Finn's return from the Irefaery Realm.

Never had Finn dreamed that the Anordúla village, so different from his own, would ever feel like home. Yet with every passing day, he felt it more and more.

However, Finn often thought of his former home.

"I just wish I had some way to know what was going on there," Finn said to Laisren as they walked away from the dining pavilion.

Behind them, some villagers cleaned up while others continued to drink and cackle and howl like lunatics.

"It would be too dangerous to send anyone from our village there," Laisren said. "And more dangerous to send you."

"I know." Finn stopped and looked downward. "Just talking, that's all. Just worried. For all I know, the Dayigans could have burnt down the whole parish. For that matter, the Dayigans could've give up on the whole thing and buggered off back to their empire. I guess I just feel guilty being happy here when who knows what is happening back there."

He took Finn's hand in his. "All you're doing here—your training, your study—is to help them, you know."

"'Tis just taking a long time, so ..."

"Chief Laisren," Nekesa shouted from the sky. She landed before continuing. "We have spotted Dayigans in the area."

"This far north?"

"Yes, my chief. We saw them crossing the border from the Allar lands to the Feah lands. They have Drevite prisoners, my chief. Most likely Allars."

CHAPTER SIXTEEN

Under the somber glow of the two moons, Laisren and Finn crouched on the high limb of an old tree. They watched.

The four Dayigan soldiers, all Human, kept a small fire with two skinned rabbits above it on a makeshift spit. Coarse wool blankets, one for each man, had been laid out in no particular configuration. Nearby sat two handcarts, each with square wooden beds framed in foot-high plank walls, two large wooden wheels, and poles off the front so someone could pull or push it. The carts held nothing out of the ordinary—a few trunks and barrels.

Laisren turned back to Nekesa on a limb behind him. The tromlee lay beside her.

"You said they had captives," Laisren whispered.

"They did, my chief. I am certain of that."

"I believe you."

Laisren jumped down, landed firmly, and kept his large black wings open as he stood tall.

The Dayigans reacted, jumping up and drawing swords.

"I wouldn't move if I were you," said Laisren.

Beside him landed Mephistus, his eyes glowing as he hissed at the soldiers.

Laisren scratched behind the tromlee's ear. "Drop your weapons. My cat hasn't eaten in a long time and is starving."

The Dayigans reluctantly threw down their swords.

In the tree, Nekesa tapped Finn's shoulder. "Come on." She jumped past him.

He followed.

Nekesa positioned herself on one side of Laisren, and Finn took the other. She armed her bow, drawing back the string, and slowly swept across the soldiers, watching.

Finn followed her lead in actions, but not in confidence. As he held the crimson bolt, staring down its length at his potential targets, he feared he'd need to use it.

"Where are the prisoners?" Laisren demanded.

One of the Dayigans, the group's leader Finn assumed, answered scornfully. "Do you see any prisoners, savage?" He kept his nose upturned and seemed annoyed by the entire situation.

Laisren turned to Nekesa with a look that asked, *are you sure?*

She raised her eyebrows and nodded.

"If you're finished wasting our time," the leader said, "I would appreciate you removing yourselves and your Demon from our campsite."

Laisren turned Finn's way. "Search the carts."

Another Dayigan leaned toward the leader, his head lowered as if it somehow concealed his words. "That's the one, Lieutenant, the pervert what murdered our man."

Laisren rushed the man who'd spoken, drawing his knife en route.

The blade was at the speaker's bearded throat.

Laisren, teeth clenched, leaned into his face. "Think you that a wise comment?"

Before the man could answer, Laisren carved a deep gash across the man's neck. He shoved him to the ground to bleed out.

Aghast, Finn stared at his love.

"Check the carts," Laisren said harshly.

Finn stared.

"Please." Laisren calmed.

A drop of blood fell from the knife at Laisren's side and tapped the loose dirt as a small crimson crater.

"Yes, Chief," Finn said.

"You're welcomed to check, if you must." The lieutenant remained casual. "I hardly think you will find some Drevites in our trunks."

Finn opened trunks and baskets and boxes and jars to find a varied assortment of items, from jewelry to plain wooden cups to wheat, bread, and fruit.

"Just looks like normal trading stuff." Finn placed a cup to the wooden tap of a barrel. He filled it. "That's the cleanest water I ever set me eyes on."

"Have some, if you like," the lieutenant dismissed, "since you've poured it. We have barrels."

"'Preciate it." Finn lifted the cup.

"Finn, wait!" Laisren said. To Nekesa, "Watch them."

He neared Finn and took the cup.

"'Tis not poison," Finn assured. "Like I said, 'tis the clearest water I've seen."

Laisren gazed into the cup. "There are clear poisons." He swirled the water. "But that's not what this is. 'Tis ..." He looked at Finn. "... actually worse."

"Stay where you are!" Nekesa commanded.

Finn looked to see a soldier diving for his sword.

Nekesa shot him in the lower leg, the arrow piercing through his calf in a spray of blood.

The other Dayigans wasted no time snatching up their swords.

Laisren drew his mace and ran into conflict.

Finn fumbled to pull his bow from the sheath on his belt. He drew back the bowstring, arming it with light, and released.

The bolt of chaos shot into a Dayigan's shoulder. His veins near the impact darkened with crimson, showing through the skin as they grew larger. He screamed, flailing to the ground as the effects spread throughout his body.

Finn had never used the bow on anything living and watched with horror as the soldier shrieked while clawing at his own skin.

The soldier collapsed, motionless.

Both Laisren and Nekesa fought hard, their maces against Dayigan swords.

The tromlee fought, claw against blade. He grabbed the Dayigan's weapon and threw it aside. He scratched the soldier's chest, claws ripping through tabard, mail, skin, and bone.

Finn froze, heart pounding.

Laisren maintained a strong fight against the lieutenant.

Nekesa, too, fought well. But even as her opponent limped with an arrow through his leg, he delivered powerful blows.

She screamed through clenched teeth as their weapons locked.

He kicked her in the stomach, sending her to the dirt.

Sword raised, the Dayigan charged her, ready to kill.

Finn shot.

The crimson bolt of light hit the soldier's center chest and passed through his clothes and armor. He dropped his sword and cried out. The dark veins spread through his visible skin as he fell, screaming.

Nekesa jumped up and hurried to Laisren's aid.

In a two-to-one fight, the lieutenant didn't last long. Soon, he was on his knees as Nekesa tied his wrists.

Laisren checked the two men Finn had shot. "They live."

Finn sighed in relief. "Thank the Mothers for that."

"Mephistus," Laisren said. "They're yours."

The tromlee leaped up, grabbing both men by the ankles. He dragged them into the woods.

"What will he do to them?" Finn asked.

"They're asleep. That's the tromlee's domain. I wasn't lying when I said he hadn't eaten in a while."

The lieutenant struggled against the ropes. "You'll receive a handsome ransom for me if you return me to our trading post. I'm a lieutenant and a lord."

"Silence, you." Laisren returned to the handcarts and grabbed the cup from the ground. He refilled it from the tap on the barrel.

Again, he stared into the water as Finn approached him.

"You can attach magic to items," he said to Finn. "Liquids are items. Typically, a potion combines magic and ingredients to work in tandem. But 'tis possible for the ingredients to add nothing, just a blank base to which the magic clings."

"Water?" Finn asked.

Laisren nodded. "Aye." He looked around before spotting a stick. He grabbed it from the ground.

"It contains a message." Laisren stirred the water with the stick.

"Message?" Finn asked. "What's it say?"

Laisren glared a moment at the lieutenant. "Let's find out, shall we?"

Kneeling to the ground, Laisren cleared an area of dirt with his hand. He dipped the stick in the water like a quill in ink.

Closing his eyes, Laisren began scratching letters into the dirt.

Finn watched impatiently as words formed, one after the other.

Finally, Laisren set the stick in the cup and opened his eyes.

"What's it say then?" Finn asked.

"Clever," Laisren said. "Clever, clever."

"By the ancestors, Laisren," Finn said. "What's it fecking say?"

"'Tis a command." Pointing to each word, Laisren read, "*When you are unseen, fly five miles straight up and continue to the Dayigan fort. Stay unseen. When you arrive at the fort, descend sharply and land safely in the fort's courtyard. Then, go to sleep.*"

"You mean ..." Finn looked at Laisren. "They were making our people capture themselves?"

He nodded solemnly. "If someone drank this and was alone within a day, it would compel him to follow the command."

Nekesa screamed and punched the lieutenant in the face. "Do you even understand what happens when a person flies that high? It is agonizing. Your lungs tighten in your chest from the lack of air and your blood vessels and organ expand and could rupture."

The lieutenant spit blood but said nothing.

She drew a knife and readied a strike.

"Nekesa, enough," Laisren commanded. "I'm sure the lieutenant is aware of the state in which our people reach his fort. We need him alive."

"At last," the lieutenant said, "someone with reason. As I said, the trading post will pay handsomely for my return."

Laisren approached the soldier and crouched down to him. "You misunderstand me, Dayigan." Laisren's words were hateful as he neared his face to the soldier's. "I didn't mean we were *keeping* you alive. I just don't want to waste your death energy in the woods."

—

On the hill centered on the Anordúla village, Finn sat, his back against the rough bark of one of the hazel trees that formed the ring. The village was empty. Nocturnal insects droned, combining as the dominant sound.

Finn also heard peaks in conversations from the villagers. All thirty-six were behind him, within the ring of trees, mounds, and ditches, all within the ráth.

He tried not to think about what was happening within.

He heard footsteps behind him, swishing on the grassy ground. Finn looked back.

"We must do this," Laisren said. "We have no other choice."

"We don't have to kill him."

"That Dayigan lieutenant has captured who-knows-how-many of our people, most likely selling them into slavery. And he knows your location."

"Still, we don't have to be like them. When me and me brother, Cal, captured a Dayigan, Cal said—"

"*I'm not your brother, Finn.*" He cut him off. "I warned you, I'm not what you want me to be. I tried ..." He sighed. "I wanted you to avoid this world. But here you are, for now."

Finn looked away.

Laisren walked in front of Finn and crouched down to his level. "This is necessary, Finn. We must perform the ritual to create a proper Anordúla temple for the Goddess of Chaos, Ignísekhet."

"The Archdemoness?"

"Yes."

"You said we could use any magic system we want to. That's what Anordúla magic is."

"Not this time," Laisren said. "Not for this." He looked down. "Your people, all the tribes, need this to defend themselves."

Finn stood and paced the side of the hill. "If you're to do this ..." He stopped, looking down at Laisren. "*When* you do this, don't dedicate the temple to the Demoness." He paused. "Dedicate it to your dark mother, Morgana."

Laisren stood and nodded. "You're right, of course."

Finn inhaled deeply and exhaled. He walked away.

"Finn."

He stopped.

"I am sorry," Laisren said, "but as the wearer of the torc, you must be part of this. A major part."

—

Finn ran from within the circle of trees and collapsed on his hands and knees. He vomited on the grassy slope.

Blood coated his hands and arms up to his elbows.

He vomited again.

Designs drawn in blood marked his upper body and face.

Finn wanted to collapse, to weep, to scream. Instead, he only stared at the sick-covered grass.

"You did well." Laisren's words were grave as he stood over him. "We grow closer to protecting your people from the invaders."

Finn vomited again.

He wiped his mouth with the back of his arm and flicked it to the ground. With teary eyes, he looked up at Laisren, standing tall, seemingly unphased, though he, too, bore designs of blood painted on his pale skin.

A translucent raven, formed in shades of red, flew down. Laisren lifted his arm, and there it perched.

"Now that we have a temple done," Laisren said, "we have a Ravenshade. See? You can send a message home. You wanted that, right?"

Still on hands and knees, Finn nodded.

Laisren forced a half smile, though sadness marked his eyes. "I'll help you write it when you're ready. You'll finally be able to know what's happening there."

CHAPTER SEVENTEEN

From a distance, Treasa watched them: the Dayigans. A few feet from the Feah Temple of the Three Mothers, they'd erected a small collection of small tents and portable stalls. Every day for months, it had gotten closer, a few feet by a few feet more, until it had reached its current position.

Though manned by soldiers, the actions were not militaristic. Four soldiers stood beside two handcarts filled with halved loaves of bread. They distributed the bread free of charge to anyone who wished to take it.

Treasa's eyes lingered on Commander Beadurinc. He acted as a sort of priest within a circle of Feah. He spoke of the law of God Déagar and the moral crisis supposedly destroying—what he called—the Drevite Nation.

The seemingly harmless scene made Treasa feel foolish for being angry, as if she were a child pouting outside a party to which she'd not been invited. But she couldn't let herself trust them.

However, a growing number of Feahs did.

Her own brother sat in the circle, listening to the commander. With Lann sat his wife, Moyra, and little Alannah.

Lann's eye met Treasa's, and she turned away in reflex.

He stood, excused himself to Moyra, and walked to his sister.

They stood there, side by side, watching the Dayigans.

Lann leaned to her. "They aren't as bad as we thought they were, you know."

"How can you say that?" Treasa asked. "You and Moyra were there in the fort."

"You mean, when *we* attacked *them?*"

Treasa opened her mouth to argue the point but stopped.

After a beat, Lann suggested they go inside the temple to talk.

—

Within the tight, dark entry tunnel of the temple, Lann and Treasa stopped. From the end open to the outside, daylight shone in, along with the murmur of conversations from the gathered people.

Lann leaned close to Treasa. "A lot of what the Dayigans say is true."

"Aye, because they twist actual True Light teachings and beliefs to their own ends. They'd see our Finn killed, don't forget. And not because of any murder."

"I didn't say everything they say is true." Lann kept his voice lowered, not quite a whisper, but he seemed nervous to be heard by anyone else. He kept glancing toward the exit. "'Sides," Lann continued. "Finn might want to keep his cock in his kilt a little more than he does. 'Tis not his sort, though, that I'm worried about. 'Tis the sort that'll be chasing after me daughter in a few years. The druidesses have never properly enforced morality."

Treasa scoffed. "I don't remember yourself being all that moral, so."

"That be true, which is why Chief Morgana should've been enforcing such things then, and why Chief Kaie should be now." He cast his intense, uneasy gaze at Treasa. "The Dayigan Empire has mortal laws. And 'percussions. The druidesses should do the very same."

"I don't think you quite know what you're asking for, Lann," Treasa said. "Besides, there wouldn't be druidesses at all if the Dayigans had their say about it. They haven't outright said, but I'm quite sure they'd see us quite dead for using magic."

Lann looked down before muttering, "They say mankind weren't meant to have magic. Says the Faeries stole the secrets and gave them to us long ago."

"It was good Faeries who gave us magic, and they didn't do any stealing."

"Right," he said. "Like I said, not all they say is true."

Treasa released something between a sigh and a groan. "I'll be needed in the Temple Grove now. You have a pleasant afternoon yourself—with your commander."

—

Through the hall lined with the skulls of the ancestors, Treasa walked around the inner sanctum and entered through the large entrance directly under the tunnel, where she'd left Lann.

The calming energies of the grove were fractured by feminine grunts and claps of wood.

Kaie, Treasa saw, stood distantly watching six of the druidesses paired in bouts of staff-to-staff combat training.

Treasa approached her.

Kaie, continuing her watch, said, "I still don't like the idea of my girls fighting. But the progress you've made, in just a handful of months, is amazing."

"I'm praying to the Mothers 'tis enough."

Kaie looked at her. "Your energies are like a storm, Treasa. What's wrong?"

"The Dayigans are what's wrong. They're right outside now. I could throw a rock from the temple and hit that commander. And I'm half tempted to do so."

"I know," Kaie said wearily. "But all they're doing is giving out bread and talking."

"More than talking. They've got my own brother believing all kinds of nonsense."

"'Tis a lot more than just Lann. And not only in the temple village, either. Throughout the Feah lands ..." She sighed. "Come here with me."

—

Kaie and Treasa passed through a stone-cased opening, leaving the inner sanctum to enter a ten-by-twenty-foot room. The walls were rough stacked stones, like uneven bricks, and the ceiling was wooden rafters and planks. It held a simple whitewashed iron chandelier.

Five evenly spaced tables lined the back wall, and furs and blankets padded them. They were unused and neat. The side walls each had a table holding various healing devices— mortar and pestle, crystals, jars of various herbs, wands, a brass cauldron, and a basket of linens—all laid out methodically.

Kaie turned to the right, to a lower table set between two benches. A worried woman sat on the bench. She slouched forward, her arms on the table, and drank tea from a wooden cup. Her arm was bandaged.

"Bévinn," Kaie said, "you know my vischief, Treasa. Treasa, this is Bévinn, tierna of—"

"Tierna of the Eorna Parish," Treasa finished with a smile. "Yes, I know Bévinn very well, though it has been some time. What brings you to the Temple Parish?"

"Nothing good, I'm afraid." Bévinn took a sip of her tea.

"That's why I brought you here," Kaie said to Treasa. And to Bévinn, "Please, go on."

Bévinn slowly nodded. "An anti-druidic sentiment has spread throughout Eorna now. Truth be told, I don't know how it started or where it came from. But near two months back, I noticed that a few people were, well, just angry at our circle without a reason. I tried asking them about it, you know, seeing if there was anything I could do to make it right with them. But I got nowhere with it. It got worse, as well, and spread to more people. All the while, I was getting reports about people disappearing—people from many of our villages, gone without a trace."

She sipped her tea. "In the end, I determined the cause of the unrest. It was some vague, silly anger about our use of magic. But it makes no sense, that. These are my own people—people I've healed with magic, people I've given protective amulets and tattoos to, people whose crops and livestock I've blessed myself to become more fruitful." She sighed. "People I called good friends before this unrest. The very same people blamed me for the disappearances of our fellow Eornans—me directly. As if they thought I did it myself. They'd gotten the fool idea in their heads that druidic magic was causing people to vanish. They referred to our—and I'm saying what they said to me here—'unprovoked' attack on the Dayigans back on midyear as some proof we've turned wicked."

"It was very much provoked," Treasa said.

"Too provoked," Kaie added. "And I'm seeing why. I think they chose Finn as the target of their accusation because he's the brother-in-law of the second-in-command of the Feah. They wanted us to retaliate."

A wave of horror throbbed through Treasa. She lowered her head. That poor Finn had suffered because of his relation to her made Treasa want to cry out in frustration. And poor Kyran, she mourned, he'd paid the ultimate cost just for being on the edge of things. Treasa stared, her heart pounding.

"How would they even know?" Treasa asked. "I doubt Finn just flew up to their fort and told them his life story. Do we have a spy?"

"Who knows?" said Kaie. "'Tis no secret. But there's more to the Eorna story."

Bévinn nodded and took another sip of tea. She rubbed the bandage on her arm. "Of course, the other pariahs, ours included, don't have temples. So I welcome my people to visit my home, if ever they need me. Last night, a group made up of men and women from various Eornan villages circled my home. I thought there was some sort of emergency, so I rushed straight out to them." She looked at Treasa. "Would you believe they attacked me right on my own doorstep, Treasa? My own people."

"That's terrible."

"That it was, yes. The injury was minor in the end. But I'm not sure if they meant to hurt me at all or if they meant to hurt me more than what they did. Or even—Mothers help me—end me altogether." She put down the cup. "Whatever the case, I fled for my life and flew here as quickly as I could manage."

"'Tis not just Eorna," Kaie said, "though it is the most severe so far. All the Feah parishes are reporting missing people and this vague anger at us."

"My brother said as much. We must remove the Dayigans from Feah shores."

"My hands are tied," Kaie said, putting her hands together as if to demonstrate. "The Dayigans have convinced our people that the death of Kyran was justified and—as far as we can prove—have done nothing else. Remember, it was Feahs, not Dayigans, who attacked Bévinn. We are servants to our people, and right now, a growing number of them want the Dayigans here more than they want us." She shook her head. "I don't understand their choice, but 'tis their choice to make."

Treasa raked her fingers atop her long auburn hair until her hand lay on her shoulder. Kaie was right, Treasa knew, which only made the circumstances more frustrating.

Silence lingered before Bévinn asked, "Are you thinking the druidesses will need to be leaving the Feah lands?"

The question went unanswered.

"Chief." A temple druidess entered the infirmary. "Forgive me disturbing you, but a Ravenshade has arrived with a message."

"Ah," Kaie said. "That'll be one of the other chiefs. I've asked them if these difficulties have spread to the other tribes, and luckily, so far, all have said no."

"I believe this is something else, Chief," said the druidess at the entrance. "This Ravenshade is red."

"Red?" Kaie looked at Treasa. "Quickly, fetch Cal and meet me in my study."

CHAPTER EIGHTEEN

As Cal and Treasa entered Chief Kaie's study, Treasa saw the chief behind a table centered in the room. Kaie had a fire burning in a brass cauldron on the table and had neatly laid out a stack of three pages, a silver feather quill, and a tiny stone pot of ink.

Kaie motioned to the red Ravenshade, perched with the others edging the room.

It flew through the fire and, unharmed, returned to the perch.

Leaning close to the flames, Kaie inhaled, breathing the smoke into her mouth and lungs. She paused, holding it within her, and exhaled a slow, smoky breath.

She did this again.

And a third time.

With her eyes closed, she took the quill, dipped it in the ink, and wrote on the page. She filled it and set it aside, then continued to the next page.

When she finished, Kaie laid down the quill and opened her eyes. "It was as I suspected. The red Ravenshade is from the Anordúla."

"Is Finn with them?" Cal asked impatiently.

Kaie nodded. "He is, yes." She smiled as she read, "Salutations, Archdruidess Kaie, Chief Tierna of the Feah. I, Laisren ó Morgana, Chief of the Anordúla, am writing to you to report the safe arrival of Finnán ó Ríona to our village."

"Thank the Mothers for that," Cal said.

Kaie continued, "The next part is dictated by Finn himself. He misses everyone here, says he, especially Cal and Lann, but he's been living nicely in the Anordúla village and there's no need to worry about him." Kaie gave a pleased smile.

"Silly fecker," Cal chuckled. "He would be having a grand time when everything's falling apart here."

"There's more." Kaie's smile faded. "Says he, 'I'm sorry, Chief, but I failed you and our people. I found the Anordúla, true, but the village is small, with only thirty-six people here. And Chief Morgana ...'" Kaie sighed. "Chief Morgana is dead." She looked up toward Treasa.

Sadness ached in Treasa's breast, sadness for a departed friend and mentor, sadness for the lost hope that the mentor would return and save them.

"She was like a mother to me," Treasa whispered.

"Aye," Kaie said, "to me as well."

"We can't let Finn go on thinking he failed us," said Cal. "We have to write back and tell him 'tis not his fault."

"We will," said Kaie. "Soon. He goes on to say that he misses us and worries about us every day. He asks that we write him about what's going on here and hopes 'twill not be long before we can safely reunite.

"This next part." Kaie looked up at Cal. Her smile returned, though slightly. "'Tis for yourself, Cal. Would you believe Finn's fallen in love now? With Laisren."

"Love?" The word was sour on Cal's lips. "With Laisren?" He glanced at Treasa. "I haven't even seen the boy since he was wee, and I didn't know him well then, besides. But he's a dark wizard now."

Treasa crossed her arms and glanced sideways at him. "Cal."

"He's a *dark wizard*, Treasa. And nothing our Finn should be loving. I didn't even want Finn to go there from the start."

"I'm afraid we have more pressing concerns," Kaie interrupted. "Laisren—who I knew very well and would babysit at times, good lad, him—he says he found Dayigans near our northern border. They possessed water enchanted with a command for people to fly to their fort unseen."

"The missing people?" Treasa asked. "But that can't be. The Dayigans are well vocal that they're against magic."

"Laisren seems sure of it," said Kaie. "He goes into detail. You said Lann goes to the Dayigan gatherings."

"He does. He should be there now."

"If he's still willing to help us, have him bring us some of the Dayigan bread. And try not to touch it."

In a disbelieving tone, Cal said, "Right, so the Dayigans are giving out magic bread is the thinking now, is it?"

"I don't know what I think," Kaie said gravely. "Please, go quickly."

—

Treasa exited the temple to find the trail end of sunset and the village crowded in a sort of festival. Half the parish was there, she estimated, if not more. About a hundred Dayigans, wearing green uniforms, strolled among them as if old friends. A few nearby people, people she'd known for years, gave Treasa mistrustful glares.

Cal followed to her side. "Why are they all here?"

"Lann said they were having a gathering tonight, but I didn't expect all this. We need to find him."

"There." Cal pointed.

Lann sat by Moyra and Alannah at the front of a gathering.

They, along with most of the crowd, held half-eaten loaves of bread, taking the occasional bite as they listened to Beadurinc speak.

Other crowds circled other soldiers, either talking or handing out bread.

"Lann," Treasa whispered as she cupped her hands around her mouth and magically threw her word to his ears.

Lann looked around until he spotted Treasa.

"*Come here to me,*" Treasa whispered ethereally. "*All three of ye.*"

After saying something to Moyra, Lann, with his wife and daughter, stood and walked to Treasa and Cal.

Lann and Moyra seemed distant. Alannah stood just behind her mother and pushed her face into the woman's leather skirt.

"Not sure if we should be talking to the likes of you then," Lann said.

"What?" Treasa showed a puzzled grin. "We just spoke a few hours ago."

"A lot's changed since then, though, hasn't it?"

"It hasn't, though, has it?"

"Lann," Cal said. "The chief's quite interested in that bread your friends have been passing out. 'Tis the good wheat kind, right? You think you could bring her a bit for a try?"

Lann glanced down at the loaf in his hand and eyed Cal and Treasa. "There's loads of bread out here."

"True," said Treasa. "But the chief's particular about that sort of thing and doesn't want to look like a fool if she doesn't like it. Besides, how would that make your friends feel if Kaie spat out their bread in public view?"

Lann nodded with dazed confusion. "Suppose that makes sense."

A tense moment passed as they stood. Lann and Moyra seemed as if they were in the company of roadside strangers.

"Come on then," Cal said. "Let's get in the temple."

They approached the hill-like temple and walked up the thin steps around the standing stone to the entrance.

Moyra placed her hand on Lann's shoulder. "You think we should ask the commander about this, wise husband?"

Cal chuckled. "Wise husband?"

Treasa shot Cal a look and shook her head.

"Right," Cal began. "Well—em—we wouldn't want to ruin the surprise, would we now?"

"If Kaie likes the bread," Treasa said, "she wants to bring all the druidesses out and have a big feast with the Dayigans. Clear up all this trouble, you know."

"No." Lann stopped, his eyes glazed. "We should be getting permission from the commander before we go entering a savage temple."

Treasa gasped and bit her lower lip. His words hurt, but she said nothing. She knew then that she'd lost him. Treasa looked out over the crowded village. *Were they all as gone as him?*

Lann began walking away. Moyra took Alannah's hand and followed.

"Wait." Treasa stepped toward them. "They've put a spell on ye. Don't you realize?"

Lann stopped and turned to Treasa with rage. "The Dayigans don't be putting spells on people. 'Tis you that does that, with your witchcraft and all. Magic is the realm of the Gods, only the wicked trespass there."

Treasa reached between her wings and drew her staff, aiming it at Lann. "Get in the temple."

Alannah screamed. Moyra clutched her daughter to her waist. Lann drew his mace.

"*Look,*" shouted someone in the crowd. "The witches are abducting our people like the Dayigans say."

"For feck's sake," Treasa muttered.

"Let me wife and daughter go," Lann said. "They're defenseless, them."

"Defenseless?" Treasa scoffed. "Moyra's more a warrior than you." She turned to Moyra, huddled against her daughter and just as frightened. "Have you forgotten that?"

Lann charged Treasa, and she blocked his mace with her staff.

"Cal," Treasa said, fighting, "get them inside."

He hesitated before grabbing Moyra and Alannah. He struggled to push them through the temple entrance.

"*Lannah!*" Lann shouted and fought harder.

Treasa didn't want to injure her brother, but it seemed clear he aimed to injure her.

The men in the village shouted and ran toward the temple.

"I'm sorry, Lann." Treasa swung her staff around and struck him on the side.

He stumbled down the thin stone steps and fell to his hands and knees at the base.

Treasa dashed into the temple.

Inside, Cal asked, "Will the temple ward keep them out?"

"No. They're our own people. The ward shields against other folks. But I might know a way." She aimed her staff at the entrance.

Thorny vines shot up from the ground at the threshold. They grew thick, twisting around one another as they faded from green to woody brown. Soon, a wall of thorns blocked every inch of the entrance.

Treasa could hear the people outside beating their weapons against it.

Panting, she looked back at Cal.

He gripped his mace as he stood over Moyra and Alannah, huddled in fright on the floor.

"I must stay and maintain the wall," Treasa said. "Get them to the chief. Have her send warnings to the other tribes."

He nodded solemnly. "Aye, Vischief."

The pounding on the wall grew louder.

"Cal," Treasa said, "she should send a warning to the Anordúlas as well."

—

"Go on. What's it say?" Finn asked impatiently.

Laisren hesitated.

They stood on the main path in the Anordúla village, in front of the home of Nekesa. She had been training Finn in archery when Laisren and Jyoti approached from the ráth.

"'Tis very short." Laisren lifted a page and read, "Dear Chiefs, the Dayigans have used enchanted food and water to twist the minds of the Feah. Our own people have turned against druidesses in multiple parishes. Currently, our people are attempting to lay siege to our temple. Take notice: Stay away from Feah lands and warn your tribes not to trust gifts from the Dayigans. We will seal off our temple soon; thus, further communication, in or out, will be impossible. Archdruidess Kaie, Chief Tierna of the Feah."

"That's all of it?" Finn asked.

"I imagine they were rushed."

"We have to go to them," Finn said. "Now."

"No," said Laisren. "We're not prepared to face the Dayigans. You need much more training."

"Fuck my training, Laisren. I'm only training to save the Feah. What good will it do saving them once there's nothing left?"

Laisren grew cross. "And what good will it do, making yourself another dead Feah next to the rest?"

"Mephistus," Finn called.

In a flash, the tromlee came and landed beside the group. He folded his bat-like wings at his back.

"How long would it take you to fly me to the temple village?" Finn asked.

"Even with the torc," he hissed, "my powers remain reduced. I cannot enter the protected village. However, I can take thee to the outer rim within two hours."

Nekesa spoke up. "How about two people?"

"'Twill be the same amount of time."

"Thank you, Nekesa," Finn said. "We should leave at once."

"No." Laisren roughly grabbed Finn's shoulders. "I've already watched you kill yourself once. I won't allow it again. The torc's powerful, yes, but all you've learnt to do with it is shoot arrows, which are only a hair better than everyday normal arrows."

Finn shrugged him off and stepped back, glaring at him for a moment. Finn sighed. Downcast, he said nothing.

Jyoti joined. "I may know a way to help him better use the torc. It is a projection, after all, and it is partially bound to him. If we fully—"

"Absolutely not," Laisren interrupted. "'Twould be permanent."

"What would be?" Finn glanced back and forth between the two. "Go on then."

Jyoti glanced at Laisren before continuing. "I know a way to meld the torc's projection to your soul. You'd still need to learn to use its power, but instead of learning to use an external tool, you'd be learning to use part of yourself, like your arms or legs."

"No," Laisren said, aggravated by the subject. "'Tis more permanent than your arms and legs. You chop off your arms and legs and you're still you, but this will be part of your soul. You can't chop that off. And my mother won't be able to transfer the torc come New Year's." He let out a heavy sigh. "You'll never be able to return to the Feah."

Finn grasped the silvery ring around his neck as he looked at Laisren for a moment. "You're an awful eejit at times, you." He smiled. "I don't have any plans to return to the Feahs. I'm already with the Anordúla permanent like, because you're with them permanent."

Laisren relaxed and looked down. "If you do what you're planning, you'll lose the choice to stay or leave afterwards."

"I'm not losing it. I'm making it now. My people—my old people—need me. And the Anordúla do as well."

"He is correct, my chief," Nekesa said. "Our village is in Feah lands. If this region falls to the Dayigans, they *will* find us."

Laisren remained silent, thinking.

"My chief, this is the reason your mother formed the Anordúla. It's time to act."

Laisren nodded. He looked at Finn with sad hazel eyes. "We need to hurry."

CHAPTER NINETEEN

Above the thick woods, through the newly born night, the tromlee—a shriveled corpse of a panther winged like a bat—flew as a black blur. In three of his clawed hands, he held Terovaes by the wrists—Finn, Laisren, and Nekesa—their wings outstretched as they glided.

Mephistus slowed and released the Terovaes, launching them to fly toward the Feah temple, still miles away.

When they landed at the edge of the temple village, Nekesa drew her mace. She ran up ahead.

"Do you feel any different?" Laisren asked Finn.

The torc no longer circled Finn's neck. In its place, crimson stained Finn's skin—as if it were a tattoo depicting the Torc of Datura. Yet it was no tattoo. The ring had melded into him, fusing permanently with his soul.

Finn touched the mark around his neck. "Still nothing, no."

"You'll need to concentrate, Finn. Sorry to pressure you, but the fate of the Five Tribes depends on your connecting with the torc."

Nekesa returned. "There are hundreds of them, my chief—Dayigans and Drevites—gathered outside the temple. Most are armed."

"The temple is warded against outsiders," Laisren said, "but not against Feahs. If they mean to invade, the druidesses have little time. We must protect the temple."

"I know a treehouse that overlooks the area." Finn looked up. "It should be empty."

"Let's go." Laisren drew his mace. "But be careful. The trees aren't safe. Our enemies have wings as well."

—

They landed on the small, unrailed porch of the small treehouse. The house's walls were thin, woven branches, with a few vines snaking between them. The roof was grass, and there was no door.

"Finn," Nekesa whispered from a crouch. "Get down."

He complied.

"You two stand watch," Laisren said. "I'll check the house."

Nekesa drew her bow, as did Finn.

Finn looked down. At the base of the towering tree, about four hundred people gathered before the hill-like temple. Many had torches and small fires burned in random spots. About a fourth were Humans in Dayigan uniforms dispersed among the Feahs. The assemblage was divided into six rough clusters, each gathered around a Dayigan who shouted at his division with angry words Finn could not quite make out. The crowd answered back occasionally, shouting with raised fists or torches.

The sight struck a deep fear in Finn—fear for those in the temple, fear for, *and of,* those controlled by the Dayigans, fear for his tiny group of Anordúlas.

Laisren returned and whispered, "The house is clear. Let's move inside."

—

Moyra screamed as she fought against the leather cuffs that bound her wrist to the table.

Treasa stood a slight distance from her side, watching her friend of many years as she fought the restraints Treasa herself had put in place. Moyra looked at Treasa with such hate, such fear, such anger.

They were in the infirmary just off the Temple Grove. Cal, beside Treasa, set his hand on his wife's shoulder.

Moyra screamed again. "What have you done with me daughter, you savage bastards?"

"She somewhere safe," said Treasa. "We're your friends, Moyra. We're trying to help ye both. Do you know who I am?"

She continued to struggle. "You're a disgusting tree witch, you, and I'll gut the lot of ye."

"At least she's remembering she's a fighter," Cal said gravely. "That's something."

Treasa nodded. "You'll have to trust us, Moyra, all right. I need to examine you so I can figure out a way to reverse the spell affecting you." To Cal, she said, "Hold her head."

He stepped to the end of the table and rested his hand on the thick brown braids that ran along Moyra's head.

Treasa lifted her staff and held it horizontally above Moyra. She closed her eyes as she slowly moved the staff in a circular motion above her friend. Treasa could see her vascular system glowing white. The veins and arteries branched out throughout Moyra's body like the roots of a mighty tree.

They bound her soul to her flesh, as trees bind the sky to land and sea.

Moyra called out and fought against her restraints.

Treasa ignored the angry screams of her friend, instead focusing on her task. Eyes still closed, Treasa whispered, "I see the spell within her."

Moyra's veins glowed with dismal green.

"'Tis unlike anything I've ever seen. Simple. But powerful."

The archdruidess stumbled backward and touched her hand to her head.

Cal rushed to her, holding her up. Treasa breathed as she stared at Moyra. "It is a twisted variation of a friendship spell combined with a hate spell."

"Can you cleanse her of it?"

Treasa shook her head. "No. Not yet. I must understand it better first."

Moyra screamed, "Give me back my daughter! I'll kill ye all."

With a heavy heart, Treasa watched her delirious friend. "I must speak to Kaie."

—

Treasa entered Kaie's study to see her standing over her brass cauldron on her table.

"Any luck?" Kaie asked.

"Not yet. The spell is thoroughly bound to her soul and mind. I believe it has a three-day duration."

"We won't last three days," Kaie said. "And I'm sure the people outside are being fed more enchanted food, restarting the duration."

"I know. I don't understand. It has a unique magical signature that I don't know how to cleanse or reverse."

Kaie nodded. "I found the very same." She moved her hand in a circular motion above the small cauldron. "I extracted the spell from half a loaf of bread we found in Moyra's bag." She lifted a wooden plate holding a three-inch quartz.

Treasa approached and looked at the crystal.

"'Tis in there," Kaie said. "Friendship and hate. But I still don't understand the nature of the magic. 'Tis divine magic, I think, but not quite like any I've seen." She looked up into Treasa's eyes. "You must speak to the prisoner."

—

"We have to rescue me daughter," Lann said to Commander Beadurinc.

They stood away from the crowd and watched the temple some forty feet away. Specifically, Lann stared at the entrance behind the large standing stone, grown over by a wall of thorny vines.

"We will," the commander said. "Trust me. What can you tell me of Vischief Treasa?"

Lann grimaced, squinting his eyes as he touched his hand to the side of his head. "She's ..." Lann started, his brain muddled. "She's a savage tree witch, m'lord. She uses magic, which is the realm of the Gods alone. She kidnaps our people to sacrifice them to Demonic false Gods."

"But she is your sister, yes? You must know more."

A sharp pain stabbed through Lann's brain. He clutched his forehead. "I ..." He shook his head. "I don't remember, Commander."

"'Tis no matter. You will lead the Feah assault on the unho-ly temple. My men and I will oversee the battle, but this is your fight. What they did to you and your people is unforgiv-able, yes?"

"'Tis, m'lord, unforgivable." Lann stared with hate at the temple. Rage flowed through him, heating his skin and pounding in his heart.

"You will save your daughter," the commander said. "And you, in the name of God Déagar, you will allow none of these detestable tree witches to live."

"Not a fucking one, m'lord. The True Light's the only way. All others will perish."

The commander grinned. "Come."

Lann followed Beadurinc as he approached the temple and climbed the thin steps.

They stopped and looked at the standing stone.

"My men and I are too holy to touch this stone," the com-mander said, "but you ... touch it."

Uncertain, Lann looked at the commander before turning to the stone. He neared his hand to it, pausing before touch-ing the rough gray surface.

"Praise God Déagar," the commander said. "Soon, we will reclaim your lands from wickedness. Go, Lann, and select a force of one hundred Drevite men to rescue your daughter. Prepare them for battle."

CHAPTER TWENTY

Cal and Treasa walked down a cramped hall, its stone walls curving up to a low vault. Mounted torches, spaced far apart, offered only a dim flicker.

They approached a closed door with a small window freshly cut through at eye level. Beside it, a druidess sat in a chair.

She stood. "Vischief. Temple guardian." She nodded. "Do be careful. He's tried to attack us before."

Treasa drew her staff from behind her back. The other druidess opened the door. Cal and Treasa entered.

The room's meager light was only the dim square ray that shone through the door. On the floor sat the Dayigan Terovae, his leather uniform grayed with filth. Treasa could smell his sweat, even from her distance.

She lifted her hand to eye level—palm upwards—and a point of purple light appeared and drifted to the ceiling, lighting the room. This was no proper dungeon—the temple had nothing of the sort—but a large, unused closet lined with empty wooden shelves on either side. From the ceiling hung an empty rack meant for drying herbs.

The captive didn't look up from his slouched seat. "I wondered when you'd show your face here." He rolled his eyes to Cal. "I should have killed you when I had the chance."

"You never had the chance," Cal said, "or you would have, that I'm sure. You definitely tried." He put his hand on his chest and rubbed the scar where the man's subordinate had tried to force a sword through him. "Why are the Dayigans abducting our people?"

The sergeant replied with a scoffing sneer, "We're saving your people. The Archbishop will bless them so they can return to the Light."

"Bless them?" Cal demanded. "What does that mean?"

"It means we're trying to save filth like you from wickedness. But I, for one, would rather see all Drevites ripped apart to burn eternally in za."

Cal jumped a step forward, but Treasa placed her hand on his arm.

She said, "We know the Dayigans are using magic to abduct our people and twist their minds."

"We don't use magic, witch. Magic is the realm of—"

"We've heard it already. Thank you." Treasa cut him off. "Is there any way Commander Beadurinc could be using magic without the others knowing?"

"*We don't use magic, witch.* The commander is a holy man, one of the last Silthex knights. Don't you try slandering his 'lustrious name with your filthy, savage mouth."

"Silthex knight?" she asked. "What is that?"

The sergeant looked at the dusty stone floor. "I don't have to answer your questions, whore. The army will find me, and you will pay for this."

"Your army thinks you're a traitor now," Cal rejoined.

The soldier looked up, glaring but saying nothing.

"'Tis true," Treasa said. "I used a glamour—a type of illusion—to make a unit of Dayigans see you and the other Dayigan Terovae helping the man who you were meant to capture. It wasn't hard making the Humans distrust Terovaes, even two of their own. I'm sorry, but I needed to make the Dayigans wary of sending any more Terovaes to our lands."

"*Fucking whore,*" the sergeant growled. He spit in her direction.

Cal clinched his fist, but Treasa set her hand atop it.

Unfazed, she continued, "If you help us, we can—"

"Praise God Déagar, the one and only God, protector from the Dark. You are the Greatest of All. I praise your name, majestic and holy, without ending. By your fire, guide me safely to Laqyigo. Astha'will-miabé."

"Come on, Cal," Treasa said. "We're finished here."

—

Lann rushed into the wooded area crowded with his fellow Feah men. He pushed his way through to see Commander Beadurinc, who stood upon the temple steps.

"Too long," Beadurinc shouted over the gathered, "has Darkness plagued these lands. Too long has this unholy temple—*led by women*—forced the good people of these lands to live in wickedness. For years, those women, *those witches*, have lied to you. They have put the souls of you and your children in danger. But I'm honest. And you know that. That's why you and so many of your friends and family are here today. I'm here to tell you the truth: the True Light is the only way; all others will perish."

Lann lifted his mace high as he cheered, his voice lost within the many around him who did the same, voicing a unified thunder.

Beadurinc shouted, "Tonight, we will take back these lands from the tyranny of the lying witches in this temple!"

The crowd lifted their weapons and roared in agreement.

"Look at all your brothers around you, ready to fight, as one, against evil. Tonight, you will. Tonight, you will prove that you are not weak but strong against those who would destroy you. Because if you do not fight for your lands tonight, there will be nothing left to fight for."

Again, the crowd raised their weapons. Again, the crowd cheered. Lann could feel the rage pounding through him, generating heat. He gripped his mace in his fist and glared at the temple. Lann hated the witches inside, hated them more than anything he'd ever hated.

"Go!" Beadurinc shouted. "And reclaim this temple for God Déagar."

With a unified shout, the Feah men pushed forward.

Thirty feet up a massive tree, Finn watched from the porch as the enraged crowd converged on the temple entrance.

"We have to do something, *now,*" Finn said.

Laisren and Nekesa stared for a moment longer.

"Do you feel *any* increase in power?" Laisren asked.

Finn ran his fingers along the crimson mark around his neck that had taken the place of the now absorbed torc. "I don't think so. I don't even know what I'm supposed to be feeling. I feel invigorated, like, but it might just be 'cause the temple's getting attacked. Adrenaline, you know."

Laisren held his fist to his mouth, still watching. "Stay together. The air gives us no advantage. We stay on the ground so nothing can attack from below. Finn, your chaos bolts only incapacitate people temporarily, so you shoot as fast as you can. Nekesa, you and I are melee. We protect Finn. But keep to non-lethal attacks. These are Feahs we're fighting. Armor check."

"My armor is good, Chief," Nekesa said.

Finn looked at the tattoo on his forearm, edged in purple but filled with crimson. "Armor good."

"Don't get killed." Laisren jumped from the tree, followed by the other two, and glided in a spiral to the ground.

The rear of the crowd was thin, with the attackers pushing toward the front and toward the temple. Laisren's group landed behind them.

"Finn, shoot!" Laisren commanded.

The nearby people turned their attention to the Anordúlas, rushing with weapons high.

Panicked, Finn pulled his bowstring and fired, one bolt after the other. He knew the people who fell screaming as their veins swelled with chaos. Neighbors, friends, cousins. Finn kept shooting, trying not to listen to their screams.

Laisren and Nekesa, maces swinging, fought off anyone who neared them, but more of the crowd turned their way, surrounding them.

Laisren cried out as a Dayigan blade cut across his stomach. The slice was shallow, his armor holding.

Finn whipped around his bow and shot the Dayigan in the chest. The soldier screamed and fell. Finn moved to another target.

"I have an idea," Nekesa said. "Cover me."

She crouched down to the fallen Dayigan and slapped her hands on his face.

The soldier began convulsing stiffly against the ground as he foamed from his mouth.

"By the infernal Grim Barron, I clutch your soul," she said. "I command your soul. I command you. Know my will and do as I bid you."

The soldier stood up, threw down his weapon, and fought barehanded against the advancing crowd.

"Finn is filling them full of chaos energy," Nekesa said. "I can use it."

—

Within the circle of ancient oaks of the Temple Grove, Treasa approached a large iron cauldron. The large standing stone towered thirteen feet beside her; on each of its rough sides, the symbol of the Five Tribes glowed purple—the symbol of the Septogram surrounding the three spirals meeting as one at their center—the air, the land, and the sea meeting as one.

Treasa's staff—leaned upside down against the cauldron—waited. Beneath the cauldron, a fire burned. Within, water bubbled and popped.

She took her position, as did two other druidesses, forming a triangle around the cauldron. In unison, they lifted their arms high above their heads. Eyes closed, they faced upward.

"We honor our physical mothers and fathers," Treasa said, "but we are older than the births they gifted us. We are born of the seas. We are born of the land. We are born of the skies above. We call to ye, O Three Mothers. Hear us as ye heard our ancestors. Join us, O Three Mothers, and grant us wisdom and guidance."

All three druidesses spoke together, saying:

"Mother Lágeya—tierna of the seas and waters that nourish us and connect us all as one—*bear witness.*

"Mother Larissa—tierna of the land that is our home and the hearth that keeps us warm—*bear witness*.

"Mother Ashatra—tierna of the sky that gives us breath and the seid that invigorates us—*bear witness*."

Alone, Treasa said, "Harm has come to our people, who are your children. Give me the wisdom to undo what the Dayigans have done."

A yellow light boiled up from the cauldron and splashed over its iron rim. It spilled over onto the grass. As a glowing yellow mist, it flowed outward, keeping low. Soon, it was a ten-foot circle wafting up to their knees.

"Grant me your wisdom, O Three Mothers," said Treasa. "Let me understand the magic infecting our people."

One of the druidesses brought her hands together before her breast and bowed her head. She moved to a small table holding a wooden plate on which lay a clear quartz containing the Dayigan spell that Chief Kaie had extracted.

Holding the plate before her in both hands, the druidess approached the cauldron. She paused before the iron rim. "Mothers, receive this." She tilted the plate, letting the crystal splash into the yellow light.

The druidess returned to her position.

Treasa approached the cauldron and lifted her staff. She held it horizontally above the boiling yellow light and moved the knobby branch in methodical circles.

"Grant me your wisdom, O Three Mothers," Treasa prayed. "Let me understand the magic infecting our people."

CHAPTER TWENTY-ONE

Finn kept shooting, his fingers raw and bloody against the bowstring. Laisren and Nekesa fought at his sides, as if they tried to stop a storm with maces. Four more Dayigans, enchanted by Nekesa, fought bare-fisted alongside them.

The attackers surrounded the Anordúlas. No longer did Finn fight to near the temple or stop the invasion. No goal remained, but survival. He shot bolt after bolt, turning, shooting, turning, shooting.

"Finn, above you!" Laisren shouted.

Finn aimed upwards, shot.

He tried not to think of the hopelessness of the situation, but the thoughts lingered, lodged at the back of his mind. The goal of survival faded, too. Finn fought on. If he could thin the enemy forces as much as possible before his death, that would leave fewer to invade the temple and fewer for the druidesses to fight. *Was that the goal?* He wasn't certain. Perhaps nothing so noble. Perhaps he simply delayed the inevitable because of some primal need to do so. Perhaps not even that. Maybe Finn fought because the task was all he had left.

Finn turned, shot, turned, shot, turned, shot. The task was all that remained. If he stopped, if he relaxed, that would be the end of him.

"Finn," Laisren said. "Give me your hand."

"I can't. I have to keep going." Finn shot and watched his bolt of chaos enter someone—someone he'd known his whole life.

The someone fell in agony as his enchanted allies dragged him back into the crowd.

"Finn, I need you to trust me now."

Finn pulled his shaking hand from the bowstring and grabbed Laisren's.

"Feel the chaos all around us," Laisren said. "Hear the shouts of anger and anguish. Feel the energy of the fight. We are the eye of the storm. Pull the storm into yourself."

Finn breathed deeply, inhaling the power of the surrounding madness.

"Now," Laisren said, "give me that power."

Finn released the chaos to flow through himself, through his arm, through his right hand, and into Laisren's left.

"Hail Dark Mother Morgana," Laisren said. "Empower me. Send agony and sorrow to those who would harm us."

A crimson wave rippled outward from Laisren, stretching twenty feet before dissipating. All assailants within the wave fell to their knees. They screamed in an ongoing chorus of anguish.

Finn watched in horror and relief. A fog came next, spiraling out from Laisren and swallowing up the sight. Only wretched sounds remained.

"We must go," said Laisren. "Now."

Laisren, Nekesa, and Finn jumped up from the ground and hurried back to the treehouse.

On the porch, Laisren searched for any pursuers. None. "Inside," he commanded.

Nekesa and Finn entered the small box of a home. She braced by the door.

Laisren entered.

"Were we followed?" Nekesa asked.

"It doesn't look like it, no. But they'll be searching for us."

"We need to rethink this, my chief," Nekesa said. "They nearly killed us for nothing."

"'Twas not for nothing."

"What did we do, my chief?" she asked. "I saw some of the same faces in the attackers that we took down before. They are recovering from Finn's magic. I would guess, in an hour, there will not be a trace of what we did down there."

"We ..." Laisren sighed. "We gave the druidesses time they didn't have before." There was little conviction in words. He was obviously worn out. All three of them were cut up, bruised, and haggard.

"My chief, we came here thinking Finn would possess some great power."

"I'm sorry," Finn spoke up as he sat on the floor.

"No," Nekesa said gently as she approached and nestled her hand on his cheek. "You fought bravely, Finn. But we are not ready for this."

She turned back to Laisren. "If we go back there, my chief, we will do nothing but add three more bodies to the Dayigan's death count. Nothing more. We need to return to the Anordúla. This is the druidesses' fight now."

———

At the steps of the temple, Lann stood beside Commander Beadurinc as a soldier approached in haste.

"They escaped in the fog, Commander," the soldier said.

"Ready a unit of Drevites and find them."

"Yes, Commander." He hurried away.

The commander turned to Lann. "Have your men recovered?"

"Aye, m'lord. It were the other teams mostly hit by the wicked magic."

"Good. We have been friends for a long time, you and I," Beadurinc said to Lann.

"That be true, Commander. You've always been a good friend to me and me family."

"You are like a son to me, Jon."

"Lann."

"Indeed. I know you'd risk your life to do what's right. You will get your daughter back. And kill every druidess in this blasphemous, savage temple."

"Aye, m'lord."

"Begin."

Lann jumped up from the ground and hovered ten feet above. "*Siege team ... go!*"

A dozen other men leaped from the ground and followed Lann the short distance to the standing stone before the temple's entrance.

They pushed against the upper half of the stone, straining, grunting and flapping their wings with force.

"Harder, men," Lann called as he shoved his arm and shoulder against the stone.

A pop rumbled up the stone as the outer edge lifted from the ground.

"*Harder!*" Lann called.

The stone fell. It shattered against the temple and smashed through the wall of thorns. Dust rose in a cloud. Smaller fragments tumbled down the steps.

—

A rumbling crash of stone against stone sounded from below. Finn dashed out onto the porch of the treehouse.

Below, Finn could see the enchanted villagers shouting as they flooded into the temple.

"I have to get down there," Finn said. "Even if I can only give the druidess an extra minute, I have to give it a try."

Laisren grabbed him, his face stern. He began to speak but stopped. Sighed. "I'll go with you. You're right; we must try. Nekesa, return to our village, if you wish. You're acting chief until—"

"We will say our goodbyes later, my chief," she said. "Right now, we have a temple to save. Maybe between the three of us, we can give the druidesses three extra minutes—before we are slaughtered gruesomely."

Laisren nodded. "My thanks," he said. "Let's go." He jumped from the high-up porch and spread his wings.

Nekesa and Finn followed.

They landed in the rubble at the temple's entrance and immediately fought against the flood of people.

"Thresholds have power," Laisren shouted to Finn. "I can use it. Give me your hand."

Finn offered, and Laisren snatched it, holding it tight.

"Agony!" Laisren shouted. "Stand firm upon this threshold and be our shield."

A spiral of crimson light spun out from Laisren, etching across the ground under the rubble. Soon, a ten-foot field carved in glowing runes—half in and half outside the temple—formed with a mist wafting upward.

Those in the field, save for the Anordúlas, cried out in anguish, crawling from the spiral. Those who dared enter met the same fate.

A sharp pain stabbed through Finn's brain as he grabbed his forehead. He fell to his knees.

"Has your hex affected him, my chief?" Nekesa asked Laisren.

"No. He nears seid depletion. He can't cast any more major spells, so neither can we. Finn, can you stand?"

He nodded, and Laisren helped him to his feet.

"With the circle blocking the door, our rear is covered," Laisren said, "but we'll have to fight our way in."

CHAPTER TWENTY-TWO

Treasa rushed into Kaie's study, her hands grasping five pages of handwritten words, drawings, and diagrams. "I've figured it out."

"The reversal spell?" Kaie asked.

"Not exactly, no." Treasa set the pages on Kaie's table. "We can't reverse it, but we can bind its effects. 'Twill only work on a few people at a time and will take continued concentration, but 'tis something."

Kaie sighed. "We're moving in the right direction, at least." She looked up and gasped. "By the Mothers!"

Treasa looked back to see another druidess, her white dress drenched with blood. She stumbled against the study's entrance, grabbing the casing to hold herself up.

"They're in the temple." The druidess panted. "They killed the other two druidesses maintaining the wall of thorns."

"Go," Kaie commanded Treasa. "I'll handle the binding spell."

Treasa rushed from the room into the grove.

"They've breached the temple," Treasa shouted. "Women, prepare for battle." She ran toward the edge of the vast room.

There, Treasa threw open a wooden cupboard to reveal a collection of staves hung evenly spaced and vertically on hooks. As each druidess approached, Treasa grabbed the owner's natural knobby, twisted staff and handed it to her.

Treasa's husband, followed by her son, rushed to her.

"How many are there?" Cal asked.

She answered so all around could hear. "The entrance is unprotected. We can assume all outside are making their way here." She handed over the last staff.

Ubaz spoke up. "Is there anything I can do?"

Treasa looked at her son—twelve years old and trembling with fear. It hurt her to see her sweet boy like that and hurt more, as she feared what the invaders would do to him.

"No, baby." Treasa forced a smile as best as she could. "I need you to hide."

The boy hesitated. "But I can use a bow."

Treasa grabbed him and held him in a tight hug as she pressed her cheek to the side of his head.

"Promise me you'll hide, son. And stay hidden, no matter what happens or what you hear. Hide until I come for you." She released him and crouched to look into his eyes, blue and sad. "Promise me that."

"I give you me word, mam, by ta Three Mothers. I'll stay hid. And a Feah must keep his word, 'cause '*he whose word is meaningless is meaningless, himself and cannot be trusted.*'"

"Yes." Treasa sniffed. "Good boy. May the Mothers guide you. Now go."

The boy flew away.

Containing her grief, Treasa turned to Cal, grasped her staff, and nodded.

They ran from the grove.

—

In the cramped stone hall, where threads of purple biolu-minescence dangled from the rafters, Finn, Laisren, and Nekesa fought their way forward.

The narrowness of the hall kept the enemy at their front—their sides were protected by walls, and their rear was empty, save for the fallen—but it also hindered their ability to fight. Laisren and Nekesa needed to keep the swings of their maces short. Finn could barely use his bow.

The tight space was a nightmare of shouts and shrieks, of violent sights in the dim purple light, of sprays of blood hit-ting Finn's skin in gruesome warmth.

Finn felt as if he were drowning, as if all the air in this hell had been sucked out to fuel the angry calls of the enemies. A sick dizziness throbbed through him. Finn fought on. Every bolt he shot pulled from his weakening life force.

Finn aimed his bow, but he hesitated to shoot. Lighthead-ed, he rocked as if his legs were failing.

Laisren stabbed his mace into the crowd. Finn wanted to tell him he was falling, but no words came. So much noise. So many people in such a small space.

Someone grabbed Finn by the wrist and tried to pull him into the enemy line. Finn braced his throbbing body, resist-ing.

Laisren clubbed the assailant. And again. The assailant re-leased Finn.

"Are you all right?" Laisren asked.

Dizzy, Finn's eyes wandered before he regained himself. He aimed his bow and shot the man who'd grabbed him.

The man screamed in agony.

Finn breathed in the surrounding chaos, letting it fill him and recharge him. He shot again.

The Anordúla continued on, fighting around the slight curve of the gradual downward ramp.

—

Treasa's staff collided with Lann's mace as her brother stared hate into her eyes.

Hundreds of invaders filled the large curved hall, which was lined with large shelves holding the skulls of the most honored Feah ancestors.

The ten remaining druidesses, alongside Cal, fought strongly with both magic and mundane means, yet the enemies continued their advance.

"This is not who you are!" Treasa yelled at Lann. "The Dayigans have twisted your mind."

He swung hard, aiming for her head and missing by inches. It would have killed her, she knew. Yet, she strove to keep her counterstrikes nonfatal. Treasa swung her staff, hitting Lann hard on the side of his stomach.

He stumbled back, but two other invaders took his place. As she fought, Treasa tried to look past her new foes to see how badly she'd injured her brother.

He was standing, arched forward, and held his side. She'd knocked the breath out of him, but he was good.

From the corner of her eyes, Treasa saw someone fly past her into the enemies.

It was a little girl with white wings and white hair.

"*Alannah, no!*" Treasa screamed. She fought to reach her, but the two she battled would not relent.

Alannah flew to her father.

Lann assured the girl that he was all right and stood tall.

Treasa screamed again, "Alannah!" as she fought.

Lann passed the girl to one of his men. "Take her back to Commander Beadurinc. She'll be safe with him."

Treasa fought harder, desperate to reach the girl as the enchanted Feah led her away. Yet Lann, recovered, joined the two who fought his sister.

Cal hurried to Treasa's side, taking on Lann and letting her fall back enough to cast.

Again, Treasa scanned for Alannah but saw no sign of her. She held her staff out vertically in front of her and began moving it outwards and inwards in a stirring motion. "Mother Ashatra, whose dominion is wind, give me strength against those who would harm us. Spiral and turn. *Spiral and turn.*"

Wind spun out, entering the enemy line to circle as a disk of whirling winds about seven feet tall and thirty feet wide.

"Spiral and turn."

It wouldn't last long and wouldn't cause much damage, but it would occupy the invaders long enough to let her allies catch their breaths and regroup.

"Is that Finn there?" Cal asked.

Treasa looked up, seeing two men and a woman in flight over the whirlwind. The center man, wielding a black bow, shot bolts of crimson into the mass of invaders.

"It *is* him," Cal said before shouting Finn's name.

Finn, with two others, landed and joined the druidic line.

"What have you done to my brother?" Cal shoved the stranger at Finn's side.

The man, in a long robe and kilt of black leather and black hair and wings, did not retaliate, but his dark eyes glared.

"Leave it, Cal," Treasa yelled. "'Tis not the time."

Lann broke free of the whirlwind and charged her, his mace high. Treasa blocked him with her staff.

"Finn is fine," the stranger said to Cal. "I'm Laisren. This is Nekesa. We came to help you."

Finn looked sick and weak. He stumbled. Cal rushed to him as he passed out in his arms.

The stranger—Laisren—joined Treasa's fight against Lann as other foes joined as well.

"Listen," Laisren said to her. "Finn cast a protective circle at the temple's entrance. If he's unconscious, the circle's down." He swung his mace, knocking a foe to the ground. "A lot more enchanted villagers are coming. We have to fall back."

"We can't do that," Treasa strained through her teeth as she fought.

"Trust me. This isn't half of those gathered against you. And we're already spent."

"I'm sorry, Lann." She swung her staff, striking him to the floor.

"Druidesses," Treasa called, "fall back to the grove."

—

Treasa and the two Anordúla fought back against the invaders as Cal carried Finn through the large stone-framed entrance into the Temple Grove. The other druidesses entered right behind them.

When all were inside, Treasa and the Anordúla hurried across the threshold.

"Chief!" Treasa shouted. "Shut the door."

Kaie stood erectly with her feet well braced and apart. She raised her hands upward at her sides.

The threshold began to rise.

Lann, leading a dozen men, charged into the grove and leaped over the rising stone slab door as it began to close.

The Anordúla fought those who'd entered as Treasa, flying to the door, cast a wall of wind to keep any more from coming through.

The door closed with an echoing thump.

Cal and Treasa hurried to the Anordúla, joining them against Lann's group.

The druidesses, rushing the invaders, aimed their staves.

Vines erupted from the ground, twisting around the invaders' wrists and ankles.

Treasa hurried to Kaie. "That won't hold them long. Is the binding spell ready?"

"It is." Kaie rushed to the altar beside the stone centered on the room. "Watch the captives. I can't be disturbed." A small brass cauldron sat on the stone altar. Within it waited a mix of dried plants—some ground, some twisted. Kaie cut her hand with a dagger, letting her blood drip into the mixture.

"By the Three Mothers, I take hold of the spell on our people here within the Temple Grove." She fisted her bleeding hand. "By the Three Mothers, I bind it."

The mixture sparked and combusted into a purple flame.

Lann struggled at the vines holding his wrists. "*I'll kill you!*" he screamed. "*I'll kill every savage tree witch in this wicked ...*" Abruptly, he stopped. Relaxed.

The eyes of the enchanted men grew heavy. They yawned and sat on the grass.

Treasa took a long, slow breath before she raised her hand to eye level. She twirled her fingers.

The vines holding the trapped villagers crumbled into dust. They looked at one another with silent confusion and dismay, her brother amongst them.

Treasa approached him. "Are you all right?"

Lann stared before shaking his head. And then realization: "Lannah," he said, dismayed, "I handed her over to—"

"We'll get her back," Treasa assured with a hand on his shoulder.

She looked around. Many in the area were injured. Of the twelve druidesses, only seven survived, plus the archdruidesses—Kaie, Treasa, and Bévinn from the Eorna Parish.

"Right, you three," Treasa said to a few uninjured druidesses. "Circle the chief and lend her your energies. She'll need your help to maintain the binding against the Dayigan spell. All other druidesses treat the injured, including yourselves."

They hurried away.

Treasa heard Cal behind her. "Get away from my brother."

The Anordúla man crouched over Finn, unconscious on the grass. Cal stood over them, ready to fight.

"I desire no fight with you," Laisren said, "but I will help Finn."

Treasa approached. "Laisren, right?"

He nodded.

"We can help Finn," she said. "He's seid depleted. We need to set up a circle to help the One Soul flow into—"

"The One Soul can do nothing for him." Laisren cut her off. "Finn is chaos attuned."

"You mean you twisted him up with dark forces," Cal said as he lunged forward, flexing back his shoulders and clenching his fists.

"Finn made himself into what *he* needed to be to help you. All of you. 'Twas his choice, and nothing I wanted for him."

"You corrupted him," Cal maintained.

"*Temple guardian,*" Treasa commanded, "stand down."

Cal glared her way. "Yes, Vischief." He stepped back.

Finn stirred some and opened his eyes. "Laisren." His voice was weak.

Laisren hurried to his side. "I'm here, Finn."

Finn closed his eyes and was still.

Laisren looked up at Treasa. "The enchanted villagers try to beat through the grove door."

"I hear them, aye," she said.

"If I lay Finn by the door, their chaotic energies will help him."

Treasa paused before nodding reluctantly. "Do it."

"Nekesa," Laisren called.

Nekesa hurried to Laisren, and they helped Finn toward the door.

Moyra ran from the infirmary to Lann. She hugged him tightly. Treasa couldn't hear what Lann said to her, but Moyra wailed with a broken heart. She punched Lann's arm and side, punches growing weaker down him as she crumbled to the ground. Lann knelt to her and embraced her. They wept.

Treasa looked at Cal, who looked broken.

"I ..." Treasa began. "I don't know how to fix this."

CHAPTER TWENTY-THREE

Treasa meandered through the grove. An uneasy calm had settled over the area despite the constant thumps and clanks against the massive grove door. The people within had clustered into frightened huddles, trying to console each other. All were healed or bandaged with moss. Only a slight few remained in the infirmary. They feared the people outside while also fearing *for* them. Friends, relatives. No one knew who was alive or dead outside of this massive cell.

Within the circle of ancient oaks, Treasa laid her hand on the rough standing stone that centered the temple. Above it, the large portal led to the sky, but thick vines twisted around the brass bars that formed the star across the portal, blocking any sight of what was beyond.

Was it day or night? Treasa wondered.

Beside the stone, Kaie stood within a triangle of druidesses, their fingers to their foreheads. They'd kept the position for an hour.

Behind Treasa, a man asked, "How long can they maintain their concentration?"

Treasa turned to Laisren and shook her head. "I'm not sure. Kaie has blocked the effects of the Dayigan spell, but the people are still enchanted. As soon as her concentration falters, these people around us will return to fighting us."

"Can the druidesses extend their will to those beating their way into the grove?"

"In theory, they could. But they're already straining just to suppress the spell within those in the grove. 'Tis a per person effect, not an area effect. And they're already binding the spell in more people than we'd planned."

Laisren nodded.

"Has Finn recovered?" Treasa asked.

"Nearly. He's sitting up and conscious. I never meant his brother must stay away."

"He stays away of his own choosing," Treasa said. "You have to understand how our people see chaos magic."

"I know," he said coldly. "I grew up here, in this temple."

"Right, of course. Morgana's son. I think I might have met you once or twice. You'd gone away to school before I began my studies as a druidess, but Morgana became like a mother to me as well. I still can't believe she turned to wicked magic."

"Mother did what was necessary to help the Feah. As did Finn."

"Maybe wicked's not the word. But *forbidden*, and with reason. Chaos magic twists the mind and soul, opens our lands up to dark Faery attacks, sends decay into nature, and makes the caster's soul vulnerable to capture by the Fae. Ugly stuff."

"And yet, we need it."

"Does Finn know all that?"

"All in the Five Tribes know the old stories. The druidesses have regaled us with the dangers of chaos since before our wings had feathers. But I never had the chance to tell Finn specifically, no. He literally jumped into the fire before I could tell him a thing."

"He is rash, our Finn. I'll give you that."

"I love him, though." Laisren smiled. "Capture by Irefae is a non-issue. The walls between our realm and theirs are closed."

"Because of the druidic circles." She smiled.

"Indeed." Laisren tilted his head in a nod. "And we need them to stay closed, not only for the Five Tribes, but for the entire world of Perdinok. The Anordúla have never disputed that. But—on the matter at hand—our magic can help you. I should be able to disenchant these people completely."

"I tried that, myself," Treasa said, "but the reversal spell would need to be in the same form of magic used by the Dayigans."

"Then that's what I'll do," Laisren said. "As Anordúlas, we can use any form of magic we like. But I need to understand it."

Treasa ran her fingers through her hair, sliding her hand down her neck to her shoulder. "You wish to perform chaos magic *here*, in the temple of the Three Mothers."

"My magic can save everyone here," Laisren said. "And save those trying to beat their way in."

Treasa looked at him for a moment. She sighed. "The Dayigan commander is a Silthex knight, whatever that means."

"In Vohcktara—where I went to school—I heard stories of the Silthex. They are the special army of the Church of Déagar—at least they were until the knights were wiped out five years ago. There were rumors they practiced magic but nothing verifiable. If I'm to use their magic, I have to start by figuring out the God they worship."

"God Déagar," Treasa said. "You said it yourself."

"True, but I need to understand the Silthex's *specific* version of Déagar. For instance, what is the color of God Déagar?"

"Well, we've always known it to be red, but the Dayigans think 'tis green, for some daft reason."

"Exactly," Laisren said. "And many would say Déagar has no color at all. It was stolen at the beginning of time. It doesn't matter what is true. What matters is what the Silthex believe."

Treasa nodded. "The commander once told me that God Déagar is the only God, and the rest of the pantheon are demigods. Oh, and they think za is a torturous afterlife."

"Perfect." Laisren smiled. "That's the sort of thing I need to know. I'll also require all your research on the Dayigan spell. Your brother was one of the enchanted, right? I'll need to speak to him, as well."

———

In Kaie's study off the Temple Grove, Finn stood next to Laisren and Nekesa. Cal, Lann, and Moyra were there too, but they remained distant from the Anordúlas, both in their dozen feet of separation and in their manner. Finn's attempts to talk to Cal and Lann had proved futile. He'd assumed they'd be happy to see him. They weren't. Now, they shot occasional angry glances Finn's way while mostly ignoring him.

Treasa entered and approached Laisren.

"'Twas hard to find," she said as she lifted a five-inch prism of pale green quartz. Its six sides were smooth and its ends, pointed. "'Tis prasiolite."

"Gratitude," Laisren said as he took it. He handed it to Finn. "Lann, right?"

Lann nodded with angry eyes.

"I must know all you know of the Dayigan belief system," Laisren said. "Even more than you realize you know. You just need to think of them and concentrate. Nekesa will pull the required information from your mind and give it to me."

"I thought I'd just be talking to them," Lann said to Treasa. "I'm not having some wicked sorcerers rooting 'round in me head."

"Our people need you to do this, Lann," Treasa said.

Moyra set her hand on Lann's shoulder. "Our sweet Alannah needs you to do this."

Lann glared at Laisren and then at Finn. "Fucking wicked Faery magic," he grumbled. "Do it."

Stepping between Laisren and Lann, Nekesa placed her left palm on Lann's forehead. "Close your eyes and say the commander's name. Concentrate on him and everything he has said or done." She placed her other palm on Laisren's forehead.

Lann closed his eyes. "Commander Beadurinc."

"Say it again," Nekesa whispered. "Slower. Concentrate on the name."

"Commander Beadurinc." Lann scrunched his face in pain, and Finn couldn't tell if it was from Nekesa's actions or from the memories he was reliving.

After a few seconds, Laisren stepped back and rubbed his temples.

"So much hate," Laisren whispered. "Against all of us." He breathed. "I have what I need to evoke the egregore of the Silthex God. Finn, give me the crystal and hold my hand."

"No," Cal objected. "You're not using Finn's magic, are you now? He's only just recovered from before."

"I have no other choice," Laisren said. "And we cannot wait. If the enchanted people break down the door—"

"'Tis no bother, Brother," Finn spoke up. "I'm all well and rested now."

"Ancestors fucking help us," Cal grumbled. "If you kill my brother, I'll ..."

"Cal," Treasa said, with a threatening look.

Finn grabbed Laisren's hand.

Holding the green quartz in his clenched right hand and clutching Finn's in his other hand, Laisren spoke in loud, clear words. "Praise God Déagar, the one and only God, protector from the Dark. You are the Greatest of All. I praise your name, majestic and holy, without ending. By your fire, guide us safely to Laqyigo."

Nekesa bowed her head and closed her eyes. "Praise Déagar." She lifted one hand, palm up, slightly above her head. "God of fire and lightning."

"In your holy name, Almighty Déagar," Laisren continued, "we ask that the curse set upon the Feah lands be broken. In your name, O Greatest of All, we ask that all magic performed by the Dayigans be undone. In your mighty name, O God Déagar, we ask that you bind the magic in Commander Beadurinc, that he may do no more against the people of the Drevite tribes or the Anordúla. Shine your divine might into this crystal, O mighty Déagar, that we may use it to shine your majestic power across our people to heal them. Praise God Déagar. Praises to the True Light."

Nekesa whispered. "Praise God Déagar. Praises to the True Light."

"Astha'will-miabé," Laisren concluded.

Finn gasped as he felt a great rush of power flowing out of him. A green light shone from Finn's core and flowed through his arm and hand into Laisren, through Laisren, to the hand holding the crystal.

Laisren released Finn's hand and looked at the green quartz, which was now glowing.

"Is it done, then?" Treasa asked.

"I usually take much more time studying a belief system before working with it," Laisren said, "but yes. I think so. But I've only created a key to unlock the enchantment. The druidesses must push the key out through the One Soul to cover the lands."

"Are you utterly mad? No," Treasa said firmly. "We absolutely cannot send chaos magic out through the One Soul."

"The One Soul is Mother Lágeya, yes?" Laisren said. "Do you think she would resist helping the Feah?"

Treasa looked back at the other three. "Ancestors help us." She huffed and took the crystal. "I'll give it to Kaie."

—

In the Temple Grove, Treasa gathered the Anordúla, including Finn, and called Cal, Lann, and Moyra to join them.

"Chief Kaie has successfully pushed the Anordúla spell throughout the grove," Treasa said, "and everyone here—our Lann and Moyra included—is free of the Dayigan enchantment and showing no adverse effects. Kaie will soon begin pushing the spell through the entire temple and beyond it. Soon, all Nature in the Feah lands will radiate Laisren's spell, thus curing everyone altogether."

"Won't it affect Nature?" Cal spoke up. "Dark forces flowing through it like that."

"It won't, no," Treasa said.

"'Tis not technically *dark* forces," Laisren began. "'Tis—"

"We tested it." Treasa cut him off. "'Twill be fine. But it will take the combined, continuous concentration of all the remaining druidesses other than myself and Bévinn, the tierna of the Eorna Parish. They can't help us in what's about to come."

Lann crossed his arms. "I hope *what's about to come* is clearing our lands of every fucking Human that set foot here."

"It is," Treasa said gravely. "'Tis the only choice they've left us with. When our people awaken from the spell, they'll be confused and disorganized. Cal, Moyra, and Lann, ye must organize them. See that all fighters are armed and arrange evacuation for all non-fighters and children. Send them west to the Rúcah lands. The severely injured will come here to the temple, where Bévinn will lead the infirmary. She'll be needing assistants and guards. After that's arranged, ye and the fighters will push the Dayigan back to their fort. As for myself, I'll go to the fort directly. I need an Anordúla with me. Nekesa, will you fight with me?"

Nekesa looked at Laisren. "Chief?"

Laisren nodded. "Stay safe. Both of you."

"Thank you," Treasa said. "Nekesa and I will go for the prisoners in the Dayigan fort. Including Alannah." She looked at Lann and Moyra.

Moyra nodded somberly.

"We *will* save them," Treasa assured. "All of them. Laisren, I'll need you and Finn to go after Commander Beadurinc." She paused. "Do your best to capture him alive so he can stand trial."

"Finn is *not* a fighter," Cal spoke up.

"Finn *is* a fighter, Cal," Treasa said. "And Laisren needs the power within Finn to fuel his own magic."

"I'll be all right, Brother," Finn said. "Me and Laisren will protect each other."

The words didn't ease the angry fear in Cal's expression. "I should have never let you go to that hexed village of theirs."

The pounding on the grove door grew louder as fractures crackled up the large stone slab.

"Whatever we feel about the Anordúla," Treasa said, "we can feel it when this is done. Right now, we have to work together."

Treasa looked back and shouted, "Chief, 'tis time."

Kaie stood within a circle of seven druidesses. She looked at the glowing green crystal cradled in her hands and lifted it to her forehead.

The cracks in the stone slab blocking the grove's entrance widened. Smaller bits fell to the grass. Another impact from the other side caused the stone to shatter into chunky fragments, crashing down onto themselves.

"Go!" Treasa commanded.

The group, rushing toward the door, drew their weapons.

With the door crumbled, those outside flooded in, shouting angrily with weapons raised.

A circle of green mist fanned out from Kaie. The wave grew larger, passing through the people who had forced entry.

The invaders' anger faded into confusion. They lowered their weapons and began looking around as if newly awakened and lost.

"It worked." Treasa said. "Quickly, we must organize them."

CHAPTER TWENTY-FOUR

Outside the temple, Lann stood in the rubble that had been the standing stone at the entrance. People hurried around and in front of him, preparing for battle and evacuation.

His wife landed beside him.

Lann looked down at the rubble. "I did this here. I remember doing it."

Moyra set her hand on his shoulders and looked into his eyes. "Fight now, mourn later."

He nodded.

"*Cal*," Moyra shouted.

Cal hurried to them. "What did you find?"

Moyra answered, "The Dayigans have regrouped just south of the temple village. About two hundred of them."

"How many fighters do we have?"

"More just arrived from the surrounding parishes," Moyra said. "So we're at about five hundred, ourselves, but most don't have weapons training or armor."

"Mothers help us. 'Twill have to do. Find us twenty fighters—decent but not our best—to head up the evacuation. And give them a hundred poor fighters. They'll need to stay back and protect the temple and protect the nonfighters, injured, and children traveling from the Feah temple to the Rúcah temple."

"Aye, temple guardian," she said.

"Lann." Cal turned to him. "How's your side of things?"

"That druidess from the Eorna Parish—"

"Tierna Bévinn."

"—is on her own doing the healing, but she's pulled in some villagers to help her out. She's healed loads of people, but she's just getting them healed enough to be transported to Rúcah lands. The ones she's released are gathered with the other evacuees just north of the temple. We'll need to be moving them soon."

"Do we know how many deaths?"

"Dozens. At least. But 'tis hard to get a good count with so many folks missing."

Cal nodded. "Go with Moyra and help her select the evacuation teams. They'll answer to Tierna Bévinn. For the rest of the fighters, we move on the Dayigans in one hour."

—

Under the pale blue larger moon and the lavender-tinted smaller moon, Treasa crouched on a high limb of a shore-side tree, her hand resting on its rough bark. Her eyes remained locked on the Dayigan fort.

"I should tell you," Treasa said to Nekesa without looking back. "I've been here before."

"In this tree?" Nekesa sat on a limb just behind her.

"I have, yes. But I meant on a rescue mission in the fort. It was a horrible failure."

Treasa turned to Nekesa—she watched the fort and seemed unfazed by the news.

"Did you learn anything?" Nekesa asked.

"I learnt not to blow all my magic on a big spell before going into battle."

"There you go. Something learnt. We will do better this time, yes?"

Treasa nodded. "There are more Dayigan ships. There were only three before. Now, I count five."

"Look." Nekesa pointed. "At the fortress door."

Treasa turned to the doors; it opened wide as hundreds of Dayigan soldiers marched out.

"They'll be headed to the temple village," Treasa whispered.

"Our allies will manage."

"Will they?" Treasa watched the grim parade. There were easily four hundred soldiers, their steps like thunder.

Nekesa opened a bag on her hip and pulled out a folded cloth. She unwrapped four, five-inch bars of crimson light without touching them.

"That's chaos, is it not?" Treasa asked.

"Yes. Finn gave them to me. I worried they would fade away, but they look to be fine." She rewrapped them and returned them to her bag.

With the last of the soldiers through, the fort's door slammed shut.

"Are you ready?" Nekesa asked.

Treasa looked at the fort and remembered Kyran—beaten and bloodied and staring at her with eyes begging for help. She remembered him lying face down in the dirt as the commander stabbed his blade through his back.

"I am, yes."

—

Where the river's shore turned from sand to grass, but before it turned to woods, a small village nestled within a fence of woven, horizontal twigs. The twelve homes clustered together were simple cottages with short circular walls supporting steep thatched roofs.

Dayigan soldiers filled the village. They walked the paths and chatted. They sharpened their weapons and prepared for battle.

"This is my home," Finn whispered to Laisren as they crouched behind a cottage. "This one right here." He pressed his body against the rough wall as he hid.

"You'll need to use this." Laisren offered an arrow. "For Beadurinc. Aim to kill."

Finn looked at the arrow without taking it. "I'm fine with my chaos bolts. They'll stun him, and we can arrest him like Treasa said."

"How? The village is crawling with soldiers. If you stun him, they'll simply take him somewhere to recover."

"Right." Finn nodded and tentatively took the arrow.

"Look." Laisren pointed.

With four other soldiers, Beadurinc walked amongst the commandeered homes.

Finn lifted his bow and armed it with the arrow. He aimed the deadly point of sharpened flint.

The other soldiers chatted with the commander, blocking Finn's shot.

Waiting, Finn kept his bow steady. Waiting, he watched Beadurinc. Finally, the other soldiers moved, leaving Beadurinc unobstructed.

Finn drew back the arrow against the bowstring. "No." He relaxed the arrow. "If we kill the Dayigan commander," Finn whispered, "we lose all chance of a peaceful compromise."

The commander entered a cottage.

Laisren grunted in frustration. "I suppose you forgot the Dayigans want us dead. Not a lot of room for compromise there, my love."

"There has to be more to it. If we can get Chief Kaie and the commander to talk—"

"Listen," Laisren whispered.

Finn heard marching on the shore behind him. He looked back.

Hundreds of Dayigan soldiers approached.

"We have to go," Laisren said.

—

Treasa and Nekesa landed in the Dayigan courtyard and braced themselves back to back—Treasa gripping her staff and Nekesa, her mace.

Treasa examined the tight, shadowed spaces between the freestanding houses on either side of the courtyard. She scanned the railed second-story walkways running alongside the thin doors leading into rooms in the fort's walls. She looked above the green-tiled roofs to the tops of the walls, at the walkway behind the parapet of sharpened logs. The area looked empty, but there were a lot of entries and hiding spots.

"This way," Treasa whispered as she turned toward the fort's front.

The large door from her last visit was absent. The tree she'd formed was long gone, as were the broken boards. A few splintered bits hung from bent hinges.

Treasa and Nekesa cautiously entered a long, wide, empty space. The area maintained the same sandy ground from the courtyard and was walled in thick logs. It set between the door she'd broken and the fort's exit—a pair of large, thick doors painted green.

Treasa motioned Nekesa to a much smaller open door to their right, but she placed a finger on her lips. She heard soldiers. Nekesa nodded, most likely hearing them, too.

Quietly, the two women entered this new large hall. Like the previous, the room was walled in thick logs but had a plank floor with thin rugs. Hefty tables and chairs clustered where functional. Dayigan flags hung on the walls above the fireplace. A taxidermized bear stood atop a pedestal while other creatures were but heads on plaques.

Treasa feared she might end up similarly stuffed as her eyes stayed focused on the dozen Dayigan soldiers. They gathered around a rough table as two took turns throwing dice.

Treasa remembered Beadurinc's tour of his "trade post" and remembered seeing the holding cells. The door leading to them was just a dozen feet across the room. But no stealth would be enough to get her there unseen, much less to allow her to unlock it and enter. They'd need to confront the soldiers.

The soldiers watching the dice game called out—some in victory, some in playful defeat.

Nekesa, moving forward, gave Treasa an attempt at a reassuring nod. It was not reassuring. Instead, Treasa eyed Nekesa, fearing that the other woman might run out and attack. Gripping her staff, Treasa readied herself for whatever would happen.

Carefully, Nekesa set her right hand on the bag on her hip, the bag holding the bolts of chaos. She gradually lifted her left hand, pulling it back before thrusting it forward.

"By the infernal Grim Barron, I clutch your soul," Nekesa muttered. "I command your soul. I command you. Know my will and do as I bid you."

A soldier called out in pain. He began convulsing rigidly, foaming at the mouth.

The other soldiers hurried to his aid, circling him. Some looked around, drawing their swords.

"*Witches!*" a soldier shouted, pointing. He was shoved by the formerly convulsing man.

This man, now enthralled by Nekesa, drew his sword and clumsily fought his allies.

Other soldiers charged Treasa and Nekesa.

The women leaped from their hiding place and started fighting.

Treasa thrust her staff into a soldier's stomach, knocking the wind out of him before she swung around and smashed her staff into his head. He fell.

Nekesa called out, as a sword cut her arm.

Yet Treasa was surprised to see that, like with her own unseen armor, Nekesa was protected, the cut shallow.

"You have Feah armor?"

"Yes," Nekesa said, as she fought. "Your former chief was like a mother to me."

"Same." Treasa swung her staff.

Nekesa pushed her mace against a Dayigan sword. "I guess that makes us sisters." She relaxed her mace and dodged the soldier as he lunged forward. She slapped her hand to his face.

The soldier began convulsing, his mouth foaming. Quickly, he became another thrall, fighting alongside the women.

Even with the enthralled allies, the women remained greatly outnumbered, and Treasa could barely think fast enough to keep up with all who attacked.

"We need to fall back," Treasa said. "Outside."

"We cannot."

"Trust me. I do better with my feet on natural ground."

When Treasa got the chance to break combat, she shouted, "Go!"

They ran out into the courtyard.

Midway into the yard, Treasa stopped with Nekesa by her side. They watched the soldiers charging forward.

When the last Dayigan exited, Treasa held her staff high.

"In the name of Mother Ashatra, who is Death, I call retribution from the earth." Treasa slammed the base of her staff to the ground.

Swirling winds spiraled from her, striking the sand before the soldiers. Dozens of massive thorns, some as tall as seven feet and as sharp as knives, erupted from the ground. They impaled the soldiers in sprays of blood and shouts of agony. Red pooled in the dirt.

Panting, Treasa stumbled. Nekesa caught her, and they watched the horrors Treasa had conjured.

Most had died outright, but some moaned in suffering.

"This is not what druidic magic is meant for," Treasa said, watching the dying.

"A debate for another time. Now, we must hurry."

—

The door opened, casting light into the narrow, dark hall. Treasa and Nekesa entered. They couldn't see much, but they could see that there were no soldiers. Treasa relaxed somewhat.

As her eyes adjusted, Treasa saw eight doors divided into four on either side of the hall. Each held a small barred window.

Treasa hurried to the first window and could see—barely—that people huddled on the floor. "'Tis all right. We've come to save you." She turned to Nekesa. "Would you watch the entrance for us please?"

Nekesa dashed away, taking a stance beyond the door.

Treasa inserted an iron key into the lock. She hurried from lock to lock until all the doors were open.

The captives—about fifty—were from various Feah parishes. She recognized a few. Most bore some sort of injury, and Treasa lacked the energy to heal them all.

Treasa helped a dusty man to his feet. She noted his wings. The eleven primary feathers—those on the outer top of each wing, if extended, but currently, as they were folded, just behind the man's calves—had been chopped raggedly in half. She looked around. The captives' wings had all been similarly clipped. They wouldn't be able to fly for at least a year.

"Can you walk?" she asked the man.

He shook his head weakly. "No, not on me own."

"*Alannah*," Treasa called. "Are you here?"

No response.

She touched the shoulder of the man she supported. "With the healing waters of Mother Lágeya, I imbue you."

His injuries faded, and he stood on his own.

"I don't have the strength to heal everyone," Treasa explained, so all could hear, "but I can surround each of you with a powerful force that mimics your being healed. 'Tis temporary and, once it wears off, your injuries will return like before. You must get to the temple so they can heal you properly."

They nodded.

Treasa hastily stabilized the most seriously wounded and made sure that everyone could walk. All the while, she kept glancing back at Nekesa, standing guard in the light of the main room. If any Dayigans discovered the carnage in the courtyard, it wouldn't take long to find the trespassers.

She touched a woman's shoulder. "With the healing waters of Mother Lágeya, I imbue you."

Finally, Treasa ushered everyone out to the main room, where the soldiers had played their dice game.

"My niece is not here," Treasa told Nekesa. "Please get these people to the temple. I'm staying to search for Alannah."

"You cannot stay here on your own."

"I can't risk the lives of these people, and I can't abandon my niece. These people need you to help them. I'll be fine."

Nekesa lifted a Dayigan sword and held it firmly. "Be safe, my sister. May Morgana and your ancestors guide you."

"And may yours guide you."

—

Within the woodlands of their ancestors, the ragtag Feah force fought with desperate determination against the trained Dayigan invaders. Wooden maces tipped with brass collided with sharpened Dayigan swords. Half-naked warriors clothed in leather stood against soldiers in suits of chainmail covered by emerald green tabards.

Blood splattered the fallen leaves and grass.

Cal hovered ten feet above the shouting, clashing hordes, twenty men and women to his sides. They shot their arrows into the Dayigans. Their height gave them good vantages, but also left them exposed. A Dayigan arrow hit Cal's stomach, cutting a bloody slice across his abdomen. His armor held, but the fresh wound only added to the many others across his body, seeping blood and stinging in a unified ache. Cal held firm and shot again.

The woman next to him was not so lucky. An arrow pierced her heart. She called out as she fell from the sky.

Cal could see the farthest Dayigans turn and head away. Likewise, the Dayigan front backed away while they fought.

Cal descended to Lann and Moyra, both fighting on the ground with maces.

"The Dayigans are falling back," Cal said.

"I see that," said Moyra. "But why? We're not exactly winning here, are we now?"

"They're planning something," Cal said. "But we have to pursue them and end this."

"Agreed." Moyra wiped blood from her face with the back of her arm. "But be ready for a trap."

"*Feahs!*" Cal shouted. "Stay with them, but stay alert."

Within the makeshift Feah army, Lann and Moyra raised their maces and shouted as they charged the soldiers.

CHAPTER TWENTY-FIVE

The beach offered no cover as Nekesa hurried the group of fifty freed captives toward the woods. Nekesa looked back, seeing hundreds of Dayigan soldiers amassing on the beach between the tree line and the fort. With their wings clipped, her group was grounded, so Nekesa had to take them the long way around, down the Hyvile River and—once they'd made some distance—head toward the trees.

She knew if any soldiers spotted her limping, weary group, it'd be their death.

Nekesa rushed back to the stragglers at the rear of the group. "We *must* hurry." She ushered them forward. She eyed the soldiers.

Treasa's spell was fading. Injuries, cloaked before, returned on all the rescued.

Nekesa saw two shadowed figures approach from the night sky. She braced herself, holding her stolen sword firmly as she held out her left hand, ready to cast.

It took her a moment to recognize the chief and Finn. She breathed.

Laisren landed. "These are the captives from the fort?"

"All we found," said Nekesa. "The little girl was not with them. Treasa stayed behind to find her. I must go back for her."

Laisren nodded. "We lost the commander, but we think he's headed back to the fort."

"*I* lost the commander," Finn spoke up. "I had him in my sights."

"Enough of that. Nekesa, you're with us. We'll go back for Treasa and the commander."

Nekesa looked back at the many soldiers between them and the fort.

Laisren followed Nekesa's eyes with his. "The commander cannot escape," he said, "or this whole thing could start again." He turned to the rescued. "The Dayigans group on the beach and on the grassy area beyond it. Get to the woods and head towards the temple. The Feahs have people gathering the injured who will find and assist you."

"We cannot leave them," Nekesa said.

"They'll be fine. Trust me, *you will all be fine.* Just stay low until you reach the trees. Go."

The people hesitated before scurrying away.

Laisren turned to Nekesa. "When Finn and I were in the sky," he began gravely, "we could see the Dayigan Army. There are far more than we expected. About six hundred."

"Yes. Treasa and I saw them too. There are more trained Dayigan soldiers than untrained Drevite warriors."

"We better get moving then."

She turned and faced the many distant soldiers. Sounds of battle erupted as the Dayigans and Feahs collided at the tree line down the shore.

"Glory to the Dinikimeran ancestors," Nekesa said. "Glory to the Drevite ancestors. Give us strength. We fight for you."

—

Treasa sneaked through a vast room within the riverside wall of the Dayigan fort. Small windows facing the courtyard allowed in moonlight, illuminating thick columns supporting heavy beams and many rows of wooden tables with benches on either side.

It appeared to be where the soldier ate their meals—it had seating for hundreds—and it flowed into the area for food preparation. She passed a cold, sooty fire pit framed in blackened brick, hoisting an iron spit.

Another dead end.

Treasa hurried to the courtyard, exiting from a door in the back corner and navigating one of the freestanding houses.

The thorns she'd conjured had mostly dissolved, leaving the impaled dead in drying gore.

She'd looked everywhere. No living soldier. No prisoners.

Treasa jumped up, stopping to hover ten feet above the fort's walls.

She stared at the five large ships rocking on the Hyvile River, just behind the fort.

Treasa flew toward them.

—

Blood, mud, and sweat covered Lann as he fought next to his wife within the chaotic collision of Dayigans and Feahs. The shouts of pain, the cries of battle, the impact of swords and maces—he was surrounded by the deafening sounds. He could drown in the sounds alone. His body was numb and aching. He'd seen longtime friends fall and was forced to trample their broken bodies as he pushed forward. Lann feared for his wife. He feared for his life. No part of him thought he'd survive this, but if he just kept going, just killed one more invader, then another, that would be less for others to battle.

To his right, the sun cast its first golden rays down the river shore, lighting the horrors of the grim morning. Lann stared farther into the Dayigan forces. They seemed to go on forever, soldier after soldier after soldier.

A loud bang sounded above the noise. Looking up, he saw a massive net launched from the Dayigans. Harpoons at its corners, it hurled through the sky at the Feah archers.

The rope from its center snapped taut, causing the harpoons to turn inward, wrapping the net around a dozen men and women. It snatched them from the sky, pulling them behind the Dayigan line.

Cal's voice sounded above. "Archers, scatter!"

Another net launched. Its catch was slimmer, yet it yanked down five more archers and pulled them into the mass of soldiers.

Lann fought hard, trying to reach the place where he'd seen the nets fall. But the wall of soldiers made advancing impossible.

"They're gone," Moyra shouted to him. "Stay on task."

Above, Cal saw the nets writhing with the captured Feah. Bodies broken from their impact with the ground, the bloodied people tried with desperate terror to escape the gruesome nets.

Cal concentrated his aim at the soldiers circling the captives, but his arrows, though fatal in their strikes, did little to stop the group overall. The Dayigans thrust their swords through the net—honorless kill after honorless kill.

Other soldiers already loaded other nets into the two strange wooden devices roughly a man's height. Each was like two, six-foot crossbows tiered at a forty-five-degree angle and atop four grooved wooden shafts holding harpoons at the corners of the net. Ropes pulled back the thick bowstrings from a lower iron crank. This was all mounted on large wheels.

Cal shot an arrow, hitting the man at the crank. He fell, but another soldier replaced him.

A barrage of Dayigan arrows targeted Cal. He tried to dodge, but there were too many. Arrows ripped across his skin.

A greater pain burned from his forearm and throbbed through his body as Cal's armor popped.

"Archers, abandon the skies," Cal called. He dove to Moyra and Lann, sheathed his bow on his belt, and grabbed his mace. He fought on.

The end, he knew, was near.

—

Treasa, her back against the outside wall of the fort, crouched behind an old wooden barrel, weathered gray, resting her hand on its side. It was clustered along with others of its kind, jammed in between crates in a haphazard stack.

Boards leveled the ground from the fort's walls to the river and continued out as two T-shaped docks where five moored Dayigan ships rocked gently on the Hyvile River.

The ships stretched eighty feet long and rode high above the water, with a raised section in the rear taking them higher. Centered on the vessel, a single mast towered, holding a rectangle sail striped in thick vertical bars of off-white and faded green.

Though the ships were only a quick sprint from Treasa, the long shadows of the rising sun offered little concealment. She saw a few dozen soldiers, some on the ships' decks and some on the docks. A handful patrolled, sword in hand, while most tended to ropes or moved cargo. However, all the soldiers were armed, she guessed, and all would rush her way if they discovered her.

Setting her fingers to her forehead, Treasa thought back to Midyear's Eve. She envisioned a soldier who'd accompanied Beadurinc, a Human with shoulder-length blond hair and a thick blond beard. The memory was over five months old, but it was the closest she'd been to a Dayigan for any length of time. She pictured him, calling up as much detail as she could recall.

"Cloak me, O Three Mothers," Treasa whispered. "Obscure my form within another."

A mist twirled up from the ground, surrounding her and taking the shape of the man she'd envisioned. Soon, she appeared like him, though nothing about the glamour was solid—definitely not enough to touch. If one were to look too closely, he'd see Treasa within the misty form. Still, from a distance, it would do.

Treasa stood and approached the closest ship—a one-in-five chance of finding Alannah, if she was on one at all.

A soldier approached at an amble, not *to* her, exactly, but toward her. If their paths crossed, a friendly greeting would be enough to see through her disguise.

Treasa increased her pace—not running; running would draw attention. She hurried between two ships, their heights more imposing from the narrow dock.

The man she'd passed called out. *"Captain Osgar."*

Treasa rushed to the wooden ramp that had been set up for boarding the ship. She looked back. The man did not pursue. She released her held breath.

Continuing up the ramp, she found no one on deck or on the raised stern deck at the back.

Dizziness struck her. Treasa pushed her hand through the fading glamour of the captain's head to her actual forehead. She'd held the disguise as long as she could. With a wave, the form dissipated in a mist.

Undisguised and exposed, Treasa looked around hurriedly. This ship was unlike anything she'd seen this close: an entire structure of solid wood. Feah boats were tiny in comparison, holding just a handful of people in a pinch, but ideally two or three. This ship could hold a village. The scholar in her had a million questions, and she wished to explore.

Instead, she found a large square hatch at the base of the mast. Through its grid of woven strips of iron, Treasa glimpsed Terovaes cowering in the lower hold.

Pressing her face to the grid, she whispered, "I'll get you out of there."

"*Intruder!*" someone called behind her.

Treasa scratched and grappled at the edges of the metal lid for some means to open it.

Two soldiers ran up on the deck, their footsteps echoing hollowly.

Treasa grabbed her staff and aimed, sending a twisting wind. A soldier flew backward off the boat, splashing in the river.

She re-aimed.

The other man flew back.

Treasa found the latch and gave it a firm twist. She struggled to open the heavy hatch as its hinges shrilled.

The prisoners had already crowded the ascending steps, and they stepped higher with their covering lost.

"You must fly high," Treasa said, "over the battle outside."

"Can't. They clipped our wings."

Treasa rammed her fist against her forehead and whispered a scream. "Mothers, give me strength." She looked up. "You must jump from the boat then and swim. 'Tis the only way. As quick as you can, get to the temple. They'll help you. Please, has anyone seen a wee girl with white wings?"

The replies were nothing but shakes of heads, and someone added, "We have injured in here."

"I'll take care of them. Go."

Fifty people ran from the hold and toward the starboard edge. A Feah man took an arrow in the back and crashed onto the deck. Others leaped and splashed. Arrows shot into the river struck frantic swimmers, releasing red to mix with choppy waters. However, most of the escapees dove deep enough to flee, and the Dayigans didn't pursue.

Within the dim chamber framed in heavy beams, Treasa rushed to the closest of three injured Terovaes, slouching against the wall.

"I'm low on magic, but I should have enough to heal you temporarily."

Before she could begin, a soldier ran into the hold, his boots stomping the boards of the steps.

Treasa aimed her staff and sent him against the hull.

Pain ripped through her mind. She called out as she grabbed her head with both hands. It was too soon, she knew, too soon after the fight alongside Nekesa. She'd nearly depleted her seid.

Six more soldiers ran into the hold.

Panting, Treasa regained herself, gripping her staff. She bluffed a brave stance but knew she faced too many soldiers to fight by mundane means. She took a breath. *One more spell should be fine.*

The soldiers stepped forward at once.

"Fear me," Treasa hissed in echoing words. "*Fear me.*" She roared like a bear, though an unearthly, elongated sound. The roar filled the hold, filled the soldiers' minds, overtaking them.

The soldiers stopped, grabbing their heads before they screamed in terrified madness. They darted about, unsure where to go, trying to escape. Some beat their fists against the hull. Finally, they dashed up the steps.

Treasa called out in pain as she fell to her knees. Her body weakened, flashing hot and cold; she tried to press on, yet the sharp pain behind her eyes radiated out, clouding her thoughts and sickening her stomach.

She reached back and grabbed the nearest captive, dragging him toward the stairs as she dragged herself.

Treasa made it more than halfway there, but weakness struck her hard. She collapsed fully to the deck. *I have to keep going.* Her breaths came quick and shallow as she stared into the speckled dark. *I must keep going.* She couldn't move, no matter how hard she tried to will it. Her body throbbed in numbness, tingling. Her vision grew dark. *I must get up.*

Footsteps approached on the stairs. Someone snatched her by the hair and turned her limp head to face him.

Through half-closed eyes, Treasa recognized the blurry image of Commander Beadurinc.

"You've gone and depleted yourself, haven't you?" he said. "Stupid witch."

He slapped her with the back of his fist, and she crumpled to the floor.

Treasa couldn't move. Despite her struggle to keep her heavy eyes open, they closed. She could still hear the heavy steps of the commander as a distant echo moving around her. Perhaps there were more boots and more soldiers. *Mothers, help me.* However, her ears failed her, sounds fading away as she lost the slow, sickening battle with unconsciousness.

CHAPTER TWENTY-SIX

Finn shot bolts of chaos into the wall of soldiers. A Human fell, but the slim gap left by the absence disappeared in seconds as other Dayigans fought forward.

Nekesa and Laisren—both upgraded to Dayigan swords—fought next to Finn, as did four enthralled soldiers.

But too many soldiers closed in around the Anordúlas.

Finn shot bolt after bolt as quickly as he could. "We have to return to the sky," he shouted to Laisren.

"We can't." Laisren strained his blade against a Dayigan's. "They're shooting nets. Nekesa, we need more thralls."

"Four is the most I can control at once." She swung her sword.

Laisren shouted as he punched a Human. "To the skies then," he relented. "We're retreating to the Feah line."

"We have to get the commander. He needs capturing." Finn shot a bolt of chaos. "And Treasa needs rescuing." He shot again.

"Finn, we'll die. Fall back. Now."

The three jumped from the ground.

—

Fighting side by side with Cal and Moyra, Lann maintained the losing battle. The Feah line had pushed no farther forward, and the raging sea of soldiers seemed no less daunting. The only change, it seemed, was that Lann had grown wearier.

Suddenly, Moyra called out in an agonized shout that twisted into gagging coughs. Lann snapped his attention to her to see a Dayigan's sword thrust to its hilt through her gut. It seemed unreal—an impossible sight, even within the surrounding horrors.

The soldier kicked her off his bloody blade.

"*Moyra,*" Lann shouted, dashing to her. He grabbed her and dragged her back from the line. "*Healer!*" he called.

The battle kept going, as if it didn't matter, as if no one cared or noticed that he held his dying love in his arms.

Pressing his hand on the gaping wound, Lann tried to keep her blood from pouring out.

"Healer." His voice cracked around the word, a sound lost within the shouts and clashing weapons.

Moyra coughed blood, and Lann cradled her head. He looked into her sleepy eyes. "Fight now," she groaned. "Mourn later."

His thoughts returned to Midyear's Eve to that night just before the world fell apart.

Tin cup of beernog in hand, Lann laughed with Moyra and Finn and Cal and Treasa. They were near the enormous bonfire. Cheery music flooded the area as happy villagers danced and joked. Strings of yellow flowers decorated everything.

"Lann," Cal said with a smile as he raised his cup. "We have to move. The Dayigans are pushing forward."

"What?" Lann asked, confused.

The memory faded as Lann stared at Moyra, bleeding out on the battlefield. Her face was lifeless, her hand cold. His wife was gone.

Lann's body throbbed. His ears were deaf. He stared.

Lann knew he needed to fight, but he couldn't let go. Cal was trying to tell him something, to pull him away. But he couldn't abandon his wife on the ground.

Lann thought of Lannah. His sister would have her in the temple by now. He would need to be the one to tell her of her mother. And he knew he could not let sweet Lannah have two dead parents. Lann needed to survive for Lannah. He needed to fight back against the Dayigans, for Lannah.

He heard Cal shout his name. Lann turned slowly, confusedly toward him.

"Lann, *we have to move, now*. The Dayigans are pushing forward."

Lann returned his eyes to Moyra and lay her softy on the grass.

"Fight now, mourn later." Lann whispered Moyra's words. They were little comfort.

Cal reached out his hand and pulled Lann to his feet.

Cal stopped with a sharp jerk. His eyes widened as he groaned in pain as a steel blade, bloodied, burst from his stomach. Blood dripped from the sides of his mouth as he opened and closed it wordlessly.

The Dayigan soldier, retracting the sword from Cal's back, shoved him forward, falling onto Lann.

"No!" someone shouted, with immense anger and utter sadness—Finn.

Finn shot a bolt of chaos into the man who'd stabbed Cal, and the soldier, falling to his knees, screamed in agony as his veins swelled. He rushed to his brother.

"I'm sorry," said Lann, holding Cal's limp body and looking into Finn's sorrow-filled eyes.

The two men lowered Cal to the grass beside Moyra.

Laisren, Nekesa, and three enthralled soldiers moved between Finn and the battle. They fought.

"I'll get you help," Finn said to Cal.

"Keep going." Cal's voice was shaky. "I'm going to the ancestors now. I know it."

"Don't say that. You'll be fine."

Cal, his hand wet with blood, grabbed Finn's hand and looked into his eyes. He said, "I'm dying, Finn. There's nothing you can do for it. Just keep fighting."

"I don't believe you." Finn's eyes watered. "You can't. *Healer!*"

"Listen to me, silly fecker," Cal said weakly. "I was wrong about your Laisren. He's a good man, him. Be happy with him." Cal closed his eyes. "And take care of each other." His body relaxed.

Finn laid his hand on the Septogram tattooed on Cal's chest—no beat beneath it. "No," he whispered as he stared.

The Irefaery Star on Finn's chest glowed like embers around its edges.

The grass around Finn wilted and browned. In a growing radius, the blight spread past a bush. Its green leaves shriveled, browned, and fell to the dirt.

"No," Finn said, staring at Cal.

Finn stood and looked at the man who'd killed his brother.

The soldier writhed in agony.

Finn shot him again.

His screams doubled as a soldier-colored mist formed around him. His fingers dissolved as wafting ash.

Finn shot him again.

The Dayigan's veins burst open, emptying blood into the dirt.

Finn showed little reaction, only glaring as he watched the thick red liquid flow and seep into the ground.

A crimson mist flowed up from the ground, maintaining a foot-thick carpet with a ten-foot radius around Finn.

All nature in the mist died. All people within the mist—Dayigans and Feah alike—fell to their knees in agony.

"Get back." Laisren grabbed Nekesa and yanked her away from Finn.

Finn screamed—a continuing, otherworldly sound that echoed over all others. All heard it, looking up as they fought. Thunder sounded. A chill wind blew over the battlefield as black clouds gathered.

Laisren watched Finn and feared whatever would happen next. He'd never seen him so angry.

Hate filled Finn's eyes—fading from blue-gray to light-flecked crimson—as he watched the conflict before him. He stood unnaturally still, his hands clenched in fists, his head lowered, just staring.

Finn stepped forward. The mist followed, keeping him centered as he advanced into the Dayigan line.

Many soldiers backed away. The few who dared remain near fell in pain. Arrows shot Finn's way but crumbled as dust when they crossed the circle's border.

"This was a peaceful land," Finn's voice echoed over the field. "But you have created *chaos* here. *Look what you made!"*

He lifted his hand to the sky. Thunder sounded. A dozen feet above the battle, a thick mist appeared, a mile-wide mist formed of countless streaks of crimson rapidly twisting around one another.

"Look at the chaos you have made on *our* shores."

Thunder rumbled.

The battle ceased as all eyes locked on the strange mist. Fear washed over all—Dayigan and Feah alike.

"Hail Morgana," Finn shouted. "Hail to the Dark Mother." He lifted his hands to the sky. Thunder echoed. "Hail, Morgana. Hail to the Dark Mother. Let me feast on the chaos around me. Let me drink in the shouts and clashing of weapons and the pain."

Finn lifted from the ground, but not by his wings, which stayed at full span and motionless.

Thunder echoed, and the wind grew stronger and colder. "Let me drink in the anger and the fear. Hail Morgana! Empower me. Let *everything* these Humans did to our people be a weapon in me. Hail to the Dark Mother!"

The entire mist moved toward Finn. It funneled into a stream flowing into Finn's mouth and eyes. His head and back arched as he faced upward. His arms, legs, and wings thrust rearward.

Laisren jolted toward him, wanting to end this, but stopped. He knew he could only watch.

Finn's pale skin paled further, freckles fading until he was as white as snow. The Irefaery Star on his chest glowed crimson, as did the tattoo of the torc.

When he had absorbed the entirety of the mist, Finn released a feral roar that spoke of pain and power intertwined. He opened his eyes, sockets wholly filled with crimson light.

He thrust both his hands at two Dayigan soldiers, and crimson light shot from his palms as twisting rays, striking them.

Both soldiers cried out as their uniforms faded, aged, and ripped. The mail beneath it rusted and broke apart. The leather cracked. Their skin rotted on their slick red muscles and their muscles rotted too. Foul fluids spilled onto the ground. The decay continued to their organs as the stench of vile putrefaction wafted out. All the while, the soldiers screamed in utter agony until they no longer possessed the organs for voice. Finally, as meaty bones, they fell.

Horror, like a wave, exploded throughout the Dayigans. In panic, the soldiers fled, even as their leaders ordered them to stand and fight.

Finn ascended, casting his hands toward the frenzied Humans. He cast a broader ray of light that swept across the crowd.

Each soldier brushed by the light screamed as they putrefied.

No longer did the Dayigan leaders call for attack but for retreat.

Finn followed, flying above them as he cast ray after sweeping ray with unrelenting hate.

Hundreds of soldiers fell screaming in rancid decay. The nightmarish sound deafened. The horrible stench sickened.

The soldiers passed their fort, hurrying straightway toward their ships.

Finn followed, but faltered. He cried out in pain and fell from the sky, hitting the ground with force.

Laisren rushed to him. "Finn, you must stop this. You are using magic far beyond your abilities."

With shaking arms, Finn pushed himself up from the ground and looked at Laisren. Blood dripped from his eyes and nose. "They killed him." He panted. "They killed my brother." Finn lifted his shaking hand. "I can't let any of them escape." He cast light at the nearest ship.

A large section of the ship's aft rotted away and splashed into the water, yet the ship stayed afloat, rocking in the disrupted tide.

All five ships began departing—men cutting through mooring lines and heaving ropes into the water—even as the remaining soldiers rushed to board.

Finn pushed himself up and attempted to run toward the ships. He managed a few hurried paces before stopping and setting his hands on his knees.

"Finn," Laisren implored, "if you continue with this, you'll die."

"*Let me die, then!* As long as I take them with me."

Laisren looked toward the sky filled with black clouds. "*Mother, please.* Remove this power from him. 'Twill kill him."

"No," Finn said through clenched teeth. "I can't let *any* of them escape." He attempted a limping run toward the ships.

Finn stumbled. He cast again yet hit nothing. He returned his hands to his knees and panted.

"Mother, fuck's sake, *please*," Laisren shouted to the sky. "I can't lose him. I need him." He looked to Finn, so wearied, yet still trying to fight. "I love him, mam."

The black clouds shattered into countless ravens and flew away.

Finn fell to the sand.

Laisren checked Finn's heartbeat, which was weak but beating. Though unconscious, he lived, though barely.

On the gruesome field littered by hundreds of decaying dead, Laisren kissed his lover's lips and held him in his arms.

CHAPTER TWENTY-SEVEN

Within the Temple Grove, within the circle of ancient oaks, Lann stood and watched Chief Kaie.

Her eyes closed, Kaie stood postured and serene within the ring of seven druidesses. They all maintained the same calm, as if they slept peacefully though standing.

Lann dropped his mace with a thud on the grass.

Their tranquility was such a contrast to the hell he'd just departed that seeing it overwhelmed him. The beauty of it hurt him, as if he gazed at a blue sky after years in darkness.

Even the people in the Temple Grove just outside the ring of oaks clamored in a panic as Tierna Bévinn and her assistants rushed to attend to the injured. The infirmary overflowed with casualties, with more laid out on the grove's grassy floor.

But that was behind him. Here was peace. Lann hated to disturb it. However ...

"Chief," he whispered. "'Tis important, Chief."

She opened her eyes and looked his way.

"The Humans are gone, Chief," he said, his words joyless. "All of them. Gone altogether from our lands, them."

Kaie sighed in relief. "Praise the Three Mothers." She smiled, but only for a moment. Her cheer faded at the sight of him. "But that's good news, aye?"

It should have been. Lann knew he should have been elated, but he felt as if he would weep or vomit. He kept seeing his wife's lifeless face with every blink of his eyes.

"'Tis, yes," he mumbled.

"Druidesses," Kaie said, "report to Tierna Bévinn. We must put all of our efforts into healing."

The women, including Kaie, rushed away.

Lann followed. "Chief, have you seen me sister? She should've brought me daughter back here."

"No," Kaie said as she walked, "but I've been in the ritual. *Tierna Bévinn*," Kaie called.

Bévinn approached. "Chief." She nodded. "If you're ready to take command, I—"

"No need. 'Twould take too long to get me caught up, and you're more than capable of maintaining command. My druidesses are at your disposal, as am I."

"Thank you, Chief."

"Have you seen Treasa?" Kaie asked.

Bévinn shook her head. "She must not have come back yet."

"What about my daughter?" Lann spoke up. "Lannah."

"I'm afraid I don't know your daughter, but we've set up a camp for unattended children. I'll find someone to show you the way."

"Is Ubaz there?" Lann asked. "Treasa's son."

"I'm sorry." Bévinn began away. "I'm not really sure who's there. 'Tis been confusion."

"Healer!" a shout sounded as Laisren and Nekesa rushed into the grove. They carried Finn, unconscious, by his shoulders and ankles.

"Someone help us," Laisren called, his voice cracking around the words. "He's severely seid depleted." He spotted Kaie and hurried Finn to her.

"Set him down," Kaie said.

Laisren and Nekesa complied, and Kaie knelt over him.

Kaie lay the back of her hand on his forehead. "I can't get a proper reading on his seid levels, but his body is shutting down. Get him to the infirmary."

"I'm sorry, Chief," Bévinn called as she tended to a man with a deep stab wound through his arm. "The infirmary's full. Many people are in critical condition."

"*You will help him*," Laisren shouted. "This man single-handedly drove away the Dayigans."

"*Laisren*," Kaie rebuked. "Would you be disrespecting the druidesses like that if your mam was here? I think not. Morgana wouldn't have had it, and neither will myself."

"Apologies."

Kaie gave him a stern look. "Get Finn to the altar in the center of the grove. I'll get supplies." She dashed toward the infirmary.

Lann neared Nekesa. "Do you know where Treasa's gone to?"

"We got separated," she said as she helped lift Finn. "The little girl was not with the other captives, so Treasa stayed behind to find her."

"In the fort?" Lann asked.

"I doubt she is still there. It was some time ago." She hurried away with Finn.

Lann watched them leave, carrying his injured friend. He worried for Finn, for his sister and daughter. He mourned for his wife and Cal. His world had collapsed around him, and he felt sick.

"Does anyone know where Ubaz is, at least?" Lann called to no one in particular.

A passing druidess answered back. "Treasa told him to hide. He's in the temple somewhere." She hurried along.

Lann nodded.

—

In a cavernous room just outside the Temple Grove, Lann stood, the stone-cased doorway behind him. This place was dark and calm. On either side of him, one- and two-story wooden structures towered, nearly touching the curved stone ceiling. Doors led into separate apartments where the druidesses lived. But his eyes remained on the yellow door. Cal and Treasa's home.

Ubaz was not there, Lann knew. Home was not a hiding place.

He jumped from the floor and flew to the top of the building. It was a tight squeeze between the flat wooden roof of the apartments and the curved stone ceiling above them, but he grabbed onto the roof, folded his wings, and pulled himself into the murky slot.

Years of dust coated the roof in thick layers. Lann crawled on his hands and knees, lowering himself to slide on his stomach under the lower sections.

"Ubaz," he called as he searched. "Ubaz, 'tis me, your Uncle Lann."

No answer. He kept searching. The rough ceiling above him sloped gradually lower the further back he crawled. Soon, on hands and knees was no longer an option. Lann continued on his stomach, dragging himself through who knew what and barely able to see. Dust lingered as a cloud around him, leaving a chalky taste in his mouth.

"Ubaz," he called again.

He heard a noise, slight but indicating some sort of motion. He began toward it as quickly as the cramped space allowed.

At last, Lann saw the vague silhouette of a small Terovae curled on his side.

"'Tis me, Ubaz. Your Uncle Lann."

"You're enchanted, you," Ubaz said, inching back. "I heard 'em talking."

"I'm not enchanted no more, boy. Come on. I came to get you. The Dayigans are gone now."

"Me mam said to hide 'til she came for me." There was fear in his voice.

"Your mam's out. Probably helping people. There's loads of people that need helping right now."

"Hurt people?"

"Aye, loads of hurt people. You know how your mam is. She'll be making them better now. She's a good one, your mam."

"She *is* that," said Ubaz. "And my daddy, he's out helping people as well?"

Lann sighed, blowing dust. "Ubaz," he started. He couldn't say it. All the hurt Lann was trying not to feel swelled up in his throat, choking him far worse than any dust.

"Ubaz, our Cal, he ..." He'd started now, no changing the subject. Lann would either need to lie or continue. He hadn't spoken the words aloud to anyone, and now he'd need to say them to a twelve-year-old boy. He wished he could see Ubaz's face, but he was equally glad he couldn't. It would make it harder, seeing him. Perhaps such horrible news was best whispered in the dark.

"Our Cal didn't make it, Ubaz. The Humans killed him dead."

"No!" Ubaz cried as he scooted back as far as the confines allowed. "No, you're lying. You're enchanted, you."

"He died brave, your da." Lann tried to keep his words strong but failed. "He was fighting for the whole Feah tribe, him, for you and us and everyone."

"I don't believe you."

Lann needed to get to him, to hold him, as much for Ubaz's sake as his own. Lann heard sobbing from the silhouette. And as if the boy had given him permission, Lann's own tears fell.

No words could console this moment. Lann didn't try. He couldn't speak, even if he wanted to. And so they remained in the dark, hidden from the world, mourning the people they'd lost.

—

Ubaz hadn't spoken since he and Lann had left the hiding spot. Rejoining the desolated world wasn't something either of them wanted, but Lann needed to find his daughter, and Ubaz needed to find his mother. The common goals drew them out of hiding.

They walked through the Temple Grove. A growing number of bloody injured people filled it, and druidesses rushed about in frenzies.

Lann and Ubaz walked through the area outside the temple, where more people rushed about, everyone looking for someone.

Lann's panic and anger drained, leaving him quiet and distant, like the world around him was something he wasn't quite a part of. Ubaz became a walking, teary corpse.

Even before they reached the area for unaccompanied children, Lann could hear it, a choir of sorrow, unlike anything he'd ever heard. Some children they passed were so young that they'd yet to grow feathers on their wings, but these babies cried in anguish and fear beyond what any of them should know.

Lann wondered how many of these children had received the same grave news he'd given Ubaz—the same news he'd need to give his daughter when he found her.

"Lannah," Lann called to no point in particular. It was but one name among the many being called out.

Lann saw a woman who appeared to have authority over the area and approached her.

"Have you seen Lannah? Or Treasa?"

She cupped her hand on the back of her neck, rubbing. "No, I haven't seen either of them."

"But they should be here by now. I know Treasa would've brought Lannah here."

She looked up at him. "I'm sorry, Lann. I haven't seen either of them."

Lann nodded. "Could you do us a kindness and watch after the lad here? He hasn't ate since all this started."

"Of course."

Lann turned to Ubaz. "I'm off to go find your mam and your cousin. I need you to stay here and have some food, all right? Your mam would want that."

Ubaz just stared at Lann with sad blue eyes.

"Come on." The woman lay her arm across Ubaz's shoulders. "We'll get you well fed and you can play with the other children."

She ushered him away.

—

Lann remembered grinning ear to ear and staring into Moyra's eyes as the two of them stood face to face. Kaie wrapped a rope—braids of white, yellow, and purple—around their hands, joining them. Their friends cheered and threw flower petals.

Now Lann stood despondent, just inside the Temple Grove's circle of oaks.

Beside the impressive standing stone marking the grove's center, Chief Kaie stood over Finn. He lay on a stone altar at table height.

It was the spot where Moyra and Lann had been married.

Finn appeared to be sleeping, as if nothing were wrong, but the worried looks on Laisren and Nekesa, who watched over him, told another story.

Lann hadn't had the mental space to worry about Finn. Now, as he looked on, he thought of their silly antics, always getting into some kind of fun trouble. When Cal had moved to the temple village, he'd asked Lann to look after his brother, and Lann had, even more than Cal had meant.

Lann approached Kaie. "Is he doing better?"

"He is a bit," she said.

"Chief, I still can't find me sister or wee Lannah."

"Laisren told me about Cal and Moyra. Mothers help us."

Lann nodded sadly.

Finn stirred some and opened his eyes. Lann and Laisren rushed to his side.

"I'm here." Laisren took his hand.

"Are they gone?" Finn asked weakly. "The Dayigans?"

"They are, yes," Laisren said. "All of them, as far as we can find."

"I didn't get him," Finn mumbled. "That bastard commander."

"You can't be certain," Laisren said.

"I'm certain." He seemed shocked, his eyes wide. "I saw them all with my mind. Hundreds of them, killed I. Two hundred and twenty-two. And I watched them die, so awful. So fecking awful. I heard them screaming and screaming, but I couldn't stop meself. No." He panted. "But the commander wasn't one of them."

"Why *two hundred and twenty-two?*" Laisren asked.

"I'm not sure. To be honest, I can't count that high. 'Tis just the number that came to my mind, so I knew it." Finn turned his eyes to Laisren. "Does it mean something?"

Laisren glanced at Kaie, and they shared a look. "It doesn't matter right now," he said.

"What about Treasa," Lann asked, "or Lannah?"

"Lann," Kaie said gently. "Finn needs his rest now."

Lann nodded.

Kaie led Lann a few paces away, and Nekesa approached.

"I am very sorry about your sister," Nekesa said. "I tried to go back for her, but there were too many soldiers. She was a brave woman."

"She *is* a brave woman, her," Lann said firmly. "You said she was looking for more prisoners?"

"Yes. We emptied the dungeon by the main gate, and Treasa went to see if they held the girl anywhere else."

Lann looked at Kaie. "Treasa said you and her were in that fort of theirs before, when it were new. Had a grand tour, said she. Is there anywhere else they'd've kept captives?"

"Not that I saw," Kaie said. "And that commander would have shown us, I'm certain. He was flaunting his fort's might and defenses."

"On the boats then," Lann said. "That's where they must have put me daughter. And Treasa would have figured it out and went there as well."

"The ships have been gone for quite a while," Nekesa said. "And the Dayigan Empire is massive."

Kaie pinched the bridge of her nose and sighed. "There might be a way to figure out where they are." She looked up. "*Laisren*, could you come here to me, please?"

Laisren, who had remained at Finn's side, excused himself with a kiss on Finn's lips. He joined the others.

"Laisren," Kaie said. "Finn is on the path to recovery, so you have no reason to worry about him any longer. If you would, I need you and Lann to go to a Dayigan we've taken prisoner. I'm sure your sort of magic will make him *cooperative*."

The words seemed to make Laisren uncomfortable, but after a pause, he nodded.

"These are desperate times now," Kaie said as she folded her arms. "And we need to be restoring the peace in the Feah lands." She looked away. "I give you my leave to make that Dayigan tell us where they took our people. Take as long as you need and"—she closed her eyes—"use whatever means are necessary to do it."

"I understand," Laisren said. "I will make him talk."

"My chief," Nekesa spoke up. "I mean, Chief Laisren. I may have a better way to make the Dayigan talk." She looked at Kaie. "But I will need herbs and other materials."

Kaie nodded. "Right, thank you, Nekesa. Whatever the temple has to offer is yours to use. I'll show you to our herb pantry."

—

"You captured this Human?" Lann asked Laisren as they walked a hall just off the Temple Grove. Lann had barely spoken a word to him before. He didn't trust Laisren—this wizard of wicked magic—and it was hard to wrap his head around the fact that this was the same scrawny dirty little boy Lann had known, somewhat, as a teenager.

After a pause, Laisren said, "I'm told he's not a Human, but I haven't seen him myself. The Feahs captured him before I arrived."

"A Terovae then," Lann said. "Must be one of them that chased Finn when he left home."

Laisren stopped. He looked away. "Finn mentioned this man to me. Back home, we found Dayigans near our village. We fought them, and most died, but the last one ... Finn pleaded with me to let that last man live. He spoke of a Dayigan his brother had let live—this captured Terovae up here, I'm certain. I told him we needed to protect our location, but he was so upset." Laisren looked down. "Now, so much blood stains the hands of my love."

"Finn did what he needed to do."

"True. But he shouldn't have needed to, not him, not *Finn*. I fear he'll never be the same."

Lann said nothing, but he knew Laisren was right. And not just about Finn. The Feahs had lost much more than the dead and missing. A part of every remaining person was gone as well. Not two hours ago, the chief archdruidess had all but asked Laisren to torture a prisoner. Lann wondered if the Feahs would ever be the same.

Laisren lifted his palm, holding a small off-white bag the size of a chicken egg tied with brown twine. It was the spell Nekesa had made. "We should get this over with," said Laisren.

They continued down the hall.

Entering the makeshift cell, Lann and Laisren found the rectangular wooden herb rack from the ceiling had half fallen with one end to the floor. A belt was looped around the fallen section, with the leather loop's other end around the Dayigan's neck. His arms dangled limply. His lower half sat awkwardly—at least one leg was broken—in a pool of dried blood.

"*Fucking bastard!*" Lann shouted. He charged the dead man and punched him in the face. He kept punching, even as thick, putrid blood coated his knuckles.

"Lann!" Laisren grabbed him and pulled him back.

"I have to know where they took them."

"'Tis over, Lann."

Lann panted. "I'll find them on me own then. I'll search their whole fucking empire, meself."

"Their whole empire?" Laisren grabbed Lann's shoulders and looked into his eyes. "You must understand what that means. The Dayigan Empire starts a hundred and forty miles down and across the river from the Feah lands, and it borders the river for well over two thousand miles—*two thousand*—with countless ports. About halfway along that distance, it begins to border both sides of the river, with more ports there too." Laisren released Lann and breathed.

"Condolences, Lann, truly, but your sister and daughter, they're ... they're just gone."

CHAPTER TWENTY-EIGHT

Three days after Cal's death, Finn stood within the singular circular room that made up his twenty-foot-wide house.

The room was nothing special, but Finn liked its simplicity. The roof was straw over exposed log rafters. The wall was a mix of dried mud and straw smeared over an unseen interior of woven sticks. An old, beat-up shelving unit held pots and crockery shoved in haphazardly. The bed against the wall was simple. In the center of the dirt floor, within a ring of random rocks, a low fire burned. Instead of anything fancy, like benches, Finn kept a few short horizontal logs for seating around the fire. Cal's son, Ubaz, sat on one of the logs, but the two said nothing.

The room comforted Finn. His attire did not.

Finn hadn't worn a shirt in a long time. The dull gray, long-sleeved tunic—this, with a laced V-neck and a low, laced V-back—suffocated him. Every time he lifted his arms, he pulled at the thin wool fabric. Every time he bent his arms, the tubes of cloth constricted his shoulders and elbows.

Perhaps it was easier to be annoyed with some shirt than to remember why he wore it.

Finn looked at Ubaz, who wore a similar shirt. The boy's shoulder-length ginger hair was clean and combed. His face was clean, too, for the most part. But his expression was blank with despair.

"Come on, lad," Finn said gravely. "'Tis time to say good-bye."

—

Under a clear, cool night, a thirty-foot-tall tree towered above a grassy field. Vines of purple wisteria in bloom twisted up the mighty trunk. People entered the field and filled it. Sad people. Lost people. They roamed, occasionally pausing in melancholic conversations. Trivial words were little comfort, but they tried. "She'll be missed." "He's with the ancestors now." "I remember her fondly." Most remained quiet. It was too much for anyone to digest. So many deaths at once.

Finn walked aimlessly, with lost little Ubaz trailing behind him. Finn had cried a lot and would again, but now he wasn't. He supposed that was good.

Stopping, Finn stared up at the tree. He couldn't make out the large wooden platforms built in its highest branches.

Ubaz looked up too. "D'you know which one me daddy's on?"

The boy's words cut through him. Finn gritted his teeth as his eyes watered. He tried to speak, but his aching throat formed no words. He breathed. "No," Finn sniffed. "No, there's too many up there. I'll ask the druidesses later, all right."

Ubaz nodded.

Finn looked at the druidesses circling the top of the tree, guarding the dead.

And he looked toward the grimmer circle farther out, the ring of vultures and other carrion birds.

"Finn," Nekesa said as she approached. She wore a long, backless purple dress with a long black cloth over her left shoulder. A purple scarf tightly circled her head, its base covering her ears and following the top of her forehead. Its peak was pleated and formed a halo. "I offer my comfort for your loss." She bowed her head. "The chief sent me with his apologies for being late. He is working on something very important."

"I need him here with me."

"*Very important.* Or he would be here. He will arrive soon, he assures."

Finn sighed, paused, nodded.

"What is this place?" asked Nekesa, straining her neck to look up.

"This is the Tree of Silence here. My people think 'tis wrong to put the dead in the ground to rot and contaminate nature. So, the druidesses cleanse the bodies and place them high up on platforms above. Then they covered them up with a nice white cloth. Tonight, we say goodbye. Some people fly up there to say it directly, but I won't be doing that—unless the boy wants to. After the ceremony, the druidesses let the vultures come in. *And to Nature, they will return.*"

Ubaz sniffed. "I don't want the birds to take me da."

Finn placed his hand on the back of the boy's head and gently turned it so Finn could gaze into those sad eyes. "Your da's not up there, lad. He's done with that body, now. 'Tis empty. Our Cal's ..." He paused, trying to stay strong for the boy. His voice cracked around the words. "Cal's with the ancestors now, in za. Mother Ashatra's getting him ready for a new birth, a new body, a whole new life."

"But I don't want him to be some wee baby, either, crying all the time." Ubaz grew angry. "I want him to be me da, like before." He jerked himself from Finn's hand.

Nekesa touched Finn's shoulder. "If I may?"

Finn nodded and stepped aside, allowing Nekesa to near the boy.

"Your father will not be a baby for a while," said Nekesa. "For now, he will watch over you and guide you, along with the other Feah ancestors. But tonight, you must say goodbye to him."

"I don't want to say goodbye to him either." Ubaz jumped from the ground, spread his orange wings, and flew away.

"Should we go after him?" Nekesa asked.

Finn shook his head. "The boy knows these woods and knows not to go off far. I think he needs some time on his own. To be honest, I'm about ready to fly off meself."

"Should I leave you alone?"

Finn shook his head. "No. Thank you for coming. Should we walk?"

"If you like."

They began a somber amble through the mourning people, navigating weeps and sobs and unhappy hugs.

"You look nice," Finn said.

"Thank you. The druidesses gave me the cloth and the dye. In Dinikimera, purple is the color to honor Mama Ashatra."

"For us as well." He motioned to the wisteria twisting up the Tree of Silence. "The druidesses keep them in bloom for all except for the two coldest months of the year. Is your people's funerals much like this one here?"

"My people are the Anordúla now, and most are from the Five Tribes. I assume this is what we would do, but we have not yet needed to. Only two have died since our formation. As you know, there was nothing left of Chief Morgana. For the other, the Anordúlas closest to him returned him to his former tribe. They returned to us with only a skull."

"Yes," Finn said. "After the excarnation is done up in the Tree of Silence, the druidesses come back for the skulls."

Some of the people Nekesa and Finn passed gave them strange side glances, as if the Feah were uneasy with the two being there. Finn tried to ignore it, but it kept happening.

Finn continued with Nekesa, saying, "Then there's the placement ceremony. The druidesses carve the skulls of the honored dead well nice with designs and then display them on the shelves in the Hall of Ancestors in the temple. That's rare. They stack normal folks in the crypts behind the shelves or wherever the family thinks is right. Loads of people bury their dead under the fire in the center of their homes."

Another two people stopped talking when Finn neared and gave him that uncomfortable glance before looking away.

"Why do they keep staring at me like that?"

"They remember," Nekesa said.

"Remember what?"

"These are the same people who we fought."

"Aye, when they was under the Dayigan's spell."

"I am sure they know that on a conscious, rational level. They know, too, that you saved them and the Feah lands. But on a deeper, primitive level—where fear comes from—you are the monster who shot bolts of chaos into their chests. Too, we are the wicked witches from their faery tales."

Finn looked around, catching more stares before they turned away.

"I don't want my people to fear me."

"It is what it is," Nekesa said. "If uncomfortable looks bother you, you have not been an Anordúla long enough."

As Finn continued to scan the surrounding crowd, he saw a figure far different from the rest. The stranger—seven feet tall—wore a black hooded robe obscuring every part of himself, except for his hands, which were only bones. A raven perched on his shoulder.

The people near him altered their course just enough to avoid him, yet without seeming to notice he was there.

"You see him?" Nekesa asked.

Finn nodded, staring.

"If you want to worry about someone watching you, that is the one who should concern you. The Grim Baron, Mama Ashatra's collector of souls, has been watching you for a while."

Finn looked at her. "Why? Because I killed all them soldiers by the river?"

"He has been watching you much longer than that. Since Chief Morgana snatched you from his bony fingers."

Finn returned his eyes to Death, and fear ran cold through his veins. "Why didn't you tell me?" He couldn't take his eyes off the otherworldly figure. His heartbeat throbbed in his ears.

"What good would it have done you to know?"

Finn rushed toward Death, pushing his way through the crowd.

As frightening as the Dark One looked at a distance, he looked ten times more frightful up close: his towering height, his bone hands, the fog wafting up his tattered robe.

Finn had had it in his mind to demand answers, but he melted. Slouching, Finn's words were a meek query: "Why are you following me?"

The Dark One was silent as he gradually turned his head Finn's way. Finn could see the face within the shadow of the hood—a nightmare of leathery, mummified skin clinging tightly to his skull. His eyes were hollows.

"I need not follow thee, Finnán ó Ríona," said Xanorael, his voice a slow, groaning whisper. "Lo, thou dost rush towards me of thine own accord."

A hand touched Finn's shoulder. He jumped.

"Sorry," Laisren said. "I didn't mean to shock you. Who are you talking to, then?"

Finn looked back to where the Dark One had stood. Nothing. He looked around. Gone. Finn looked back at Laisren.

"Glad you made it here," Finn said. "Finally."

"I was working on something to help protect the Feah. But it proved futile."

"Against the Dayigans? You think they'll return."

"I do, definitely."

"As do I, as well."

"We'll discuss it later. It looks like I'm just in time." Laisren motioned.

At the base of the towering Tree of Silence, its trunk wrapped in purple wisteria, Kaie stood, her head bowed. The mourners gathered around her.

"Tonight," Kaie addressed the crowd, "we gather to say goodbye to our brothers and sisters, mothers and fathers, husbands and wives, aunts and uncles. And children. This horrible tragedy has touched everyone in the Feah lands. But we must remember that *death is but a transition*. The time our loved ones spent here in their garments of flesh—now laid peacefully above us in the tree—was only a fraction of their existence. They lived many lives before and have many lives yet to come. And when we meet again—though we may not recognize them with our eyes or our minds—we will know them with our souls and hearts and be together."

Finn didn't feel present in this unreality. Laisren wrapped his arm around him and held his hand. Finn pressed himself against Laisren's side, trying desperately but futilely to gain just the tiniest comfort from the sorrow he felt.

"But for now," Kaie continued, "as much as it pains all of us, we must say goodbye to our loved ones, as the Dark One leads them down into the shadowed land of za. There, Mother Ashatra will welcome them in and give them a recess to rest, recuperate, and learn as they prepare to live again."

Finn wept into Laisren's shoulder. A part of Finn, a small part, thought how ridiculous he must look, a grown man. A part of him reminded himself that there were ways adults should behave in public. Finn tried to contain himself, but the grief was uncontainable. The loss was too much to hold inside.

Kaie raised her hands high and shouted, "Hear me, spirits! We release you from the world and from the bodies that were never truly you. Go into the arms of Mother Ashatra, for your work here is done. Go into the arms of Mother Ashatra, for your obligations here are done. Go into the arms of Mother Ashatra and prepare to live again. We will remember you and hold you in our hearts forever. We will honor you!"

Finn sobbed, unable to care who saw him this way. His brother and so many others were gone. And he'd killed hundreds of soldiers. Even as sorrow flowed from his eyes and sounded from his mouth, it seemed much more remained within him.

People began shouting out the names of their lost loved ones and releasing them from the world. There was no order to it, just whenever the family thought it right.

Finn knew it would be his place to do this for his brother. His throat ached, and he couldn't speak, much less shout. But he needed to do this.

Finn inhaled a shaky breath. "Cal ó Ríona," he shouted, "I honor you and release you."

CHAPTER TWENTY-NINE

Snuggled on a fur-lined cot about half a foot above the dirt floor and supported by a frame and legs of bark-enveloped branches, Finn stirred. The cot wasn't meant for two people, but he didn't mind being close to Laisren, especially on the chilly morning. Laisren's heat pressed against the back of his bare body. Laisren's arms wrapped around him.

Glimpses of sunlight filtered in through the gaps in the circular mud wall and the beat-up wooden door. More light beamed through the thatch of the steeply pointed roof with a smoky apex, black with soot.

Finn stood carefully, trying not to disturb Laisren, whose face was contented and peaceful. He grabbed his kilt from the floor and wrapped it around himself.

He stepped softly to the center of the room and grabbed a long stick. He poked the orange embers in the fire pit and tossed the stick in.

Nekesa, on a fur-coated mat on the opposite side of the hut, rolled under her thin sheet to face him.

"Awake so soon?" she asked, yawning.

Finn glanced back toward Laisren before nearing Nekesa. He whispered, "I'm going out to get us all some breakfast. Be back in a bit."

She nodded and closed her eyes.

—

Finn stepped out of the rough door of his house, softly closing and latching it. He stretched on the threshold. Today was that first chilly morning that told of autumn's approach. A light fog from the river lingered over the village. He pushed his wings forward, wrapping the sides of his bare shoulders in feathery warmth, and walked to the side of the house to piss on a post.

Afterward, Finn strolled through the collection of twelve homes that made up the fishing village. Each cottage—some smaller, some larger—had a short, round outer wall coated in a mix of mud and straw. The roofs were large cones of river reed that hiked a little higher in the front to allow the height of the door. The placements of the houses were random, with the surrounding sandy grass worn by years of bare feet. A few small rectangular structures of similar construction stood on stilts and contained the communal grain storage, along with a few other food items. Finn knew that three goats roamed within the village, but he didn't see them.

More than the goats were missing, Finn realized, and the few people who were about gave him those side glances he still hadn't gotten used to. He felt like a stranger with these people he'd known his entire life, and it didn't quite feel like home, not now. Yet, with all that had happened, he needed a home more than ever.

"Finn," a man called. He was one of three, about Finn's age, who sat on a grouping of logs beside the door to a house. The man, called Martin, smoked a long-stemmed pipe and used it to signal Finn over.

"Where are you off today?" Martin asked.

Finn took the pipe, took a long draft, and handed it back. "Fetching breakfast. Have you seen Lann around?"

Martin inhaled from his pipe. "Oh, 'tis a sad thing about Lann, to be sure. He's shattered by what happened to Moyra and Lannah. The poor fella's been in that Human fort, lurking like some lost black dog, him. 'Tis a shame, it is."

The other men nodded in downcast agreement.

Finn looked toward the fort, not visible from where he stood, and fretted for Lann.

"Are your eyes staying like that, then?" Martin asked. "With the red irises?"

Finn shrugged. "I suppose so, aye."

"So you know," Martin said, "me and the lads here aren't afraid of you like the rest of the village."

"The rest are afraid of me?"

"They are, yes. Some in the village—with wee ones, you know—took their families off to visit friends for a while. But not us. Them Humans got what they needed to get, and we're glad you gave it to them. Even if you did have to sell your soul off to the dark Faeries."

Finn nodded, glancing around the village. It had seemed nearly empty, but there'd been many deaths, and he knew many people had traveled to visit relatives. He hadn't realized that people had also left because of him.

"We were wondering, though," Martin continued, "how long are them other folks to be staying 'round yours? One dark wizard we might can live with, but a dark trio ..." He chuckled. "Mothers help us."

Finn folded his arms and looked down. "Laisren and Nekesa are just visiting. That's all."

"I didn't mean nothing by it. 'Tis just we're a respectable place here. You know that, Finn."

"Right," Finn said sadly. "I need to be getting on me way now. Good morning to ye."

—

Finn held his reed pole and cast his line into the water. The Hyvile River was the only part of his home that remained the same—an old friend who didn't care if he'd joined the Anordúlas. However, it was being rather stingy with the fish today. Finn stood on the shore, staring out across the water, trying not to think about the rest—the village, the deaths, the missing. It was just him and the sparkling water stretching as far as he could see. Puffs of fog drifted in a few random spots.

Despite his attempt to have a pleasant day by the river, Finn's pain lingered like a dagger in his chest that he tried to ignore. He sighed.

Nekesa walked up and stood beside him. "You would never know my homeland is just across that water."

"I've seen it myself," Finn said, "when I fly high enough. 'Tis all grayish-blue silhouettes, but I could see land. Is your city across there?"

"No. That is Dinikimera, but not my city. Alemiberi is much farther west. Out here, it is mostly forests and villages, somewhat like the Drevite lands." She paused. "I plan to return there. Soon."

"You're leaving us?"

"For a while."

Finn watched the great span of water—twenty-five miles, from what he'd heard. "'Tis a long way to fly over water—

nowhere to land and the lift isn't as good as on land. Dangerous stuff."

She chuckled as she took a seat on the shore. "I had planned to take a boat, actually, if the Feah could spare one."

"Oh, right."

She inched her toes into the water. "My people need to know what the Dayigans did here. I will try to gain an audience with the king."

Finn jabbed his fishing pole into the sand and sat down. "Do you think he'll help us?"

She shook her head. "No. If we'd known beforehand how bad it would get here, I would like to think that the king would have sent aid. It's hard to guess. But he definitely would not help now that the Dayigans are gone."

"They *will* return," Finn said.

"I believe you are right. But there is no way to know for certain. And a king must know for certain to act. Dinikimera's neutrality is very important for all our trade routes. You must understand, our trade does more than line the pockets of our merchants with coins. People need it to survive. Not just Dinikimerans, but other peoples, too. There are places *far* to the west where the land is nothing but sand." She scooped a handful of beach and let it slide through her fingers. "Miles and miles of dry sand with very few plants or life. It is called the desert, and the people who live there must trade rocks and metal for food. Otherwise, they die."

Finn looked at the sand and tried to imagine an endless beach with no river. "I understand. I think." He sighed. "I think I have to stay here." He glanced at her for reaction. "Here in the Temple Parish."

She continued to watch the water. "Have you told Laisren?"

"No. I don't know how to tell him that. Have you told him you're to go to Dinikimera?"

"Yes, I told him last night. But my news is less complicated than yours."

"Very complicated, mine. Laisren can't leave the Anordúla, and I don't want to leave him. Too, this is not my home no more, not really. The people don't want me here. But I have to protect the Feah."

"Home is home, even when they cast you out." Her eyes remained on the distance. "It is a sad reality, but you must help your people, if you can."

"True." Finn nodded, knowing she meant the words as much for herself as for him. "Will you be seeing your family in Dinikimera?"

"I plan to go to the capital city, not the city where I'm from."

"Two cities in one nation?"

She laughed. "We have much more than two."

"It must be a grand place. Still, you should visit your family even if you're not getting along with them. I've learnt recently ..." He looked down. "Well, sometimes you don't have as much time as you think you'll have."

"*Finn,*" Laisren shouted down the shore. "*We need to be going. We're to meet Chief Kaie soon.*"

"*I'm getting breakfast.*"

"*We'll need to skip it.*"

"*Right, I'm on me way then.*" Finn turned to Nekesa. "Promise me you'll visit with your family. At least for a bit. To be fair, your father had good reasons to not want you to leave and go do chaos magic. Just show him you're doing well and he has no reason to be concerned."

"I promise. And you promise me you'll talk to Laisren."

Finn nodded.

CHAPTER THIRTY

In the infirmary of the temple, Finn lay on one of the timbered examination tables as Chief Kaie slowly moved a large, clear crystal over his stomach, chest, neck, and head. At some points, the crystal glowed brighter; at some points, it dimmed. Kaie paused over the two extremes as if they meant something, taking some sort of mental note, but it meant nothing to Finn.

"What do you see?" Laisren asked.

Kaie shook her hand. "'Tis not good." She set the crystal beside Finn on the table. "Right after the battle, Finn's readings were clouded. Still, seid depletion seemed like the obvious cause of his sickness."

"What do you mean, *seemed*?" Laisren asked. "That's what was wrong with him. And he should be recovered now."

"'Tis much more complicated than that," Kaie said. "He's not depleted at all. On the contrary, he's still full of the chaos he drank in from the battle."

Finn sat up on the table.

"Finn." She took his hand. "People usually work up to magic on the grand level you used. Not only does someone normally take years, even decades, to learn to do what you did, but in that time she'd be strengthening her mind and soul to accommodate the powerful magics she's learnt. And that's after being born with high coronal seid levels from the start."

"But I had to do it fast, Chief. To save the Feah."

"I know. I'm not trying to ..." She sighed. "Finn, your soul's been severely damaged. Your strikes on the Dayigans caused large rips in your soul. The smallest are healing, but not the same as before. To put it in physical terms, they're leaving pronounced scars, scars infected with chaos."

"Will he be all right?"

"This is one of the very reasons why you need a higher power to guide you on your spiritual journey, Laisren. They help you avoid missteps."

"Will he be all right?"

She answered to Finn. "As long as you don't cause any more damage to your soul, you should be fine, I think. But you can't use any more magic, not until you're healed. *Or you will die.*"

Finn nodded. "And how long's that? 'Til I'm healed up?"

Kaie paused. "You must understand how very rare it is for someone to go from altogether unable to perform magic to able to use magic like you did. There's no real prescience for soul damage on this level. I consulted with the ancestors, but they weren't able to tell me much about the matter. I wish I could talk to Morgana. Can you?" She looked to Laisren.

He shook his head. "No."

She set her other hand on Finn's. "From what I've gathered, I'm thinking 'twill take centuries to heal."

"Centuries?" Laisren asked.

"Aye. These issues will follow Finn through a few lives."

Silence fell over the three as the gravity of the situation lingered. Finn's future selves, he knew, would not understand what had happened to them.

Laisren slammed his fist on the examination table. "'Tis not fair to our Finn. After all he's done for us."

"'Tis no bother, this," Finn said. "I saved the Feah. And maybe even all the Five Tribes and Anordúla. If I'd known beforehand that doing all that would cut up my soul, I would have still done it all the same. But I ..." He looked at Kaie. "I can't protect the Feah no more when the Dayigans come back."

"No," she said. "Not by any magical means. Physically, you should be fine."

Finn nodded with disappointment. "And Chief Morgana can't transfer the torc to you come autumn"—he looked at Laisren—"not now that I've made it a permanent part of me?"

"That is correct." Laisren turned away.

Finn touched the crimson depiction of the torc around his neck as he watched the floor. "I think I'd like to go now, if 'tis all the same to you."

"There is the matter with the boy," Kaie said. "The temple doesn't mind looking after him, but he really should be with family."

"Right," Finn said. "I'm not fit for that, am I. But I know where Lann is."

—

Finn landed centered on the sand of the Dayigan fort's courtyard. The fading evening filled the place with shadows, adding to its cold emptiness. It stunk of old death from the dozen soldiers abandoned on the ground. Foot-wide punctures had opened up the bodies and carrion birds had ripped up the rest.

Finn stared at the scratched-apart meat and scattered organs and recognized that he should feel something—disturbed, disgusted, distraught, anything. Instead, he felt some mild concern, but not for them; Finn felt concerned about his lack of concern. The *him* from a few weeks ago would have felt something, and he wondered what it meant that he didn't.

"Fuck the bastards." Lann's voice sounded across the yard.

Finn looked to see Lann by the opened door of a square house in the fort's southern corner, toward the river.

"I've been looking for you," Finn said as he approached. He could see into the house's shadowed interior, full of shelves stocked with various types of food.

Lann sat with his legs out straight and his back against the wall. His hand loosely grasped the handle of a tin cup on his lap. Beside him, a wooden barrel lay on its side with its uppermost board smashed in. Dark beer trickled from its cracks.

"They're not here, Lann."

"I know that." His voice was hopeless. "I know. Moyra, dead as a stone. And me sister and sweet daughter, long gone. I talked to Morgana's boy—the one you're keen on. The Human empire, says he, has got more ports than I could search in two lifetimes. And there's not a reason to think they'd keep them in a port town at all. They're just fucking gone, all of them." He leaned his head limply against the wall. "I just want to know what happened to them, that's all." He went silent and sat as still as a corpse.

Finn started to say something, but no words formed. He crouched down to Lann's level. "You need to be coming home now."

"Home? Bollocks." He threw the cup.

It didn't hit Finn, but it got close enough that he leaned to dodge, stabbing his hand into the sand to keep from falling over.

"What home's that, then?" Lann asked. "That fucking empty house with all their stuff in it? Those bastard Humans took everything from me. They can at least share their shite beer."

Finn looked down at the sand. "You've always been a good friend to me, Lann, looking out for me and all. I'm sorry I didn't stop the commander sooner. I let him get away."

"Now I've lost me fecking cup," Lann said.

Finn stood, snatched up the cup from the sand, and handed it to Lann.

Taking the cup like a prize, Lann proceeded to climb up on the barrel. It rocked and splashed. Lann dipped the cup through the broken side. Careful but shaky, Lann returned to his seat without spilling a drop.

Lann took a long drink. "I remember, you know. If them bastard Humans were to put a spell on me, they could've at least had the decency to make me forget what I done. I remember breaking down the temple ward. I remember fighting the druidesses. Killed one, me. Killed her dead. Those eyes, staring at me. And I remember handing over me one and only daughter. 'Go to the Human commander,' said I. 'He'll keep you safe.'"

Finn sat down, folding his legs under himself and slouching. He chewed his thumbnail. "I'm sorry, Lann. I should have killed that commander. He's still out there."

"You killed loads of them, though. Who would've thought, our Finn? Bastards deserved it." Lann lifted his cup. "To our Finn, the bastard-slayer." He drank. "Guess you're the one keeping us safe now with your magic."

Finn nodded sadly. "Right."

—

Finn's mace collided with Nekesa's with a wooden clap. His feet dug into the sandy beach as he pushed forward against her. He could see the determination in her grimacing face as the firelight flickered across her dark features.

She pulled back and swung low, aiming for his legs.

Finn jumped back, dodging, but he tripped. He fell to his butt on the sand.

Seizing the moment, Nekesa leaped forward and aimed the wooden tip of the mace to the center of his chest.

"You are getting much better," said Nekesa, drawing back her weapon and sheathing it. She reached out her hand to help him up.

"'Tis not enough, though." Finn grabbed her hand and jumped up.

Laisren approached. "Bit late for training."

"I needed it," Finn said. "The Dayigans'll come back, and I have to be ready for them. I might not have magic, but I'm getting skilled with a bow, and I'm learning the mace as well. I might could be the new temple guardian."

"Temple guardian." Laisren furrowed his brow. "You mean stay. Here."

Finn looked away from him, uncertain what to say.

Laisren sighed. "You might be right. The Feahs don't trust us, but you're still their hero. Magic or no, you're a symbol they can't afford to lose right now. It might be best if we stay."

"We?"

"Of course *we*, you idiot." Laisren smiled. "Unless you're trying to be rid of me."

"No, not at all. To be honest, 'tis been eating me up trying to figure it all out. I didn't think you could leave the Anordúlas."

Laisren took Finn's hand in his. "We'll figure it out, you and I. We both want the Feahs safe. We're both from here. But"—he looked to his left—"we'll discuss it later. Right now, we have a visitor." He nodded. "Chief Kaie."

"Chief Laisren." Kaie returned the nod. "Sorry about popping in on ye so late, but I couldn't pull myself away from the temple any sooner."

"'Tis not the slightest bother, Chief," Finn said. "We were just talking that I was thinking about—with your permission, I mean—I might take over Cal's position as temple guardian."

She smiled with a touch of sadness. "Right, thank you, Finn. But I think Lann would be better suited for it, in truth. I am delighted you're still driven to help the Feah, though. I may have a task." She looked across the black waters lapping against the shore. She slowly extended her arms, lifting her purple velvet cloak from her sides and letting a gust of wind wash over her and flow around her white dress.

"'Tis a beautiful night," she said at length. "I never get out to the river as much as I'd like to." She walked a few steps until the water rushed around her bare feet, then her ankles, and then just above the bottom of her dress.

"Here," Kaie said, "is the intersection of water, land, and air. Even in this desperate time, Mother Lágeya consoles us if we let her." She inhaled a slow, deep breath through her nose. Held it a few seconds. And exhaled just as slowly. "But that's not why I've come. We have to do what we must, to maintain peace in the Feah lands."

Kaie turned from the river to face Laisren, Nekesa, and Finn. "For years, we feared any negative action against the

Dayigan fort would bring retaliation from the Dayigan Empire. And, by the ancestors, when we finally went negative action, we went *negative action*, you be sure."

Finn began to speak, but Kaie gently raised her hand.

"What you did," she said, "it needed to be done. What we all did needed to be done. But that doesn't change the fact that retribution from the largest empire in the world remains a threat to us."

Finn glanced at Laisren.

"Let's sit," Kaie said, as she motioned to the small fire a few paces away on the sand.

As they walked, Finn said, "I think the Dayigans are coming back as well. That's why I was wanting to be the temple guardian."

Kaie sat on the sand, as did the others. "As ye all know, Chief Morgana revived the Anordúlas to protect us from this same retribution we now face. But 'tis clear now—though let me say first, no one's to blame—that the Anordúlas will not be enough to stop another attack by the Dayigans. Some time ago, I contacted the surrounding True Light nations, but they won't help us."

"Or cannot," Nekesa added.

"That be true," Kaie consented. "The rejection from Dinikimera was kind."

"You must understand," Nekesa said, "the hands of the Dinikimeran king are tied in this matter."

"Whatever the case," Kaie said, "we must turn elsewhere if we're to survive."

"You mean Vohcktara," Laisren said, intrigued.

"I can't believe I'm as much as giving it a thought." Kaie's words were weighed by uncertainty. "But aye, them."

It seemed to Finn that Kaie had crossed a line just by broaching the topic. He fidgeted uncomfortably. "But they're Dark Light, them."

"We're not exactly True Light ourselves," Laisren said. "Are we, my love? Except for Kaie." He looked intently at Finn. "You're thinking it, aren't you? You want to say it so badly it hurts."

Finn said nothing, but he gritted his teeth as he squirmed on the sand.

"They're *wicked*," Laisren began in a sing-song mocking manner, "and they use *evil* magic. The same fecking thing the Dayigans say about the Feahs, and the Feahs say about the Anordúlas."

"'Tis different, though, with them," Finn said. "They worship devil Gods and Demons."

Laisren crossed his arms and gave Finn a stare. He raised an eyebrow.

"Not like the Demon you ..." Finn trailed off. "'Tis different, that's all."

"Personally," Nekesa joined, "I have no problem with the Vohcks. However, my homeland does. So, I know, your allying with the Vohcktaran Kingdom would ruin *any* chance, ever, of any of the larger True Light nations helping you, while giving the Dayigans more reason to hate you."

"Your concerns are valid," Kaie said. "And I've struggled with them myself. But the other True Light nations already won't help us, and the Dayigans already hate us. Turning to the Dark Light is not ideal, but ..." She sighed and turned to Laisren. "Well, you lived there. Do you think they'd even help us at all, us being a True Light nation?"

He nodded. "Yes. If they can. The Vohcks tend to only dislike the True Light when the True Light is setting them on fire. The Academy had people from a range of backgrounds. You'll remember, when I attended, I was a Feah, not an Anordúla. They encourage the exchange of ideas. When I was older, I taught a class on Drevite culture. But, as far as helping us, they aren't a militaristic nation. And they are much smaller than the Dayigan Empire."

"I'd like you to give it a try," Kaie said. "If you would. You lived in their capital, so I assume you know their king."

Laisren laughed. "I do not. But I have some connections. I can most likely arrange an audience." He turned to Finn. "You got quiet. What are you thinking, my love?"

"I think we have to do it," Finn said. "I sucked up all the Anordúla magic into me and then broke my soul. And I let that commander escape."

"You'll like the city," Laisren assured, with a hint of excitement. "Tomorrow, Nekesa plans to leave for Dinikimera. We'll head east at the same time."

"You have my thanks," Kaie said. "May the Mothers bless you and the ancestors guide ye well."

CHAPTER THIRTY-ONE

In a wicker rowboat lined outwardly in leather, Finn sat backward, an oar in each hand, as he rowed steadily at a gentle pace.

Laisren, in the boat's rear, sat in front of him, facing him and facing forward. Currently, they said nothing, only enjoying the cool autumn breeze mixed with the afternoon sun warm on their skin.

The oars, in near unison, splashed down into the Hyvile and pushed through clear water, which churned and twisted around the paddles. The oars lifted, circled, and splashed again.

To Finn's right, the coast was less than a mile off. The woodland canopy had set aside its green for now to display a mosaic of orange and yellow leaves. To his left, sparkling water stretched as far as he could see.

Finn took a deep breath, trying to inhale the relaxation, as if it were a substance in the air he could consume. He needed it. Still, an ache lingered in his chest, the ache of sadness, the ache of an unrequited anger he could not fully ignore.

For two days, he and Laisren had traveled the Hyvile, taking turns rowing for most of the daylight hours. At night, they slept together on the shore.

Two days ago, Finn had needed to say goodbye to his remaining friends. Kaie, Lann, and Ubaz had seen them off.

Nekesa left at the same time in a borrowed boat she'd promised to return, though Finn knew the owner was dead.

Nekesa would have most certainly crossed the river by now. She'd be following the Dinikimeran coast as she traveled west toward the city she grew up in and ultimately to the capital.

The oars cut through the Hyvile with the sound of water twisting around wood.

"Would you look at how nice it is today?" Laisren broke the silence.

"It is, aye."

"You should try to relax some."

"I am trying." Finn rowed two more beats. "I'm just so angry now. And I can't do a thing about it."

"We are, actually. We're going to Vohcktara now to do something about it."

"Aye, that's true. But that commander's still out there. And he's not hiding in the shadows, guilty like. 'Tis not some dark secret, no. No, he's probably telling his mates, and they're all having a fine laugh about what they did to us. They'll be lifting their pints, cheering him on, telling him what a grand job he did, killing all them *fucking savages*. I keep seeing that in my head, them patting his back like he did a wonder."

"Never mind the commander," Laisren said. "Hopefully, the Vohcks will help protect us from future attacks. As hard as it is, we need to put what happened in the Feah behind us."

Finn nodded and kept rowing. And thinking.

A quarter of an hour passed before Laisren motioned to the shore. "We're nearly there."

Finn looked toward the land, examining the narrow rocky beach at the foot of twenty-foot cliffs topped with woodlands. Gulls hopped from rock to rock, diving noisily at the water.

A feeling of excitement kicked in. "We should go to shore," Finn said. "'Tis a big deal, this. I've never left the Five Tribes and barely left the Feah. It should be a grand thing entering a whole new nation. I'd like to walk in, feet on foreign soil, like."

"If you want," Laisren said. "You've already turned that way."

Finn hadn't meant to change course, but Laisren was right; he'd angled toward the large rocks. "So I have."

When they arrived, they pulled the boat up on the narrow beach and tied it to an old gray stump in case the tide came in.

Afterward, they flew up the cliff.

Finn scanned the surrounding woods. "Where's it start?"

Laisren chuckled. "There's not a line drawn on the ground. We'll have to walk east awhile before I'm certain we're properly there."

Finn looked around at the surrounding forest—Feah lands. Although he'd never been to this part before, it was still his home. He was sad to leave it but ready.

As they ambled through thick woods without a path to guide them, Finn looked around for any change to denote a foreign land. Having resolved to walk into this new kingdom, he resisted the urge to fly, to get there faster. He found he was just as eager to see this new place as he was to leave all that had happened at home behind him.

"D'you think I'll like Vohcktara?" Finn asked as they walked.

"I've been debating that in my head since we set off on the Hyvile. I'm leaning towards yes. 'Tis very different, Vohcktara."

"Do they have a temple same as ours?"

"They have multiple temples, but they're nothing like the Feahs'. The largest is the Black Temple in the city's heart. 'Tis a massive rectangular building with grand, black marble columns—as thick as trees—edging its sides. They support a large roof that's triangular in the front and angled flat down the sides. Under the roof and within the columns is a massive room where they house larger-than-life statues of the Gods, carved in black marble and seated on silver thrones."

"Dark Light Gods?" Finn asked uneasily.

"Aye, they are."

Finn nodded, taking in the words with quiet uneasiness. "And the king lives there in the temple?"

"He doesn't. The steps of the temple lead out into a large open area paved with stones. It holds statues and fountains, and other great buildings run along its sides. On the other end of the paved area stands the Ameprilya Palace. That's where the king lives."

Finn stopped and looked down. "It sounds so different. Are there a lot of people there?"

"There's a million people there."

"A million? No. That's not a proper number, a million. 'Tis an expression, that's all, like there's a million stars up in the sky or a million grains of sand on the shore."

"'Tis a proper number and there are a million Vohcks just in the city."

"A *million*." The number frightened Finn.

"You'll love it," Laisren assured him. "'Twill just take some time to get used to it, but you will. I did—except for missing you. We should stay there until winter comes and goes. I have some coins saved in the Vohcktaran bank, so we should be good. I was thinking we could stay in the fishing district. 'Tis not where most visitors choose, mind you, but they have rooms, and I think you'll be more at home there."

"That's like my fishing village?"

"Not really. But 'tis more similar than the rest of the city."

Finn grinned. "I think I'll love it there. 'Cause you'll be there."

Laisren flashed a large smile. "I've been thinking as well— but we don't have to decide right now. I think it would be nice—if you wanted—we could get married there. There's a beautiful place in the art district that would be perfect. You'll have to see it and—"

Finn leaned in and kissed his mouth. "I'd be delighted. All of it sounds grand." Finn stepped back and held both his hands as he gazed into his eyes. "We'll stay there a few months, living in their fishing village, and we'll get married there and invite the whole city."

Laisren laughed. "Not the whole city, Finn."

"The whole fecking million. 'Twill be fantastic." Finn sighed. "I really will try to make this a new beginning."

"I think we're here. Your feet ..." Laisren made a sweeping gesture toward the ground "... are now on foreign soil."

Finn looked around. "It looks the same as before."

"Well, what did you expect? The trees to be purple?"

"You said there'd be temples and statues and all."

"In the city. We're out on the outer edge of the Vohcktaran Kingdom."

Finn stepped back and looked up at the autumn canopy and down at the tangled shrubberies. Despite his uncertain expectations, he found himself relieved that nature remained the same here. He stooped and lifted a handful of Vohcktaran soil. He sifted the moist grains through his fingers, letting them return to the ground.

"I'll set up camp," Laisren said. "*You* have to go back to the boat and bring it here."

Finn stood. "Ach, you want me to go back to Feah lands when I just got here."

"You're the one who wanted to leave the boat behind. Go on." He slapped Finn's butt. "I'll find a spot, build a fire, and you can meet me there."

—

Laisren found an enormous flat rock near the craggy beach at the base of the cliffs. The water surrounded it, their own little raised island away from everything. Laisren had made a fire by the time Finn arrived with the boat, and they had helped each other fly the boat atop the rock.

As Finn caught dinner, Laisren rolled out furs to make a bed between the fire and the boat.

Finn noticed, with contentment, how they both seemed to flow into their respective tasks, as if they'd been setting up campsites together for years.

When it came time to eat, they sat side by side at the edge of the rock, their legs over the side, and watched the sun sink into the river.

"I wish we could just stay right here," Finn said.

"We could come back after we leave Vohcktara. I wouldn't mind spending the spring, right here on this rock, with you."

After they finished eating, they stripped down and ran off the side of the rock, diving into the river. It was first a bath as they soaped up and got clean, but it turned into a playful romp, laughing, swimming, and splashing each other.

In time, Finn and Laisren returned to the rock and didn't bother redressing. Instead, they lay on the furs Laisren had laid out and embraced each other under the stars.

Their kisses turned lustful as Finn lay atop Laisren. They ground their waists together, swelling against one another. Finn grabbed both rods together, stroking along with their writhing movements. Finn's other hand rubbed Laisren's arm and side.

The kiss grew deeper as Laisren slid his arms under Finn's wings, clutching his back and pulling him closer.

The pistons thrusting together within Finn's fist pumped harder and faster.

In time, Finn's lips parted from Laisren's and called out in pleasure. Laisren was not far behind.

Finn collapsed atop him, their sweaty, sticky bodies pressed together as their breathing slowed.

"We need another bath now," Finn said.

"In the morning." Laisren wrapped his arm around Finn.

CHAPTER THIRTY-TWO

"B y the Gods," she said, intrigued. "What marvelous sight have I happened upon this morn?"

The woman's voice pulled Finn from his slumber—warm against Laisren, furs under and atop them as they lay on the large rock surrounded by water. Sleepily, Finn looked up at a wingless woman in her mid-forties.

Frightened, Finn sat up and jumped back, crawling backward over Laisren as he grabbed a bow and snatched an arrow from his quiver.

"Apologies," she said. "I meant not to startle."

"You're Human." Finn's heart raced as his mind returned to when the Human commander found him in the arms of Kyran.

Laisren put his hand on Finn's wrist, pushing down the bow. "She's a Vohck," he said, yawning.

Finn lowered his bow, but not his guard, as he examined the woman.

She was stunning, with dark hair circled atop her head in a multitiered, braided bun ringed by a thin silver band. Silver earrings dangled. In striking contrast to her pale skin, black lined her dark brown eyes and shadowed her eyelids. Her long dress of thin vermilion cloth was pinned atop her shoulders and open down the sides, with five bands of black leather ringing down each arm to hold her sleeves in place. A leather band below her breasts and around her waist secured her dress. Her sandals were of the same leather, with strips crisscrossing up her calves.

"Your face isn't hairy," Finn said.

She touched her cheek with a perplexed laugh. "Should it be?"

Laisren stood, facing away from her as he wrapped his black kilt around his waist. "Only Human *men* have beards." He put on his leather robe. "He's only ever seen Dayigan soldiers."

"Ah," she said. "Yet beards are not fashionable with Vohck men. They shave their faces. Along with"—she glanced down Finn's torso—"*other areas.*" She grinned.

Finn covered his lap with the fur.

"I am Chariklia. I come here often, to this rock, to view the sunrise, yet never has the sight been quite so pleasing as today."

"Well met. I am Laisren." He approached her. "And this is Finnán."

Finn gave him an odd glance. "Finn," he corrected.

"We travel from the Drevite nations en route to Vohcktara."

"Truly? I've only just come from there and will return three days hence. I've come home for a brief visit. In the city, I *shine* as an actress."

"Have you performed in the Skote?" Laisren asked.

"Often. Is the Skote known to Drevites?"

"No." He smiled. "No, I attended the Academy."

"A man of two worlds. Fascinating. You *must* join me for breakfast and tell of your travels. There's a little restaurant in town I adore."

"Apologies," Laisren said. "I bear no coin."

"Spoke I of coin? I invite you both as honored guests. My purse will settle accounts."

Laisren looked to Finn with a silent question.

Finn nodded and shrugged.

"Then it is settled," she said. "But you will sing for your supper—as it were. I want to hear all about you. I've never met a Drevite before."

—

After Laisren and Finn packed up all their things into their wicker boat, they dragged it down a thin, sloped section of the rock island that led to the river. There, Chariklia waited by her rowboat. Soon after, they set off across the water to the mainland.

Laisren and Finn followed Chariklia's boat a short distance to a series of docks meant for various-sized boats and ships. Some were used, but most stood empty.

Once they were all on land—or at least on wooden decking—Chariklia motioned to steps carved into the forty-foot cliff face.

"The town of Makriá is just up there," she said.

It seemed silly to Finn to climb steps when he could have flown up to the top, but more so, it seemed discourteous to leave the Human behind. Laisren seemed to agree as he walked just behind her, chatting. Finn stayed back a few paces as he looked out over the glistening Hyvile—his river, even so far from home.

"Finn," Laisren called.

He looked up to see Laisren ten feet above, waiting by Chariklia at the top of the stairs.

Finn flew the remaining section.

Months ago, Finn had traveled to another world, yet even the tin trees of the Irefaery forest seemed more familiar than the bizarre town in which he landed. The path leading from the stairs passed between two-story buildings with off-white walls of stone. Finn touched the nearest cold, smooth wall. It had no lines of mortar but was like one enormous stone block stretching up to its roof of terracotta shingles.

Sliding his finger down the wall, Finn followed it to its corner. There, a narrow street was lined on either side with similar buildings, all side by side with no separation. They had similar walls and red-shingled roofs. Some had wooden-railed balconies overlooking the busy street. Ropes, running from windows to cross high above, held clothes swaying in the wind.

Humans and Terovaes filled the cobbled road. The men of both races had short haircuts, beardless faces, and wore sleeveless, belted tunics pinned atop the shoulders. The women, Human and Terovae alike, wore tunics like the men, but longer and belted higher, under the breasts. Most of the Humans added a wool cloak. The tunics were of various colors, but most of the people, regardless of sex or race, appeared to favor black, dark gray, or indigo. Likewise, both men and women lined their eyes in black.

"What do you think?" Laisren asked.

Finn turned to realize that Laisren and Chariklia had been watching his reaction to the town. Beyond them, he saw a large mosaic of countless little tiles. It depicted, on an indigo background, the head of a black ram with sinister red eyes.

"I'm not sure." Finn looked around the area. "Are there no plants at all here?"

"Look, there's some now." Chariklia pointed to a passing handcart filled with baskets of carrots, arugula, and cabbages.

"Right," Finn said with a laugh. "I think I do like it. There's an energy here. Exciting, like."

"That's the chaos in you." Laisren lifted a hand as if to feel it in the air. "It vitalizes us. 'Twill yet be stronger in the city."

"My friend's restaurant is just there," Chariklia said and began walking across the street.

Soaking up the surrounding energy, Finn followed Laisren and Chariklia through one of a series of wide stone archways that led into a shadowed room. The narrow space ran parallel with both the street and arches and held four tables surrounded by chairs.

One table held a group of six who laughed boisterously amid conversation and dining.

A counter came next, running parallel to the wall. It was tiled in designs of earthen-colored stone and four large bowls were recessed into its surface.

"Chari!" a Human man called welcomely from behind the counter. "I feared you'd miss breakfast. Who are these you've dragged along?"

"I found two boys, fresh from the untamed wilds, naked on a rock. I simply *had* to bring them."

"The orange-winged one is nearly naked now. I know Terovaes stay warmer than Humans, but you surely freeze in this autumn wind."

Finn shrugged. "A bit."

"A full belly will warm you. What will you have? I suggest pancakes." He tapped the rim of a bowl inset into the counter, the one filled with flat palm-sized disks of bread.

"Looks good, aye."

"A dozen?"

Chariklia answered, "A dozen all around, and for you as well, good Xander. I pray you join us."

"How can I refuse? And how favors you today, lovely Chari? Sweet or savory?"

"I'm feeling ... *sweet*." She pushed her shoulder forward with the word.

"As always. And you two? Would you prefer your pancakes covered in honey or cheese?"

"Honey sounds well nice," Finn said with a wide smile. "Thank you."

"Is it feta?" Laisren asked.

"It can be."

"I'll have that, then."

"Come," Chariklia said. "We'll take this table on the end."

After they took their seats, Chariklia faced Finn, gazing before she said, "You have the most fascinating eyes."

Finn jumped as if caught and jerked away, looking at the dusty stone floor.

"He is chaos attuned," Laisren said. "We both are, but him particularly so. We use chaos energy in our magic."

It seemed to Finn an odd topic to broach with a stranger, but Chariklia seemed all the more fascinated.

"The two of you are layers upon layers of intrigue." She looked at Xander. "They're sorcerers too."

"I heard." Xander approached, holding four terracotta plates of pancakes and began distributing them. "You seldom hear of people using chaos energy." He walked back to the counter.

"'Tis an ancient and long-forgotten path," Laisren shouted across the room. "We strive to revive it."

Fearing someone might overhear their topics, Finn glanced uneasily at the people around the table on the room's opposite end and at the large archways open to the street. No one took notice.

"If I remember," Chariklia began, "that is the domain of the wrath Demon, yes?" She grabbed a pancake with her fingers and lifted it. "I played her in a play." She hesitated before the bite. "What is her name? *Ignísekhet*."

"It is." Laisren smiled as if she'd mentioned an old friend.

Xander returned with four cups and a small bowl. He positioned the cups before each person. "Do you favor nuts?" he asked Finn.

"I do indeed, sir." Finn laughed.

Xander shook his head with a smile. "Of that, I have no doubt." He set the bowl in the center of the table. "Here are some crushed walnuts if you'd like them on your pancakes."

Finn eagerly grabbed a handful and sprinkled them over the plate.

Xander took a seat. "That's the purpose of your travels to Vohcktara? To start a chaos sect?"

Finn drank from the cup. "This is that grape beer we had before."

"'Tis not actually called that," Laisren said.

Chariklia laughed. "I think that's a marvelous name for it. I'll use it myself." She lifted her cup with a nod to Finn.

Finn took another sip. "'Tis not as strong as what we had."

"This is a restaurant, good Drevite, not a wine bar," Xander said. "I serve it quarter wine, three-quarters water."

"Still good," Finn said. "And the food as well."

Chariklia turned to Laisren. "You said you go to the city to start a Demonic sect?"

"We do not. We've had trouble from the Dayigans and seek assistance in the matter."

"Dayigans?" Xander asked. He turned to Chariklia. "Think you 'twas those same men who came here a few days past?"

"If they were, they were brutes."

"Dayigans here?" Finn mumbled through a mouthful of honeyed bread.

"Their identity was well suspected but not confirmed," Xander said. "I tried to accommodate them with hospitality, yet it proved futile. They came in here—about twenty of them—and filled the place wall to wall. Which is fine, of course, even with their rowdy manner. However, they began asking questions about witches. Well, I thought they needed magical supplies, so I nearly pointed the way."

"Aren't you glad I dissuaded you?" Chariklia asked.

"Quite so. Because when they continued their gripes, I realized their purpose was for trouble. I had to call upon the legionaries to escort them out of town."

"Are they still nearby?" Finn asked, anger blotting out his merriment.

"Honestly, 'twas not something that concerned me enough to keep up with."

"We need to find them," Finn insisted.

"'Tis not something that concerns us either," Laisren said. He turned to Xander. "Yet the place you nearly directed them to—a magic shop, I assume—is of note. I'm in need of materials for a working."

"You'll need to be more specific. We're not Vohcktara, but we do have a few magic shops with specialties of their own. What is your intent?"

"I mean to summon an Irefaery."

"That's not exactly your everyday spell?" Xander laughed. "I trust you plan not to release a troll in our treasured town."

"No." Laisren smiled. "Not a troll. And well tame."

"Mephistus?" Finn asked.

"Yes. We're far from the protection of the temple village and 'twould serve us well to have him with us."

"I know a place," Xander said. "'Twould be easier to show you than to direct one unfamiliar with Makriá. I close between breakfast and lunch. After we eat, I'll see you there."

—

Finn sat on a crate on the dock overlooking the river. In tense contemplation, he stared at the cup between his feet. He dropped a leaf, and it fell straight in.

Behind him, Finn heard a flap of wings and then footsteps on the decking.

"Chariklia said you'd come down here," Laisren said. "I thought the two of you would yet be exploring Makriá."

Finn grabbed up the leaf and dropped it. Straight in. "You talk like a Vohck here."

"I know not your meaning. I speak as I have always ... No, I hear it. Yet Vohcktara was where I lived from the age of thirteen to twenty-two."

"I know. 'Tis class how you talk. Real proper, like." He grabbed the leaf from the cup. "Did you summon Mephistus?"

"I did, yes."

Finn looked back, searching the area in an attempt to see the tromlee. "Where is he?"

"On his way here, I'd imagine. 'Tis not instantaneous." Laisren glanced at the cup. "You shouldn't be doing magic."

"'Tis not proper magic, this. 'Tis just something Nekesa showed me awhile back. I couldn't do it before."

"You shouldn't do it now. Chief Kaie said—"

"I know." Finn nodded, downcast. "I'm just thinking; that's all. I was asking around town about those men Xander mentioned. They weren't wearing their tabards, but everyone figures they were Dayigans all the same. They have a camp about two miles east of town." He looked at the water. "I found out how to get there."

Laisren sat down beside him on the crate. "We're putting all that behind us for now. Our priority is getting to Vohcktara."

"We *were* putting that behind us until it jumped right in front of us and waved its dirty asses in our faces. I have to go to that camp."

"What will you even do?"

"Something. I don't know. Maybe nothing. I want to see if 'tis them. I just wanted to tell you where I was going."

"Fucking za, Finn." Laisren sighed. "We'll go, but only to confirm 'tis them and report our findings to the town guards. Whatever they do with the information is up to them."

"Right." Finn nodded, staring at the water. "We'll wait 'til it gets dark then."

CHAPTER THIRTY-THREE

An hour after sunset, Laisren and Finn landed some distance from the Humans' camp, not far, just enough distance that their feet's impact on the leaf-carpeted ground would go unheard. Laisren drew his sword as they approached on foot, carefully and quietly, hiding behind trees to look around for any outliers.

The camp, they soon saw, sat within a natural grove of trees atop cliffs overlooking the river. The underbrush was cleared, showing the ground covered in dead leaves. Three small fires, spaced yards apart, burned with wooden spits above them, holding roasting meat.

There were no tents, but a handful of small makeshift structures acted as such. Each was nothing but thin branches arranged as a free standing rectangle with smaller branches leaned diagonally atop to form a slanted roof. The shelters were not enough to house the twenty Human men within the camp. Instead, Finn could see bed-shaped piles of leaves— some topped with a blanket, some not. Personal kit edged some, though it appeared that the retreating soldiers had brought little with them.

The beds were empty. The men grouped in casual conversations or by the fire. Some ate roasted meat off sticks.

A gathering of five engaged in a hearty competition that appeared to be a game of *who can throw an acorn in a small hole in the ground from the farthest distance.*

Two sets of men appeared to be patrolling the outer edge, peering into the surrounding shadows as they sloshed through the leaves.

Nothing specifically announced these men as Dayigans. They flew none of the emerald green banners they'd flown so abundantly in Feah lands. They wore no green tabards. Finn recognized the black trousers and boots as like what he'd seen on soldiers, but these men wore tunics in shades of off-white to faded brown or variations of dingy gray.

The lack of display struck Finn as an insult. They either respected the Vohcks enough not to parade, colors blaring, through their country, or feared them. Either way, the same had not applied to the Feahs.

A happy guffaw sounded from a man chatting with others. It filled Finn with anger. His heart pounded, warming him despite the chill. These men, who'd taken so much from the Feah, did not deserve to laugh, Finn resolved. Did they even care enough about the lands they'd destroyed to give it a thought?

As the patrollers neared, Laisren snatched Finn back to crouch behind a larger tree, frozen and silent.

The soldiers passed in an amble, giving half-assed glances out into the dark. It was the search of those not expecting trouble, but ordered to keep watch anyway.

Once they'd passed, the Anordúlas breathed.

Finn leaned close to Laisren and whispered, "When they're sleeping, we need to kill them all."

Laisren gave a look that was first shocked, then sad. He grabbed Finn's hand before pulling him away from the camp.

Once they'd gained some distance, Laisren whispered, "We don't even know who they are, not for certain."

"They're Dayigan soldiers. The ones that didn't make the boats. Who else would they be?"

"Well, you clearly don't know who *you* are. Kill them in their sleep? That's not you, Finn."

Finn looked toward the camp. Even from his distance, he could hear the cheery tone of the chatter. The occasional laughter. Every note of their undeserved happiness enraged him more.

"I didn't expect them to be standing around wailing in sorrow like some banshees," Finn said. "But to see them, joking about. Fuck, I think I'm to be sick, Laz." He wrapped his arms across his stomach.

A group expelled a unified congratulatory cheer; no doubt someone got that damn acorn in that damned hole.

Laisren laid his hand on Finn's cheek and gently turned Finn's head so he could look into Laisren's dark hazel eyes.

"To be honest," Laisren said, "I couldn't care less if everyone in that camp spontaneously combusted. But I ..." He stroked Finn's cheek with his thumb. "I don't want *you* to change." He smiled. "I don't want to lose my sweet Finn."

Finn sighed. "Fine. I won't do a thing to them. But we have to search that camp. Maybe we can find something that'll lead us to that commander I let escape."

Laisren's eyes narrowed as he moved his hand to Finn's shoulder. "You mean lead us to the captured Feah? To your brother's widow? To your friend's daughter?"

Finn nodded. "Aye, them as well."

Finn hurried back to the edge of the camp and crouched behind the same thick tree as before. He scanned the camp, examining every part he could see. He wasn't sure what he was looking for or if there was even anything to find.

Laisren was soon beside him.

"There," whispered Finn, pointing to a shelter formed of branches.

Inside, lay a rolled emerald green cloth acting as a pillow, a sword within its scabbard affixed to a belt, and a small black trunk.

"That trunk must hold something important. Why else would they lug it all this way? I figure it must have maps or directions written down to tell them how to get back to the other soldiers."

"Could be," Laisren said. "Or maybe it has a map with a big red X on Commander Beadurinc's home city, a drawing of his house, and a list of the best times to find him in."

Finn looked at Laisren for a moment, confused, before realizing he was trying to be funny. Finn scrunched his face in a glare.

"'Tis important either way," Finn said. "I know it. And I aim to get it and see for meself."

He dashed away.

"Finn," Laisren whispered as loud as he dared, like a cross parent trying to call back a child without attracting attention. "Finn."

Finn continued around the shadowed edge of the camp. Each step added to the knot of anxiety growing in his gut. He tried not to disrupt the crunchy leaves underfoot as he darted behind a tree, pausing before he peeked around at the camp.

The Dayigans remained oblivious to his presence as they continued to chat and play their games. Finn found the patrolmen.

Both pairs were far off, but a set headed in Finn's general direction.

Finn moved again, maintaining the nerve-racking balance of quickness and quietness.

Another tree offered cover as Finn jumped behind it, pressing his back against it. The shelter holding the trunk was still about twenty feet away, but he could get no closer without entering the camp.

The patrollers passed between Finn and the small shelter.

Finn didn't move or breathe.

"Who goes?" a patroller called.

Had I made a noise? Finn didn't think he had. Nevertheless, he heard the metallic scrape of two swords withdrawing from scabbards. Footsteps slowly approached.

Careful and noiseless, Finn lifted his bow and drew an arrow from the quiver on his belt. Despite his growing archery skills, he doubted he could take on twenty soldiers. Flying away remained an option, but he'd abandon all hope of finding Commander Beadurinc.

The steps neared. Finn ached to look and see how close they were, but he knew better.

Heart pounding, Finn waited.

"There's nothing there," the other patroller said. He returned his sword to its sheath.

The first waited before doing the same. They walked on.

Finn let them gain some distance before he ducked low to the ground and peeked around the tree.

There were a few other trees between him and the shelter, but moving inwards, nearer the fires, meant entering thinner shadows while coming closer to the soldiers.

Laisren hurried to Finn and crouched by his side. "Stop this madness, Finn. The plan is to get help from the Vohcks."

"If we both go in the camp," Finn whispered, "that'll just mean there's two of us for them to see. So stay here."

Finn dashed away, staying low as he moved inwards. He stopped at the first tree, but it was thin, leaving him exposed. He continued in.

Finally, Finn reached the back of the shelter beside its angled roof of branches lain across a horizontal support.

The front opening faced a relatively well-lit area filled with soldiers. But the sides were open, too and less exposed.

Finn moved, inch by inch, around to the side. He could see it, the wooden trunk about a foot tall and wide and three feet long. Staying hidden while watching the soldiers, Finn reached his hand around the branches of the roof. Stretching his arm, he managed to wrap his fingers around the rope handle at its end.

Finn pulled. It was much heavier than he'd expected. He pulled again, harder, but with caution. With a bit of tugging and maneuvering, Finn slid the trunk through the triangular side opening and around behind the structure.

A large iron padlock dangled from the front latch. He'd need to deal with it later. He saw the other pair of patrolmen approaching. With no time to waste, Finn struggled to rush the heavy trunk away from camp.

Finn hid, setting the trunk on the ground as he clamped his hand over his mouth, trying to control his panting.

It seemed the patrollers walked at a turtle's pace as Finn strained to remain still. He knew that if they spotted the absent trunk, a search would ensue. But they passed.

Finn breathed.

With both hands gripping a handle at one end of the trunk and dragging the other, he hurried it farther from the camp.

He heard a steady stream of water splashing against the ground. He looked to his side to see a Human pissing toward a tree.

Finn froze.

The Human casually looked Finn's way. It took the soldier a moment before realization struck. He fumbled to stuff his wiggly bits into his trousers with one hand while fumbling to draw his sword with the other.

Unable to run or fly with the heavy trunk, Finn dragged it in a slow escape.

The Human opened his mouth to call out, but a shriveled, blackened hand clapped over his face. A matching arm encircled his chest.

The sight horrified Finn until he saw it was Mephistus, standing on his hind legs behind the Human. The tromlee jumped up, snatching the soldier into the sky.

Finn sighed in relief, heart pounding.

Laisren hurried to him.

"Take the other handle," Finn said. "'Twill take the both of us to fly this out of here. We must hurry."

CHAPTER THIRTY-FOUR

"Stay," Laisren ordered the soldier. They were now about a mile from the Dayigan camp in a small rocky clearing at the base of a hill coated with green moss.

Mephistus released the soldier and stepped away, circling on four legs before lying down. His skeletal tail swished back and forth as he watched, like a lion watching prey.

"If you stay where you are and cause no trouble," Laisren said, "you can stay unconfined. If you try anything stupid, Mephistus here will hold you in place."

The soldier said nothing; instead, he scanned the area while, no doubt, planning something stupid.

Finn ignored them. His focus was on the black trunk. He'd found a rock and, holding it with both hands, hammered against the iron padlock. Besides making noise and sparks, the effort did nothing.

Laisren approached. "The lock's stronger than the box. Hit the center of the lid."

It seemed obvious once he'd said it. The trunk was beat up and weathered. Finn did as he'd suggested, striking its top. The wood cracked. After a few more strikes, a hole formed through the black-painted wood. Finn was able to squeeze his hand in and yank up the broken board. It cracked and splintered before breaking free.

"'Tis just bits of pointless metal," Finn said.

Laisren leaned to look. "They're coins. Other nations use them to—"

"I know what fecking coins are, Laisren. I'm not *that* country." Finn dug his hand in, pushing aside the assortment of flattened, stamped metals and trying to see if there was anything else there. "I've heard of them, at least. I meant they're pointless to us."

Finn shoved over the trunk, dumping its contents to crash out. The bits of metal slid down the slanted ground. Finn raked through them, searching for anything important. He raked the last coins out of the box. Nothing. He threw down a coin to clink against the others.

Enraged, Finn rushed to the soldier and shoved him. "Where is Commander Beadurinc?"

"I don't know."

"You're lying." Finn panted through clenched teeth.

"I swear by God Déagar, I don't know. My ship wasn't part of the first unit stationed in Drevite lands. We were dispatched right before the experiment's end, as recovery, in case there was trouble from you natives."

Laisren approached the soldier and extended his hand flat before his own mouth. He blew, sending a cloud of dust into the soldier's face.

The soldier's head and eyes grew heavy, and he had trouble standing. Arms out, he stumbled toward the steep wall of the mossy hill, catching himself against it.

"What was that about?" Finn asked.

The soldier lowered himself to sit sideway against the hill.

"Nekesa made it for me so I could interrogate a prisoner in the Feah temple. But he was dead, so." Laisren shrugged. "It has forced him into hypnagogia."

"Right, so how about using a word normal folks use."

"'Tis when you're falling asleep, and you're no longer awake but not quite asleep: hypnagogia."

"Fucking magic," the soldier mumbled sleepily, his eyes closed. "Magic is the realm of God Déagar, alone. All who trespass ..." The rest was incoherent.

Laisren neared the soldier and crouched to his level. "You called the attack on our lands an experiment. What kind?"

"People like you can't understand holy works."

"Try us."

The soldier kept his eyes closed as he lay his limp head against the rock. "The Dayigan Empire is a force for good. It unified many nations with the goal of ending all wickedness, but there's still much work to do, work at home and work in other nations that threaten us."

"Our people never threatened your empire," Finn said.

"Not you. Evil fucking witches in our empire. Fucking Blue Death. They need vanquishing. They're trying to destabilize the holy nation our leaders built. They refuse to bow down to the perfect laws set by the Church of Déagar and refuse to burn for their crimes. They incite civil war. And then there's those nations north of the Hyvile uniting to stop us from making the world better. They're wicked too."

"What does any of this have to do with Dayigan soldiers coming into our lands and attacking us?" Finn asked.

The soldier opened his eyes slightly and looked at Finn. "I told you you couldn't understand our holy mission, fucking savages. You're too lost to the Dark. You think I don't know who you are? I seen you attack us. You flew above us and slaughtered my fellow soldiers when we retreated. Hundreds of innocent Dayigan men."

"Innocent, says he," Finn scoffed. "There's a laugh. Your people came to *our* land and attacked and killed *us* without any reason at all."

"Those savages died for the betterment of the world. We had to perfect our methods before using them in the real conflicts—the proper war that's coming."

His words left Finn feeling as if he'd walked through a cascade of icy water: shocked, pained, numb inside, and cold. Finn drifted his eyes to the ground. He wished to scream but was hollow. "That was it, then?" A dizzy sick vibrated down the whole of Finn's body as he lowered his head. "You didn't want our lands. Or to start trade with West Bikia or anything, no." Finn smiled a sort of mad smile. "You just needed a fucking place to practice before the proper war."

"Yes, that's right," the man said, with a sleepy grin. "You do understand. It was more than just practice, though. In the Drevite Experiment, the army developed new methods to take the law of the Church to all of Bikia, both East and West, and perhaps, eventually, to all of Perdinok. The True Light is the only way. All others will perish."

"We'll be needing him alive, Finn."

Finn had done nothing to warrant Laisren's words, but he was thinking many things: violent things, slow, violent things. Did his eyes betray him so clearly, Finn wondered as he stared at the man. Finn's mouth hung agape. Bloody visions danced through his throbbing brain as he envisioned a plethora of agonizing deaths for this Dayigan soldier.

"Are you all right?" Laisren's words vibrated through Finn. He felt them—felt the words—vibrating, tingling his fingertips. Finn smiled at how funny it felt.

Finn, looking at his hand, touched his fingertips, one by one, with his thumb. He looked past them, at Laisren. Laisren

watched Finn. *Right, I'm supposed to answer.* "I'm all right. Aye."
Finn sat down, staring at his knees as he listened.

Laisren asked, "What methods did your people develop in
our lands?"

The soldier grinned. "You're trying to trick me into telling
you something. But I'm not going to, am I? Even if I knew.
Which I don't. I'm just a footman, lowest of the ranks. They
barely told me nothing before they loaded me on the ship in
Wendian."

"Wendian?" Finn looked up. "Is that where the commander is?"

The soldier shook his head against the mossy hill.
"Wendian's the holy city where the Supreme Patriarch lives.
Everybody knows that." He yawned. "The commander was
already in the Drevite Nation. We sailed for days to get to
him. We were just supposed to help extract the team stationed there. No one said there'd be a wicked sorcerer flying
over us and rotting good Human men. We had to leave two
days early."

Finn forced calm, as if talking to a child he wanted to
strangle. *"Where is the commander now?"*

"Wherever the ship's going to take us. We missed the ship
before when we were running. So we regrouped and headed
east on foot. We were all miserable after that sorcerer killed
so many of us, and then we were in the evil kingdom filled
with witches. But the scout in the little boat found one of our
ships that had stopped to make repairs across the river. They
said they'd come back for us, so we made camp and waited.
We were in good spirits tonight since they said they were
coming for us tomorrow, but now ..." He yawned and snuggled against the hill. "I guess I'll be dead now."

"Are the Dayigans coming back to ..." Finn nearly said Feah lands but changed to "the Drevite Nation?"

The soldier didn't respond and appeared asleep.

"We won't get any more out of him," said Laisren, standing as he signaled Finn to follow.

A few paces away, he continued. "It sounds like the Dayigans were done with us. But their experiment—evidently the enchanted food—clearly failed, thanks to you. You probably saved more people than we realized. Unfortunately, a failed experiment could lead to another phase."

"I can't believe that's all we were to them. Like we were nothing. We're not even people to them, are we?"

"At least they're done with us for now. Which means we have time to get the support of the Vohcks and prevent this from happening again."

"We have to go for that commander first."

"The commander is not an immediate threat, Finn, not if his experiment is over."

"I don't care! He's the reason my brother died. He's the reason your mother left the Feah and died. He's the reason all the others died. Including me. And I, fool I am, let him get away."

"If there is another phase to the Dayigan experiments on our people, then our time is limited. It will take time to establish an alliance with the Vohcks. I hate that commander as much as you, but we must get to Vohcktara as quickly as possible."

"The commander has to die," Finn maintained, crimson eyes narrowing.

"This isn't about saving the Feah anymore, is it?" Laisren asked. "You just want revenge."

Finn looked away, staring at the ground. "Mephistus, take the soldier and leave him close to his camp. Do your nightmare thing on him and have a nice meal, but leave him so 'twill look like he had a fall. We don't want to give them soldiers a reason not to all get on that ship tomorrow." He looked at Laisren. "I'll be getting on the ship as well."

CHAPTER THIRTY-FIVE

Since sunrise, Laisren and Finn had monitored the Dayigan camp. In a tree. Waiting for hours.

Finn's troubled sleep of last night had relieved none of the horror or sickening frustration born from his learning about the "Drevite Experiment." He'd tossed and turned within the bed of the room they'd rented with Dayigan coin in Makriá. In time, Finn resolved to do Laisren a mercy and lay on the floor. In the space between wakefulness and sleep—hypnagogia, Finn remembered—he was taken back to that first meeting with the commander half a year ago when Beadurinc had called Kyran and Finn filth. Even though Finn had been insulted at the time, he had greatly underestimated the gravity of what the commander had meant. Filth.

Finn's people were absolutely nothing in the Dayigans' eyes. Perhaps Finn had felt some unknown comfort in believing the Dayigans saw something of value in the Feah, something worth taking, something that those who died had died protecting. But no. They were filth protecting filth, as far as the Dayigans saw.

"Do you think they were experimenting on us the whole four years they were there?" Finn whispered to Laisren, though whispering was unnecessary. They were about a hundred feet from the camp and high in a tree. Laisren used a branch as a seat and the trunk as the back, while Finn slouched sideways on the same branch and dangled his legs over. Mephistus lay like an enormous cat on a higher branch.

After thinking, Laisren, still staring out toward the distant camp, said, "Most likely. I assume they carried out a series of control groups—a lot, considering the timeframe—before launching such a large strike. Which is why we should head straight to Vohcktara and not remain in a tree waiting for some ship to sail us to our deaths."

"The ship's the only way to find the commander."

"We don't know that," Laisren said. "We don't know it is the only way, and we don't know if it will take us to him at all. Our only guarantee is 'twill take us to more soldiers than you and I can fight alone."

"'Tis the *best* way to find the commander, then. And I never said you had to come with me."

Laisren leaned his head back against the tree and faced upward. "I've watched you run to your death before, Finn. I know how it feels to lose you. I know I can't stop you, but I ... I would walk into torment just to be with you." He lifted his head to face Finn. "Just know, that's where we're going. Death. Two more pointless deaths at the hands of the Dayigans. The commander won't be killed. The Feah captives—who you keep forgetting—won't be saved. And there will be no one to make an alliance with the Vohcks. You're sacrificing everything for some futile quest for vengeance."

Finn slouched downward, staring through twenty feet of limbs with barely a glimpse of the ground. "The commander has to die."

Laisren closed his eyes and took a long, sad breath. "Your ship is nearly here."

Finn turned toward the cliff-side camp. Beyond the cliff flowed the Hyvile River. And there it was, a Dayigan ship, small but growing closer.

Finn was not the only one who saw it. The Dayigans in the camp gathered at the cliff. They shouted and pointed. A few had already donned their emerald green tabards over their clothes. Others gathered their possessions.

The sight set an ache in the pit of Finn's stomach. This was happening.

He looked back at Laisren. "There's no other way to find the commander," he told him, while telling himself. "If we don't get on that ship, he'll be lost altogether."

Laisren said nothing.

Finn returned his eyes to the ship. It had already gotten visibly closer. With every foot it drew nearer, Finn felt his time slip further away. He had no idea what the right decision was.

With no conviction in his voice, Finn muttered, "I have to find him."

"Wherever you go, I'll go," Laisren said sadly.

Finn nodded. "I guess we should be heading down to the shore then."

—

The Dayigan ship swayed in the glittering tide as it kept its distance from the rocky shore. It had dropped anchor, and a smaller boat had carried the first of the stranded soldiers toward it.

Finn recognized the ship by its damage. Even from his distance down the shore, he could see that its stern had been hastily reconstructed. Freshly cut, unsealed wood—still yellow, with sections covered in bark—formed a slapdash frame with uneven boards tacked on. Finn recalled lying on the shore of his homeland, distraught and weakened, as he cast out a final desperate crimson ray, ripping off the rear of a fleeing ship.

Laisren and Finn kept to a thin section of beach between the cliff wall and the river. The waves circled Finn's feet as he watched the ship. That same nervous ache remained in his stomach.

Laisren maintained his annoyed silence, his arms folded.

"You're right," Finn said. "The Feahs need help from the Vohcks, and getting that help can't wait."

Laisren raised an eyebrow but said nothing.

"And if the two of us go off to the Dayigan Empire and get ourselves killed, there won't be anyone to talk to the Vohcks at all."

"So ..." Laisren began, "you're saying we can now go to Vohcktara?"

Finn looked down at his feet in the sand. Another wave slid onto the shore and circled his toes.

"Mephistus," Finn said emptily, "grab Laisren. Hold him in place."

"What?" Laisren said, shocked.

The tromlee sprung up, stood upright behind him, and grabbed Laisren's arms.

"Finn, what are you doing?"

Finn couldn't look at him. His eyes remained on the rocky shore. "'Tis like you said before, we can't both go after the commander. One of us has to go to Vohcktara."

"Finn, don't do this."

"I'll meet you at that place you talked about: the Black Temple in Vohcktara. I'll be there at noon—I mean, not today's noon, of course, but some noon real soon. I promise." Finn looked up at him.

Laisren's eyes watered. "No."

"'Twill be all right, all of it," Finn assured him. A tear rolled down his cheek. "We'll get married there in that Black Temple. And you can show me the whole city. We'll be happy ever after like ... like in some Faery story."

"Finn, you'll die. I'm begging you, no."

Finn turned away. "I suppose that could be true, yes. But I died a while back though, did I not? This is all stolen time I'm on now. And I thank the Dark Mother for giving it to me, 'cause I got to spend it with you, and help my people. But if someone's going to risk his life, 'tis only fair it should be someone who's died already."

Laisren struggled to free himself, but the claws of Mephistus clamped tighter around his upper arms.

Finn sniffed. "'Tis not just about revenge, Laz. You saw what the commander's magic did to our people. He's dangerous. I don't know if he'll be back for more experimenting on the Feah, but either way, he learnt what he learnt so he could attack others. And from what that soldier said, those others seem a lot like us, and they're attacking the Dayigan Empire from the inside. I have to help them as well."

Laisren, his eyes circled in sorrow, said, "At least take me with you. Finn?"

"Nekesa needed to go to Dinikimera. You need to go to Vohcktara. And I must go on me own to the commander."

Finn approached and kissed Laisren's lips, slowly, sadly, lingering in that moment they both feared might be their last.

Finally, Finn stepped back and wiped the tears from Laisren's cheeks.

"I love you, Laisren."

"I love you as well, Finn. So much."

Finn sniffed and cleared his own tears with his arm. "Mephistus—"

"Finn, you can't."

"—take him to Vohcktara."

Mephistus spread his bat-like wings and jumped upward, snatching Laisren into the sky.

Finn watched them grow smaller as a receding black blur. Then he fell to his hands and knees on the sand. His heart felt as if something had clutched it, and hurt throbbed outwards, filling every inch of his being.

Finn pressed his fist to his mouth, trying to quiet the sound of his crying. He coughed, spitting up anguish to the sand.

CHAPTER THIRTY-SIX

A thin green door flapped forsaken in a chilly wind. It beat against its wooden frame, tapping out a slow, irregular tempo that no one heard. Inside, a long bunkroom held—along each elongated wall—evenly spaced, double-level beds supported by rough four-by-four posts. The coarse wool blankets remained neatly tucked, awaiting a rest that would never come. Only a few of the trunks—once positioned at the foot of each bunk—remained. These stood open and empty.

In the same room, identical doors also swayed. Outside, these doors lined a second-story walkway, which was enclosed in a rough green railing and covered by a green tile roof. Below, more doors lined the first story, leading from another bunkroom to the sandy ground. The moonlit courtyard in between remained empty, save for four houses in its corners and a dozen dead soldiers with very little rotting meat remaining on their bones. The fort's opposite wall mirrored the first, its doors tapping.

Atop the corner towers, emerald banners flapped vainly, declaring vainly, "This belongs to the Holy Dayigan Empire," though its bombastic claim was now defunct.

Nevertheless, the shadowed walls of the grim, forsaken fort, though unoccupied, looked no less ominous as they loomed over the Hyvile River. No longer did they threaten the surrounding people, yet they endured as bleak reminders of tragedy and hate.

Outside the fort, a thousand Feahs gathered. Within the crowd, torches flickered sporadically. The people—men, women, and children—all maintained a joyless silence. They'd come from all the Feah parishes, and some had come from farther lands.

Kyran's formerly intended husband, circled by his forlorn friends, had journeyed the lengthy distance from the Frelon tribe in the northwest, from his lonely home beside the Teréyi Sea. Wordless and despondent, he stepped forward, watching the fort wherein Dayigan soldiers had tortured and slaughtered his love.

Lann, within the many, grasped the rope handle of a wooden bucket as he stared blankly at the fort. He had no tears, for now, no cries, only silent misery.

Beside him stood Ubaz. The distant boy had barely spoken since the murder of his father and his mother's disappearance. He, too, held a wooden bucket.

Chief Kaie, centered alongside the other eight parish tiernas, stood at the front of the crowd facing them. The tiernas bowed their heads in crestfallen contemplation.

In time, Kaie lifted her head. "Go!" She pointed. "And cleanse our lands."

People throughout the crowd spread their wings and leaped from the ground. Lann, among them, held his bucket of grease with chunky bits of white tallow, which sloshed as he flew.

Three hundred people, their buckets in hand, flew over the fort. They heaved oils, grease, and alcohol. The clumpy mixtures splattered against the wooden walls, dripping downward in oily glops. More buckets emptied on the green-tiled roofs and on the walkways along the sharpened parapets. Some people flew lower, hurling buckets into abandoned sleeping quarters. Ubaz was with those who bypassed the fort and poured their buckets' contents in slick lines along the docks.

When all who'd taken flight returned, alighting within the crowd, Kaie addressed them:

"When the first winter came to the world of Perdinok and the first death struck mankind, Mother Ashatra said to Mother Lágeya, 'Let me offer a home to the disincarnate. Let me give them a place to rest and learn and prepare to live again.' And so Mother Lágeya fashioned a realm deep below and called this place the Za. And to Ashatra, she gave dominion.

"Tonight, on this eve of a new year, when the walls between the living and the dead are thin, we do not celebrate with our usual merriment, but we gather to remember those who've returned to Mother Ashatra. This year, we don't light separate fires in each parish, but we light one cleansing fire so that we and our lands may begin to heal." She spoke louder, saying, "Let this be a place of calm and reverence. Let this be a place of remembrance. Mother Lágeya, who is Nature, bring us peace. Mother Ashatra, Queen of Za, bring our departed peace." She raised her hand. "*Loose.*"

Archers launched countless flaming arrows at the fort. The fire spread.

The tiernas walked three slow circles around Chief Tierna Kaie. They stopped and joined their hands.

Kaie raised her hands to the night. "Departed loved ones, we remember you."

The other tiernas repeated, "Departed loved ones, we remember you." They lifted their joined hands.

The fire swirled into a vortex, swelling substantially higher as it consumed the fort. The growing popping and crackling became the only sounds along the shore. Lann watched the twisting flames ascending high to blackened plumes. A tower buckled, creaking and snapping. It collapsed, releasing orange embers to glitter in the sky.

Throughout the crowd, people joined hands, sharing the time of silence as they watched the burning fort. Some set their hands on others' shoulders, wordlessly consoling. Some embraced. Some breathed in somber release.

Another tower crumbled, sending further embers shooting into the night. With wailing shrieks and crashes, the front wall collapsed, opening a vivid view into the blazing courtyard. Twisting arms of brilliant heat reached out from every room. One of the freestanding barracks fell as fiery rubble, and the other drooped on its blackened beams, ready to follow to the ground.

"Treasa," Lann whispered, the firelight gleaming on his dismal frown, "and my sweet little Lannah, I honor both of ye and release ye."

———

The ship creaked and groaned as it swayed on the currents of the river. The cargo hold, framed in heavy beams, was dim. The only light to filter into the murky chamber came as dusty beams of daylight through a metal grid, a square hatch atop the stairs.

Nets of thick rope weighed by crates hung and swung along with the ship's motion. Other ropes secured wooden boxes and barrels stacked and tied along the wall. However, the ship's main cargo was not these things but the fifteen sullen people who sat cramped within the confines. Most were severely injured but stable. All, half-starved and hopeless, maintained a silent dread after weeks on this ship to some unknown horror.

A dusty man sat leaning against a stack of crates. Coughing, he spit slimy blood into his fist.

An older woman, her left wing broken and splinted, muttered prayers to the Three Mothers for help.

Treasa checked the bandages wrapping a man's chest. Ideally, they needed changing, but their situation was not ideal. The skirt of her white druidic dress, after cutting off strips for bandages, was already as short as a man's, and she thought it best to save the rest.

She carefully unwrapped the gruesome covering, revealing a deep gash, layered black and dark red.

There'd been only three injured people on this ship when Treasa was captured. Afterward, the soldiers brought ten more. Though they gave no reason for the increase, it was clear that they meant her to nurse them back to health. Or at least keep them alive. And true to the Dayigans' expectations, Treasa couldn't let these injured people suffer—even if it meant helping the Dayigans.

"Your wound is healing," Treasa said. She almost said "nicely," but realized that was inaccurate. She began rewrapping the same blood-caked bandage. "You'll have quite the scar, but I don't expect you'll have much bother from it after a week or so. I hate that I can't use magic to speed the process along."

She touched her thick iron collar, locked in place with a large padlock. Its rough black surface showed words and symbols engraved in green, circling its length.

"Don't you worry yourself, Vischief," he said with a cough. "With or without magic, you're a blessing from the Three Mothers all the same."

Treasa smiled, though her eyes were hopeless. "May they watch over you and make you well."

She stood, straining for balance in the creaking hold.

A girl ran up to her and wrapped her arms around Treasa's waist. The impact of the hug, combined with the rocking of the ship, nearly sent Treasa to the floor. She grabbed a thick beam overhead.

"I still have one more patient to check on. Then, I'll tell you another story."

"But the ship's making loud noises," Alannah said. "What if it falls apart again?"

Treasa looked to the aft of the cargo hold, where the rear of the ship had decayed and fell away and where armed guards had stationed themselves until it was repaired. It was a mess of hasty carpentry but looked solid.

Treasa put her hand on Alannah's back, gently rubbing her white wings. Soldiers had held down the girl and cut her primary feathers in half. Treasa hadn't seen the event herself, but she saw the result, and Alannah had told her of the nightmares. The same had happened to all the prisoners while they'd been in the Dayigan fort, but Treasa—arriving directly on the ship—managed to skip that particular torture.

"The ship won't fall apart again," Treasa said, despite not understanding what had happened the first time or if it would repeat.

"Where are we going, Aunt Treasa?"

She sighed. "I can't say for sure."

"Does the True Light hate us now?"

Treasa crouched to eye level with her ten-year-old niece.

Her face, frightened and dirty, still held a sweetness to it, even as she frowned. Her lips pouted.

Treasa wrapped her arms around her and held her tightly.

"They don't, sweetie. Mother Lágeya and the Gods loyal to her are the True Light, not the people who captured us." Treasa pushed the girl's white hair behind her ear. "But sometimes bad people do bad things and say they're doing them in the name of good, when really"—she sighed—"they aren't."

"Will we be all right?"

Treasa kissed her forehead. "I don't know."

The little girl's eyes turned toward the floor.

"Do you remember that lullaby your mam used to sing to you?" Treasa asked. "Whenever you're afraid, I want you to hum it, all right, and know Moyra's somewhere, thinking of you and hoping you come home safe."

Alannah nodded and sat down on the deck. She hummed, slow and sad. The melancholic melody filled the cargo hold. Treasa, too, found it comforting.

Listening, Treasa walked to her next patient and checked the bandages.

CHAPTER THIRTY-SEVEN

Thunder stirred Finn from his wet, uncomfortable sleep. The many cracks in the cramped hole in which he'd spent the last two days dripped and dripped. The stormy river tossed the Dayigan ship and, in turn, tossed Finn within the hastily constructed scaffolding of unfinished lumber.

The hollow section of the rebuilt stern hadn't been as large as he'd hoped—and he hadn't hoped for much. Finn couldn't lie all the way down or sit all the way up. Too, it offered little as far as flat segments, and he knew that if he fell off the beam where he sat, he'd most likely crash through the lower decking. Even now, looking down, he could see the dark water crashing and churning. The occasional spray reached up, slapping Finn's legs, but he was already soaked from the water filtering down from the sky through the wood.

Finn cupped his hands, capturing a trickle winding down a beam. He drank.

At least the rain held that benefit. The Hyvile gave him food, and the sky gave him drink. He thanked Mother Lágeya for that.

The ship stopped—or, more accurately, it stopped moving forward; it still rocked side to side and up and down, punching the river.

Were they at their destination—wherever that destination was? Finn maneuvered over the same hole he'd initially used to climb into the space and braced himself. Lying on the rocking wobbly beams, he lowered his head and shoulders upside down through the hole.

He could see nothing but the ass end of the ship and stormy, moonlit water on either side.

Annoyed, Finn inched himself farther until only his legs, hugging a beam, remained inside.

A wave hit the back of the ship, pushing it upward before it crashed down. Finn fell, finding himself surrounded by dark water.

The unexpected plunge left him breathless, but Finn gained his bearings and swam to the choppy surface. Gasping for air within the turbulent waves and torrents of rain, he desperately treaded water. It was hard for a Terovae to sink, but the river was trying. Soon, Finn found himself a good ten feet from the ship.

And then he saw it—land. A hundred yards past the forward bow of the ship, an island showed through the storm. It spread about a mile wide, with miles of violent river all around it.

Returning to the ship was futile, he knew, and that island was surely where he'd find the commander. Taking a large gulp of air, Finn submerged and extended his wings. He pushed them back, propelling himself toward the island.

Thunder sounded as lightning ripped across the sky.

Finn struggled his way toward land and hurried under a dock. The dock was the center of three of its kind, and the others held rocking Dayigan ships.

Beneath the gapping slats of the dock, the river's surface was no less fierce, yet a portion of the wind and rain was blocked.

Finn hugged a slimy wooden post, catching his breath as waves slammed against him. He let go, trying to avoid being washed away as he swam to the next leg in the line.

The worst of the storm faded, though rain continued to pour. Finn persisted, moving inward, under the dock, the water at shoulder level while his feet squished saturated sand.

Footsteps approached above him, boots stomping in a run. They passed overhead and continued a few paces out beyond him.

Through the gaps in the wet planks, Finn saw a soldier waving a torch high toward the ship Finn had left. With the storm passing, it would be safe for it to dock.

A second pair of boots approached. These stepped more slowly as another soldier approached the first.

"I have orders from the commander," the second man shouted over the rain. "Once the last ship is unloaded, prepare his ship for departure. The commander wishes to return to Dayigo to report the findings of the experiment."

"Yes, sir. When does the commander plan to set sail?"

"As soon as the storm has passed."

"The storm's nearly passed now, sir."

"Then 'tis best your men hurry, Sergeant."

"Yes, Lieutenant."

The lieutenant had made some distance up the dock before the sergeant began grumbling and cursing about young nobles, unrealistic expectations, and rain.

The news equally frustrated Finn. He growled and punched a pole. Finn, too, needed to hurry.

—

With a shrill shriek from the hinges, the hatch leading from the ship's cargo hold flew open and slammed against the deck.

Treasa grabbed Alannah and held her close as soldiers stormed down the stairs.

"Listen up," the leader commanded. "Everyone will stand up orderly and put your hands behind your back. We're disembarking, and we're going to do it quick."

"I have injured people in here," Treasa said as she put her arms behind her back. "Some can barely walk at all."

A soldier grabbed her and tied her wrists. Other soldiers dispersed among the Feahs and did the same to them.

The lead soldier said, "Anyone can't walk out: I run 'em through and throw 'em in the river. Anyone causes trouble: I run 'em through and throw 'em in the river. Anyone pisses me off ... You get the idea." He grabbed Treasa, yanked her forward, and shoved her toward the steps.

Alannah hurried to Treasa's side as they walked, huddled with fear, onto the drenched deck.

Outside, the soldier marched the Feahs onto a rainy wooden ramp leading off the ship to a long dock.

They continued past the shore into a camp, and a soldier shoved Treasa as the signal to continue.

On either side of the path, hundreds of faded green tents clustered. Most were small and triangular, with canvas taut across a center apex. Larger tents were cylindrical, with pointed roofs topped with small green flags.

A few large emerald banners on pikes displayed the Dayigan symbol, the same symbol on the tabards of the three hundred soldiers in the area.

Many soldiers worked to reset structures disrupted by the storm, but those men who were free gathered to watch the passing Feahs.

Alannah, shaking in terror, pushed herself against Treasa as soldiers shouted horrible things: accusations, obscenities, slurs, and whatever violence they wished to do to the Feahs. Some threw handfuls of mud.

Though Treasa tried to continue through the nightmare, she froze, ducking her head and clenching her whole body.

A soldier shoved Treasa; she tripped forward.

Some men laughed. Others threw more mud.

"Keep moving, savages. Straight on to the abbey."

Treasa looked up. The path led to a large chapel of pale brown blocks, its roofs sharp and tiled green and its bell tower stretching higher. It was the largest of a compound of similar buildings grouped within a stone wall. A stream ran through a watermill on its side.

Someone grabbed Treasa by her arm. "The commander wants this one."

The lead soldier looked Treasa up and down. "Can't say he don't have good taste." He laughed.

The one who'd grabbed her pulled her from the others.

"No!" Treasa struggled.

Alannah tried to follow, but someone grabbed her. She screamed.

"Alannah," Treasa called as soldiers pulled the two apart. "'Tis all right. I'll come for you. I vow."

"Aunt Treasa!"

A soldier snatched up the girl as she reached out in Treasa's direction, screaming. They took the girl with the others toward the abbey.

Two soldiers pulled Treasa, struggling, toward a large tent with a front awning. Dayigan flags fluttered on either side.

They forced her inside.

—

Finn crouched behind a tent, rain trickling down its roof to splash down his back. He clutched his ebony bow as his eyes remained locked on the prisoners approaching the abbey. It was too dark to discern faces, yet Finn knew them as Feahs by the silhouettes of wings and shouts from soldiers. And he'd heard the screams: *Alannah, Treasa.*

Finn had given up on their being alive, but they were, for now. He was too afraid to be relieved. He was a rabbit surrounded by wolves and if one so much as glimpsed him, he'd be hunted down and killed.

The people in the abbey would need to wait. "May the ancestors protect you," Finn whispered.

His attention turned as Commander Beadurinc came into view. Finn grinned maliciously as his heart pounded with something closer to desire than anger, but a twisted mixture of both.

Finn reached into the quiver on his belt. He would not lose his chance again. The commander would die. Now.

He reached deeper into his quiver but felt no arrows, even as he frantically patted around.

Quickly, Finn yanked it upward so he could look inside. He turned it upside down, only to pour out a measure of water that splashed on the ground.

"Fucking river," Finn spat as he threw down the quiver.

CHAPTER THIRTY-EIGHT

With a soldier on both sides of her and her hands tied behind her back, Treasa stood at the center of the large tent. A few weapons and shields lined the perimeter. A few trunks had been left open, revealing folded clothes, while others held brass items. A sturdy table scattered with maps stood before her. Candles burned on iron plates hung from iron stands. She tried to focus on these things, not on the cot in the corner. The commander's bed.

Beadurinc flung open the tent flap and entered. "Put her on her knees."

The other soldiers pushed Treasa to the rug.

The commander moved in front of her and grabbed her chin in a gloved hand. He yanked her head to look at him. "You cannot fathom the trouble you savage fucks have caused me."

"Do you think I'll be mourning your troubles, sir?"

He unhanded her, only to jerk back his fist and slap her face.

The impact pushed her head to the side, but Treasa recovered and straightened herself as tall as she could manage on her knees.

"You twist the True Light to your own ends," Treasa said. "You make it a vessel of *hate* and *greed*. But Mother Lágeya—"

"God Déagar's *mother* has no power in this world. But if she did, she would certainly join the Holy Dayigan Empire in ridding Perdinok of all wickedness and perversion. *Leave us,*" he said to the other soldiers.

They hurried away.

Behind the commander's tent, Finn carefully pressed the point of a Dayigan sword to the canvas wall. The blade popped through, and slowly Finn cut downwards, creating a long tear.

Finn could see Beadurinc inside. And Treasa.

Treasa forced herself to be calm. "Do they know you used magic on the Feahs?"

"My people do not use magic, witch."

"You lie so easily, Commander. We know you are a Silthex knight."

His lips formed a scoffing sneer. "Do you think that is an accusation? Or a secret? I am proudly a Silthex, and all here know it. I'm one of the last. A blue witch slaughtered my brethren, yet I, by the grace of God Déagar, was far from the event. Now, the handful of us who remain must continue our holy task in the name of the fallen. And *all* witches will burn for that spilled Silthex blood." He grabbed her hair at the back of her head and yanked her halfway to her feet.

"After the defeat in the Drevite Nation," he began.

"Defeat?"

"A minor setback. However, morale is low within the camp. You are just what I need to raise spirits. Did you know—for some reason we don't understand—Terovaes burn better than any other people?" He shoved her toward the exit.

Finn hurried around the canvas wall, dashing to another tent while keeping to the shadows. He kept Beadurinc and

Treasa in his sights, watching as two other soldiers grabbed Treasa and forced her to return to the center path.

Rushing from one hiding spot to the next, Finn followed, stolen sword in hand. He wanted to act, but there were too many soldiers too close to Beadurinc and Treasa. More Dayigans circled them as they continued.

Their destination became obvious—an unlit mound of sticks and logs just beyond the camp.

Treasa struggled as more soldiers grabbed her, lifting her from the ground. Those who gathered on either side of the path grew more rowdy and much closer, closing in around her as they shouted.

Hands snatched at her, ripping her dress as they handed her down the line of men. Treasa screamed, but no one cared. There were so many soldiers, hundreds, yet not one amongst them offered her kindness, even as they shouted of God Déagar, of the True Light, even as they called her wicked.

They slammed the ramp for disembarking ships on the mound of sticks and logs centered between the camp and the abbey. The soldiers carried Treasa up to a stake centered on the pile. They wrapped ropes tightly around her body, constricting her and binding her in place.

"Mother Lágeya," Treasa cried, "see me. Mother Ashatra, see me. Mother Larissa, please see me. True Light mothers rain your protection upon me. Help me. Please."

Standing on the ramp, Beadurinc punched Treasa in the face. "Your witchcraft will not work with that iron 'round your neck."

The men departed, pulling away the ramp.

Treasa looked down at those gathered around the mound. Some had broken into chants of "Burn the witch. Burn the witch," while most just shouted random obscenities, fists raised. She saw so much anger in their faces, so much hate, as if Treasa had wronged every one of them, personally, by her existence.

She tried to remain strong. Though they might kill her, they would not receive the pleasure of seeing her crumble. Nevertheless, tears rolled down her cheek.

"True Light Mothers," she said, "please help me. Please see me."

"Tonight," Beadurinc shouted, and the noises lessened so the men might hear, "we see what happens to those who turn against the True Light and infect the world of Perdinok with their wickedness." He raised his hands to the crowd. "Praise God Déagar, the one and only God, protector from the Dark. You are the Greatest of All. I praise your name, majestic and holy, without ending. By your wrathful fire, cleanse the world of this *wretched* creature who pollutes it with her foul iniquity. Astha'will-miabé."

The shouts from the soldiers returned, louder and more furious.

Body shaking, Finn inched from the concealment of the tent and crawled through the mud toward Treasa. Countless soldiers stood between him and her; their shouts were like an ongoing blast of hateful thunder.

Panicked, Finn didn't know what to do. He couldn't watch her die, not like Cal. Sword in hand, he crawled closer yet was no better situated to fight hundreds of Dayigans.

Low to the ground, Finn fought his drive for survival with every moment he crawled forward. He needed to stand, to get up from the mud. He couldn't.

Finn breathed quickly through clenched teeth, hyperventilating. He grew lightheaded.

There was no time for fear, no other moment to act. Finn would need to stand before the entire encampment. Or Treasa would die.

With all her might, Treasa writhed against the thick ropes, twisting her shoulders and pushing outward with her arms and legs. The ropes scraped against her skin, bruising and abrading her. If she could get an arm free, perhaps that would grant enough slack to push down the ropes. But even this minor goal proved futile.

The shouting continued as Beadurinc, arms raised, coaxed it. Anger filled Treasa as she stared at the commander. This was all a show to him. Her death was nothing but a means to encourage his monstrous troops. She glared at him as hate overrode her fear.

"No," Treasa said to herself. She breathed. "I'll not be going to the ancestors with a heart filled with hate and anger." She closed her eyes and centered herself, feeling the power of Mother Lágeya flow over her like a gentle river. Calm.

A soldier handed Beadurinc a torch.

Treasa let the angry shouts fade from her ears. "Open your arms, Mother Ashatra," she said, "and give me refuge in your Kingdom of Za."

Commander Beadurinc held his torch high as he shouted, "*The True Light is the only way. All others will perish.*" He turned to light the mound.

"Stop," Finn shouted as he flew over the crowd and landed a few feet from Beadurinc. Finn stood tall, forcing an air of confidence—*be afraid of me*—but he felt more like a pup left out in the cold.

The shouts from the soldiers ceased, and the resulting silence was slashed by the sound of swords sliding from scabbards. Enough arrows pointed Finn's way to pop his armor three times over.

"Who are *you?*" Beadurinc asked, annoyed by Finn's presence.

"I—" The question made him feel smaller. He swallowed dryly. "I'm Finn. You was looking for me all this time 'cause you said I killed that soldier on Midyear's Eve."

"Ah yes," Beadurinc said. "The pervert. Good of you to turn yourself in. Seize him."

"No. I'm not turning meself in, ya eejit. I'm doing a rescue here. I'm the one that flew over the Dayigan invaders and ..." Finn forced some bass into his voice. "... *rotted the meat from their bones*. And rotted the bones as well. To dust." Finn stuck his arms out, fingers extended in a way he thought looked forebodingly magical. "And I'll do the same to any man here that gives me reason to do so."

The blond captain leaned toward Beadurinc. "It is him, sir. I wouldn't forget that face."

Despite the commander's order to *seize him,* no one attempted to do so; no one moved forward at all, and some moved farther back. Fear shone apparent in the eyes of all the densely crowded soldiers.

Finn darted the aim of his hands from soldier to soldier as he looked around, assuring that no one moved. The only motion Finn saw was the occasional soldier jolting back when he found himself the focus of his palms.

Relaxing some, Finn stood taller. "Right." But he knew all too well that if even one of the hundreds of soldiers surrounding him called his bluff, he wouldn't survive the minute.

With his focus on the Dayigans, Finn flew up to Treasa and landed unstably on the pyre.

A stick, under his foot, rolled out and clicked down the pile. Finn tumbled a step with it, but he grabbed hold of the stake and Treasa's arm to keep from falling.

"What are you doing, Finn?" Treasa whispered.

Finn regained his balance and stood, thrusting his left hand toward the Dayigans as he drew his sword.

"What does it look like I'm doing?" Finn slid the sword between the thick rope and the stake and levered it to cut the rope. "I'm rescuing you."

The rope parted and uncoiled around Treasa.

The newfound freedom did little to put Treasa at ease. "Is it so? And why are the Dayigans looking at you like you're some sort of dragon?"

"'Tis complicated, that, but, in short, they think I can do stuff I can't really do. Least not anymore. And if they figure out I can't do what they think I can do, we're both dead. So, now that you're untied, you'll need to be the one doing the saving of us now."

"Feck sakes, Finn. I can't do magic or I would have already. They put this iron collar on me to bind my powers."

Finn looked down at the soldiers. They crowded every side of the pile and had moved closer. The archers kept their arrows nocked and aimed.

"You might have to catch me," Finn said.

"Catch you?"

"If I pass out." He nervously touched his finger to the U-bolt of the heavy padlock on the iron collar. The pain in his head was instant. Finn grimaced his face. He ran his finger across the bolt and the path his finger took rusted and cracked. He called out in pain.

The lock broke and fell from Treasa's neck. Finn fell onto her limply, nearly sliding down the pile. Treasa caught his arm, holding him up as his body slouched. She hurriedly removed the collar, throwing it aside.

"He's down!" Beadurinc shouted. "Kill them."

At once, arrows flew at the Feahs, striking them both.

With one hand holding Finn, Treasa thrust out her other. "In the name of Mother Ashatra, who is Death, I call retribution from the earth."

Swirling winds spiraled from her palm, striking the ground around the base of the mound. Massive thorns erupted, impaling the soldiers as they charged.

Eyes heavy, Finn looked at Beadurinc. The commander lived and navigated the gory spikes in a hasty retreat.

"Mother Lágeya," Treasa called, "she who is Nature, grant us your protection." She cast her hand toward the sky.

The sticks on which they stood began to sink into the ground, while thick vines shot upward around the base of the pile. Green turning brown, the vines hardened and thickened as a wall around the Feahs. The vines twisted together into a point above them, blocking out the night.

Finn lay flat on the ground, arms and legs out as dizziness throbbed through him.

"Finn," Treasa said in the darkness. "Are you all right?"

CHAPTER THIRTY-NINE

Between her folded palms, Treasa created a minor point of light, like a purple firefly, and released it to ascend a few feet above their heads.

Treasa knelt beside Finn, helping him to the coiled rope, which he used to sit up against. He looked around the cocoon of hardened vines. It was strangely beautiful.

"Your eyes are different," said Treasa. "Your irises are ... crimson?"

He nodded. "I've been told so, aye."

She glanced down with an unsaid thought. "That wall won't keep them out for long," she said. "It took three druidesses at a time to maintain the wall I set over the temple's entrance, and it was only the size of a door. Whatever you need to do to recharge your seid, you might want to do it quickly."

"I'm not seid depleted. I'm seid ... broken. Chief Kaie told me not to be using any more magic at all." Finn left off the part where she'd said he'd die. He looked at his fingertips, the middle and index of his right hand. They felt as if he'd burned them and they'd blackened. Finn tried wiping them on his arm, but the char remained.

"Is Cal here?" Treasa asked.

The question was a dagger in Finn's heart. He closed his eyes, absorbing the pain. "He's not, no. I ..." He sighed. "I'm sorry, Treasa, Cal is …" Finn looked at her, lit purple, already fretful about his answer. "He's back home with Ubaz. Someone had to watch the wee lad, didn't they now?"

"Right." She nodded disappointedly. "Moyra and Lann, they're here though, yes?"

"'Tis just me here, on me own. I wasn't planning to come here at all, but it just sort of happened like. And I figured I couldn't let you get burnt, so."

"Right." She touched her fingers to her forehead. "And you have no magic." She massaged her temples. "I don't have nearly enough to fight past three hundred soldiers."

"I had to come when I did," he said apologetically. "Otherwise, there'd be no way to find this place."

"That was truly really brave of you, Finn, to come here like you did. I'm just trying to figure out what our next move is. I saw where they took Alannah and the other captives from our ship. I assume they took the captives from the previous ships there too. If we can get to the Déagrian temple just up from the camp—"

"No, we have to go after the commander. He's the one that did all of this to us. That makes him our first priority." Finn knew how it sounded. He knew that if Laisren had been here, he'd object with that worried look of his. Finn didn't care. "Beadurinc has to die."

Treasa had the same worried look. "Finn, we need to rescue our people, and if Beadurinc stands in the way of that and gets himself killed, so be it. I won't mourn him for a moment. But we will not hunt down a person. That's not who we are."

"Maybe that is who I am now. And maybe if it'd been me sooner, that commander would be long dead, and we'd all be together at home."

Treasa put her hand on his shoulder. She took a deep breath, gathering herself. "They hate us, I know, and they've used that hate to do horrible things to us for no reason. To be honest, I've struggled myself, not to return their hate three-fold. A part of me wants their whole loathsome empire to burn right down to the ground with them in it. But we mustn't be that. We must fight, yes, but without losing our-selves to hate. Or we'll be just as lost as they are."

Finn folded his arms and bit his lip. Now he wished he'd told her about Cal and wondered if the news would quell her leniency.

"How many arrows do you have?" Treasa asked.

"Arrows. Right. So about that; I fell in the river, you see, and all me arrows—"

"Don't tell me you have none, Finn."

"Seems I don't have to tell you. Seems you've guessed it."

"Feck's sake."

"I'll use magic. I'm not running away, so my only choice is to use my magic, even if the chief says I shouldn't do."

"I'd object to it, but druidic magic isn't made to fight off an army. Or fight at all, truth be told. But *we're going to the Déagrian temple first.*"

Finn paused, clenching his jaw. "I'm an Anordúla now. You don't have any authority over me anymore."

She shot him a cross look.

He lowered his head. "Yes, Vischief."

Finn smelled smoke and looked to see a large charred area growing on the wall of the cocoon.

"Of course they'd set it on fire," Treasa said. "Of course. Get behind me—back to back—and get ready. We're staying on the ground; my magic works better foot to soil, and 'twill make us harder targets for their archers."

Finn drew his bow. "What about the ones using swords?"

"I might know something that might work."

"A lot of *might*'s in that."

The fire broke through the cocoon in various places. Swords stabbed through the openings and slashed.

Treasa reached out her hand straight in front of her, and a staff grew from the ground. She grabbed it and broke it from its roots. She held it high above her head.

"Mother Larissa, Goddess of the hearth and home, see us! I call upon your protection, encircle us. Shield us from those who'd do us harm."

The fire flared up, engulfing large segments of the cocoon.

Treasa circled her staff above her head.

The fire rotated around the perimeter, ripping through the cocoon as it gathered together, becoming two birds of yellow fire. They flew as a circle about four feet from the ground, their tails long, each nearly to the other's beak.

Treasa slammed the base of her staff to the ground. The collapsing cocoon and the thorns outside it exploded into dust, blowing out over the soldiers.

Soldiers tried to push through the ring of firebirds but found themselves severely burned. The tabards of three burst into flames before the men retreated into the crowd.

A soldier rolled under the ring and jumped up, charging Finn. Finn shot him with a bolt of chaos.

The soldier fell to his knees, but his motion left a trail of himself, like a soldier-colored mist wafting in place.

Finn winced in pain, as if his fingers burned. All ten digits blackened to his knuckles.

The soldier's every jerky movement of agony left behind more of the mist; parts of himself were being ripped from him. The soldier's form unraveled, and soon the mist and the soldier became dust raining to the ground.

Another soldier tried to duck through the four-foot space between the firebirds and the ground. Finn shot him before he entered.

On Treasa's side, she aimed her staff at an entering soldier, lifting him upward to the fire.

An arrow struck Finn's neck, cutting him though his armor held. He searched for the archer and shot. He missed, hitting another. Finn shot again, reducing them both to ash.

With each bolt Finn shot, the burning in his extremities increased while shifting the blackness farther along. He shot more bolts into the crowd of soldiers. The blackness crossed Finn's hand, nearing his wrist. It likewise affected his feet, with the burning and the blackness nearly to his ankles.

A sword swiped under the fire ring inches from cutting Finn's legs.

"Stay in the center," Treasa called, her staff locked against the sword of a soldier who'd managed his way into the circle.

The pain had distracted Finn. He hadn't realized how close he'd gotten to the edge, and now he realized the circle itself was moving. They were significantly closer to the abbey.

A soldier inside the circle grabbed Finn from behind. Finn struggled, trying to get his other hand to his bow, but failed.

A soldier ripped away the ebony bow and threw it—over the circle, over the crowd.

"No." Finn reached vainly toward it.

With newfound courage, more soldiers entered under the circle. Treasa battled two. Others pulled Finn toward the circle's fiery edge.

"It wasn't a magic bow, Finn," Treasa shouted as she fought. "It was just a focus."

A soldier pushed Finn's head toward the ring of fire as Finn strained with all his might against him.

"*What does that mean?*" Finn screamed.

"It helps you focus your magic, but you don't need it." Treasa received a boot in her stomach and fell to the ground.

Finn slapped his hand to the arm of the man who held him. The arm began to crumble amid torrents of blood. The soldier cried out, releasing Finn.

Finn, now free, glared with a grin before he cast his hands toward two other soldiers in the circle. Bolts of crimson shot from his palms.

Another soldier raised his sword above Treasa on the ground.

Finn cast chaos into him. He fell, falling apart.

The excruciating blackness burned past Finn's elbows and knees. The pain left him breathless, but he gritted through it.

The circle of firebirds, now empty save for Finn and Treasa, neared the short stone wall of the abbey.

"Line yourself up with the gate," Treasa shouted. "When the firebirds go over the wall, we'll need to go through, or we'll be trapped on this side."

Finn nodded, grimacing as the last of the pain throbbed through him. He lined himself up like she'd said while facing outward, hands held ready, toward the gathered soldiers.

The first firebird neared the wall and ascended a sharp turn up the stone and over. When it passed to the other side, it collided with something unseen. Dispersing, it flared out—gone.

"No!" Treasa called.

The other firebird was not far behind. Gone.

Fire ring lost, Treasa held her staff out with both hands. Straining, she created a rippling wall of wind against the surrounding soldiers.

Finn hurried toward the gate.

"Finn, stop." With all her might, she pushed out her staff, holding back the crowded Dayigans. "It has a ward. We can't enter. And I can't push them back for long. You must fly away whilst I'm holding them back."

"I'm not leaving you here on your own."

"Go, Finn." She strained to push her staff forward. "You only have seconds."

Finn braced himself, standing firm. He crossed his arms across his chest, forming an X with his fists on his shoulders.

Staring hate at the soldiers, Finn growled. "Hear me, Dark Mother. Give me strength against my enemies." He flung out both hands as he shouted.

Forty Dayigans at the front of the mob fell to their knees. They screamed in agony as their motions blurred into trails of mist. As dust, they crumbled to the ground.

The other soldiers, terrified, fell back and fled.

Shouting in anguish, Finn fell to his knees. His entire body felt as if it burned. Both arms were already black to the elbows, as were his legs to the knees. Now black veins ascended higher, twisting up his legs and up his arms onto his chest. The tattoo of the Star of Irefae on his chest burned and blackened, as did the tattoo of the torc around his neck.

Treasa shouted his name, but Finn was deaf to all but the pounding of his heart. She grabbed his shoulders, but he felt only pain.

Finn's orange feathers shriveled and curled inward on themselves, as if too near a fire. Brittle, they broke away. The skin underneath cracked open, seeping thick blood. Finally, like burnt meat, the flesh from his wings fell as black chunks melting off bones. Next, the bones themselves shattered.

In a nightmare of agony, teetering on unconsciousness, Finn fell to his side.

"Finn, listen to me. I can't imagine what you're going through, but we have to go. The soldiers will return soon."

Numb and limp, Finn stood with Treasa's help and leaned against her. He looked at his back. Less than a foot of each wing bone remained, this dripping with burnt meat. The sight sent his head spinning.

Treasa held him up. "We have to retreat to the woods. We can find a place to hide there, and I'll figure out a way to treat you. But I need you to stay with me."

Finn tried to nod but wasn't sure if anything happened.

"Don't use any more magic," she said. "*None.*"

CHAPTER FORTY

Through a wooded area of the island, away from the camp, away from the abbey, away from the many soldiers, they ran—or hobbled quickly, in Finn's case. Treasa kept stopping and running back for him, helping him along.

Finn stopped, propping his hands on his knees. "If they was chasing us, we'd be caught, slow as I am."

"I'm shocked you're running at all." She lightly touched one of the two broken bones protruding from his back. "Does it hurt?"

"Not as much as it seems it should. Do we have a next move?"

Treasa placed her hand on her forehead and pushed back her auburn hair, keeping her hand atop her head. "I'm at a loss. I'm at the edge of seid depletion. My armor's popped. There's a ward on the temple keeping us out. And you—Mothers give me strength—you are literally falling apart. I don't understand it. What have you done to yourself, Finn?"

"Like I said, Chief Kaie told me not to use magic."

"She knew this would happen?"

"Not exactly, no." He sat on the ground and panted. "The chief said that if I used any more magic, I might could, maybe, well, you know, die. Perhaps."

Treasa huffed with frustration. "Feck's sake, Finn. You should have said."

"And what? 'Tis not as if I was doing magic for laughs back there. If we both hadn't done what we did, we wouldn't be here but dead. Plus, you said yourself that you're near seid depletion, which is just as fatal as my thing."

Treasa was silent before chuckling, a distraught sound rather than mirthful. "Would you look at this mess we're in? Who would have believed it? I'm on a Dayigan island fighting soldiers with our wee Finn, who's turned wizard. Mothers help us. Cal will be flabbergasted when I tell him of all this."

"Aye. Cal." Finn looked downward. "I'm not a wizard no more, though. I tried a spell back there when we were running and nothing happened."

"Right." She glanced down. "I'm going to fly up to the treetops and see if I can't see the soldiers. I know the Anordúlas don't meditate, but you'd do well to try it."

"I wouldn't know where to start, to be honest."

"Then sit and rest. You'll need your strength." She spread her wings and flew upward.

Finn stood, muttering. "Sit and rest, is it? Like I'm a child." He looked and found the top branch where she'd landed. He spread his wings—no. They were gone. He'd felt them for a moment.

The limb holding Treasa seemed so far away, so unobtainable. The night sky, Finn's playground as a child, was so much farther. He would never go to the skies again, he realized. The loss of it all struck him and weighed him down. He felt small, bound forever to the ground.

Finn sat down, letting it sink in.

Treasa returned. "They're coming."

Finn jumped up. "How far out?"

"You can see them if you look. There."

A shout sounded from a distant soldier. "They're here!"

"What do we do?" Finn asked, frantic.

"We run, Finn. That's all we have left now."

She took off, away from the soldiers, and Finn followed just behind. Their steps were loud against the leafy ground. Brambles cut their feet. The untamed woods offered no paths, sending them through the sharp fingers of the obstructing limbs, which reached out to scratch their skin.

The heavy, booted steps of the soldiers drew closer, stomping nightmarishly loud.

Finn stole a glance behind him and could see at least a dozen soldiers gaining ground.

The Feahs neared the woodline, and Finn could see the sandy ground beyond it. Next, stretched the vast dark waters of the Hyvile River.

"You have to fly off the island," Finn said.

Treasa didn't respond. Her eyes widened as soldiers marched into view on the shore.

Finn and Treasa stopped within the thick trees, soldiers all around them.

Treasa grabbed Finn from behind, locking her arms around his chest. She flew, yet her flight was low and labored.

"You have to let me go," Finn said, "so you can fly higher."

The soldiers closed in under them. Finn cast his hands forward, but no crimson lights formed.

"Treasa, drop me and fly away. There's no use us both dying here."

The Terovaes were twenty feet up, but above the same area they'd taken flight from.

"'Tis this cold autumn air," Treasa said, straining. "Poor lift. But if I can just get a good wind, I can glide us."

"Glide us where? We're on an island. On your own, you can fly over the water."

Arrows flew their way.

Treasa struggled to dodge while losing elevation.

"You have to let me go." Finn pulled at her hands around his chest, trying to release them, but she had locked each of her hands around each of her wrists.

More Dayigan arrows flew. One pierced Treasa's upper wing, cutting feathery flesh.

They fell, hitting the ground hard. Two soldiers were quick to grab Finn as he struggled. Another grabbed Treasa.

Finn closed his eyes and concentrated. He envisioned those who held him falling apart as dust. Nothing happened.

Within the thick woods, a hundred soldiers crowded, forming a dense circle around the Feahs. Finn looked to Treasa, struggling against the grip that bound her.

"I'm sorry," Finn shouted to her. "You could've gotten away."

"You shut your mouth, Finn ó Ríona," she said, forcing a sad smile. "Not a bit of this is your fault. Not one bit."

"I'm sorry," Finn said.

Commander Beadurinc, sword in hand, entered the circle; his posture, pompous; his stride, unhurried. He approached Finn.

The commander eyed him up and down. "What are you?"

"I don't know, to be honest."

The commander angled his head mockingly and placed his sword flat on Finn's chest, the blade not an inch beside the neck. "I should kill you now for all the trouble you've caused here. The Drevite Experiment is over, yet you follow us to our own empire and attack us."

"Is it over then now?" Finn asked with bitter sarcasm. "Really? So you'll be releasing the people you took from our lands? So you'll be bringing me brother back to life as well now?"

"Your brother?" Treasa gasped.

Finn looked at her, into her crestfallen eyes. The revelation seemed to take the last of her.

"I'm sorry," Finn said. "It didn't seem right to tell you, with all the troubles."

"Where's my wee Ubaz?"

"*Silence*," the commander said. He lifted the sword away from Finn's chest. "The archbishop will want to study you. Alive."

He walked a few paces to Treasa.

"But you, Vischief ..." He raised his sword to her stomach. "We know everything we need to know about druidesses."

He thrust his sword through her gut.

"No!" Finn shouted.

As Beadurinc withdrew his bloody sword, the soldiers released Treasa. She crumpled to the rocky yellow grass. Her blood flowed into the dirt.

"No," Finn cried. He struggled to free himself, but another soldier grabbed him.

"Release the creature," Beadurinc said. "Let the filthy savage see what happens to those who stray from the Light."

Shoving off the soldiers, Finn dashed to Treasa. He knelt beside her and cradled her with an arm under her shoulders. His other hand held hers on her stomach. She coughed, blood oozing from her lips, and stared up at him with heavy lidded eyes.

"Promise me you'll take care of Ubaz," she choked. "Keep him safe from the wicked church."

"I promise." Tears ran down Finn's cheeks.

"And promise me you'll save the people in the Déagrian temple. Sweet Alannah and the rest."

"Aye. I vow that as well."

Treasa smiled weakly as she closed her eyes. "Our Cal will be flabbergasted when I tell him about all we did here."

"Tell him I miss him."

"I will. And how brave you've become. Don't lose yourself to hate, Finn." Her body relaxed and her head rolled to the side. She breathed, "May the ancestors guide you and ..."

CHAPTER FORTY-ONE

Finn kept his arm under Treasa's shoulders. He held her cold, limp hands. He stared, his vision blurred. She was gone.

"She was a good person, her," Finn muttered. He looked up at the many soldiers gathered in a circle around him. "*She was a good person!*" he yelled.

Treasa's body turned to dust in Finn's arms and sifted to the ground.

Finn stood. "Do ye Humans even care? She was always trying to make herself better. She was a good healer and a good mother and ... a good friend as well."

"She was a witch," Beadurinc said flatly. "She chose her path, and this is where it led."

"You hear your man here?" Finn motioned to Beadurinc. "The man you follow? Treasa didn't choose the path to death. She chose a path of healing and kindness and teaching"—he sniffed—"teaching the virtues of the Three Mothers. *You* made her a fighter to protect our people. Her path ended in death because *you* chose to shove a fucking sword through her gut—*no other reason.*" He nearly choked on his words, burning in his throat.

Beadurinc chuckled. "Do you think the blasphemous ravings of a monster can turn these virtuous men?"

Finn looked down. "I'm not sure. But enough people have died." He looked up at the soldiers gathered around. "Treasa said, if everyone's lost to hate, everyone's lost. We can stop this, now."

The Dayigans were stone-faced as they watched Finn. None showed signs of remorse. Most seemed to wait impatiently to fight.

"Ye have to see 'tis your commander that's the wicked one here."

"Enough," Beadurinc said. "You want Dayigan soldiers to follow you to darkness and perversion, so be it. Men, listen up. If any of you wish to join this savage, you may do so. I vow, by the Greatest of All, to let you—and him, if you join him—leave this island unharmed. I'll give you a ship. I'll even release the savages we captured."

Finn looked around the circle, looking deep into the crowd, only to see hundreds of faces turning from him.

"No one?" Beadurinc spoke louder. "If only a single man stands with this savage, I will spare his life and release his comrades. Anyone? Pray, assure they heard my offer in the back rows."

Someone threw a rock, smashing against Finn's face. He touched his fingers to his bleeding cheek and shouted. His heart pounded with growing anger as he clenched his fists and stared at the rock on the ground.

The men laughed. One yelled, "Burn in za, you filthy savage."

"You're bastards," Finn shouted. "The lot of ye." Heat ran through his veins. "Fucking bastards."

The laughter from the circle of soldiers grew louder.

Beadurinc grinned as his cold eyes stared into Finn's. "My men know the True Light is the only way. All others will perish. *Seize him!*"

A soldier rushed from the crowd toward Finn. The Human reached out to grab him, but Finn shoved him in the chest.

As dust, the soldier exploded backward, raining on his brethren.

Finn called out in agony as his lower right leg shattered, crumbling into dust. He fell to a knee, blood pooling beneath him.

Panting through clenched teeth, Finn stared hatefully at Beadurinc. Finn was like something feral, anger cloaking pain.

"*You will die,*" Finn said. "All of ye will die."

The soldiers, before so callous at the plight of Finn and his people, now showed fear.

Finn inhaled their terror like an elixir, vitalizing his soul.

Beadurinc slapped an iron ring to a soldier's chest. It was the one they'd forced Treasa to wear, with green symbols etched along its length. "Collar him."

The soldier gripped the collar anxiously and stepped forward.

Finn stared him in the eyes, daring him to approach.

"Go with him," Beadurinc said.

Another soldier approached. The two were like frightened trappers approaching a lion, each step slow and timid.

They leaped at Finn as one.

Finn pushed them away, one hand toward each, and as dust, they exploded outward.

Finn roared as his other lower leg shattered. He fell to his stomach and arms. Growing weak from the loss of blood, he strained to hold himself up.

Through blurred vision, Finn saw two translucent figures at the edge of the circle.

The Reaper, Xanorael—cloaked wholly in his back misty robe, save for his skeletal hands—watched from the shadow of his hood.

By his side, the Dark Mother, Morgana, stood nobly, her hands together at the waist of her long black velvet dress, her raven wings folded behind her. Her shadowed eyes, too, watched Finn.

Both were unnaturally still as they waited.

"You're falling apart, monster," Beadurinc said. "But I assure you, I have much more men than you have body parts, and they all know to die in the service of God Déagar assures them a place in the paradise, Laqyigo. Put the collar on. Let us take you alive, so the archbishop can study you."

"Aye, I might be falling apart, true enough, but if I'm left as just a grain of sand, I'll fling meself in your eyeball and *scratch it out.*"

"Men, attack as one. Rip that fucking savage apart."

The soldiers roared as they drew their swords, a burst of chaotic energy filling the area. Finn gained an enormous smile as he lifted his hand from the ground and flexed it into a fist.

The soldiers were a foot from Finn, readying a dozen swords to pierce his flesh.

Finn punched the ground, shattering his hand past the wrist.

The ground rippled outwards, rumbling and shaking. The grass wilted and crumbled. Three trees cracked and fell apart, their fragments crashing down as they collapsed.

The soldier halted in fear and began searching their surroundings.

"Death," Finn whispered.

A crimson mist rose around Finn and spiraled outward over the gathered soldiers.

The Dayigans called out in agony as they fell to their knees. Those farther out tried to flee, but the mist spread quickly, seizing them and pulling them to the ground.

The sound of screaming echoed in the night, as flesh rotted from bones.

And around Finn, the Dayigans flailed about in torture as their blood soaked the ground.

Finn knew he should feel sympathy, even for them. The Finn of last year would have cried at this gruesome horror show. But the wide smile remained on his face as Finn watched the soldiers slow and stop. Their slick muscles decayed off their bones, spilling organs to rot on the ground. Soon, their bones crumbled into dust.

Silence and stillness moved over the dusty shoreside woodlands, and the crimson mist faded.

As the mist lifted, Finn saw a large orb of green fire, like fire curved within walls of glass. It was seven feet tall and stood, Finn realized, approximately where Beadurinc had stood.

"Fuck's sake." Drained, Finn fell to the ground.

The orb twisted away, leaving the commander standing with a smirk on his face.

"You should have let me capture you alive, monster," Beadurinc said. "You didn't truly think your wicked magic would kill a man of Déagar."

Finn couldn't lift any part of his throbbing body. Cheek against the ground, he watched Beadurinc step closer.

"Your witch friend was wrong when she said the Knights Silthex practice magic. Partly wrong. Even when our numbers were great, only a handful in the order practiced divine works. The Supreme Patriarch gave these select few special dispensations. He deemed it necessary—fight fire with fire, as it were. Your burst of wicked sorcery proves our point. Nevertheless, the Church maintains concerns that public knowledge of our power might *confuse* the common man— using *magic* in the war on *magic* and such. Thus, we took a vow to keep our divine gifts secret and never use them around anyone else. Do you see anyone else here, monster?"

Finn couldn't speak or move.

Beadurinc glanced around the area. All that remained of the Dayigan soldiers was scattered as wind-blown piles of dust.

"Looks like we're alone." Beadurinc held his hands together at his chest and thrust them outward, expelling a large ball of green fire.

It roared through the air, striking Finn. Finn's body, singed, lifted three feet from the ground and crashed to roll limply.

Exhausted beyond movement, Finn could do nothing but lie how he had landed and struggle laboriously to breathe.

CHAPTER FORTY-TWO

The rain returned, splashing mud around Finn as he lay on the ground. Brown drops splashed up on his face, but he could do nothing but let them drip down. He felt his body giving out, his numbness growing, his eyes heavy. Finn's legs—missing just below the knees—had stopped bleeding, as had his right arm—gone just past the elbow.

Beadurinc launched another green fireball, lifting Finn a foot before crashing him down.

Finn coughed blood, feeling it ooze down his cheeks.

"Get up and fight, monster," said the commander. "Or hurry up and finish dying."

Beadurinc's words would have been Finn's own words to himself, if he could speak. He only managed a feeble groan as he rolled over to his side.

Finn looked at the two dark figures watching from a distance. The Dark Mother. Death. They barely move in their solemnity. The rain passed through them without touching.

"Help me," Finn pleaded weakly.

The two did nothing. They were like statues overseeing the event. Yet Finn saw concern in Morgana's hazel eyes. She would help him, he decided, if she could.

Those dark, beautiful eyes were like Laisren's. Finn knew he'd never see her son again. Even with the pain of his failing body, the hurt from the loss of his love rang out.

"I'm sorry I left him," he muttered. "I should have gone with him to the city."

"Who are you talking to?" Beadurinc demanded. "There's no one left to save you."

The rain dripped down Finn's face as he turned toward the mud.

"No one left," Finn whispered.

Beadurinc stepped closer, his boots trudging heavily, and cast another fireball.

Finn thrust his remaining hand upwards and caught the fire, burning himself. He weakly threw it aside.

It hit the ground, exploding as plumes of green.

"No one left," Finn whispered, "but me." He pushed himself to sit up. "There's no one left to save me but myself. There's no left to stop you, but myself."

Beadurinc threw more fire. Finn swatted it away.

"Hail Ignísekhet," Finn growled, "she who creates herself. Give me the strength to create *my* self."

The commander held both of his hands together at his chest and thrust them forward, casting a larger ball of fire.

It struck, exploding against Finn. Finn fell into the mud.

"What can you do to me, monster?" Beadurinc said mockingly. "There's barely anything left of you."

Face down, Finn glared in hate, letting the anger fill him like fire in his blood. Finn pushed himself up on one arm and looked at the commander.

"You killed my brother, my friends. You destroyed my home."

"As they deserved. And after I kill you, too, I'll assure no being, not so much as a squirrel, remains living in your savage homeland." He threw another fireball.

It struck Finn, and he called out in pain, but he did not fall. "Hail Ignísekhet, she who creates herself. Goddess of Chaos. Archdemoness of Wrath. I invoke you."

Thunder sounded above, as lightning struck a tree.

Finn looked at Morgana at the side of Death. She kept her arms and eyes raised to the night.

Finn sat up and looked into the stormy sky. He lifted his arms as the parts that were missing reformed as crimson mist.

"Hail Ignísekhet. I invoke you!"

Beadurinc backed away nervously.

Finn stood up on feet that reformed as black hooves. His lower legs, now black, had skin like burnt bark. His black fingers elongated and his nails grew sharp and blood red. The skin of his lower arms matched his legs, with black veins twisting up to his chest. The rest of his skin paled white, save for the tattoo of the star and torc. His irises glowed crimson.

The commander stumbled backward, keeping his balance on a tree. His words were quick whispers. "Praise God Déagar, the one and only God, protector from the Dark. You are the Greatest of All."

As Finn watched him, he gained a large smile, baring sharpened fangs. "You want me to be the monster you hate?"

Finn spread his wings of crimson mist as they solidified to leathery black, like those of a bat. "But I will be the monster you fear."

Thunder sounded above.

Horns, black and sharpened, burst from Finn's forehead, causing blood to drip down his face. They extended two inches at the front of his spiked white hair. The tips of his ears rose into points.

Beadurinc threw the iron collar at him.

Finn caught it and roared as the iron burned his hands.

Beadurinc took off running through the woods.

—

Into the empty Dayigan camp, Finn flew, bat-like wings wide as he circled, searching. "Run, Commander. I don't care. Wherever you go, I *will* find you."

Beadurinc, on the path leading to the center of the camp, held a large burlap sack from which he poured the last of an ash circle around himself.

"I set this circle that no enemy may enter." Beadurinc raised a hand high and thrust it down toward the ground. A flash of yellow light flowed along the ring of ash, hardening it into place.

Finn landed, black hooves striking mud, and approached the commander. Finn thrust both his hands forward, radiating twisted rays of crimson light.

The light struck the unseen wall of the circle and blasted outward as a ten-foot radius. Everything within the radius—patches of grass, rocks, tents, and equipment—decayed to dust. However, the interior of the circle remained unharmed.

"You should appreciate this, savage," Beadurinc called. "This is ash from your own village's fire on Midyear's Eve. They say it deters wicked Faeries and their magic. 'Twould appear they were correct."

"Bastard," Finn said, his voice bestial, "using our own sacred ways against us."

"I admit 'tis less than ideal. God Déagar will, of course, protect me from your wickedness, but why waste his divine gifts on defense"—he drew his sword and its blade ignited with green, ethereal flames—"when I could use them to strike you down?"

Beadurinc thrust the sword forward, expelling a continuous stream of green fire.

The fire stuck Finn like a dragon's breath. He roared in pain as the fire lashed around his body. He struggled to remain standing.

Spreading his wings, Finn leaped from the ground, but Beadurinc adjusted his aim, keeping the vortex of fire on Finn.

Unable to endure more, Finn fell to the ground, a knee and a fist to the mud. He extended his wings forward, forming a shield around himself.

Still, the pain continued. Finn gritted his sharpened teeth and growled as the fires burned him. He concentrated, forcing his focus within the eye of the storm. Finn pushed his wings against the force of the flames before, with a roar, he thrust his wings open, ripping apart the fire.

The flames dispelled, shoving Beadurinc back and knocking him to his butt in the circle.

Finn, weakened but not visibly harmed, stood and glared glowing eyes at Beadurinc. "Is that the best Déagar can do?"

Finn jumped up and flew toward the circle. His clawed hands extended, aimed for Beadurinc's throat.

Yet Finn hit the ring with force, sending him backward in waves of yellow ripples. Finn crashed into the ground, sliding as the dirt parted around him in a crackling rut.

He lay where he fell, aching.

Beadurinc stood and chuckled. "'Tis a shame I couldn't capture you alive. 'Twould be interesting to discover what you are. You're no Demon, despite appearances. Judging by your weaknesses, you're something in the Irefaery Court. An over-grown imp, perhaps. The knowledge of how a man becomes an imp could have proven valuable to our army. Yes, a shame."

The commander aimed his sword forward, and green lightning erupted.

The bolt struck the center of Finn's chest and branched out along his burning body.

Finn moaned like a beast before shouting, "I will not die before I kill you!"

Pushing his shaking, clawed hand into the excruciating lightning, Finn pushed the bolt away. It dispelled, again pushing the commander back, though the Human didn't fall.

Finn jumped from the ground and hovered about twenty feet above the camp. He had little left in him; he struggled to remain aloft, and he knew he could only take a few more strikes before the commander ripped him apart.

Finn looked to where they'd nearly burned Treasa. A ring of twenty dead soldiers, their bodies opened by thick im-palement wounds, surrounded the spot.

Centered there, Finn saw the long rope they'd used to bind her to the stake.

Beadurinc thrust his sword again, casting a fireball.

Finn dodged it and dived near a tent. He pulled himself up just in time to miss its canvas roof, but he struck the green flag, breaking it from its peak.

Finn looked at the rope again and flew toward it. He snatched it up, coiling the heavy thing over his vein-twisted shoulder.

Beadurinc reared back his sword, preparing another strike.

Finn leaped up and flew away.

"Cowardly imp," Beadurinc shouted from his circle. "Come back here and face me."

—

Finn crouched behind a faded green pup tent and watched Beadurinc.

The commander paced within the circle of ash. He called out, *"Where have you gone, imp? Do you fear the wrath of Déagar?"*

Finn's clawed hand moved atop the tent, and he inched forward like a stalking cat ready to pounce.

Beadurinc stopped and called, *"Savage imp."* He looked at the surrounding skies. *"Get back here and fight me."*

Waiting eagerly, Finn stared, crimson eyes glowing.

The commander, still searching the sky, began to turn away from him.

Finn moved farther forward. *Not yet.*

Beadurinc turned his back to him.

Spreading his bat-like wings, Finn jumped, silent as a breeze, to the sky.

The rope, clutched in his blackened hand, dangled ten feet, ending at the iron collar—which was hinged open.

Finn continued to fly steadily but quickly, dreading every moment that the commander would turn his way.

Just before Finn reached the protective circle, he arched his wings forward, stopping himself in air while letting the iron swing out toward the commander. To Finn, the forward inertia appeared in slow motion. He concentrated on the perfect trajectory, like a leaf falling precisely into a little wooden cup.

The collar crossed over the barrier of ash and continued toward the commander's neck.

It struck hard. The commander turned, but the hinged front had already swung around, closing around his neck.

Finn yanked, pulling the commander to stumble out of the circle. Without losing a moment, Finn dove, grabbing the commander from behind, one arm across the Human's chest. Finn's other hand fought toward the iron collar.

Wrestling to hold him still, Finn said, "Feck me. I'm well certain you're the ugliest fish I ever caught."

Finn grabbed the collar's closure; the iron burned his fingertips, which sizzled with steam. He maintained his effort, however, causing the closure to rust, merge, and unrust, melding together.

He released the struggling soldier. Beadurinc ran, but Finn held the leash tight, even as the commander fought to pull himself free.

Watching him struggle, Finn smiled at his victory, a crazed smile of bared fangs.

"You have no magic now, Commander." Finn felt almost giddy. "As it should be. Magic is the realm of the Gods, you know. All that use it are trespassers in their big God house."

"Damn you to za, insolent imp." Beadurinc grasped the collar with both hands, trying to pull it open. "You will release me at once."

Finn smiled even bigger, crimson eyes widening with pleasure. Giddiness welled within him, a sort of ticklish lunacy. He laughed as he watched this man, who'd taken so much from him, trapped so comically.

"You've lost your mind," said Beadurinc.

"Have I? Maybe so. Some say that if you're not careful with chaos, it can twist the mind up and twirl it around." The smile remained. "If that be true, you should be well concerned, I think. Very much so."

Finn tugged at the leash and began walking away, pulling the commander behind him.

Marching happily along, almost skipping, Finn dragged the commander behind him. The twisted merriment only increased within him, filling him with a strange energy. The enormous smile remained; his crimson-irised eye barely blinked; his heart pounded.

As Finn approached the circle of corpses where they had nearly burned Treasa, he cast out his clawed hand.

From the center of the circle, a thick pole of choppy charred wood grew from the ground to tower nine feet high.

Beadurinc's struggle to escape heightened as he saw the destination.

Finn stopped and looked back. "What are you doing that for, ya eejit?" he said through a clenched smile. "I've planned something well fun for us." His whole body tingled with an almost pleasant feeling similar to passing out.

Finn yanked the rope and continued into the circle. He shoved Beadurinc against the pole and tied the rope around him.

"Now, it were you, yourself, Commander"—Finn, rope in hand, circled, wrapping the commander like a grim maypole—"that said a good burning at the stake would boost morale up. And after the night we've had, I think we all could use it. Look at them there." Finn motioned to the circle of corpses. "Just laying about, sulking like."

"If you do not release me, God Déagar will punish you everlastingly."

"Will he now? You don't say." Finn tightly tied the end of the rope. "Don't you worry there, Commander. This'll all be done with soon, and we can all get back to normal. Well, not you, yourself, but ..." He patted the Human's chest. "Keep your morales up, though, Beadurinc." Finn looked at him for a moment, his eyes narrowing as he thought. "*Beadurinc.* That is a stupid name, that." He thumped the commander's forehead. "You should get yourself a better name, and you wouldn't be such an arsehole."

He stepped back and admired his handiwork as the commander struggled against it. "Nice." He gave an approving nod.

"Look here," Finn spoke loudly, as if to a crowd. "Tonight, we see what happens to them that turn against the True Light and infest the world of Perdinok with wickedness."

Finn lifted his hands to the rainy night. "Praise God Déagar," he said, "the one and only God, protector from the Dark. You are the Greatest of All. I praise your name, majestic and holy. Bring your fiery wrath down on this wicked commander."

Thunder sounded as green lightning bolted from the clouds, striking Beadurinc. Fire ignited, twisting around him and swallowing him as he screamed.

Finn watched a moment, smiling blankly as the light reflected on his face. "Praise Déagar." He grunted in pain and pressed his fingers to his forehead just below his horns. Tiredness swept over him.

Listening to the screams, Finn lay on the ground by the fire and relaxed.

With his wings extended out flat, Finn folded his arms under his head and stared up into the rain.

It was over.

Finn's horns melted and joined the water dripping down his face. His wings, too, dissolved. His renewed appendages went next, flowing away to the mud. His skin's color faded, white to freckled pale. All the injuries held back by magic returned, including new deep burns from the fire bolts that the commander had launched against him. The pain and weakness returned, too, but mostly the pleasant tingling, a throbbing tingling accompanying sleepiness.

Finn closed his eye and felt as if he were sinking away.

His racing heart slowed.

Calm.

CHAPTER FORTY-THREE

A wave pushed up on the sand, circling his toes before receding away. Sitting on the shore of the Hyvile River, Finn crossed his vibrant orange wings behind him so that he could lean back and gaze toward the sun. It was nearly overhead and warm on his face. He sighed in calm contentment.

Lann smacked the back of his head. "What are you doing here still? Everyone's waiting on you."

"I'll be along soon. I'm just relaxing a bit before the start."

Laisren and Nekesa landed beside them.

"We thought we'd find you here," Laisren said with a laugh. "You're late for your own celebration."

With a lazy smile, Finn looked up at him. "Can't they just celebrate without me?"

Laisren grabbed Finn's hand and pulled him to his feet. He squeezed him in a hug and kissed his lips.

Their foreheads together, Laisren said, "They can't start without the guest of honor. You're the hero who defeated the Dayigans."

"I'd rather stay here and fish, to be honest. I'll show you how, if you like."

"You showed me how when we were boys. And I was never any good." He gave him a quick kiss. "Still, I'd be delighted."

Lann shouted down the shore. *"He says he's not going now."*

Finn looked back to see Cal and Treasa approaching.

"The chief's gone to a lot of trouble to make this grand for you," said Treasa with a smile. "And there are more people in the temple village now than for a fire festival. All to celebrate you. You're quite the hero."

Finn shrugged his freckled shoulders. "I'm just me, s'all."

Lann slapped Finn's shoulder, gripping it. "If our hero wants some time with his friends before the main event, so be it. But you will need to be going soon. *Moyra*," he called toward the fishing village, *"join us, would you, love?"*

She jumped over the woven fence marking the village border and flew the short distance to the group.

"Have you seen Alannah?" she asked Lann. "I can't find hide nor hair of the wee lass."

"Our Finn was supposed to get her," Lann replied.

An ache formed in the pit of Finn's stomach. "Was I?"

"Don't you remember?" Treasa spoke up. "You promised you'd go get her. It was my dying wish, no less."

"I ..." Finn began. The entire area darkened, as if the sun itself had dimmed by half. "I had to kill the commander first."

The entire group, smiles fading to concern, watched Finn.

Treasa's voice was a whisper behind his ear. "I told you not to lose yourself to hate."

—

Jolting awake in a fit of dry coughs, Finn lay flat on the ground, staring up. No wings, no legs below the knees, and a missing hand. His body was drained beyond exhaustion. Within the murky sky, the sun was nearly overhead, cooking his face. His skin felt dry and tight.

With effort and struggled breath, Finn turned to Beadurinc, a blackened corpse with very little brittle meat remaining on his bones. It hunched over at the base of the broken stake.

With his remaining hand, Finn turned himself away, facing the Déagrian abbey.

"Lannah," he wheezed.

He rolled himself to his stomach, groaning all the while. Straining, he dragged himself toward the collection of masonry buildings within a masonry wall.

Every inch forward was a struggle, as Finn's body seemed near to giving out. The rocky ground scraped against his stomach and forearm, drawing dots of blood along his dirty skin.

Finn only managed six feet before the task proved insurmountable. He stopped, panting shallow breaths, and lay his cheek on the ground.

A repetitive sound grew louder—crunch ... crunch ... crunch—and Finn's exhausted, mangled mind needed a moment to recognize it. A pair of boots approached on gravelly dirt.

Without the strength to move, Finn could do nothing to determine the sound's source. He could only wait as the boots drew nearer.

They stopped right behind him. Silence followed. Dread filled him, and he tried to will himself to move. Even if Finn could not escape, he wished to know who stood inches behind his head. The silence became torture as the stranger only stood.

Finn's face remained on the ground, staring at dirt. If he'd had the breath to do so, Finn would have called out in rising terror, but his tight lungs worked their limits to maintain his shallow breathing.

A boot planted itself against Finn's shoulder. It rolled his aching body to face upwards.

The man towering over Finn was wingless, Human perhaps, but far older than any Human, nay person, he'd ever seen. Hundreds of years older, by the look of him. His loose, wrinkled skin hung from a brittle frame as if it might soon drip off in fleshy glops. Yet, it was the green of regal clothing that frightened Finn like a captured mouse. The man wore a long green cloak of fine fabric enhanced with gold designs.

"Who are you?" Finn croaked through a scratchy throat.

The man leaned downward, peering at Finn with yellowed eyes. "I am the Most Reverend *Blastilv*, Archbishop of Klikate Forest, Abbot of Blessed Hand Abbey. A better question asked is, what art thou?" His words were slow and sinister, with an undertone of annoyance. He poked Finn with a sword, pricking a drop of blood. "Frail and unremarkable as thou appearest, thou hast killed mine army, every man, including my valued protégé, fierce and righteous Beadurinc."

A few feet to Blastilv's side, Morgana and Xanorael stood like wavering mirages. They watched.

"Help me," Finn groaned.

"Help thee?" Blastilv chuckled, jiggling the hanging flesh of his throat with each quick chortle. "I came to watch thee die, O savage reprobate. Alack, I regret only that I do not have the time to enjoy thy prolonged suffering. Other matters— service to our holy God Déagar—require my attention. Lo, with our experiment having failed tragically and Beadurinc slain brutally, I must begin a new plan to cleanse the world of Darkness. Thou"—he stabbed Finn in the shoulder, blood flowing to the dirt—"hast set us back nigh unto a decade, *boy*.

Thus"—he withdrew the sword—"magnanimous as I am, I will end thee quick and be away."

"No," Finn whimpered, no strength for more.

Blastilv stabbed his sword through Finn's chest.

Finn coiled in pain as his eyes lit up, and crimson fire blackened the sockets. His voice was bestial as Finn hissed, *"The Firechild will be your end. And I will be the guide."*

Withdrawing slowly, the blade plucked out Finn's heart, snapping the slick organ from its veins and arteries.

Staring, the archbishop held the bloody, beating thing before his eyes. "Know thou, fiend, good doth ever stand triumphant over evil."

The heart crumbled to dust, twisting away with a breeze.

Finn became still, unbreathing. His eyes stared lifelessly. His body cracked down the center and crumbled as dust into the dirt.

And Blastilv walked away from the corpse as slowly as he'd come, his boots crunching on the rocky ground.

—

Touching his hand to his heart, Laisren sighed and thought of Finn. He sat on a nice bench, Mephistus beside him, reclining like a panther on a branch. With melancholic thoughts, Laisren gazed into the shallow, rectangular pool—thirteen feet by six—set centered in the gray marble floor of the massive, malevolent room. The pool's floor of polished copper reflected light through clear water.

The long, colossal room towered sixty feet to a vaulted ceiling, resembling a ribcage like a dragon's. Between the granite bones were scale-shaped tiles of red marble cut so thinly as to permit ruddy daylight from above. The sternum split apart in a pointed oval, thirteen feet long and opened to the sky.

The walls were black marble. Thick black columns, set five feet inward on either side, lined the room and towered to a horizontal lintel of gray marble. Shorter columns continued farther up.

This architectural wonderment glorified two statues near the back of the room. The forty-foot Gods, formed of black marble and clothed in silver, sat on silver thrones.

To the right, the male God bore a bestial yet Human face. Two horns, like a ram's, crowned his bald head. His eyes shone lustrous red. His Human chest and stomach—left bare, with only a drape of silver over a thick shoulder—were exceptionally muscled. In his clawed hand, he held an iron bident, its handle extending to the floor. His legs, shown beneath the silver cloth atop his lap, met cloven hooves below.

To his left, the Goddess wore atop her long straight hair, a silver circlet from which five spikes shot upward to sharpened points. An indigo gem was set within the center spike. Her fierce eyes were lustrous indigo. Her thin face spoke of dark authority. She wore a necklace of nine silver skulls. Her body—wrapped in a low-cut gown of silver—was mighty and seductive. Though she appeared otherwise Human, the Goddess had four arms—one pair, black marble, the other, silver. In one of her hands, she held a silver trident, its handle extending to the floor.

These Dark Light Gods atop their thrones set on a black marble stage. Its six-foot front held silver reliefs portraying soldiers and Demons, side by side, preparing for battle.

Every day since his arrival in Vohcktara, Laisren had come here to the Black Temple. He'd come even that first day, though all his rational faculties knew it would have been im-

possible for Finn to be there so soon. Every day, Laisren waited, arriving half an hour before noon and leaving two hours
after.

The dread that Finn would never come lingered constant-
ly in Laisren's mind. When he walked the various forums of
the city, seeing masterpieces of sculpture and architecture
and fountains flowing with clear water into sparkling pools,
Laisren tried to imagine how wonderful it would be to show
these fantastic things to Finn. He imagined Finn's excitement. But in these same moments, Laisren feared he'd never
show him them at all.

A slight rain began to fall through the opening in the ceiling, splashing directly into the pool underneath. Laisren
watched the rippling surface as he placed his hand on
Mephistus's head, scratching behind his ears.

"You needn't wait here every day with me," Laisren said.

Mephistus scooched closer, setting a forelimb over
Laisren's leg and laying his head atop it. Laisren cupped his
hand on the tromlee's neck above his wings, rubbing gently.

Mephistus jerked painfully.

Thinking he'd somehow injured him, Laisren yanked back
his hand.

The tromlee jerked again, roaring.

Laisren stood up, searching for any cause of the effect, yet
saw nothing.

A crimson mist surrounded Mephistus as he withered.
Soon, he shrank into a black housecat with the wings of a bat.

"No," Laisren whispered, eyes welling with tears. "Finn."
Finn had been Mephistus's link to the Irefaery Realm, the
power that had allowed the tromlee to grow large.

And Laisren now knew—his heart broken—that link was
gone. Finn was gone.

He felt sick and empty.

"No!" Laisren's shout echoed in the marble room. The handful of people within the cella turned his way. He didn't care. He couldn't care. His pain was too overwhelming to contain.

Laisren fell to his knees and folded his arms on the bench. He laid his head atop them, trying to hide his face as he wept, ugly and loud. Each sound echoed. People whispered. Laisren tried to stop—*You're in public, for fuck's sake*—but he couldn't halt the absolute sorrow that erupted from his core. He coughed, choking on his sadness.

Mephistus neared, rubbing the soft fur of his side against Laisren's head. The minor comfort settled him.

Laisren looked up, eyes watery and red. He sniffed.

"Finn." He wiped his eyes with his finger. With broken, breathy words, Laisren said, "I honor you and release you."

Continue at

JEREMIAHCAIN.COM

CPSIA information can be obtained
at www.ICGtesting.com
Printed in the USA
BVHW041931200223
658865BV00001B/38